FANCY DANCER

Other books in the series:
Noir Rehab (2020)
Ibizan Run (2023)

FANCY DANCER
A Jake Jakes Mystery

CARL WALDMAN

OUTER CITY PRESS

For Mavis ...
Keep dancing in mind and body.

CONTENTS

PROLOGUE

"Let us see, is this real, this life I am living?"
– from a Pawnee song

DRUMS? NATIVE DRUMS? No ... hands banging on the van.

"Wake up, chief!" a man's voice called out.

"Don't be parking on private property, dirtbag!" That voice was younger.

"Go back to the rez, redskin!" As was that one.

Jake rose up. The van now rocked, hands pushing it. He moved toward the front from the rear sleeping area. Through the windshield he could see an imposing moonlit figure standing a short distance away. He wore overalls and held something in his hands – a baseball bat.

How to play this? Jake had tools under the sleeping platform that he could use as weapons. Maybe he should grab one. That was one adrenaline-fueled idea. Flight was a more sensible one.

"I'm leaving!" Jake yelled as he slid into the driver's seat, adding, "racist assholes," under his breath.

"Well, hurry the fuck up!" one of the younger-sounding voices yelled.

With the doors locked and the windows only slightly cracked, Jake had felt confident in leaving the key in the ignition. A good decision, following the bad one of parking where he had. He turned the key. The engine kicked into life. He turned on the headlights.

"Back away, boys!" the man with the bat yelled. "Let him go! This piece of shit isn't worth the hassle."

Two boys, apparently teenagers, moved next to the older man. Their loving daddy? He handed the bat to one of them.

"Get going, Injun!" one boy yelled.

Jake eased the van back onto the road. He looked in the sideview mirror and saw the boy with the bat break into a run after him. Jake accelerated just in time to avoid the boy's lunging

1

swing. The bat missed his taillight, getting only air. Jake laid on the horn as he sped away.

It took him a good while to calm down. His thoughts kept rebelling. He'd been targeted as a Native American. Because he was near Seminole lands? He'd pulled the curtains on the back windows tight, and the cargo van was windowless along its sides behind the seats. But perhaps one of the family gang of three had spotted him relieving himself after he'd parked. He certainly could pass as part-Native regardless of his ancestry. Take this as a sign who his own father actually was – prejudice and harassment leading to an epiphany?

The encounter carried him back to his recent past and beyond. His descent into the vortex of polydrug abuse had started in his hometown in upstate New York, then accelerated during his time as an artist in New York City. He'd ended up homeless before this home on wheels. He'd been shunned plenty and even roughed up. To keep his mind off alcohol and other drugs and to keep simmering anger no more than that, he'd started roleplaying detective and following people randomly, leading to a real case that led him all the way to Florida.

Now, on the very night of the day he'd overheard those strange words in the Seminole Brighton Casino at Okeechobee leading him to a new case, Jake was experiencing all-too-familiar druggie cravings.

Stay on task, his brain intoned yet again. Don't succumb.

PART I: TREK NORTH

"This is my heart as I travel all over, my spirit, my life and living."
– from a Flathead song

A Legend Now

ADORNED MEN MOVED to the center of the circle of spectators, their costumes unique combinations of wildly colorful regalia. Now, finally, the Fancy Dance. From online research Jake knew that Fancy Dancers drew on traditional dances. The centuries-old Grass Dance of the Plains Indians, a victory dance after warfare, had been the original inspiration. This modern version was a contest for cash prizes.

Elders – men and women both – had begun the various competitions with their individualistic Straight Dance. Their moves were powerful in their own right, subtly so. Next, the Tiny Tots, child dancers, had improvised moves with reckless abandon. Ladies had then performed the Shawl Dance, like birds in flight. Now, the Fancy Dancers were set to compete.

The music began. Drummers sat nearby in a circle around the host drum, pounding in unison and singing arc-shaped melodies. The drumbeat and vocal accompaniment pushed the dancers, who responded with shuffling, shaking, gliding, hopping, leaping, and spinning. At the end of beats, contestants froze in dramatic poses, sometimes even in splits. Fancy indeed.

"Fancy Dancers don't commit murders."

What to make of that bizarre statement he'd overheard when passing two apparent Native Americans at the Brighton Casino? It occurred to Jake, caught up in the spectacle, that perhaps the dignified Straight Dancers didn't do so. Nor the Tiny Tots, still innocent despite their abandon. Nor the elegant and lofty Shawl Dancers. The Fancy Dancers, however, while in frantic motion, seemed capable of any passionate act, including a killing.

Jake decided not to take photos with his cellphone. A sign said photography was acceptable at this powwow. Some spectators clicked away. But it would detract from the moment for him.

The drumming crescendoed and abruptly ended, the dancers freezing in place. Spectators cheered. They cheered again when the winner was announced, a young Creek Indian decked out in orange and white. He glowed with sweat and pride. All of the dancers had a proud glow about them. They all knew they were good and their stances indicated they would return for another contest.

The closest spectator to Jake was a black-haired woman, wearing a ribbonwork shirt. She stood a comfortable distance away, the new public normal even after a vaccine gave people new confidence following the coronavirus pandemic. She apparently was the mother of a colorfully costumed Tot, who, after his own earlier dance, had returned to her side and intently watched both the Shawl and Fancy Dances. As spectators dispersed, he practiced more of his moves.

"Does he dance at a lot of powwows?" Jake asked the woman.

She looked him over, her dark eyes more curious than distrusting. "This is his fourth powwow this year," she replied.

"He sure seems to love it.

"Yes, he does."

"How old is he?" Jake asked.

"Seven."

"I'm new to this. The dancers are like rock stars."

That got a slight smile. "My son also drums," the mother said.

Jake smiled back. "Cool."

"You indigenous?" she asked.

"Maybe. My mother wasn't sure who my father was."

"What tribe?"

"Maybe Mohawk."

She nodded, studying his face. "Yeah, you might be."

"Are you Seminole?" he asked her.

"Miccosukee. The boy's father is Seminole."

After the resolution of his last case, Jake had visited three Seminole reservations. At the Hollywood Reservation outside Miami, he'd visited the Seminole Okalee Indian Village, with its open-sided and thatched dwellings known as *chickees*. He'd

4

also seen alligator wrestling there, a tradition in which a tribal member taunts, tests, and finally tames the primordial creature. At Big Cypress he'd spent time at the Ah-Tah-Thi-Ki Museum. At Okeechobee he'd visited the Brighton Casino, where he'd heard the Fancy Dancer comment. He'd seen mention online of the upcoming Leesburg Powwow and its dance competitions and had driven north beyond Orlando to attend.

Jake hadn't made it to the lands of the Miccosukee, Seminole relatives to the south. Yet he'd read up on them, wondering about Native themes and how they might relate to him.

"You grew up in the Everglades?" he asked.

She nodded and said, "If you have more questions, you can come to my husband's table. Over there." She pointed. "Maybe buy something," she added with not-so-subtle emphasis.

A man also in a ribbonwork shirt sat behind a table displaying wood carvings.

"I'm Jolene," she said. "This is Joe, Little Joe. My husband at the table, his name is Joe Panther. He's a master carver."

Jake had seen a live cougar – commonly known in Florida as a panther – at the Indian Village on the Hollywood Reservation.

"I'm Jake." He turned to the boy. "Nice dancing, Little Joe."

Little Joe nodded as if to an obvious truth, then followed his mother as she turned away.

Jake perused items for sale at different tables – leatherwork, beadwork, woodwork, and stonework. He reached Joe Panther's display. Jolene now was sitting next to her husband, eating a sandwich.

Joe Panther looked up and said, "Hello. You're the one called Jake. I'm the one called Joe."

The carver had the same dark and probing eyes as his wife. Jake, still not certain in this post-pandemic age whether to extend a hand, fist, or elbow as a greeting – or anything at all – offered an elbow. Joe accepted a fist bump and Jake turned his attention to the carvings.

"Prices are on the bottom," he stated.

"Can I pick them up?"

"Gently," Joe advised.

"One carving was of a figurine painted in bright colors with attached feathers. It reminded Jake of a Southwest Indian kachina doll, but this one in a dance crouch. A sticker on the bottom next to Joe Panther's inked signature listed the price as *$110*.

"A Fancy Dancer?" Jake asked.

"Right."

"This poplar?" Jake knew different woods from his time as a builder in upstate New York.

"Right. Cottonwood, we call it in these parts."

"And the feathers?"

"Parrot on this one," Joe replied matter-of-factly. "I use feathers from many birds,"

Jake decided to buy it. It would be a nice gift for his sister Caitlyn. He'd bought her a calendar and a collection of postcards at Walt Disney World to share past memories but here was a gift for the ages. And the purchase might help get him information.

"Sold," he said. "I got to see my first Fancy Dance today. Nice way to keep the memory."

Jake noticed Jolene's smile of approval. Joe wrapped the figurine in layers of paper and put it in a small recycled cardboard box. Little Joe had moved away from the table and was dancing with a small wooden hoop, trying to move it back and forth between his arms. Jolene stood up and joined her son.

Jake drew bills out of his wallet and handed them to Joe. "I heard something strange at the Brighton Casino," he broached. "It's been puzzling me, even more after I saw the dancing here. Has there been a recent killing involving a dancer? A murder?"

Joe counted the money, then looked up. "Jolene said you might be part Mohawk."

"My mother told me I was probably either half-Mohawk or half-Italian."

"Where're you out of?"

"Shaleville, New York."

Joe's dark eyes were piercing. "In that case, you should know what happened. What'd you hear that was so strange?"

"Someone said, 'Fancy Dancers don't commit murders.'"

Joe's eyes widened in surprise, then he gave what might have been a smile. "Indigenous people and everyone else have a lot to say about this. The person the cops are looking for is a dancer. He's a big winner on the circuit and an idol to young dancers." He glanced at his son.

"What tribe?" Jake asked.

"Raised Seneca but with a Seminole grandmother from Oklahoma."

Jake knew that some of the Seminole had been relocated to Oklahoma in the 19th century, about the same time as the Cherokee Trail of Tears. And he knew that the Seneca are the westernmost tribe in the Iroquois Confederacy of New York, Quebec, and Ontario, and the Mohawk, the easternmost.

"This happen in Seneca country?" he asked.

"Not far from it. Some new organization sponsored the powwow."

"When?"

"September ... soon after the Fancy Dancer in question won first prize. You'd think he'd have other stuff on his mind than killing someone, wouldn't you?"

"Who'd he allegedly kill?" Jake asked.

"A retired cop."

"Uh-oh. How?"

"A knife." Joe tossed his head to the left. "Tell me, Jake, you with White Eyebrows over there?" The question had a sharp edge to it, like the referenced knife.

Jake turned to look. Several tables away, a tall, middle-aged, hatchet-faced man, with gray hair and pronounced white eyebrows, was looking over books and pamphlets. He wore khakis and a plaid shirt, with a camera around his neck and sunglasses on his head.

Jake looked back at Joe. "No. Why?"

"Because he's full of questions, like you."

"He brought up the killing?"

Joe nodded. Jake looked over again at the man with the white eyebrows. He'd moved on to the next vendor's table, one with blankets and t-shirts.

"Claims he's a retiree and tourist from up north," Joe said. "Says he's part Crow but when I mentioned the Absaroka, he acted like he didn't know what I was talking about."

"Absaroka?"

"Another name for the Crow. White Eyebrows smells like a cop. And you? You know what Haudenosaunee means?"

Jake, armed with knowledge, gave a little smile. "Testing me? I'm no cop ... that's for goddamn sure. But I'll play along. Haudenosaunee ... that's the Native name for all the Iroquoian-speaking tribes of the League of Six Nations. It means People of the Longhouse."

"What are you then? You a *tourist*, too?"

"I guess you can call me that. I did go to Disney World. I followed a woman there who didn't want me to. But I passed the test, if that's what it was, and since I might be part Haudenosaunee like the Fancy Dancer, I'd sure like to know his name without having to look it up."

Joe gave a little grunt. "Fair enough. You can find out on your own, anyway. And you bought something from me. White Eyebrows didn't. And my wife told me she thinks you're okay. The Fancy Dancer everyone's looking for, his name is Grant Guyasuta."

"And he's missing?"

"Either hiding out or dead. Either way, he's a legend now."

Jake thanked Joe for the information and for the Fancy Dancer figurine, nodded goodbye to Jolene and Little Joe, then headed for a food truck. He ordered an Indian taco and a lemonade. A woman yelled out the order and a man yelled it back – unnecessarily loud but in obvious good fun.

Food in hand, Jake sat at a picnic table to eat. Childhood memories had risen up. He'd first experienced a powwow and eaten an Indian taco – typical taco ingredients but on frybread – at the Iroquois Indian Museum in Howes Cave near his home in Shaleville, New York. That was the same day his mother Grace had first told him his father might be Mohawk. Caitlyn, Jake's half-sister, knew who her father was although she hadn't seen him in a long time. Hugh Edmonds had moved to Alaska after he'd split from Grace. Caitlyn had his last name. Jake went by his mother's maiden name: Jakes. His biological father remained a mystery.

Enough of his wanderings in Florida, Jake resolved over his food. The Fancy Dancer comment had motivated him, along with his possible ancestry, to visit more of Seminole country. Now, after what he'd learned from Joe Panther – that Grant Guyasuta was Seneca and that the killing had happened in western New

York – he had additional incentive, besides seeing Caitlyn, to head back north.

The powwow was winding down. The crowd was thinning out and some of the vendors had started breaking down their tables. Jake gathered up his trash and tossed it into a can, then headed for the parking area. He turned for one last look at the powwow grounds. Joe and Jolene were carefully wrapping Joe's artwork to load in their van. Little Joe was now practicing with two hoops at once. No sign of the self-proclaimed tourist, dubbed White Eyebrows by Joe Panther.

Jake reached his van and climbed behind the wheel, placing the boxed figurine on the seat next to him. He activated GPS on the new phone Disney officials had provided him and reviewed his route north. He then followed the line of vehicles to the designated exit and beyond.

After his interrupted sleep the night before and the long day, his whole being ached with fatigue. Get a motel? It was tempting: security, a hot shower, and a real bed. Still another reason to do so: December nights were getting cold this far north in Florida. Even so, to save money, he would rough it.

With the growing darkness, Jake found himself blinking his eyes hard to stay awake. He decided to stop for a nap. At a stretch of road with a wide shoulder and no house in sight, he pulled over, shutting down the engine. As usual, he locked the doors, cracked the side windows, and left the key in the ignition. This time, however, he stayed in the driver's seat, angling it backward, rather than bed down in the rear of the van. To his relief, it wasn't long before his agitated thoughts dissipated ...

Mickey Mouse, the Sorcerer's Apprentice, comingle with Tiny Tot dancers. Inside a giant wigwam Mickey orchestrates a frenzy of dance to a soundtrack of drumming. Someone else is watching ... White Eyebrows. The wigwam becomes a drum and Jake and all the others are tossed about like feathers inside it. No, not the belly of a drum ... the belly of a vibrating van ...

Jake woke up. Disney characters and powwow dancers faded as he found his bearings. Hands weren't banging on the van this time. It was rain. How long had he slept? Hours? Minutes? He checked his cellphone. He'd gotten an hour and a half of sleep. Good enough.

After nearly three more hours driving in the intermittent rain, Jake made it to I-95 near Jacksonville and, before long, a rest stop. Truckers were parked there, sleeping in their cabs.

Jake parked near one of the big rigs and felt safe. Sort of.

Spirit Guide

JAKE AWOKE at first light. He'd been caught up in yet another confusing, unsettling dream. But the drone of traffic on the highway caused the dream threads to dissolve, leaving no conscious memories.

He moved his van closer to the welcome building and went inside. He was in no mood for people. All he wanted was a restroom, coffee, and snacks for the road. In what counted as a general store at a stop like this, he bought a coffee, water, and some power bars, all overpriced.

Jake, somewhat refreshed, took to the road again. How long had it been since he'd driven in the opposite direction along I-95? Weeks felt like months. Time had expanded for him once he'd reached Florida. Now, like the road stretching toward the ever-changing vanishing point, time again registered as linear.

Georgia presented itself, Florida receding behind him. Memories leading up to and during his time in Florida kept pace, however. He knew that even as he created new memories, he would revisit the recent loaded ones time and again.

Jake had the urge to call Caitlyn and tell her he was heading back to upstate New York. His sister's enthusiasm would do him good. But he decided not to promise a visit just yet. The road played tricks.

Without a working FM on the van radio, AM stations – with limited music and one-sided negative political and evangelical rants – provided his only company. Jake was reminded of the assailants near the Brighton Casino who had assumed he was Native. Their words had revealed bigotry and venom beyond anger over his trespassing – the same hatred he'd witnessed at Disney World against a Sikh family. Opportunistic politicians had fueled the great divide, making it open season for hatred. At least weather reports were positive, with no heavy storms predicted.

Jake looked at the box on the seat next to him. He reached over and, keeping one hand on the steering wheel, he used the other to liberate the Fancy Dancer figurine. He propped it up on the console between the van's front seats. It would be his Spirit Guide, leading him some thousand miles north to Haudenosaunee territory in upstate New York.

He thought about the roots – rather, possible roots – journey he'd made years before. He'd visited three reserves in Canada: Six Nations of the Grand River, Akwesasne, and Kahnawake. He'd visited Grand River first because his movie-obsessed mother had made a big deal about *Key Largo* – and not just about director John Huston and stars Humphrey Bogart, Lauren Bacall, and Edward G. Robinson – but also about the Mohawk Jay Silverheels, who played a Seminole in the movie before going on to play Tonto in the *Lone Ranger* films and TV show. Silverheels had grown up on the Grand River Reserve. The only person Jake had talked to while there had been in a gift shop and the conversation had been mostly about the actor. The owner had informed him that Silverheels had been a star lacrosse player and boxer and had started work in Hollywood as a stuntman and bit actor in the late 1930s before his breakthrough. Jake had bought a copy of a signed photograph for his mother. She'd seemed genuinely moved when he'd given it to her, even commenting that the photo meant more to her than the memory of her affair. She knew little about her Mohawk lover and the possible father of her son other than his tribal affiliation and that he liked rock'n'roll. She wasn't even sure of his first name – Brent or Brant, she'd said. Jake had found out on his own that the latter was more common among the Mohawk, after the 18th-century leader Joseph Brant, whose Native name was Thayendanegea.

With the designated Spirit Guide looking on, thoughts of Jake's possible Mohawk father and the Mohawk actor who had once been cast as a Seminole, along with scattered knowledge about both tribes and memories of reservations, casinos, powwows, and Fancy Dancing, occupied him through a good many of the drawn-out hours behind the wheel.

~

11

Jake traversed South Carolina, finally reaching North Carolina's border. After almost five hundred miles that day – seven-plus hours – with just one stop at a rest station, he was ready for a motel bed. He took advantage of the remaining light on this short December day and, after another hour, he left the highway. Before motel-searching, he filled up the van's gas tank at a convenience store on Cumberland Street in a small city called Dunn, cleaned up in the restroom, ate a sandwich, and went online to check out the area.

A public library, just off Cumberland, offered one more hour till closing. He decided to take advantage of a more comfortable way to search the internet than on his phone. He would look for a motel afterwards. He found parking near the library. After tucking the figurine under his sleeping bag on the van's platform bed, he headed for the entrance. The librarian greeted him with Southern hospitality, something Jake sure appreciated after the lack of it near Brighton.

Sitting in front of a library computer, he searched for anything on the powwow killing involving the Fancy Dancer Grant Guyasuta. He found a report from the *Associated Press*, posted the previous September:

"Man Found Dead at Native American Powwow. The body of Richard Baines, a retired Buffalo policeman with a residence in Bradford, Pennsylvania, was discovered in the woods on the grounds of the Arrow Alliance headquarters, situated on the edge of the small hamlet of Seneca Hills, NY, by a group of teenagers the morning after the final night of an intertribal powwow. There was no sign of a robbery. Baines was last seen in the presence of Grant Guyasuta, a 28-year-old tribal member of the Seneca Nation of Indians and a resident of Salamanca, NY, who is now missing and is being sought as a person of interest by the police. No weapon has been located."

Other newspaper reports were as brief. Searching the Arrow Alliance led to a page stating "website under construction." Jake eventually found another mention of the incident in an editorial in the newspaper *Indian Country Today*, published by the Oneida Indian Nation of New York:

"Powwow violence will not be tolerated. It is a sorry state of affairs to think that personal matters can lead to violence at the expression of artistry and joy basic to Native powwows. While facts in the case at the Labor Day Weekend powwow are still undetermined, it is known that the death occurred on lands owned by the Arrow Alliance near Seneca Hills in western New York, during the Alliance's first such gathering.

Many Nations were represented. In past centuries, powwows were social gatherings and celebrations, including feasting, dancing, and singing, often prior to a council or hunt. In modern times, the concept of both gathering and celebration are still central, with powwows offering a coming together of Native peoples and non-Native guests, as well as a celebration of enduring Native America. Powwows are all about unity and peaceful interaction.

We would hope that any participants in these gatherings leave personal feuds behind and that Natives and non-Natives can find common ground. We appreciate that the Arrow Alliance's chairperson, Chad Catamount, has spoken out so passionately against this incident as an aberration contrary to what the Arrow Alliance stands for. When Catamount echoed the famous words of Chief Joseph of the Nez Perce, 'My heart is sick and sad,' he spoke for all of us."

Jake searched for Chad Catamount, which led him to a website for the Erie-Mingo Nation. It was a simple site with text only, other than crossed arrows in the letterhead. On its "about" and "history" pages, he learned that Catamount had organized the Erie-Mingo tribal entity and that anyone who claimed Erie or Mingo ancestry with some documentation to back it up could join. Any registered Iroquois could also have a voice on the council because of the historical connection to those peoples.

An article, again in *Indian Country Today*, stated that Catamount had also founded the Arrow Alliance, a not-for-profit intertribal organization that sought to put revenue from bingo and casino revenue into causes relevant to all Native Americans. With donated funds from the gaming First Nations, the Alliance had purchased lands near Seneca Hills and was building new offices and a cultural center known as the Turtle. The Labor Day Weekend powwow had been the first event on the new lands. An earlier event in June, just after the founding of the Alliance, had taken place at the New York State Capitol in Albany. In an interview Catamount had called that event a "cultural celebration as well as a political intervention."

Jake also found some decade-old information about Catamount as the star of Kenton College's lacrosse team – the top scorer as both a freshman and sophomore.

And Jake found a notice about an event the next day in Washington, D.C.:

> "Chad Catamount, council chief of the Erie-Mingo Nation and chairperson of the Arrow Alliance, has challenged real estate developer and casino owner Andrew Sharp to a debate on the subject of casinos in Native America. The not-for-profit human rights organization E/E (for Empathy/Empowerment) has agreed to sponsor the event at its offices on Prospect Street in Georgetown, scheduled for 7:30 p.m. Mr. Sharp has yet to respond to the challenge. Catamount has stated that, even if Sharp is a no-show as expected, he, Catamount, will give a talk on Native sovereignty and the gaming issue."

The E/E website included a quote of Catamount's:

> "Andrew Sharp is a modern-day land baron. His company Sharp United, famous for changing the skylines in numerous America cities, has also invested in casinos from Atlantic City to Las Vegas. With the competition from Native-run casinos and the downturn in Atlantic City gaming, Andrew Sharp is lobbying Congress to amend the Indian Gambling Regulatory Act of 1988. He refers to 'an uneven playing field between Native and non-Native high-stakes casinos.' Doesn't he have a big enough piece of the pie? Native Americans must find a way out of their dire poverty. Andrew Sharp and other assumed landlords of Native ancestral lands will not keep indigenous peoples down."

Jake was aware of billionaire Andrew Sharp. It was hard not to be, especially for anyone who followed news stories in and around New York City, where Sharp had grown up and where Sharp United was located, although most coverage seemed to be about his personal life and mistreatment of women. He had read once about Sharp taking issue with Native casinos. Chad Catamount of the Arrow Alliance apparently had been pushing back.

Jake now knew where he would stop first after the drive through North Carolina and Virginia ... Washington, D.C.

Blood on the Sidewalk

JAKE REACHED the Beltway around Washington by midafternoon the next day. It took him another hour and a half in traffic to make his way to Georgetown. Darkness was descending and the temperature, dropping.

The E/E building was just east of Georgetown University. Rather than take on the challenge of street parking in this city, Jake pulled into the Georgetown Court parking garage on Prospect Street. An Asian restaurant was located nearby. With Happy Hour still underway, he was able to pass the time inexpensively with a beer and appetizers. He was just one of a few customers.

At 7:00 p.m., Jake exited the restaurant and headed west along Prospect. Not counting the city-like sprawling Disney World, he hadn't been in a true big city for about a month now, and the stimuli were jarring.

Sirens, loud and biting, added to the noise and intensity. He turned to see the accompanying light show – emergency vehicles approaching. Here in this political city and what with the current political climate, Jake had the momentary thought that U.S. storm troopers were on their way, as if in an apocalyptic movie, to round up dissenters. But an ambulance raced by, followed by two police cars and a van. They stopped a block-and-a-half away.

Jake soon realized that their destination was the same as his – E/E headquarters, one of several brick rowhouses on the block. It stood four stories tall with two dormer windows jutting from the roof, like bug-eyes on a long face. One of them was open, peering askance at the fuss below. Other official vehicles arrived from different directions, a fire truck among them. Onlookers had already gathered. Police used a vehicle to block traffic, then some among them hustled to set up yellow barrier tape to keep people away from the building's entrance.

Passing a group of foreigners – Scandinavians, he guessed from their chatter, both in English and otherwise – Jake advanced far enough to catch a glimpse of a covered body on the sidewalk, surrounded by medics and police. Two women standing nearby were crying. A man a few feet away shook his head in dismay. Two men approached the man from an unmarked car and began talking to him. Jake pushed farther through the crowd. Reaching the barrier tape, he sidled past other onlookers to a uniformed policeman.

"What happened?" he asked.

"Read it in tomorrow's paper," the cop answered without looking at him.

The plainclothes police were now interviewing the two distraught women. They all looked up at the dormer with the open window, then back down at the victim as a man carrying a doctor's bag approached. He crouched down and, pulling the blanket slightly back, examined the body. He stood up and nodded. The medics wheeled up a collapsible gurney, slid the body onto it, then raised it and wheeled it to the open back doors of an ambulance. Other cops covered the stain on the sidewalk with a plastic tarp. A police car led the way as the ambulance pulled out onto 34th Street, then drove off, lights flashing without siren.

The crowd gradually dispersed, including the three witnesses. Only a few onlookers stayed to watch, Jake being one of them. The temperature continued to drop and he shuffled and stomped his feet to keep his blood flowing. Police entered and exited the building. After almost an hour, someone closed the dormer window. After another twenty minutes or so, two policemen appeared in the doorway, escorting fourteen people.

Another policeman pulled aside the barrier tape to let them pass. Two young women out of the fourteen eventgoers headed west on Prospect – one, athletic and blond, the other, diminutive and pale, with brown hair tinted silver and an abstract tat up her neck. They both carried large shoulder bags. Jake sauntered after them, then stopped several feet away.

16

"Excuse me," he said. "Are you Georgetown students?"

"Yes," the blond replied, continuing on.

She looked emotionally drained. They both did.

Jake walked alongside them. "I noticed that you were at the E/E building. Was that for the Chad Catamount event?"

"Yes. It was canceled," she said with a southern accent.

"I was heading there myself. I hate to bother you at a time like this. What happened?"

They stopped walking and both began to talk at once. The brunette went silent to let the blond make her point.

"A woman fell from a window."

"She probably jumped," the pale brunette added. Her accent also sounded southern.

"Was she there for the talk?" Jake asked.

The brunette answered: "We saw her in the audience. She was sitting several rows in front of us."

"How do you know she was the one?"

"The police described her," the blonde said. "She wore a blue headband with beads."

"Native American?"

"She looked more African-American," the blond offered.

"Maybe a student?"

"A graduate student maybe," the brunette said. "Never saw her before."

"The talk hadn't begun yet?"

"No, she ..."

The blond interrupted: "A man ... a young man ... came over to her and said something to her and she left with him."

"Was it Chad Catamount?"

"No, I'd recognize him from the poster. Someone else. Younger."

"Also Native?"

"I'd say."

They both were chewing their lips, letting out stress. Time to wrap this up after one more question to redirect their thoughts.

"Did you attend the talk for a particular class?" Jake asked.

The brunette replied: "We're taking a course on Native American politics."

"Thanks, I appreciate it. How terrible it all is."

The blond shuddered. "Worse than terrible."

Her friend nodded in agreement and the two moved away. They would no doubt be talking about what had happened for a long time. Violent death leaves scars for anyone in range.

Jake returned to the barrier tape and waited a while longer. The police escorted two more people from the building. They looked Native American, one a head taller than the other. They both had their heads down, and Jake couldn't make out their faces. Catamount, he assumed, and perhaps the younger man who had led the victim away.

The two men were driven off in a police car. The remaining police began removing some of the barrier tape. Jake and the other stragglers dispersed. As Jake headed back east along Prospect, two city vehicles approached and passed him – one a sedan and one a van, both marked "Department of Public Works."

Arriving to clean the blood from the sidewalk, Jake guessed. He wouldn't stay to watch that.

Escape Artist

"HI, AKI. IT'S JAKE."

"Jake. Holy fuck," his photographer friend responded. "All okay? You clean? I mean that both ways. Daily hygiene?"

Jake had taken a shower at the truck stop, readying himself for a question like that and hopefully setting up a meeting.

"All good. I just took a shower."

"And no telltale symptoms, viral or otherwise?"

"Clean bill of health."

"Whose bill?"

"The fates?"

"Okay, fuck it, that's good enough. My therapist tells me I shouldn't even ask those questions. But given your fucking ways, I made the exception."

"Believe me, I'm honored. I'm passing through on my way upstate. You in Brooklyn or Manhattan? I thought I should fill you in. I'd love to do it in person, but I know how it goes."

"I'm at my Manhattan studio. I'm actually doing better with not sheltering-in-place. I have to. I'm doing some shoots in my new studio. Yee gads, people. And I've been going out for lunch regularly, but only to restaurants that have their social distancing together."

"So that's a yes?"

"Yeah, let's meet at Fanelli's. They've removed some of their tables and it seems okay now."

"What time?" Jake asked.

"About one."

"Okay. I'll call if I get delayed driving in."

"Fine," she said. "Wait ... a rental?"

"No, my own wheels ... from my sister."

"You been with her the whole time?"

"No, I'm returning from Florida."

"Florida? Jake, please tell me it was for a good reason."

"I'll see what I can come up with."

"It better be good," she said and signed off.

Jake pulled out of the truck stop located about an hour south of New York City. On leaving Washington, D.C., in the middle of the night, he'd decided to break up the trip with a stopover in his old stomping grounds. After Maryland, rather than cross Pennsylvania, he would cut through Delaware and New Jersey toward the Big Apple. He'd put off calling Aki until today and wanted to reassure her about how he'd used her money – that is, not a penny spent on drugs. When she'd paid him for having used one of his sculptures as a basis for an art photo, she'd encouraged him to take up his art again. He'd continued his sleuthing and wanderings instead.

On this latest leg of his journey, Jake's thoughts kept returning to what had happened in Georgetown. At an earlier rest stop, he'd used his phone to research the incident and found a couple of posts. It was reported as a likely suicide. *Indian Country Today* mentioned that the deceased – Salali Jenkins, a Lumbee Indian from Pembroke, North Carolina – had been an employee of the Pelican Wing Casino in Atlantic City, owned by Sharp United. Andrew Sharp, the famous mogul – he whom Chad Catamount had called a modern-day land baron, as quoted on the E/E website – was Sharp United's CEO.

Traffic was relatively light entering the Holland Tunnel leading under the Hudson River. As the tiled tube carried Jake onto a city street, he had the thought that the island, like other lands he'd recently passed through, possessed a rich Native American history. The name Manhattan – or Manhattoe, an alternative English spelling of a tribal name – was a powerful reminder of that, even in the shadows of concrete, steel, and glass.

Jake also knew that a Mohawk community in Brooklyn had formed over the years because of the tribe's tradition of high-steel construction, including work on the Empire State Building, the George Washington Bridge, and the United Nations buildings. Many of them were from Kaknawake, the third reserve he'd visited on his roots journey years before.

Jake made his way north and east to the Manhattan neighborhood south of Houston Street referred to as Soho. Jake Soho was the handle given to him by a street friend during his homeless period and he knew the neighborhood well. Some of its streets offered parking except between 11:00 a.m. and 12:30 p.m. If lucky, he would find one, necessitating staying with the van only a half-hour. From there he would walk to Fanelli's at Prince and Mercer to meet Aki.

Success. He located an open spot on King Street just west of MacDougal and south of Houston and eased the van into it. He killed the engine and settled in, watching city life around him, pondering the good and the bad from his inner-city past.

~

"Bizarro life you're leading, Jake."

Jake, over soup and a sandwich, had just recounted his travels to Aki since last seeing her. While poking at a salad, she'd listened with a skeptical grin and occasional comment.

The final one had been: "At least you fessed up to your sister. I'm not sure driving far and wide, sleeping in a van, and playing detective is finding yourself but, hey, you seem to be doing okay."

"It's all helped me stay clean. Look at me. No hard drugs and no grime. Plus I got the vaccine, even though I'm pretty sure I fought off the virus beforehand."

"Yeah, same for me. I dealt with my fear of doctors' offices and needles to do so."

She suddenly looked like a doctor herself, as she tilted her small head – small but brainy. She even sniffed like a police dog. The label obsessive-compulsive only scratched the surface with her. Aki's phobias reached to her bone marrow. The fact that she was in a restaurant sitting opposite him was a triumph for her – just as it was for formerly homeless him.

"You look healthier," she asserted. "Gained some weight. And you don't smell like a sidewalk. Think you'll get back to sculpting?"

Their last encounter had started with his sleeping in a doorway on her block and had ended with her first payment to him for using his sculpture as a basis for her career-building "Infinite Web" photo. The money had helped him break free of his homeless stagnation.

"Not sure. Being a sculptor and heavy user went together. I need to keep moving."

"You really think you can solve this Fancy Dancer thing?"

"I want to try."

"You think the leaper in Georgetown is connected?"

"Not necessarily a leaper."

"The Andrew Sharp connection is sure newsworthy. That odious guy's all over the place. This Catamount is an interesting character. Sure willing to take on the one percent. I guess I can see why you're hooked on this case. But wouldn't it be nice if someone actually hired you instead of your roleplaying? You'll run out of money soon. What then?"

"I've decided at the very least to visit Seneca Hills. Try to meet this Chad Catamount."

"I mean longterm."

"I don't know. I can stay with my sister. I owe her work on her house for the van. And I can find other construction work in my hometown."

"And party with the good old boys? Go all alcoholic and druggy again?"

"Yeah, I know. I'm as scared of the Shaleville me as much as the New York City me."

"New York, New York," she said sarcastically.

"You love it," he jabbed.

21

"Beats the alternatives." Her eyes locked on his face. "So you might be half-Native American," she said. "You never mentioned that one before. You really think so?"

"My mother got around a lot. She also had a thing with a Sicilian about the time she got pregnant. She doesn't remember much about any of the guys from that period of her life. Too many one-night stands. She was nineteen."

"Maybe it's better you don't know your father ... at least if he's as tight-assed as mine. If I didn't know mine, I wouldn't have to work so hard not to be like him."

Aki tossed off her words, but Jake knew they came from down deep.

"You visiting Japan this year?" he asked her.

"No way. Their turn to come to me."

She looked at her watch, then played with her hands, getting fidgety.

"Anyway, Aki," he said, "I wanted to reassure you that I've been okay since you paid me and that I've been mainlining moderation."

She laughed. "That's a good one. Well, keep going with that and your detective thing if it helps you." She shook her head at him. "You and your film noir. Now you have this Fancy Dancer mystery playing in your head to replace the one co-starring that chameleon-haired Leandra."

"Yeah, it's working for me. My sister's scolding has also helped me stay clean ... you too, with your generosity."

Aki looked down at the table, then up again, then one more time down and up, all the while fiddling with her orange cashmere sweater. Jake had never seen her without some article of orange clothing. Even her pajamas were orange, he recalled from the short period she'd let him sleep on her couch. She nodded to herself, the light of a decision in her eyes.

"I might be able to help some more," she said.

"How so?"

"You're going to your hometown, then setting out again?"

"That's the plan."

She nodded to herself and to him. "I have an idea that I think you'll like. More gas money for you."

"I'm liking it already."

22

"You know how psycho I am when it comes to traveling. Back and forth between Brooklyn and Manhattan has been challenging enough."

"I'm impressed you're doing lunches like this."

"Nothing like success to help me cope. Artists have to schmooze to keep that success growing. My latest thing is photo collages. My first true collage was based on some photographs taken by some tourist friends from Japan. Have a look."

She reached in her tote, pulled out a tablet, and turned it on. Her slender finger danced on the screen and she found the image she wanted. It was a striking collage of doctored cityscapes. The overall effect was abstract, like the inside of eyelids, yet with fascinating details for a viewer to decipher.

"I sold it to a Japanese collector for good money. He wants more of my work, based on images from all over the U.S. So I need collaborators, people who like to travel unlike yours truly. I just lined up a model friend who works out of Miami. She'll be going to L.A. soon. You're also perfect for this. Get me photos from wherever you go. Lots of them. I'll pay you a grand at first. Maybe more ... depending on what I get from you and whether collectors are collecting."

"What an offer. Can I use my cellphone as the camera?"

"Not that old one I gave you."

"Disney gave me another one on appropriating mine." He pulled it from his pocket and held it up.

"Perfect. I'll text you the link for a lens to attach to it for better quality. Order one."

"Will do."

"You email the images as you go. I'll be photo-shopping them and overlapping them with others, so you don't have to worry too much. Let the camera be the smart one. Just be trigger happy."

"You're a savior, Aki. Once again."

"I'm not gonna tell you how much I sold the first collage for. You'd hold out for more money. I can give you an advance today. Three hundred."

"Great."

She pulled a checkbook out of the tote and began writing, then handed him the check, saying, "We can use PayPal from now on if this all works out. You got PayPal?"

"No."

"Well, get it. Digitize even more, Jake. That way we never have to meet in person again."

"Ha, ha."

"I'm joking of course. But you know how I roll. So we shake on it? So to speak. I don't wanna catch whatever hitchhiked a ride with you."

"Give me an elbow bump at least," he said, extending his arm.

She did – well, really an air elbow bump – but a breakthrough just the same.

~

Before leaving the city, Jake meandered through some of his former territory – up MacDougal Street into Washington Square Park and back. The park was quiet at this time of year – the new normal? – just a few people ambling about. The sounds and smells of the neighborhood brought back negatives from his recent past – the cauldron of drugs, his sidetracked art career, his failed relationships, and his homelessness. Yet he was clean other than minimal beer and pot, and he'd cut back on tobacco as well. Although admittedly a short stretch, his clearheaded moments were adding up on the big life clock. As ever, he had to be wary and not let negatives eat at him.

He stopped at Citibank and deposited Aki's check in his dwindling account. From sculptor to photographer, with the latter now doubling as a cover for shamus. The trip to this branch made him wonder about his street friend Mackerel, whom he'd last seen panhandling outside it. Was he alive and coping? Winter would be hard on him and Jake's other street friends – Tenor, Mary, and Ricky Rad.

He bought a coffee from a deli and crossed over to the Playground of the Americas, located at the corner of Sixth Avenue and Houston Street, the closest thing he'd had to a home while living on the street. He found his favorite bench to sip and ruminate. Some of his thoughts went to all the women he'd known in the city – lucky enough to have known, although it sure hadn't felt that way when it became time to move on from each and every one. He was sure fortunate to have reunited with Aki

– never a lover but always a friend and with no lingering ill-will between them. Now, she'd even become an employer.

Besides Aki, Caitlyn was the only other woman who was relevant now. He pulled out his phone and texted her and told her where he was and that he was setting out momentarily for Shaleville.

His sister texted back, "Fuck yeah!"

He returned to his van, snapped on his seatbelt, and fired up the engine. Time to make his escape. He'd only been on Manhattan Island a few hours and he was beginning to feel trapped again. The city had that effect, as if the Big Apple's skin were impenetrable from the inside. He pulled out of his parking spot and turned north onto Sixth Avenue, heading for the George Washington Bridge and lands beyond.

Despite his breaking free all those weeks ago and now doing so again, he remained tied to this city and its art scene thanks to Aki – a scene that had helped him define a creative self until a destructive one had won out.

Photo Shoot

"MOVE A LITTLE to your left," Jake told his sister.

She was standing in front of the green 19th-century saltbox house.

"You sure Aki wants people in them?"

"I'll tell her this isn't for reproduction. I just want to show off my sister in front of her house."

"Your house, too," Caitlyn said. "Make it a selfie."

His sister had bought out Jake's potential share of their mother's house with money her father – his sort of stepfather – had sent her, allowing Jake to move to New York City back when.

"Aki knows what I look like," he countered.

"Oh, all right. Just hurry up and take the goddamn picture."

"You sure are camera shy for such a doll."

"I always was and still am."

She was at that, Jake well knew. Even as the lead singer in a band her senior high-school year, she avoided standing at the center of promo photos. She also was painfully nervous before gigs, even though she performed so well.

"Camera shy or a doll?" he teased.

"Both, smartass."

He clicked away. Today was sunny yet cold. Caitlyn wore a red wool cap over her protruding blond hair and a white fleece coat. She'd given him a winter coat, a brown flannel-lined canvas one she'd bought at a thrift shop in anticipation ... anticipation and hope, she'd reminded him ... of his return.

"So graceful," he commented as she shifted her slender self from one modeling pose to another, with a seemingly unforced smile on her face.

"Don't use that word."

Grace, their mother, had made a joke out of being "graceful" whenever she danced in front of them – typically when drunk. Jake and Caitlyn had started using it to refer to their mother as inebriated.

"I meant graceful as in Grace Kelly."

Their mother's collection of classic movies was a positive memory, and thankfully so because the sequel to the neo-noir movie *Chinatown* – *The Two Jakes* – had inspired his mother's choice of his first name.

"Okay, I'll go with that," Caitlyn assented, her tone typically playful.

Jake checked the photos, then looked up at the house. "Now, I have some pics of you in front of the house's peeling paint to remind me of the work I promised to do come spring."

"Send them to me, so I can send them back to you to remind you again." She joined him at the end of the snowy footpath. "Okay, that's a wrap for this model."

"You did great," he said. "Want to see them?"

"Spare me. Where to now, Mr. Professional Photographer?"

"Let's walk to the end of Elm, then maybe visit a few other side streets. I'll wait for the new lens to arrive before I take on Main Street."

The street was quiet on this early Saturday morning. A plow hadn't come through yet and there were no car tracks in the three-inch dusting of snow. And without any wind, the powdery snow remained intact on rooftops and branches. Shaleville at its pristine winter best. No doubt Aki would make the small-town preciousness edgy in her collages.

Caitlyn pointed. "There's an eyeful. Ugh."

In front of a small two-story house stood an inflatable Santa. Next to him a snowman waved at the world with an inflated arm. Jake got a picture of that.

She pointed to a Victorian. "That's a nice sight, a neatly stacked woodpile."

In that big house's side yard, a pile of firewood stood four-logs deep in near-perfect symmetry.

"I get the message," Jake said.

Caitlyn had had a delivery of wood the previous day that needed stacking.

"I'll help." she said. "Saves me on gym fees."

Jake had already decided to stay in Shaleville through Christmas. After the recent nighttime nastiness in Florida and the grinding thoughts on the road, he wanted more of the comfort zone his sister and childhood home offered. He could accomplish a lot for her in two weeks in addition to keeping her company through the most emotionally charged of all holidays for them, thanks to their inevitably drunk-on-Christmas-Day mom.

Having abandoned Caitlyn for the past two-and-a-half years before being here, Jake wanted to come through for her. The Fancy Dancer mystery would have to wait.

He hadn't yet told her about it, but he would tonight. No more hiding his behavior from his sister as he had for too long on the last case. Enough of that foolishness.

~

"I don't trust you, Jake."

He thought it was a dream. Wrong.

Caitlyn, silhouetted against the hallway light, had opened the bedroom door – his childhood bedroom converted to a guest bedroom – and she was speaking to him.

"Hey, sis," he managed, blinking away sleep.

"I woke you?"

"Yeah, guess so."

"I thought you'd still be up ... a night owl still on city time."

"Road time. All I need is a pillow."

"Sorry," she said, turning to go.

"No, wait. Whattya mean about not trusting me?"

She turned back to face him but took a moment to reply. "I'll sleep well tonight because you're here. When you're gone, I lie in bed tossing and turning, wondering about you. After you left in November after being away so long, I worried that something bad had happened, like the city had swallowed you up again."

"It didn't. I missed Thanksgiving but I'm here for Christmas."

"I'm worried about what'll swallow you up next. Now, you're trying to solve some death that has nothing to do with you or anyone you know. What the fuck? Why seek out trouble?"

Jake had told her over dinner about the Fancy Dancer mystery and his plans. He'd framed his trip to western New York as a way to continue distracting himself from drug cravings, as well as a way to satisfy his curiosity about Native America, given who his father might be. He obviously had to do a better job convincing her.

"You can say the city swallowed me up," he continued. "But the pull of drugs started right here in Shaleville. I don't want you to be my minder, worrying every time I go off with any of the old crowd. What if I drink too much, which leads me to popping a pill, then someone offers me a bump of coke, crank, or horse, no doubt laced with fentanyl, and, you know ..." he trailed off.

"Sure, all the drugs are here, but at least I get to see lots of you and know whether you're turning them down," she said quietly.

"I'm determined not to succumb again. Living here with all the memories would be a challenge. For now, I'm better off staying on the move and keeping my mind on other people's fuckups."

Caitlyn retreated into silence. He couldn't see her face clearly in the shadows but he could imagine her expression showing worry, resentment, and love all at once.

She finally spoke, her voice now louder. "Okay, okay, Jake, but while you stay ahead of your own demons, watch the fuck out for other people's."

She turned away again, this time closing the door behind her a little too hard. Jake was left with his thoughts ... thoughts of his years in this town and in this bedroom ... thoughts of his sister and mother ... thoughts of his substance-abuse past ... all intermingled with thoughts of where his new path might lead him.

PART II: PROBE WEST

"Keep your head up, look around, don't make any mistakes that will lose you the game."
– from a Maya song

Western Door

A BLANKET OF SNOW covered the passing hills along New York State's Southern Tier Expressway, tree trunks gray against the stark white. Forecasts indicated clear weather over the next several days, including New Year's. Christmas in Shaleville and surrounding areas had been a white one – as much as six inches – and flurries had continued intermittingly since then. As of now anyway, it seemed that Jake could relax about driving conditions.

Over the holidays, Caitlyn had turned down invitations and had stayed at home with him. On his arrival, he'd shared his Disney purchases with her but had saved the Fancy Dancer figurine for Christmas. She loved it. She'd given him a sweater she'd started knitting since his visit during his first case. She'd made a vegetarian lasagna, a dish she'd learned from their mother. They'd watched movie after movie from their mother's collection of old VHS tapes in a laboring video player, among them Alfred Hitchcock's *Rear Window*. Jake had suggested watching that one because of his Grace Kelly reference on their photo shoot walk, telling her that, while in New York City, he'd tried to track down 125 West 9th Street, the apartment building with a rear window opposite that in the apartment of the laid-up photographer who becomes fixated with a possible murder. It had turned out to be a nonexistent address.

"Such a sleuthhound, just like the James Stewart character," Caitlyn had teased him. "What's his name?"

"Mom would know."

Every time their mother had watched that particular movie, she'd reminded her kids that it was based on a story by Cornell

Woolrich. He was one of the writers, like Dashiell Hammett and Raymond Chandler, among whose books, new or used, Jake inevitably got as Christmas presents – presents he was supposed to pass on to his sister when he was done with them. Caitlyn had chosen her own teenage reading list, however.

Remembering childhood Christmases – the relatively good ones – they'd tried to phone their mother in Oklahoma City. Not surprisingly the latest number Caitlyn had for her wasn't in service.

"She'll call when she calls," his sister had said, waving off hurt and worry.

Jake had seen no one else he felt obliged to talk to during his Shaleville visit, except the couple and their daughter who ran the hardware store. He'd stayed busy piling wood, cleaning up the basement and attic, building shelves to help Caitlyn organize stored possessions, and tuning up the van.

A truck pulled out in the passing lane. Jake eased up on the gas pedal to let it speed by. No need to race other vehicles, especially not tractor-trailers going too fast. He'd departed Shaleville early to have mostly daylight to reach the Seneca Allegany Resort & Casino in Salamanca, the Fancy Dancer's reported hometown. He'd booked a room for a night.

This journey with a mission had begun at a Native-run casino in Florida, and he would visit another one, hoping to pick up helpful information. Afterwards, he would head for Seneca Hills, where the killing had occurred.

Jake knew that the member tribes of the Iroquois League thought of their combined ancestral territory as one big longhouse, originally extending across New York State and eventually including lands in Ontario and Quebec. The Seneca are considered the Keepers of the Western Door, and the Mohawk, the Keepers of the Eastern Door. In between the ancestral lands of those two peoples, west to east, are those of the Tuscarora, Cayuga, Onondaga, and Oneida.

The van reliably hummed. It had served Jake well, carrying him thousands of miles. Today, he was counting on it to manage at least two hundred more. So far so good.

The sense of security evaporated as he happened to glance in the side mirror. A cop car – State Police – drove behind him.

It remained in the right-hand lane behind him. Checking the listing for the plate number? Cargo vans were suspect in the age of terrorism – as Jake had worried on the last case – and perhaps his van even more than others, given its beat-up look. Was this vehicle profiling?

Why feel threatened? He had a valid license. The vehicle had a current inspection sticker. He was clean. The van was clean. Not even an ashtray with a roach in it, not a big deal anyway given the changes to cannabis laws.

After the first few moments, the tailgating felt like harassment. The Statie was just earning his living, right? The cop finally pulled into the passing lane and cruised next to the van long enough to get a look at Jake's face. Or so Jake surmised. Jake had been advised back in his druggie days that it was better to glance at cops while driving than not. But he kept his eyes straight ahead, ignoring the representative of road law.

The cop car sped off.

~

Darkness came early on this short winter day. To stay alert on the final stretch to the casino and hotel, Jake rolled down the van's window, letting the cold air hit his face.

He exited the highway at Salamanca and angled toward the towering lights of the resort protruding from the otherwise moonlit hillscape. Make arrival as easy as possible for visitors; start gamblers' good luck with ready parking, easy access to the lobby, and a warm greeting from a cheerful receptionist. And so it was for Jake.

After checking in, he easily found his way to his room on the eighth floor. What money can buy. He was still appreciating hotel luxury after his recent months of homelessness. Earth tones in the room hinted at the Native connection, enhanced by Native-themed artwork. A hotel room photo-op for Aki. Would there be video cameras here to monitor him, like in the gaming rooms? What an invasion of privacy that would be. Control paranoia, he reminded himself. Be hardboiled. Live up to his self-proclaimed calling, or just stop kidding himself and go back to hiding behind booze and all the rest.

After showering, Jake ventured forth into the evening – or the presumed evening. No night, day, or seasons existed within the casino's perpetually lit and climate-controlled confines. He rode the elevator down from the hotel tower to the lobby and made a right to the casino's entrance.

Even though Jake knew what to expect, the casino's sights and sounds jolted him, with their intense lighting, piped-in pop music, humming slot machines, and visitors in manic gambling mode. He wandered about the big room, from the slots to the table games. Cards danced in dealers' hands. Craps and roulette possessed a Bondian elegance. Many of the props themselves – especially the roulette wheels with their polished wood and golden spindles – were finely crafted objects.

Odd to think, surrounded as he was by the confusing morass of cross-cultural aesthetics, that he walked on Native lands. Not all Native-run casinos are situated on tribally held territory, he knew. This one rises up from hills within the limits of Salamanca, the only U.S. city located on a Native Reservation – the Allegany Reservation of the Seneca Nation of Indians – with both Native and non-Native residents.

Jake made his way to the circular Casino Bar and sat down. A beefy, middle-aged bartender took his order. Jake chose a local beer, Buffalo Lager. For him, in his present state of mind, the name referenced a Native connection to an animal, not just to a city. The bar was quiet – no crowd drinking away gambling winnings, or more likely exorcising gambling losses. The bartender stayed busy, fussing with bottles and glasses.

"I missed last summer's powwow," Jake said. "Anything going on this winter?"

The bartender shrugged. "Not my cup of tea," he said, moving away. He looked non-Native with his faded blond hair. "Hey, Sandy," he called over to the female bartender on the opposite side of the circle. "Question for you." He tossed his head Jake's way.

Sandy approached him. Her hair color matched her name and she also looked non-Native.

"Hi, I'm Jake," he said. "I was wondering about an indoor powwow around here this time of year."

"Not much going on until the big one in Salamanca come July," she replied.

"Yeah, saw that online. Hope to make it."

Her blue eyes studied him. "What's your tribe?"

"Mohawk, but that's family hearsay. No documents to prove it. I was raised in a small town over Albany way. You?"

"Irish Catholic," Sandy replied. "Raised in Buffalo's suburbs. I married a Seneca."

She said the last proudly.

"He a dancer?" Jake asked.

"Used to be. Has a bad knee. He drums now ... when he's not making jewelry."

She held out her wrists covered in bands of silver, some of them with multicolored stone inlays.

"Nice," Jake commented. "Will he have a table at the July powwow?"

"That's the plan. If you're interested in the Seneca and the other Iroquois, you should go to the Seneca-Iroquois National Museum on Broad Street. My husband has jewelry for sale in the gift shop."

"I'll do that. What's his name?"

"Stan Porter," she said proudly. "He's got a website. StanPorterJewelry.com."

"I'll check it out."

Sandy went off to another customer, returning after a few minutes.

Jake had more questions ready: "Will there be a dance competition at the summer powwow?"

"Of course."

"I read about what happened at the Arrow Alliance on Labor Day Weekend. Were you there?"

"No."

"So unlikely, something like that at a powwow."

"I'll say. People are worried around here."

"About more violence?"

"No ... worried for the prime suspect, Grant Guyasuta. No one thinks he did it. My husband and I know him from the powwow circuit. We also know people who grew up with him. Not a militant guy at all."

34

"Wasn't he seen with the ex-cop who got killed? Baines?"

"Who was probably hassling him."

"Didn't he run away?"

Sandy lowered her head and sighed, then looked back up at Jake. Showing impatience?

"Some of the vic's friends might've jumped to the wrong conclusion and taken Guyasuta away and done who knows what to him," she said.

Jake absorbed that, then asked, "You ever see him dance?"

"Many times. He's awesome. Dancing is everything to him. He appreciates his audiences whether they're Native or not."

Other folks sat down at the bar – two happy couples exalting over some blackjack winnings – and she started toward them.

"Nice talking to you," Jake said.

She nodded neutrally.

Just after putting a ten on the bar and stepping away, Jake heard shouting from the casino floor: "These slots are too fucking tight!" Then, sounds of glass breaking.

Jake moved to the Casino Bar's entranceway and watched as Casino employees, some in uniform and some in plainclothes, darted from different directions to haul the disgruntled gambler away. The scene reminded Jake of Disney's Epcot Center on Thanksgiving when security went into high gear. Thankfully, this time, he wasn't involved in any way.

Jake headed for the casino exit and entered the lobby. He walked past the elevators and found the staircase to the second floor. He was hungry. There were several choices on this level: The Western Door Steakhouse; Patria, offering Italian dining; and the Seneca Café. He chose the café.

He had a beer and a club sandwich. This second beer after the one at the Casino Bar relaxed him – unlike back when he'd needed a twelve-pack for the alcohol to register – and made it easier for him to be social and try for more information. The waitress didn't look Native and showed no interest in his queries about local events, so he let it go and didn't bring up powwows or Fancy Dancing. But he'd done well on this first stop in Seneca territory. He'd learned from bartender Sandy that local sentiment leaned toward Guyasuta's innocence, similar to the sentiment expressed at the Brighton Casino by the two men, and at the Leesburg Powwow by the carver Joe Panther.

Riding the elevator into the sky, Jake reflected on how the man who might have fathered him was a descendant of the Keepers of the Eastern Door. Did his mom's Mohawk lover ever visit this Western Door? Did he attend powwows? Did he frequent casinos? She'd told him he liked rock'n'roll. No doubt he appreciated part-Cherokee Jimi Hendrix. Did he also like Redbone, encouraged by Hendrix to put together an all-Native band? Caitlyn, who liked oldies, had sung both some Hendrix covers and the Redbone hit "Come and Get Your Love" in her band.

Jake reached his room and the big bed. While lying in it, he had the thought that it felt good to be connected to Native America, at least in concept if not by blood. And he realized that he wanted the Fancy Dancer to be innocent.

Suppress that thought, he told himself. Stay objective while on a case – noncommittal, skeptical, and even cynical, like his teenage heroes, the fictional private eyes – and be ever vigilant, in survival mode. There was a killer out there and maybe more than one if Sandy had it right about Baines's friends taking matters into their own hands and doing "who knows what" to Guyasuta.

Cross-Cultural

"WHAT'LL IT BE?"

"Just coffee and a poppyseed bagel with butter."

The sleepy-eyed waiter – at the end of an all-night shift? – moved away. Jake had chosen the Bear Claw Café on the far side of the casino for breakfast. While waiting for his order, he read the magazine *Seneca Today* that he'd taken from the hotel room. Some articles related to casino and gaming issues; others celebrated Native arts and crafts.

He checked out just before 11:00 a.m., then headed to his van in the hotel parking lot. He climbed in and drove a short distance away, then pulled onto the shoulder. Stepping outside, he snapped some pictures of the massive resort. Reflected sunlight from the glass and steel made for good images to send to Aki.

He located a parking spot just a half-block away from the Seneca-Iroquois National Museum and walked along Broad Street to its entrance. The modest one-story building seemed just enough museum for Jake to take in before wandering Salamanca's streets.

Inside, he wandered through sectioned-off displays of Iroquois history and artifacts from ancient times to the present. Several other folks milled about. He learned that the municipality of Salamanca had leased its lands from the Seneca Nation of Indians for a dollar a year beginning in 1892, then had renegotiated the lease a hundred years later in 1991, trying to address both Native and non-Native interests. The new lease was for a period of forty years.

Jake also studied several maps. He now had it straight that, in addition to the Allegany Reservation where he now stood, the Seneca Nation of Indians also has the Cattaraugus and Oil Springs Reservations, plus two small pieces where other casinos had been built – the Buffalo Creek Territory in downtown Buffalo and the Niagara Falls Territory in Niagara Falls. Another tribal entity, the Tonawanda Band of Seneca Indians, has the Tonawanda Reservation.

Inside a glass case in the gift shop, Jake saw a silver and black stone necklace made by Stan Porter, the bartender Sandy's husband. He thought about using the necklace as a starting point for conversation with the Native woman behind the counter but let the idea go. From a necklace to a Seneca murder suspect was a long way to go conversationally with a salesclerk in a retail setting with other people nearby.

Outside again, phone-camera in hand, Jake walked the streets. As Aki had suggested, he became trigger happy. She would do her near-abstract thing with the photos. Yet there were also photo-essays in this city, with its unique landlord-tenant relationship. The sorry state of many of the homes spoke to the tension between the two factions. Smoke shops with giant signs offered cigarettes at discount reservation prices.

The cross-cultural strangeness of this place felt like simmering fuel – fuel for violence. Like at the Arrow Alliance powwow?

~

37

Steel-gray clouds hung low in the sky. Not quite halfway between Salamanca and Cattaraugus, beyond a stretch of well-kept houses dotting the landscape, Jake made a right off Route 353 onto Eagleton Road. After less than a mile, he reached Seneca Hills. The one-stoplight hamlet sure felt familiar, like a mini-Shaleville. This stretch of Eagleton – now marked as a street, not a road – offered a church, bar, diner, hardware store, gas station with convenience store, and the Red Jacket Motel, where he'd reserved a room in advance.

A red neon profile of an Indian with a one-feathered headdress announced the motel. It was named, Jake assumed, after the Seneca leader Red Jacket, famous for his oratory in the decades after the American Revolution, and not referencing the red coats of British soldiers. The large central cabin held the office, flanked on each side by five smaller ones. Jake stepped out of the van into colder air than earlier that day, stretched, and entered.

A portly bearded man in striped shirt and suspenders sat at the counter. His chair was positioned so that he only had to move his large hands to check Jake in. The fan of an electric heater purred behind him like a big robotic cat, putting out more heat than necessary for the small room. The man took Jake's debit card, then handed him a form to fill out.

"I'll probably be here a week," Jake said.

The man looked up from the debit card. "The weekly rate is the same as four days. That means even if you leave early ..."

"Understood. Sign me up."

The man stroked his beard. It was a full one and fit the rest of his bloated face. Jake wrote his name, address – his sister's as on his license – and the license number and handed the form back.

The man studied it for at least a minute.

"This a work thing? Arrow Alliance business?" he finally asked.

"Could be," Jake replied.

The man grunted a "Huh?"

"I heard about the Arrow alliance Center being built. Thought I'd check it out. Maybe find some work."

"Work's stopped for now. That's why I have empty rooms. Word is they're gonna start up construction again come warm weather if they can afford it."

"Any doubt about that?"

"They're gonna have the money. Casinos are making a ton of money and this guy Catamount knows how to work tribes with casinos."

Jake nodded.

The man now had his eyes fixed on Jake. "You Injun, Jake Jakes?" he asked.

"Maybe some Mohawk blood."

"Might help get you work being one of them."

Jake wanted out of this stifling office and away from the man's surly presence. But he was on a mission. Keep the conversation going.

"Hope so. You own the motel?" he asked.

"It's my baby."

"The pandemic must have hurt business."

"Yeah, of course it did, but people around here ain't chickenshit. I had my medicine." He pulled a bottle of Everclear from behind the counter and waved it. "A high-proof sanitizer inside and out."

"Yeah, just don't be drinking Lysol," Jake quipped. "Anyway, you gotta be happy about the Arrow Alliance building their headquarters here to keep going strong."

The motel owner didn't look happy. Jake thought about the bias directed at him in Florida – bias backed up by a baseball bat. More of that sentiment here apparently.

"Sure, up to a point," he admitted. "I like filling the cabins but I don't like the bullshit that goes along with it. That Catamount fellow asked me to change the motel's name and take down the sign. I brought in WiFi for the out-of-towners. Hell, ain't that enough?"

"Why'd he want you to change the name?"

"He said it's undignified to use a Seneca chief's name like that. That was his word. 'Undignified.' Hell, Catamount's not even Seneca. He's Erie-Mingo, whatever that is. He offered the cost of a new sign, but no friggin' deal. The motel was called the Red Jacket when I bought it and I'm keeping it that way."

"What about the killing last September? That must make people around here nervous."

The man grunted affirmation. "We had cops and roadblocks everywhere. People thought that the Fancy Pants would show up on their back porch. I bet he's long gone and never coming back. Lots of reservations where he can hide out."

"You think he's guilty?"

The man guffawed. "He hightailed it out, didn't he?"

"And the motive?"

"Doesn't take much."

"Guyasuta's quite the dancer, I understand," Jake said.

"Wouldn't know about that stuff. So you got an appointment with Chief Catamount?"

"No, I'll just head on up there. They call it the Turtle, right?"

"Yeah, that's what they call it. It's gonna be shaped like one when they finish the damn thing."

Jake had had enough.

"Thanks for the info," he said. "I didn't get your name."

"Sam Collins," he said, handing Jake a key. "Last cabin thataway." He pointed with his big thumb.

Jake pointed in the other direction. "The Jack and Jill Diner ... how late is that open?"

"Nine. Try the meatloaf sandwich."

Jake gave him a thumbs-up and left. He re-parked his van in front of the designated bungalow and, key in hand, walked to the door.

The room looked clean. The walls seemed freshly painted. No radio but cable TV. And WiFi, as reported. No artwork – just a Billy's Hardware Store calendar, a business in a neighboring town, Little Valley. Support local businesses? The Arrow Alliance wasn't getting that treatment. To Sam Collins, Native Americans – the First People – were outsiders. Jake felt the tension, even from his motel room, and thought about some beer. He'd do food instead.

Redirect agitation, he reminded himself. Concentrate on this photo op. Get more images for Aki. He went back outside and shot the Red Jacket sign, the exterior of the office, and the row of cabins. Maybe she could do something with contrasting establishments – the glistening Seneca Allegany, the rundown houses in Salamanca, and the budget motel with the controversial neon sign.

Back in the room, Jake put his bag on the chair and headed to the john to wash up before checking out another local business venture, the diner. After Sam Collins, he felt anxious about that.

Small towns and their small-mindedness could be more daunting than even a big city.

~

The cold had even more of a bite to it. Snow that might have melted earlier was now icing over. Jake, bundled up in the coat from Caitlyn, paid attention to each step.

Two snowmobiles were parked in a small lot next to the Jack and Jill Diner. Jake entered through the glass door. No one sat in the diner's three booths or at its two tables. Just two people were at the bar. Their heads turned toward Jake for a quick glance. They belonged to a giant of a man probably in his late forties with whitening blond hair, and a woman of about the same age but a lot smaller, with hair that had been dyed a few shades lighter than the man's. They wore snowmobile suits. Against the Formica-and-chrome backdrop, they looked like they might be early space pioneers of the 1960s, wearing their space suits to dinner. Christmas music sounded forth from a single wall-mounted speaker. Time to move on from the Christmas music, Jake thought as he approached the counter.

A woman in white apron over sweats, coffee pot in hand, appeared from a doorway behind the bar. She was probably a decade older than her customers but, without makeup or hair dye, she wore her years well. Was this Jill? Expressionless, she looked at Jake.

"Still serving?" he asked.

"Uh-huh." She seemed stern, or was she just weary after a long day's work? "Sit at the counter?"

"Sounds good," Jake said, taking the stool next to the man.

The woman turned to the other customers. "More coffee, Big Ben ... Little Nell?"

"A half-cup will do, Jill," Ben said.

"Not me. I'm at my beddy-bye limit," Nell said.

Jill poured Ben's cup, then turned to Jake. "You?"

"Yes, please."

Jill grabbed a cup from under the bar, placed it in front of Jake, and poured.

"Milk, sugar?"

"Black is good." Before she could hand him a menu, he added, "I'll have the meatloaf sandwich. Recommended by Sam Collins."

"Fries or mashed potatoes on the side?"

"Mashed potatoes."

Jill nodded her approval, then said, "I take it you're staying at the Red Jacket."

"Right."

"Good, he's getting some business. Help stop his complaining." As she reentered the kitchen, she called ahead, "Jack ... meatloaf sandwich!"

Jill and Jack. Ben and Nell. Now to start a conversation. Jake had grown up where weather was a preoccupation.

"Clear driving these past days. That's a blessing."

Ben replied: "Just enough snow on the ground to snowmobile. Where you hail from?"

"Shaleville, west of Albany."

"Never heard of it."

"I have," Nell put in.

"Uh, Nell ... let me guess," Ben said drily. "You bowled there."

Small-framed Nell puffed up. "I bowled there all right. Place called Maggie's."

Jake smiled at her. "That's great. Maggie's an old pal. You get to talk to her?"

"I sure did. She liked us. We're legendary."

"Go on, tell him already," Ben prodded Nell. "I sure know you're going to." His sarcasm was gentle.

Jill returned from the kitchen with a napkin and utensils for Jake. She stayed at the bar.

Nell puffed up even more, head thrust forward. "My girlfriends and I have bowled every bowling alley in New York State, except in New York City and Long Island. That's what we do."

"That's awesome," Jake said.

This felt good so far, unlike at the Red Jacket. The positive side of small towns.

"Legendary status sure comes in handy when meeting strangers," Ben commented, again drily.

"What're you doing in these parts?" Jill asked Jake.

42

"I needed a break from the same old. Maybe get some better-paying work for a stretch. Thought I might talk to the folks at the Turtle."

"You in a tribe?"

"No ... maybe some Mohawk blood though."

Were Jack and Jill, like Red Jacket Sam, critical of the Arrow Alliance? Its presence in Seneca Hills had to have helped their business.

Jill spoke again: "They're not hiring. They just turned down someone I know. Someone your age who wanted office work. Maybe it's different if you're Indian."

"They hired Smitty to paint," Nell offered.

"He didn't last long," Jill said.

"Not surprising," Ben offered. "I wouldn't trust him with a paint brush on my place."

Jake sipped his coffee. He wouldn't bring up the killing to this bunch yet. Ben and Nell seemed accepting of outsiders. But he wanted to be sure he'd won Jill over before any probing.

He resorted to the weather again: "Any storms predicted? I haven't checked the forecast in a while."

"Just lake effect stuff through New Year's." Ben stated. "Hopefully enough for better snowmobiling."

Jack appeared from the kitchen, delivering the plate of food. His long face on top of his lanky body gave nothing away.

The others talked while Jake ate – mostly about the Christmas basketball tournament in Little Valley. Jack eventually returned to the kitchen. Ben and Nell stood up to leave.

"I'm Jake. Ben and Nell, right?"

"That's us. Big Ben and Little Nell."

They left. Jill cleaned and organized behind the counter. Jake finished his food. He commented on how good it all was – he meant it except for the bland white bread – and asked for the check. On settling up, he told Jill he would be back for breakfast. She gave a slight nod as he turned and made for the door.

That night, Jake dreamed of Shaleville, emotions running from nostalgia to anxiety to panic ...

A high school gym ... the noise, the smells. Then ... never quite making it to class ... ridiculed by teachers. Time crawling, walls closing in, suffocating him. Breathe ... wake up!

43

He did so and forced his thoughts to what was right about his adolescence ... little sister Caitlyn.

Turtle Island

JAKE FOLLOWED Eagleton Road northward. Less than an eighth of a mile beyond the hamlet's residential area, he stopped at the end of a driveway on the left. A freestanding post held a carved wooden turtle and two wooden signs. The larger sign, black over green, had a row of four connected circles forming a cross; lettering underneath announced *Arrow Alliance*. A smaller sign, black on red, announced *Erie-Mingo Nation* above a double-lined hoop containing two crossed arrows.

Jake drove westward up the inclined driveway flanked by forests. It soon leveled out and divided. One black on green sign pointed to the left: *Staff Parking*. A second one pointed to the right: *Guest Parking*. He angled to the right.

The trees soon opened up, revealing a partly finished structure. At its southern end Jake saw a domed oblong in the shape of a turtle's head and neck. It was covered in cedar shakes except at the neck's back end, presently sealed off with heavy-duty clear plastic. Extending about two hundred feet from the head, a concrete foundation outlined the rest of the unfinished structure – a turtle's shell, legs, and, on its northern end, a tail. He parked and stepped onto the otherwise empty guest lot, near what would become the tail. The grounds along the edge of the foundation had been re-excavated and resurfaced as a red flagstone walkway. He followed it.

After rounding the jut in the foundation for the Turtle's left front leg, Jake reached the head and neck. A double wooden door represented the mouth; windows bulging above it, the eyes. The door was recessed, creating the effect of a turtle's overbite. The staff parking lot opposite held two cars: a black Volvo station wagon and a red Ford sedan.

Jake approached the door. A sign on the structure's cedar shakes announced *Welcome to the Turtle*. Smaller versions of the two signs at the driveway's entrance were mounted beneath it. A fourth sign, this one handwritten and mounted on the door, told him to *Please Enter.*

He did so and proceeded through a wood-paneled vestibule into a large office, also paneled with stained boards. Two desks were situated under the Turtle's eye-windows. A couch, a stack of folding chairs, and shelves holding publications lined one wall. A stone chimney rose up along the opposite wall, with a barrel-shaped woodstove in front of it and a woodpile nearby. Native-themed artwork filled some of the empty wall space. On the far wall directly opposite the vestibule, a back door led to what Jake assumed to be the Turtle's neck.

An elderly Native-looking woman sat at one desk, her frame tinier than Nell's, even with her bulky sweater. She looked up from a computer screen, revealing a small, pointed face.

"*Kwekwe?* May I help you?" she said.

Her gray hair was pulled back in a bun. Her smile accentuated her wrinkles. Jake guessed her age at pushing seventy. A second woman, maybe early thirties, sat at the other desk. With her black hair and deep complexion, she also looked Native. She wore a flannel shirt. She glanced up briefly, then back down at her computer screen. She had angular features balanced by full lips.

Jake approached the older woman's desk, stopping at a strip of yellow tape on the floor, a typical six feet away.

"Hi, I'm Jake Jakes," he said. "I'm taking some photos of my travels for an artist friend. I hoped to get some of the Turtle."

She tilted her head, studying him momentarily. A nameplate identified her as Ehnita Feather.

"For personal use, these photos?" she asked.

"My friend, Aki Sato, is a photographer out of New York City. She's doing a series on America for Japanese clientele. She asked me to document my trip ... wants landscapes and buildings more than people. She makes collages of them. She has a website."

"Are you from New York City?" Ehnita asked.

"I grew up in Shaleville, over near Albany. I'm staying at the Red Jacket. My mother says my father might be Mohawk. I stayed in Salamanca last night."

She turned to the younger woman, "Ona?"

Jake saw that a nameplate identified the younger woman as Onatah Makens.

45

"Ehnita is Mohawk," Ona said without looking up from her computer. Then: "Spell the photographer's name, please."

He did so, then added, "Her site is under Aki Sato Photography."

Ona entered the information, her slender fingers moving fast on the keyboard. She then used her mouse, moving it around and clicking.

"What's the name of the Mohawk who might be your father?" Ehnita asked him. "Is it Jakes?"

"No, that's my mother's maiden name. She married years after I was born and told me she doesn't remember last names of anyone who might've fathered me if she ever knew them at all. It's like that. She also was with an Italian-American man about that time."

"You could get a DNA test," Ehnita said.

"You should know even if you don't get one," Ona added, still gazing at the screen. A pleasant lilt to her voice softened the pointed comment.

"That's why I'm visiting Native lands ... to find out if I know," Jake countered.

That was partly true.

Ona finally looked up, her eyes hanging quizzically on him.

"I like your friend's work. Excuse me," she said.

She stood up and headed for the back door, walking brusquely yet with a bounce. Her tight faded jeans revealed her as fit. Jake didn't let his eyes linger too long, turning back to Ehnita.

"Where'd you stay in Salamanca?" she asked.

"The Seneca Allegany."

"Did you gamble?"

"A bit."

"I've been known to gamble there some. At least my losses go to the People. What else did you do in Salamanca?"

"Walked the streets ... and I visited the Seneca-Iroquois Museum."

"You're just touring around, taking pictures and learning about the People?"

"That's the idea. I'm also hoping to land some part-time work so I can afford to keep traveling."

Ehnita's eyes again moved thoughtfully over him. "What skills do you have besides photography?"

"Actually, I'm kind of new to photography. Smart phones make it easy. Just helping my friend out while on the road. I'm a builder. I worked on a lot of houses around Shaleville. In New York City I got it in my head to be a sculptor."

"Any success?"

"For fifteen minutes or less."

She gave a half-smile. "You pick up any computer skills while on your life journey?"

"The basics."

"I'm striving for the basics myself. One other question ... did you get the latest vaccine?"

"The latest as far as I know. And I think I was one of the asymptomatic positives who got immunity that way, too."

"Glad to hear it. At my age I have to stay paranoid. So why don't you have a seat while we wait for Ona, Jake Maybe-Mohawk," she said, the last with another half-smile.

She returned to her screen. Jake walked over to a shelf, picked up a magazine – *Native Peoples* – and sat in the nearest chair, beginning an article on Native athletes. Jim Thorpe of the Sac and Fox was the lead.

Ona opened the inner door and told Ehnita, "Chad wants to talk to you."

The older woman stood up, nodded knowingly at Jake, and headed toward Ona in the doorway. She also, despite her years, walked with a bounce. Ona handed her a cellphone. Ehnita disappeared through the door, and Ona returned to her desk and computer screen. Jake turned the pages of the magazine, reading about another Olympian – the Lakota runner Billy Mills – absorbing what he could despite the loud silence.

Ehnita was gone about five minutes. On returning, she carried the phone to Ona at her desk, who spoke into it in Iroquoian, then listened a moment. After touching the screen to end the call, she looked over at Jake.

"We held council by phone and came to a decision," she said. "I'll talk to Aki Sato. If she agrees to our terms by email, you can take photos on her behalf. You'll have to sign an agreement, too. We'll also be providing you both with a statement about our nation, our organization, and our center. Many of Ms. Sato's photos run from impressionistic to abstract. She might want to represent the shape of a turtle in at least one of them. If so, we want it known who we are and what the Arrow Alliance is all about. Can you give me the best number to get in touch with her and let her know I'll be calling her? I'll need your number, too. I'll be in touch with you."

Focused and efficient, Ona was. He gave her the contact info and said his goodbyes. She returned a perfunctory nod.

Ehnita spoke:"*O:nen*. That means 'goodbye' in Mohawk. Learn it."

Jake repeated it back to her. Ehnita smiled, a full one now, causing her eyes to smile as well.

~

The Jack and Jill Diner had a late breakfast crowd. Lots of heads turned to eyeball Jake as he moved to the only empty seat at the counter, the end one on the left. He nodded hello to Jill and she nodded back ever so slightly, just like her goodbye nod the evening before.

A waitress taking care of the customers at the booths reminded Jake of his mother. She had the same lean build with muscle tone long gone, hair dyed blond too many times, and premature deep lines. The waitress looked happy enough with her lot in life. His mother would have been scowling to be trapped there.

Jake picked up a nearby menu and gazed at it although he already knew what he wanted. Jill came over with a cup of coffee for him. He ordered eggs, home fries, and wheat toast – nothing controversial for an upstate hamlet, such as egg whites and a slice of avocado. The man next to him was deep into a newspaper. Staring into the distance, Jake waited for his food.

After a breakfast without conversation, he returned to his motel room and lay in bed, researching the region on his phone and waiting for a phone call from the woman known as Ona ... Onatah Makens.

~

"Let me know whenever you want to stop and take a photo," Ona said.

"Okay, thanks."

On the far side of the Turtle, after following a path through a partly snow-covered field, Ona led Jake along an icy path up a forested hillside. He held back, taking the lead from her social spacing. She wore a green down parka and hiking boots. He was glad he also had a decent coat and decent boots. He tried to keep his eyes on his every step rather than on her shape moving in front of him. Sunshine, competing with passing clouds, came and went.

Ona gave little away. One exception: On phoning him to set up a time for the tour, she'd told him that she'd spoken to Aki and that she liked her. Unpredictable Aki had evidently come through. She probably took some pleasure in verifying Jake's assignment even though she knew his other motive for being where he was. Inquisitive Aki would want a full report from him on the Native woman who had phoned her. He would check in with her that night.

Ona stopped to let Jake catch up on the steep incline.

"Is this all Alliance land?" he asked as he reached her.

She looked at the trees – mostly pine – around her. "No, it's a state reforestation area from the bottom of the hill upward."

He wanted to keep her talking. "I've been reading up some on the Seneca, Erie, and Mingo. Are you Seneca?"

"My father, who was from Oklahoma, grew up among the Seneca-Cayuga but also claimed Mingo blood. My mother was full Seneca, raised in Salamanca by Thomas and my grandmother. She met my father at a gathering in Canada and he moved here."

Jake noted that she'd used the past tense for her parents.

"They named me Onatah for the Haudenosaunee Spirit of Corn," she added.

"Beautiful."

The name indeed was, but he still felt awkward after saying so.

"Thanks," she said quickly.

"The Mingo were a branch tribe of the Haudenosaunee ... do I have that right?" he asked.

She met his gaze. "You want the history lesson?"

49

"Please."

She seemed to look inward, gathering her thoughts before speaking. "The Mingo people branched off from the Haudenosaunee and, in the early 18th century, settled in Pennsylvania. Their name is derived from Mingwe which had been used by other First Nations for any of the Haudenosaunee. In the mid-1700s, the Mingo joined the Shawnee and other Native peoples resisting the British. A century later, some of their descendants moved to the Indian Territory with Seneca and Cayuga bands. That group became known as the Seneca-Cayuga Tribe of Oklahoma. Seneca-Cayuga are proud of their part-Mingo ancestry."

Her soft, modulated voice, no longer neutral, was mesmerizing.

"And the Erie?" Jake asked.

"The Erielhonen ... the 'long-tailed ones' ... are more of a mystery. Early 17th-century French traders called them the Nation of the Cat because of the animal-skin robes they wore, complete with tails typical of the mountain lion. They lived west of the Seneca mostly in what is now Ohio. They warred with the Seneca over hunting grounds, a conflict spurred on by Europeans who supplied firearms to the Seneca in exchange for furs. The Erie were killed, dispersed, or absorbed. Some of them are thought to have joined the Mingo."

She let him absorb the information, then added, "Ehnita tells me you visited the museum in Salamanca. I give history talks there to school tours."

"You explain it well. I read online that Chad Catamount founded the Erie-Mingo Nation and the Arrow Alliance. What's his background?"

She hesitated, then said, "Yes, we did. Chad was born in Oklahoma. His father was part of the Seneca-Cayuga Nation like mine. His mother, also from Oklahoma, was half-Shawnee, half-white. His father felt connected to the Erie, the Cat People, and adopted the name Catamount ... a name used for various wild cats. He brought his family to Salamanca about the same time my father married my mother here. They all ran a general store together."

She'd used the past tense for both sets of parents.

"The fellow who owns the Red Jacket ... Sam Collins ... doesn't seem to realize that Chad is part Seneca," Jake said.

"The Erie-Mingo thing has confused many of the locals ... even though we've gone to great lengths to explain what we're all about. Many non-Native folks don't realize Native folks are mutts, too. Chad probably shouldn't have pressed him so early about changing the motel's name. I bet Sam mentioned that."

"Yeah, he did."

Since they were discussing so many tribal entities, Jake considered asking Ona about both Grant Guyasuta and Salali Jenkins. That might ruin the mood. Later for that.

"Let's go to Turtle Overlook," Ona said.

She continued up the hillside. Jake paused to take photos of a nearby towering pine tree, then hurried to catch up again. They reached the crest. The path veered southward to the left. At an opening in the trees, they could look down below and see the expanse of the unfinished Turtle, its head jutting out from the foundation's outline. The sun was cooperating and Jake snapped picture after picture.

"Why a turtle shape?" he asked.

"According to Haudenosaunee oral history, Sky Woman fell down to Earth when it was covered with water. Various animals tried to swim to the bottom of the ocean to bring back dirt and create land. Muskrat succeeded in gathering dirt and placed it on the back of Turtle. It grew into the land known today as North America. Turtle Island or Turtle Continent, it's called by some. Many First Nations have sacred lands with important historical or mythological meaning. This is becoming a sacred place for us."

Jake wanted to say something meaningful. All he managed was, "There's magic here ... that's for sure."

Was "magic" the right word? It could have negative connotations. Chill, he told himself. He'd already acknowledged being uninformed.

Ona offered more information: "The Turtle shape has elements of traditional dwellings of many First Nations ... the communal longhouse of the Iroquoians and the domed wigwam of the Algonquians. It'll have offices and a council room. We also intend to build smaller lodges so we can house staff and guests on the grounds. A row of them will be located at the base of this hill.

"Will you live here?"

Was that too personal? Chill, he again told himself.

She seemed unfazed. "Some of us have been sleeping in our offices. We want someone on the grounds at all times. Eventually we'll move to the lodges. Construction starts again come spring. That's the plan anyway if things work out. We're always trying to raise money. The SNI ... the Seneca Nation of Indians ... have been generous. They originally provided us office space in Salamanca, then gave us matching funds for the land in Seneca Hills. We've been reaching out to casino tribes far and wide to move forward. Unity among Native peoples feels especially urgent. We didn't think we'd see progress at the federal level, even as slow as it's been over the decades, grind to such a dramatic halt as it has in these trying times."

"I hear you."

She fell silent, her concern palpable.

After a few seconds, Jake asked, "Will you build a casino here someday?"

"The Erie-Mingo, given the fact that we've only recently adopted those tribal names, will never get federal recognition, which is necessary for a gaming compact. Anyway, we wouldn't want to compete with the Seneca casinos in the region. Arrow's mission is broader than that." She turned slightly toward him, probably assessing his grasp of what she was telling him. "We're trying to change public perception about Native economic development surrounding high-stakes gambling. We've also been speaking to member First Nations of the NIGA ... the National Indian Gaming Association ... about rediscovering the traditional aspect of gaming and using it to educate all Americans about Native history and culture. Our ultimate goal is an intertribal sharing of profits to offset a struggle between the have and have-not First Nations."

She turned her head sharply away, then fixed her gaze on something in the distance. Jake looked in the same direction. At another opening along the crest farther to the south was a bearded man in camouflage winter clothing. He was looking at the construction site below through a pair of binoculars. He turned the binocks on them before receding out of sight into a stand of trees.

Ona looked tense. A cloud passing in front of the sun dramatized the moment.

"Is he trespassing?" Jake asked.

"It's state land."

"Oh, right. A hunter?"

"Probably."

Jake took a chance: "Maybe hunting for Grant Guyasuta?"

Ona gave him a thoughtful look. "I think Ehnita's right. I think you do have some Haudenosaunee in you. You notice things. So you know about the trouble we had at our powwow? From Sam Collins?"

Jake lied. "Yes."

"The police seem to have given up on a manhunt around here. Some local vigilantes haven't."

"Where'd you hold the powwow and the dancing?"

"Where the Turtle's being built. Before the foundation walls were lain. We had a tent set up. Right down there ..." she pointed as her voice trailed off.

Jake wanted to keep her talking about the killing, but she turned back toward the path down the hill.

The tour had ended.

Radio Catamount

JAKE, LYING DOWN, head propped up by two pillows, struggled to keep his eyes open while waiting for the radio broadcast. Twice, when he started slipping down toward sleep, he unexpectedly envisioned the bearded, camouflaged, binocular-holding figure on the hillside. That brought him back to wakefulness.

At Aki's emailed request, he'd returned to the Seneca Allegany Resort in Salamanca. If possible, she wanted photos from inside the casino as well. He'd wandered the gaming rooms and hallways to do so, holding his phone at thigh level, discreetly shooting low angles without a flash. She'd told him not to worry about the casino's policy regarding her use of any of his photos since she would hide anything that gave this particular casino away. But he still felt like a thief carrying out a heist.

Jake had another reason to be here. Ona had informed him that Catamount was giving a talk at the University at Buffalo to be aired on the school's radio station, WRUB. His hotel room offered a radio, not just WiFi as found at the Red Jacket in Seneca Hills, and he was certain to be able to hear it live here. The fact that the topic related to a casino setting – Native gaming – made being at the resort that much more compelling.

After a listing of upcoming college events, Chad's talk was announced. A student organizer of the Intercultural & Diversity Center thanked students along with members of the greater Buffalo community for attending. He then introduced Chad Catamount, citing his Seneca background, the Erie-Mingo Nation, and the Arrow Alliance. The applause was scattered.

Jake pulled himself further upright on the hotel bed.

Chad's voice sounded out over the airwaves: "*Scan-noh.* Greetings. Thanks to those students here with me during your winter break and local members of the greater Buffalo community ... and to the radio audience far and wide ... and thanks to the university and WRUB for giving me this opportunity. I'd intended to communicate my thoughts on Native gaming recently at the Empathy/Empowerment center in Georgetown, but due to the tragic passing of a dear friend ... Salali Jenkins of the Lumbee Tribe of North Carolina ... that event was canceled. Sharing them with you now is especially meaningful for me."

He paused briefly, then continued: "I'm going to do my best to give a context for the growth of Native gaming."

"Should we give you a grade?" a man shouted out, followed by some audience tittering.

"Let's go with the pass-fail system," Chad flatly responded, barely missing a beat. "My first point ... because of the dislocation from the vast majority of our traditional land base, we Native Americans have been limited in our pursuit of economic opportunities.

"In 1976, the U.S. Supreme Court ruled that states have criminal and civil jurisdiction over First Nations, though not regulatory powers. The following decade, in 1987, the Supreme Court upheld a Florida ruling regarding the Seminole, deciding that because states lack regulatory authority on indigenous lands, state laws against gambling cannot be enforced against First Nations.

"The next year, 1988, Congress passed the Indian Gambling Regulatory Act, granting First Nations the right to pursue compacts with states for high-stakes gaming, that is, not just bingo. Presently, First Nations have the right to purchase additional lands and start gaming businesses on them that become exempt from federal taxes. Native peoples have thus been provided with new economic opportunities to help them achieve self-sufficiency."

"Giving them an advantage over others!" an audience member, again a man, interrupted.

"Remember," Chad countered, "any advantage First Nations have in an economic venture has been shaped and negotiated over centuries. It's been a long and arduous journey."

Chad went on to explain how, in the 17th century, the first reservations were created in the British colonies, and how, the next century, after the American Revolution, a number of federal articles, ordinances, and acts were designed to deal with issues of Native sovereignty. In the 19th century, he further explained, during the post-Civil War period, many new reservations were created and the reservation system was shaped. In the 20th century, the Indian Reorganization Act of 1934 solidified tribal self-determination.

"The concept of protected lands and limited sovereignty on those lands are the underlying principles of Native rights," Chad explained. "First Nations have powers to govern themselves although only under federally imposed regulations. They receive assistance for services in the same way that states receive subsidies for social programs, education, transportation, health, and so on. First Nations also receive additional federal aid as many private corporations do ... in the form of tax relief and funds for research and development and job training.

"Without the necessary capital for development, some tribes have had to make deals with outside investors, receiving a small percentage of profits, especially in the early years of Native gaming. With that small percentage has often come a disregard for Native well-being by the business community ... and the degradation of Native lands."

Chad paused again before continuing: "That's just a broad view of some of the history of federal Indian policy. Detailed information is out there for those who want to understand all the legal implications of Native sovereignty and gaming on and off reservations."

"Out where?" a woman yelled.

Chad replied that the Erie-Mingo Nation could direct anyone to specifics, such as books, websites, and noted academics. "Now, I want to discuss some of the misleading generalizations applied to the Native gaming issue," he added.

"Go for it!" It sounded like the same woman.

"Thank you," he replied, sounding sincere. "First of all, let's examine the term 'Casino Indian' ... the new stereotype about Native Americans after so many other stereotypes over the centuries."

A man let out a war whoop, then yelled, "Stereotypes like that?"

"Yes, like that," Chad said with an exaggerated sigh.

Jake wondered if that particular audience member meant to support Chad or mock him. Chad's tone implied the heckler was an ally, helping communicate his point.

"The warrior/brave stereotype still persists with some sports teams ... happily fewer and fewer. As for the label Casino Indian, that, like all the stereotypes, marginalizes what it means to be Native. There are gaming First Nations and there are non-gaming First Nations. Many involved in gaming in some capacity do not even sponsor casino-style gambling. In fact, casino gaming relates to a minority of First Nations ... only about one-third of the nearly six hundred federally recognized First Nations in the U.S. Moreover, the casino tribes engage in other enterprises as well."

Chad was talking faster, in rhythm. Jake readjusted his pillows. He thought of his restlessness sitting in classrooms in Shaleville. Lying comfortably in bed helped his concentration. So did interest in the speaker and subject matter and how his lecture might fit in with solving a mystery.

"Another generalization that doesn't hold is that the gaming First Nations and their tribal members are all rich. Gaming has been a boon to some First Nations, yet profitability varies significantly. The gaming business, like gambling itself, is a high-risk enterprise.

"Still another generalization relates to the financial deals between First Nations and outside investors ... that corruption is inherent to them. Many different kinds of deals for bingo halls and casinos have been made. Some have been fraught with problems. Organized crime has made some inroads, especially in early deals. Some casinos have benefited individuals over tribal interests. But viewing Native Americans as innocents who fail to learn from past mistakes is one more stereotype.

"As the idea of incompetence is propagandized, so in fact is the opposite ... that Native Americans are tricksters, hoodwinking state governments into giving them unfair economic entitlement with their gaming compacts. States have profited significantly from their revenue-sharing agreements with First Nations, receiving percentages of profits from Native casinos just as they do from non-Native casinos and lottery games.

"Another negative generalization about casinos relates to both their cultural and environmental impact. Granted, mistakes have been made. Yet First Nations have learned to minimize such impacts. And the profits from gaming have been used to encourage cultural awareness of Native themes through the building of cultural centers and the sponsoring of educational programs. Development of any kind can cause new problems, especially without proper infrastructure planning. First Nations are savvier than ever about such matters. And funds from gaming have been used to address other environmental issues, such as longstanding pollution of Native lands by industries conveniently located next to reservations."

Chad's delivery had gotten edgier, a pushback against prejudice.

"One last kind of stereotyping I want to mention is the question of Indianness. Non-Natives often judge Native Americans who physically manifest non-Native ancestry ... the proverbial blue-eyed Indian or the African-American Indian ... as scam artists if they seek federal recognition and the right to pursue gaming compacts with states. As I mentioned, there exists a legal process with the federal government. Every tribe with a casino has fulfilled a strict set of requirements for federal recognition. Many groups have been turned down in their attempts to be federally recognized. The terms of each state gaming compact ... the degree of profit-sharing ... are negotiated according to the laws of a given state. Some states allow no form of gambling at all. Nothing in any of these procedures is automatic. Native Americans are condemned as lazy if they accept their poverty and condemned as scam artists if they demonstrate entrepreneurial and capitalistic spirit!"

Some applause came, along with some shouts of encouragement. One female audience member yelled, "Occupy their minds!"

That gave Jake pause, reminding him of his first case.

"The minds of all asshole politicians, including the Asshole-in-Chief!" a man shouted out.

"But casinos are so goddamn cheesy and phony!" another man yelled.

"Hear, hear!" a woman affirmed.

Jake heard voices from nearby, the hotel hallway – two voices, apparently a man and woman arguing loudly. He couldn't make out their points and counterpoints and didn't want to, what with his attention on the radio.

Chad spoke again: "What about the cultural implications of gambling? Does gambling compromise tribal cultural integrity? Know that games of chance are as Indian as the buffalo and the longhouse. They've been played for centuries by indigenous peoples from all over the Americas. In traditional guessing games ... including the hidden-ball game, the stick game, the moccasin game, and the hand game ... participants tried to guess the location of hidden objects, often betting prized possessions."

A "Fuck you!" came from the hotel's hallway It was the woman's voice. "You're gonna have to make up your stupid mind!"

"I have! You're a fucking bitch!" the man shouted back.

Both sounded drunk. Big surprise.

Chad continued his flow, his now-gentle urgency in contrast to the hallway spat: "Many different varieties of dice have been played over the centuries by indigenous peoples. Pieces of wood, stone, bone, shell, reed, or fruit seeds were marked or numbered. In the traditional Haudenosaunee version, known as 'peach bowl game' or 'peach stone game,' six peach stones were prepared by grinding them down and blackening them on one side. They were shaken in a bowl by striking it on a ceremonial blanket. The object was to have five or six sides of one color showing. Opposing players, often the different kin groups of a communal longhouse, wagered articles of clothing. Guessing games and ice games were often a part of harvest and renewal ceremonies. Indigenous peoples also bet on foot races and horse races."

"Giddyup," someone heckled.

Chad ignored that comment. "As for 'cheesiness,' there is a formula for designing casinos involving glitz mixed with the practical purpose of making money. I don't always agree with the esthetic of a particular casino's architecture and design. However, before you lump all Native casinos together, I'd recommend visiting a number of them. You'll be surprised at the wonderful artwork that can be viewed.

"Let me close by saying that, according to the belief systems of many First Nations, deities play games with humans. Human affairs themselves thus resemble games of chance. Native peoples, in their move toward gaming for economic development and funds to combat centuries-long social ills, are playing a high-stakes game. The challenge has become for First Nations to maintain control and not succumb to the pressures of big business or organized crime for the sake of quick money. A further challenge is to unite First Nations and use a percentage of the profits for the good of all Native Americans. That's what we at the Arrow Alliance are trying to do.

"Believe me, we Native Americans undertaking this challenge are sensitive to consequences. We don't all agree on what paths to take. First Nations have been divided on the gaming issue, even to the point of violence. For or against the casino path, we're well aware of what we face regarding outside influences, cultural compromise, and public perception. We at the Arrow Alliance hope to find common ground on these issues.

"Thank you, my friends. *Da neho.*"

Loud applause sounded out along with some shouts of approval. All in all, despite some voices of dissent, the UB audience seemed to like what Chad Catamount had to say. Jake wondered if any of the residents around Seneca Hills felt the same way. Had even one of them listened? If Sam Collins did, it was to reinforce his resentment. Jack and Jill would be too busy with the diner. They certainly wouldn't have aired it there. Maybe Big Ben and Little Nell, who seemed openminded, had tuned in to learn more about their new neighbors.

Nice to think there could be some acceptance in these parts, Jake thought. He turned off the radio, got out of bed, and walked over to the hotel room door. Opening it, he looked both ways. The hallway was empty and mercifully silent. Peace of one sort or another – more likely a truce – had been reached by the angry couple. Or maybe they'd just gone their separate ways.

Jake returned to the bed, burrowed under the covers, and turned off the light. Chad's words and their meaning ricocheted about his brain ...

A room full of gamblers. Is this a lucid dream or just a movie memory? Is he watching a movie dream with his mother and sister, the eerie surreal one inspired by Salvador Dali? A slender man uses giant scissors to cut drapes decorated with giant eyes. A woman serves the tables. At one of them a game of blackjack is underway. One of the players is a bearded man. He wins with a hand of twenty-one. But his cards are blank. A masked man angrily interrupts the game. Cut to both men on a rooftop. They're fighting. The rooftop has become a forest. The woman from the gambling house has shapeshifted into a giant bird. Jake looks for but doesn't see a wheel with spokes symbolizing a revolver in the masked man's hand. This must be a real dream, not the celluloid one. One of the men holds something else, something small and shiny. Not a gun in this real dream. A knife!

Jake woke up. The radio clock said 4:44 a.m. His dream had been in black and white, like so many of the films he'd seen time and again, now interwoven with the real in his subconscious. His mother often had a movie repeatedly playing throughout the day as background to whatever she was doing, and typically involving murder. The dream that had become entwined with his own was John Ballantyne's, as played by Gregory Peck, in Alfred Hitchcock's *Spellbound*.

The oversized dream scissors helped Jake cut through his entangled thoughts as he sunk back into sleep ...

First Night

JUST AFTER 10:00 P.M., New Year's Eve, Jake's cellphone sounded out, his crickets ringtone evoking summer. Caitlyn? Aki? He checked the screen and saw that the number had the local area code. He answered.

"Hello, Jake?"

Jake recognized the cogent voice from the radio talk. "Speaking," he said.

"This is Chad Catamount. You at the Red Jacket?"

"Right."

"What, no revelry for you tonight?"

"The revelry, such as it is, is on TV."

"Mind if I join you?"

Jake was taken aback but quickly replied with, "Sure. Last cabin to the left of the office. You'll see my white van parked in front of it."

"I'll be there in about an hour," Chad told him. "I'll bring a deck of cards and some beer."

"I've got five beers left of a six-pack."

"I'm a two-limit guy."

"We'll have leftovers then."

Jake had resigned himself to a lonely New Year's Eve at the Red Jacket. He'd considered staying at the Seneca Allegany one more night. But he never liked the forced celebration anyway and he probably would have just stayed in the quiet of that costlier hotel room and either watch the ball drop or ignore it. He'd picked up beer at the convenience store as his only acknowledgement of the supposed big moment to come. As it turned out, Jake was finally going to meet Catamount ... at the motel with its undignified use of a Native name. How would Sam Collins feel about that?

Chad's purpose? The visit made some kind of sense despite the First Night timing. When Jake had first visited the Turtle, Ona had consulted with the Alliance chairperson by phone. He also had to know about Jake's visit to Turtle Overlook with her. This was his follow-up.

To what end?

~

At 11:10, Jake saw the lights of a car through the window's curtains. A green Subaru Outback pulled up. He hit the mute button on the TV remote, then went to the door and opened it. Catamount ambled toward him. Jake recognized his body type from outside the E/E Building in Washington, DC – tall with rounded shoulders. He wore an open charcoal-colored peacoat, black jeans, and brown leather work boots.

"Hi, I'm Jake. Come on in."

Catamount gave him a fist bump on the way through the door.

He removed his coat, revealing a purple sweatshirt that said "Six Nations Lacrosse." Like Ona, he looked about Jake's age, early to possibly mid- thirties. Longish black hair and olive-toned skin. Muscular, with the hint of a paunch.

"Great to meet you," he said. "Heard all about you from Ehnita and Ona."

"Some powerful women there."

Chad agreed in a smile. "They keep all of us in line ... me too ... or at least try to. I understand Ona took you on a tour of the grounds."

"I learned a lot. From your talk on the radio the other night, too. She suggested I listen."

"She tried to get all of western New York to tune in. She was worried about attendance between Christmas and New Year's with so many students gone. Glad to hear her public relations attempts worked with at least one person. I think we were able to line my talk up only because there's little else going on for the campus station this stretch. Since many people still shy away from public events anyway since the pandemic, especially indoor ones, I figured radio might be a good way to get my message out there."

"How big a room and how full was it?"

"It was the main campus theater ... about a third full."

"A lively audience, sounded like."

"Right. At least they stayed awake." He pulled an unopened deck of cards from his pocket. "You play poker?"

"I know the rules, sort of."

Chad raised his eyebrows and said jokingly, "You wouldn't be hustling me, would you?"

"I barely graduated from Go Fish."

Chad laughed. "Okay, we'll keep it simple and play blackjack till the ball drops."

"Sounds good."

Jake got them each a Buffalo Lager from the motel ice bucket. They sat on the edge of the bed opposite the TV. Jake left it on mute so they could talk. Chad opened the cards and deftly dealt some onto the bed covering.

The game was secondary, just a facilitator to conversation, as were the TV's flickering images leading up to midnight. Chad asked a lot of questions and Jake opened up – the edited version with nothing about amateur sleuthing or about Florida, but lots about growing up and working in construction in Shaleville and about New York City and its art scene. He even talked some about his drug history and his months being homeless. On being asked about his present habits, Jake replied that he'd learned his lesson. Some beer and some cannabis were now his limit.

Chad, his tone somber, commented on how he had way too many friends growing up who had been alcohol and other drug casualties. "With the opioid crisis made worse by big pharma's oxycodone and hydrocodone, and especially the super-powerful fentanyl, many more are at risk. For those who can't get the pills anymore – black-market or otherwise – heroin, now sometimes laced with deadly fentanyl, has returned to the reservations with a vengeance."

Chad revealed little about himself, however. Jake didn't learn if he 'd ever dabbled in drugs at all. When Jake asked about the Alliance leader's family after discussing his own mother and sister in detail, Chad repeated what Ona had already told him about tribal affiliations. Then, tapping his sweatshirt, he said that playing lacrosse had given him a connection to his ancestry.

"You played in college, I read," Jake said. "Kenton College, right?"

"Yeah, that's the place. I was a college jock but I always had a sense of the game's traditions."

Chad went on to explain how lacrosse was a Native-invented game, played by eastern peoples long before contact with Europeans. He spoke with underlying passion: "Teams sometimes had hundreds of players, with the goals a half mile or even more

63

apart. Games lasted from sunup to sundown. Hard-ass stuff ... lots of injuries, even deaths ... sham warfare, serving as training. Even the more benign modern version of the game helped me prepare for life's challenges."

"You still play?"

"I'm too busy to be part of any of the local leagues right now. I sometimes play in pickup games to stay in shape." Chad looked down at his cards. "I spend more time at blackjack and poker."

The big moment was close. Jake turned up the TV volume. They watched the countdown and the ball dropping. Flashing lights, crowd exaltation and noise, leading into Auld Lang Syne.

Jake hit the remote's mute button again.

Chad spoke: "Traditional Native celebrations are aligned with the natural world, unlike this one."

His cellphone clanged.

He glanced at the screen and answered, saying, "Hey, Rick." He listened, his face tightening. "Oh, man. On my way."

He stood up.

"Problem?" Jake asked.

"Nothing new ... a friend in trouble. That was the owner of the Woodbine. Want to take a ride?"

"Sure," Jake said, grabbing his vintage baseball cap, black with orange lettering – NY for the Giants baseball team that had moved to San Francisco long ago.

"Nice hat," Chad said.

To relieve the sudden tension, Jake figured.

Once underway in the Outback, Chad told him that it was Oren Feather – Ehnita's grandson – who was in trouble. "I told him if he wanted to step up to more responsibility, he'd have had to avoid situations like this. He's been doing fine till now."

"One more reason to ignore New Year's Eve," Jake said.

"You got that right."

Chad drove along Eagleton southwestward past the Jack and Jill Diner and pulled up a half-block shy of the Woodbine Tavern. As they hurriedly approached on foot, Jake saw a crowd of about a dozen whites standing in a jagged semicircle in the small parking lot flanking the tavern's side wall. Without hesitation, Chad hustled along the back of the crowd and, at the first small opening, pushed the rest of the way through. Jake followed, getting jostled. He broke free and looked around. He stood next to Chad at the center of the semicircle, close to parked cars. One youngish man in the crowd held his nose, trying to stop a trickle of blood. Another young man turned and joined Chad – Oren no doubt. His narrow face was flushed, but it was hard to tell if from excitement or from liquor. His small, wiry frame was tense and fists ready. He wore a gray hoodie, green carpenter jeans, and a black baseball cap with a red "Native Pride" logo. Chad looked at a middle-aged man next to the one with the bloody nose. "Okay, Rick, fill me in."

Rick, coatless like the others, looked sweaty despite the cold.

"Seems like your boy Oren here got caught messing with someone's car," he said. "What'd he do when he got caught? Smashed Ronnie's nose."

"He's not my boy. He works for the Arrow Alliance." Chad turned to Oren. "What's your side of this?"

"I was leaning on his car, talking on my phone. I hadn't even gone inside the bar yet." Oren pointed at the man holding his nose. "He and two others came out to smoke and started shoving me around."

"He sucker-punched me!" the bloodied man said.

Chad looked him up and down. "That's the charge ... sucker-punching? Or is it leaning on a car?"

Some other young man stepped forward from the crowd. "Let's make trashing an Indian the charge?"

Chad turned to Jake. "You getting all this? Threats. Racism. Take some photos. Better yet, video, so we have evidence for the Staties. I'll call them. Let's tie up the first few hours of New Year's with legal bullshit."

He pulled out his phone. Jake did the same, thinking about how sleeping in a vehicle in the wrong place in Florida had gotten him in trouble and that leaning on one had been the catalyst here. He activated his phone's camera app, but Chad's ploy had worked. The crowd, grumbling, began to disperse.

Chad nodded to Rick, saying, "Thanks for the head's-up."

Rick nodded back and looked at Oren. "Do me a favor, will you? Don't be using customers' cars to lean on. I don't need this shit any more than you do."

Rick headed for the tavern's side door. Chad took Oren by the arm and led him away from the Woodbine down the block toward the Subaru. Jake fell in stride next to them.

"My car's the other way," Oren said.

"I'll drive you to it," Chad told him. Then: "Why the hell come out here on Amateur Night? Did you plan on drinking?"

"Three more months and I'm legal."

"Meaning you're still illegal. Who were you on the phone with? Someone to come and buy you drinks?"

"No one you know."

"Give it up, Oren ..."

"Okay, okay. Her name's Jess. She's a waitress I met at the steakhouse in Little Valley. She was supposed to get off work at 11:00. She called to say she got delayed."

Jake could see Oren's grandmother features in him – the narrow, pointed face.

"How old is she?"

"Twenty-one."

"Tell her to meet you somewhere else from now on, and you drink goddamn soda till you're legal. Resentment's simmering and you just made things harder. This is Jake by the way. You owe him thanks for helping you."

Oren looked Jake's way. "Thanks, I appreciate it."

His apology sounded sincere, even a little conspiratorial, his dark eyes now smiling the way his grandmother's did.

Into the Fold

"COME WITH ME," Ehnita said. "Meet my man."

On New Year's Day evening, Jake had gone to the Woodbine for two beers. Even more so than at the diner, he'd been reminded of his Shaleville existence and too much time sitting at bars. Rick, the owner, hadn't been there. The bartender had said he knew nothing of the incident the night before other than that it had been one fight the cops weren't needed. Jake had wondered if anyone there would recognize him and show some kind of attitude. The other three men at the bar had seemed oblivious, and he'd returned to his motel room with no new information.

66

This following morning, Jake had wondered what to do next – give up the Fancy Dancer case and move on? But then Chad had phoned to invite him to the Turtle. He hadn't given a reason.

Ehnita, waving Jake to follow, stood up and moved spryly to the door at the rear of the Turtle's big outer office. In what was the Turtle's neck, a hallway – wood-paneled like the outer office – had two doors on each of its side and another one at the far end. The closest door on the left was marked as a restroom. Ehnita opened the second door to the left and led Jake through. An elderly man with long white hair and deep lines sat at a corner desk.

"Jake," Ehnita said, "this is Thomas of the Seneca ... Thomas Dion'dot, the Arrow Alliance's shaman, Ona's grandfather, and my boyfriend. Thomas, this is Jake Maybe-Mohawk, known to some as Jake Jakes."

Thomas stood up. He was about a head taller than Ehnita.

"I'm surprised you listed me as boyfriend last," he said facetiously to her. Then he looked at Jake, saying, "*Scan-noh*. Welcome to the Turtle. By the way, the name Maybe-Mohawk coming from Ehnita is a huge compliment."

He wore a traditional Native shirt – tan-colored cotton, two blue velveteen panels in front, and leather shoulder strips fringed along their edges. A button pinned to one of the panels stated *Proud to be an Elder*. Weathered looked good on some. It sure did on Thomas Dion'dot.

Ehnita spoke: "Why don't you two get to know each other. Chad and Ona will meet with you soon. I'll be at my desk."

She left the room. Jake looked around the shaman's modest work space, a small version of the outer office, with wood paneling, shelves, file cabinets, a desk, two chairs, and artwork.

"They gave me my own office. I must be relevant," Thomas said drily.

"Such a great building," Jake offered.

"That it is and will be. Have a seat. Tell me about your home and your family."

Thomas sat down behind his desk. Jake took the opposite chair. He filled Thomas in on his mother, sister, and hometown. He gave the short version. The Arrow Alliance shaman probed deeper. Jake was forthcoming about his mother's alcoholism and his teenage drinking. Thomas also wanted to know about how

Jake related to his work, first as a builder, then as an artist in New York City.

Thomas seemed nonjudgmental and genuinely interested and Jake felt comfortable opening up to him, as if in a therapy session. Of course he didn't share what had led him to Seneca Hills – the Fancy Dancer mystery – although he felt compelled to do so.

"I understand you'll be visiting other Haudenosaunee lands," Thomas said. "What do you do on your visits? Talk to people?"

"In some stores and museums. Mostly I just drive around and look at things."

Thomas nodded in thought. "Let's go to Chad's office."

The Alliance shaman led Jake across the hall and through the first door on the right. This room, in addition to the office furniture, had a cot in the corner with a pillow and blankets. Ona sat at the desk chair, looking at the computer screen. Chad, standing, leaned over her shoulder, watching what she inputted. They both looked up. He smiled; she didn't.

"One moment," Ona said and typed a bit more.

She finally looked up again and asked Thomas, "How's everything?"

"Everything is just fine ... just fine," he replied, heading back out the door. "I'll go see what my better half has in store for me the rest of the day."

Chad bent down, opened a desk drawer, pulled out a camera, and extended it to Jake, saying. "I know you use your cellphone as your camera, but can you help us with this one? It's digital ... a recent, pricey Nikon."

Jake took it and looked it over. "I'll need time with the manual. Maybe lots of time. But I'm decent at reading plans and instructions from experience as a builder."

Chad looked at Ona and they both nodded slightly, communicating a decision, it seemed.

Jake deduced that, after reports to Thomas from the others, the shaman had now also interviewed him and had discreetly let the others know of his approval for what they had in mind.

"Take a walk?" Chad asked. "I want to fill you in on the lodges we're planning to build. You might have some suggestions."

"Sure thing."

He led Jake through the outer office past Ehnita and Thomas standing together at the woodstove – she waved and he gave a knowing nod – then outside onto the walkway along the western side of the Turtle. A path branched off to the left and they followed it farther westward. Ona had led him along this same footpath on the way to Turtle Overlook.

At the foot of the hill, to the south of the path leading up to the Overlook, Chad stopped. He looked along the forested hillside running north-south.

"Here we'll have lodges resembling the wigwams of New England Algonquian First Nations, seven of them for seven generations – the symbolic Haudenosaunee number for protecting the Earth for future inhabitants. Their doors will face east toward the Turtle." He looked back in that direction, then added "Feng shui, Native-style."

He went on to explain that east is typically associated with birth and renewal; west, with completion, the end of cycles; south, with growth and abundance; and north, with wisdom, knowledge, and purification. The four circles on the Alliance signs represent the four directions, he added.

Chad then picked Jake's brain about construction decisions, mostly about green materials and which of them would make sense on small structures. More interviewing?

As Chad led Jake back toward the Turtle's head and around it, he pointed and described how, along the south branch of the driveway, a field would be cleared to hold an amphitheater as well as large tents for artisans and vendors at Alliance gatherings. On the opposite side, flanking the driveway's north branch, would be a field for camping. Near the tail and the guest parking lot, a garage would be built for equipment. Between the driveway's branches, an area would be cleared for event parking.

Chad led Jake back to the staff parking lot and the van. Jake waited for the sendoff.

"Want a job, Jake? We can offer you a salary for a variety of Alliance-related tasks, some skilled ... photography, construction ... others just routine like driving and helping keep an eye on things. For now, we can offer you two-hundred-and-fifty a week, a six-day week along with continued lodging at the Red Jacket. I know it's not a lot but you said you have other income from your photographer friend."

"Sounds just fine."

"You have health insurance?"

"No."

"We can't offer that. We can help with other options ... unless politicians don't further sabotage progress toward healthcare for all. First thing tomorrow, you'll be on the clock and we'll call it a full week as a welcome bonus."

"That's generous."

"You'll be working with Oren. That could be a good thing for you. He grew up with his mother and grandmother at Akwesasne. You can pick his brains about your possible people. Like him, you'll be at the beck and call of several of us, not just me ... also Ona, Ehnita, and Thomas. Okay?"

"Agreed."

"To seal the deal, we'd like you to join us in a sweat this evening hosted by Thomas."

"I'd be honored."

"Good. I'll pick you up just after sunset. Remember, sunset comes early on these short winter days."

Chad nodded farewell, then headed for the Turtle entrance.

It was true what Jake had said. He did feel honored. But honored with a degree of guilt because of his mystery-solving agenda.

~

Chad pulled out a pouch of American Spirit tobacco – organic tobacco from a company based in Santa Fe – and, leaning against his green Subaru in front of Jake's motel room, rolled a cigarette.

"Want one?" he asked Jake.

"Yeah, sure. I've been good. Trying to keep it at not more than three cigs a day."

"I haven't been good but this is my replacement for lacrosse."

Chad handed Jake the rolled cigarette and started another.

"I thought the replacement was poker," Jake kidded.

"That too," Chad said with a smile. "We'll smoke out here. Ona hates riding in a car that smells of the stuff. I remind her that tobacco is a Native tradition ... an offering to the Spirit World ... and she tells me that throwing it on the fire is tradition enough. She's hard to disagree with, given her shamanic insight passed to her by her grandfather Thomas."

Jake leaned against the vehicle next to Chad, who handed him a lighter. Jake lit his cigarette and gave the lighter back. Taking more drags, which sure tasted good, he scanned the horizon. Snow still covered the hills despite the dry spell. It had reached above freezing that day, causing some melting, especially when the sun peeked through the cloud cover. Now, with the sun below the tree line, the temperature was again dropping.

"Upstate winters seem trickier than ever," Jake commented. "Early storms, late storms. January and February thaws mixed in with scary cold."

"Winter as a Trickster figure," Chad replied, "reacting to the impact of humans, too many of them mindless about that impact."

Jake was again talking about the weather to fill silences. But Arrow's chairperson had responded meaningfully.

They finished smoking, took their seats in the Outback, and drove through the darkening hills southward toward Salamanca. Jake mentioned how Thomas and Ehnita had such a great way about them, mixing wisdom with humor.

Chad smiled. "Thomas is the Arrow's spiritual grandfather, and Ehnita, the spiritual grandmother. Without them Ona and I would be floundering." He went on to explain that elders, especially grandparents, were revered in many First Nations as keepers of wisdom, and that for some First Nations the concept of Grandfather and Grandmother were synonymous with the Great Spirit.

He and Ona were both effective teachers and a powerful couple, he thought. A couple or a duo?

On the outskirts of the city, Chad turned onto a smaller road. After about a quarter-mile more, the paved surface ended and the Subaru bumped over washboarded gravel. Chad slowed down along a partly fallen stone wall, pulling up behind a black station wagon – the Volvo Jake recognized from the staff parking lot. Beyond the wall were the remains of a house – a damaged foundation and a half-chimney. The grounds had been cleaned up, but the remaining block and stone were stained black from a fire.

Jake now saw three small polished granite headstones between the stone wall and the house site. Chad walked over to them, waving at Jake to follow. On reaching them, Chad closed his eyes and hung his head, as if in meditation or prayer.

Jake read the inscriptions: "Da Neho. Michael Jeffers-Catamount, 1962-2014. Susan Jeffers, 1963-2014. Sarah Jeffers, 1994-2014."

They'd died the same year, he noted. He would look into that.

After a few more moments of silence, Chad turned to Jake. "Jeffers is my father's birth name and mine. This is where I grew up and this is where the ashes of my family rest." He paused. "*Da neho* ... Iroquoian for 'It is finished.' Of course it isn't. It never will be." His last words were spoken with extra intensity.

Some distance away, a campfire flickered, next to which someone was crouched.

"Come on," Chad said, heading in that direction.

Thomas Dion'dot was hunched over the fire, pushing a rock into it with a stick. He wore a beaded leather shirt and, over his now-braided white hair, a headdress – a wool cap with a decorative silver band and a single upright feather. Around his neck hung a small suede pouch. He looked up and nodded at them both, then turned back to his task.

A domed shelter stood a safe distance from the fire. Blankets and canvas tarps covered a frame of maple branches about six-feet across and at least as high. A loose piece of canvas hung over the doorway. A creek flowed beyond the structure, the sound of the trickling water a constant over the changing rhythms of crackling embers.

That afternoon, after the invitation to the sweat by Chad, Jake had gone online and had learned that contemporary Iroquois borrowed the Lakota model of a traditional sweat, altering it somewhat. The sweatlodge, like the Alliance building, symbolizes a turtle. Thomas, the Keeper of the Fire, would be tending what is known as the Sacred Fire.

Chad stripped to his shorts, leaving his clothes in a pile near the doorway. Jake did the same. He noticed a third pile, consisting of a buckskin shirt, dress, and moccasins.

Thomas approached them. He carried a cluster of dried herbs, lit at one end and giving off smoke. He smudged them with it, moving the smoke around different parts of their bodies. Chad nodded to the Alliance shaman, pushed the lodge's canvas door aside, ducked down, and entered. Jake followed.

Candles flickered, casting lambent light. In the middle of the lodge, a pit had been dug into the earth. Ona sat at the far end on the straw-covered floor. A blanket covered her legs but she was naked from the waist up, her black hair loose and touching her shoulders. She looked at Chad but not at Jake. Ehnita sat next to her, wrapped in a blanket. Jake sat down to one side of the pit, wondering if Oren would also be coming, then tried to empty his mind while waiting.

Without fully entering, just leaning through the doorway, Thomas used a pitchfork to place a hot stone into the central pit. The stone represents a particular ancestor, Jake knew from his readings. The shaman retreated back outside. Ona picked up a wooden bowl and sprinkled herbs – sweetgrass, white sage, and cedar – onto the stone. Chad added water out of a ceramic jug. The steam shot up and filled the domed sanctum with the herbal odors.

Outside Thomas now pounded a slow beat on a drum and chanted in Iroquoian. The three Alliance members joined in on some of their chants. The temperature in the lodge climbed. They drank the Water of Life from another jug, passing it to Jake. The process was repeated a total of four times in the course of an hour, for four ancestors and the Four Directions.

After their incantations, Chad, Ona, and Ehnita sat with eyes closed. Sweat beaded up on their brows. Jake avoided looking at Ona. The ceremony was about purification and he tried to think pure thoughts.

The heat became stifling and Jake had a hard time breathing. Nausea crept up on him. In order to stay relaxed and motionless, he tried to concentrate on the sound of the chanting and the shape of the Iroquoian words. Although this was a life detox opportunity, the setting made him yearn for a mind-altering drug. If he could only attain wakeful dreaming. When he glanced at Chad, he saw that his position and expression remained unchanged.

Ona stood up first. Jake watched her duck through the doorway. Ehnita followed.

After about ten more minutes, Chad spoke: "We'll bathe in the stream now."

He rose up and headed for the doorway. By the time Jake had stepped into the refreshingly cold night, Chad was already running naked toward the water. Jake glanced at Ona. Dressed now in buckskin, she was drying her hair at the fire still being tended by Thomas.

Jake heard a splash and broke into a run himself. The rough ground hurt his bare feet. He didn't care, feeling as if he were part of the earth and air. He then became part of the cold water as it shocked his system. He splashed around, enduring it, then stood up when Chad did. They walked, dripping wet, back to their clothes and the fire and dressed in silence.

Chad headed for his parents' and sister's graves. Jake sat down at the fire with Thomas, Ona, and Ehnita.

Chad rejoined them after a few minutes. He'd obviously been crying.

Thomas began to speak in quietly urgent tones, one hand clutching his medicine pouch: "Jake Maybe-Mohawk, I see you on a path of learning and doing ... helping others to help you find out who you are. Do you see this path extending before you?"

"Yes," Jake said.

"Ehnita, I see you poking me and all the rest of us, pushing us forward, but keeping us on the path. You see this, too?"

"I do."

"Chad Catamount, I see your father sitting in council as one of the league's Pine Tree Sachems. I see your parents selling groceries. I see your father at his fireplace, your mother talking to him, advising him as she weaves sweetgrass into the ash-splints of her baskets. I see your sister laughing and dancing and tossing her head back in her own special way. I see them all looking toward you and I try to see what they see.

"Through your father you have blood from Seneca leaders of the Turtle Clan. Through him you also have blood from the Erielhonan, the Cat People. Through your mother's Shawnee ancestors, you witness Tecumseh uniting the First Nations. Through her you also have French blood, just enough for you to walk with ease among the White Eyes. If I see what your parents and sister see, I see you walking a new path among all the peoples.

I see you taking action, doing what is necessary. Do you see it, Chad Catamount?"

"Yes, I do," Chad answered. "The vision burns bright and hot."

"Do you see this same path, granddaughter Onatah Makens?"

Ona, her eyes closed and her hands clenched, remained silent. They all watched her, waiting as she looked inward.

"What do you see?"

The seconds stretched out. Her expression seemed far away. To a distant future?

She collapsed into herself, then onto her side. She'd fainted.

PART III: EXPEDITIONS EAST AND NORTH

"My friend, this is a wide world we're traveling over, walking on the moonlight."
– from an Omaha song

Small City

EHNITA HANDED Oren a brown paper bag and hugged him. He nodded, put the bag on the back seat of the Volvo station wagon, and slid into the driver's seat. Jake took the passenger's seat.

They were driving Ona's car to Foxwoods rather than Oren's old pickup. Ona would ride with Chad in his Subaru. After the trip to Connecticut – first Foxwoods, then a "cultural celebration" in Hartford – Chad and Ona would head to Philadelphia for a meeting, and Oren and Jake would again use the Volvo to return to Seneca Hills.

Jake watched as Thomas gave his granddaughter a farewell hug. Ona hadn't been at the Turtle the past two days; Jake hadn't seen her since she'd fainted at the sweat. Oren had told Jake that she'd been dehydrated and was recovering at Thomas's house in Salamanca. Dehydration and something more perhaps, Jake couldn't help but wonder. At the time, it seemed that Thomas's questions had prompted her fainting spell. Stress from the past? Losing her parents? Thomas had mentioned Chad's parents selling groceries while addressing him; Ona had mentioned her parents running a general store with them during Jake's walk with her. The powwow killing? Jake knew how that preoccupied everyone at the Alliance. She looked fine now, full of early morning vitality. She wore a black sweater and jeans, her down parka under one arm and a tablet in her opposite hand.

Chad and Ona climbed in the Subaru. They closed the doors and pulled away from the Turtle. Chad tapped his horn in farewell as did Oren, falling in behind them. Jake looked over his shoulder to see the receding figures of Thomas and Ehnita near the Turtle's mouth. Tribal elders. Concerned elders, it also seemed.

Oren drove in silence all the way to Salamanca and onto the Southern Tier Expressway. He soon moved into the passing lane and sped by the green Outback. Chad glanced their way but showed no reaction.

Jake broke the silence: "Will we caravan all the way?"

"I told 'em we'd meet 'em there," Oren replied. "We'll get there first. Chad likes to make good time. Ona will wanna stop a lot. It's gonna be probably seven hours to Foxwoods. My grandmother packed us some food and drink. So we're all set with that. Let me know if you need a pit stop. I'll coordinate it with a cigarette stop. Can't smoke in this car."

"You've been there?"

"Once. Never by this route. From Akwesasne the last time."

Jake looked out the window and watched the countryside rushing by. During his first days working with Oren – thinning out the woods with chainsaws where the lodges would stand – Jake had let him lead their conversations. They'd talked mostly about the job at hand and future building plans. He'd told Oren that he'd driven through Akwesasne once when he'd first learned his father might be a Mohawk. But Oren still hadn't revealed much about himself. Jake knew that he'd come to Seneca Hills from Akwesasne the summer before and had been living at Thomas's house with his grandmother. He also knew from the New Year's Eve incident that Oren was twenty years old and that he was seeing twenty-one-year old Jess from Little Valley.

Time to probe. "The weather's been easy on us."

"Supposed to storm tonight, but we're ahead of it," Oren replied.

"Upstate winters ... I've had my share. You too? Cold wet wind off the St. Lawrence at Akwesasne, right?"

"Yeah, right to the bone."

"You plan to go back there to live?"

"I might."

"You still have family there?"

"My mother. Unlike you, Maybe-Mohawk, I know who my father is but he's long gone." Oren tossed out the words, but Jake sensed the underlying emotion.

77

"You know where he is?"

"California, last I heard. I don't give a fuck."

"What's he do?"

"Now that he's not a Warrior? No idea."

Jake wasn't sure how to take that. "A warrior?"

"You know, the activists ... Mohawk Warrior Society," Oren said, now with a hint of pride.

"Oh, right."

Jake had read that the Warriors, a militant pan-Indian organization, involve themselves in a variety of causes, especially sovereignty and land rights, on different U.S. reservations and Canadian reserves. A lot of Chippewa have joined up with Iroquois members. Some have called them heroes; others, mercenaries. Whatever their individual convictions, reports typically depict them as hardcore and, with their hunting rifles and other weapons, they've given authorities pause about breaking up Native occupations.

"Fuck him for abandoning my mother," Oren added, discarding any trace of pride.

"When did your grandmother move to Salamanca?"

Oren counted in his mind. "Two years ago."

"Because of Thomas, right?"

"Yeah."

"Where'd they meet?"

"In a gift shop."

"They seem great together."

"Yeah, real lovebirds, living in a cozy little love shack." Oren wore a half-smile a lot of the time, like Ehnita. With him though, it seemed more like a smirk.

Jake redirected the conversation: "Chad and Ona ... they an item?"

Oren didn't answer right away. Then: "They grew up together but don't live together. My grandmother says they're like brother and sister. I think it's more than that."

"I understand Chad's real sister was killed in a fire with their parents."

The night after seeing the gravestones, Jake had researched Michael, Susan, and Sarah Jeffers online. He'd learned that they'd all died in a fire at their home, now in ruins near the site of the sweat. An investigation had ruled out arson, declaring the conflagration an accident caused by a kitchen grease fire.

"Yeah," was all Oren said regarding that.

Jake kept probing: "I understand Ona also lost her parents."

"Drunken driver. Outside Salamanca. A Seneca friend."

Oren didn't elaborate and Jake let the subject go other than a quiet "Fuck."

After some more miles of silence, Jake asked, "You know Grant Guyasuta well?"

Oren again took some seconds to reply. "Yeah, he worked at the Alliance all of August, helping us get ready for the powwow. His sister Anna helped, too."

"The Labor Day Weekend powwow?"

"Yeah."

"Were you the photographer for that?"

"Yeah, me, Ona, and Anna. Glad I don't have to bother with that anymore." He glanced over at Jake. "You can have that one."

"You get any photos of Grant dancing?"

Jake had found a few on his phone along with some videos, but not enough to get the full effect of his abilities.

"Yeah. They never got used."

"I see the Alliance website's still unfinished and not much activity on the Erie-Mingo one."

"There was an Alliance site up but Ona removed it. I think she used not liking it as an excuse to take it down after what happened at the powwow. She's been working on a new one. She's kept social media current. Some of my photos are posted ... none of Grant."

"Time for me to re-up my social media," Jake said, trying not to come off as all about the subject of Grant. "I got fed up after my art career nosedived and deactivated my accounts."

"I hear ya'. It gets aggravating. I stay the hell away unless for work.

Jake kept the conversation going: "I understand Grant's a great dancer."

"Sure is."

"His sister lives in Salamanca?"

"He's gone. She's gone. She cleared out to New Mexico after all the crap." Oren said the last with extra feeling.

"You think he killed that ex-cop?"

"No way."

"Maybe the ex-cop Baines deserved it," Jake said.

"Oh yeah. But Grant wouldn't do it that way."

"What do you mean?"

"No way with a knife," Oren insisted. "He never carried a knife. He would've used his fists if someone was messing with him. He'd dance circles around anyone. I know what I'm saying about my Native brother."

"Then why'd he run?"

"Because everyone thinks he's guilty," Oren said impatiently. "Had to be a setup. Do it at a powwow so Indians get blamed. Easy to blame Indians."

Enough probing, Jake told himself. He pretended to settle in and doze. But his thoughts raced ahead of the car.

~

Despite some rush-hour traffic, they made it to Ledyard by late afternoon. Jake now had a headache and growing motion sickness from researching Foxwoods on his small cellphone screen.

They followed the signs to the resort casino. Dusk was in play on this short winter day, and they could soon see the lights of its towers against the gray sky.

Oren found parking in the Great Cedar Garage. He and Jake grabbed their bags and walked along a passageway to the spacious hotel lobby, then to the desk to check in. Three rooms had been comped to the Arrow Alliance by the Mashantucket Pequot Tribe that owned the resort. Oren and Jake would share one of them. Oren asked the concierge if others in their party had checked in yet. Chad and Ona hadn't but a Will Thatcher had done so earlier that day, the clerk informed them. Jake wondered if Chad and Ona would share the third room.

On the ride up in the elevator, he asked about Thatcher.

"A lawyer dude ... college friend of Chad's," Oren told him. "He's been helping Arrow. Chad claims he's a legal eagle but he sure acts like a dumb fuck a lot of the time."

Their shared room on the fourth floor reminded Jake of hotel rooms everywhere – more so than his room at the Seneca Allegany with its décor that reminded guests that it stood on Native land. This more typical hotel room still offered an Americana photo-op and, while Oren was in the bathroom, Jake took some pictures for Aki.

Oren told Jake it was free time until 10:00 the next morning and that he planned to order in something to eat, watch some TV, and nap before going out this evening. Jake unpacked. When he entered the bathroom to wash up, the blower was still on. It didn't mask the odor of cologne Oren had used, or the other odor the cologne was masking – one that Jake knew well – that of marijuana smoke. So Oren had a stash, and he apparently wasn't yet comfortable enough with Jake to share it.

Jake set out to explore what he now saw as a small city, with a maze of corridors and rooms he could hike well into the night. Jake had read online that Foxwoods comprises six casinos, offering hundreds of table games and thousands of slot machines. Between the casinos are restaurants, bars, stores, spas, and theaters. It had opened in 1992, six years after the Mashantucket Pequot Tribe had begun its bingo concern and twelve years after it had achieved federal recognition. It was the first of the Native-run Vegas-style casinos and, for a time, the largest casino in the world before some Asian concern topped it. The worn quality of faux facades lining the corridor – like something out of Disney World without an abundance of kids – somehow made the tack and glitz more appealing for Jake. But he saw few Native themes, other than some pieces by an Apache sculptor.

In his university talk Catamount had spoken of the controversy surrounding Native gaming. Jake had learned from his research that since its founding, Foxwoods had been central to the national controversy, including the state politics surrounding its birth and growth, the behavior of some tribal members with their sudden wealth, and the impact of development on this part of Connecticut. Internet postings further revealed that it had been Foxwoods's great early success that had started Andrew Sharp on his openly anti-Native path.

Jake had come upon a number of statements about Sharp and his stance from different sources. One was "Andrew Sharp already owns Boardwalk and Park Place in his lifetime Monopoly game. Does he really need to control more properties?" Another: "Native casinos – Foxwoods and Mohegan Sun – have long been part of the region's landscape and of Connecticut's economy. Celebrate them. Don't undermine them as Sharp United has tried to do."

Chad apparently had wide-ranging company in his criticism of Andrew Sharp and Sharp United.

Comments about the Mashantucket Pequot Museum and Research Center, built by the tribe with gaming profits, were positive. One post referred to it as "a vital center for historical and cultural studies of New England."

Along with Foxwoods and the Pequot, Jake had looked for more about the Mohegan Sun Casino in nearby Uncasville and the Mohegan Tribe operating it, and had learned that the two nations' histories were entwined over the centuries right up to the present.

The Arrow Alliance mission was to promote the positives, Jake knew. The upcoming event in the nearby state capital of Hartford, with both Pequot and Mohegan involvement, was supposed to do that.

He felt a vibration in his pocket from his cellphone, its beep drowned out by the noise from the nearest gaming room. He checked his phone and saw that the text was from Ona.

"You 2 at Foxwoods?" it read.

Jake leaned against the hallway wall to write a text saying that they were. She texted a reply stating that she and Chad had stopped for some phone conferencing so they were still an hour out. She added that both she and Will Thatcher had called and texted Oren but he wasn't responding. Jake texted back that he was exploring Foxwoods while Oren napped.

"I'll tell Will to wait to hear from him. Thx. See u later," came back.

Jake decided that after eating at the Regina Pizzeria in the Great Cedar Food Court, he would wander about Foxwoods to further get his mind around the geography of this labyrinthine place. Perhaps he would even sneak some more photos for Aki. Having that concurrent project helped remind him of his circuitous path here ... where he'd come from and what he hoped to accomplish. He liked his new friends. He admired what the Arrow Alliance was all about. But Grant Guyasuta cast a long shadow on all of them. If he were guilty, they'd all been duped. If innocent, someone else's shadow enveloped them.

On Call

JAKE WOKE UP to the hotel door opening and Oren entering. He glanced at the room's digital clock. 5:07 a.m. When he'd returned to the room the night before just after 11:00, Oren had been gone, leaving a scribbled note saying only, "Seeking my fortune."

"You find your fortune?" Jake asked drowsily.

Oren collapsed onto his bed. "For once in my goddamn life I won," he said.

"At what?"

"Craps. It's a fucking miracle," Oren slightly slurred his words. "Thatcher, he lost bigtime. But he's a lawyer. He can afford it."

"You ever connect with Chad and Ona?"

"My sort of stepsister and I've been texting. I spotted Chad in the poker room. He was deep in, so I left him alone."

"We're scheduled for ten this morning."

"Yeah," Oren said, his voice fading toward sleep. "Wake me ..."

"Such responsibility."

"Oh, and don't mention to Ona about my present underage state."

"More responsibility."

Oren let out a sound; it could have been snoring.

~

Jake was awake again by 9:00 a.m.; Oren, not surprisingly, still sound asleep. Jake showered, then made some coffee provided in the room. He was about to rouse Oren when another text came in from Ona.

"C & I at museum auditorium for meeting with tribal reps, then lunch. Meet you both at Rainmaker Square for PR photos. 1:00 prompt. Tell Oren who doesn't reply. Thnx."

Jake texted a thumbs-up emoji, then picked up his wallet and key card on the bedstand. Oren stirred.

"Change of plans," Jake told him. "They're at a meeting. We're good till one. Wake you at noon?"

Oren managed an "okay" and Jake headed for the door. He had several free hours so he decided to take the long walk over to the MGM Grand side of Foxwoods and the MGM Food Court. Afterwards, he would make a point of playing one slot machine in each of the six casinos. That would give some shape to his time and make it easier not to detour to a bar. He would have preferred the sanity of visiting the museum across the grounds, learning something about Pequot history. He reminded himself to be patient and thankful that he was again a working man with comped shelter. Appreciate the lulls, he told himself. The winds will pick up.

~

At Rainmaker Square a giant color-changing glass Indian – the Rainmaker – aimed an arrow upward at a glass portion of the ceiling. Jake recognized the figure from one of the Foxwoods logos. On a nearby bench sat Ona, looking elegant with her hair up and wearing a business-style black pantsuit; silver and turquoise pendant, earrings, and bracelets provided contrasting color. A man sat next to her. Will Thatcher, Chad's "legal eagle"?

They stood up. Ona made introductions. Thatcher, when introduced, started to extend his hand to shake Jake's in a pre-pandemic greeting, but caught himself and shrugged a hello. His brown hair was thinning. He had the flushed look of a heavy drinker. His clothes looked like he'd slept in them. He smiled at Oren, his gambling and drinking buddy from the night before.

Ona spoke to Jake: "Chad should be here soon. He's coming with representatives of both the Tribal Council and Elders Councils, along with dancers who will be with us tomorrow. We'll want a group shot in front of the Rainmaker. We'll eventually put the best photos you get up on our website."

The last was to let Jake know not to blow it. He wished Aki, the professional picture-taker, were there. He'd been practicing with the Nikon after studying the manual, taking indoor and outdoor shots, and he was getting familiar with it. The pressure was now on to deliver images of a planned event.

Ona turned to Oren. "Take some photos with your cellphone as backup."

Oren gave a negligible nod.

Chad arrived with four men and a woman, two of them male dancers. Introductions were made all around. Lots of bowing. Chad wore a multicolored beaded headband, a ribbon shirt, sports coat, black jeans, and brown work boots. The Pequot tribal rep, probably in his forties, wore a sweater and slacks. The tribal elder – in his sixties or maybe even seventies – wore a white shirt decorated with beads. The probably thirty-something woman, introduced as the head of Foxwoods's public relations, wore a skirt and blazer and had a camera around her neck. The dancers wore full Fancy Dance regalia, including beaded bodices, moccasins, leggings, feather bustles, and roach headdresses with feathers. One sported blue and white colors; the other, black and yellow. They were young – probably early twenties.

The publicist took over, positioning everyone at the base of the Rainmaker – Chad and Ona at the center, flanked by the two Pequot reps and the two dancers. Even though this was a photo op and not a dance performance, some Foxwoods visitors stopped to observe.

Jake snapped photos from various angles as the subjects held their smiles. Oren, as instructed, shot backups with his cellphone. Ona and the PR rep did their best to offset any awkwardness. Chad, the tribal rep, and the dancers all stood dignified and proud.

~

A knocking, irregular at first, then patterned. Native drums and dancers. One of the dancers is Ona, covered in feathers. She spreads her wings ...

Jake surfaced. There was knocking on the hotel room door. Oren without his keycard?

Jake in t-shirt and boxer shorts pulled himself out of bed. Oren's was empty. He glanced at the clock. 2:32 a.m. The light was on in the bathroom, illuminating the little hallway.

"Oren, you in there?" Jake called out.

No reply.

Jake moved to the door and opened it. It was Ona. She wore a bathrobe over pajamas. She looked little-girlish – not like the office Ona he remembered, or the hiking and teaching Ona, or the sweat Ona, or the PR Ona from that afternoon at Rainmaker Square. Or dream Ona, he realized, remembering that she'd just haunted one of his. He opened the door wider but she didn't enter the room.

Jake blinked to clear away the traces of REM sleep.

"Ona. What is it? Everything okay?"

"Is Oren here?" she asked matter-of-factly.

"No."

"Chad and Will are still out as well. No one's responding. I have a good idea where Chad is."

"The poker room?"

"Can you do me a favor and remind him how early we're leaving for Hartford? Keep an eye out for the others, too. Will's no doubt in a bar if not watching Chad. Oren better not be. Everyone's gotta be at his best tomorrow."

"Sure."

"Thanks. I hope you can get back to sleep afterwards so you're rested."

Her eyes held his briefly. So radiant, he thought, even when upset.

She stepped back and turned to go. Jake watched her move along the hallway, then closed the door.

He got dressed and headed out. Although it was the middle of the week and the middle of the night, a good number of patrons moved along the main hallway. Some were keyed up, others zombie-like.

Jake was now wide awake and relieved to have purpose again. After the photo shoot, he'd spent most of the afternoon alone in the hotel room, waiting to see if he would be needed again. Ona had taken the camera to download all the pictures onto her laptop. But he hadn't been summoned, not to retrieve the camera or even to join any of the others for dinner. Oren had found his own dinner companion, he'd reported to Jake, a young female Pequot artist. Jake had wondered at the time if he'd added the artist bit to make the dinner sound professional.

Jake had had a long phone conversation with his sister in the early evening and had brought her up-to-date on his whereabouts. She'd then asked him about his sleuthing.

"I can't push too hard," he'd said. "I have their trust. That would evaporate if they knew what I was up to."

"Just be careful," she'd advised, his little sister acting more and more and more like a big one.

"Being on the street taught me to watch my back. I'm sure learning a lot about Native America though. They call me Jake Maybe-Mohawk."

"You feel Nativeness in your bones?" Caitlyn had asked. "You want your dad to be mom's Mohawk lover?"

"It sure seemed kind of cool when she first mentioned the possibility."

"Still cool?"

"The idea makes me feel at home in Seneca Hills and even here in the weird Foxwoods reality. But it's fascinating no matter whose genes I can claim or blame. Enough talk about me, sis. What about you? How's school?"

Caitlyn had expressed how challenging school was after half a decade away and how strange it was being older than most of the other students. He'd shifted to big brother mode and gave her a pep talk, telling her there were kids out there who were going to be lucky in landing her as their teacher.

Now, in the middle of the night, Jake wound his way around the Rainmaker archer and descended a staircase past a faux waterfall to the World Poker Tournament room below.

The ambience changed immediately. He found himself in a big room where poker players – men and women both – sat in life-and-death silent seriousness, pondering their cards and fingering their chips. Jake moved from table to table, looking for Chad. At first, he felt awkward but noticed others hovering around the tables, watching the players, although of course not close enough to see their cards.

He almost missed spotting the Alliance leader because he was wearing a baseball-style cap, black with a red Saratoga Race Course logo. He sat at table near another staircase at the room's far end. He looked tired and resigned – no doubt because of his tiny chip stack. No sign of Oren or Will.

Chad glanced up, revealing not a flicker of recognition, then quickly back down. The four others at the table paid Jake no heed. After another bet, Chad beckoned Jake closer with a finger. Jake moved around the table behind him. He lowered his cards as Jake leaned in.

The poker maven spoke: "Ona sent you on a retrieval mission." It was a statement, not a question.

Jake answered it anyway. "Right."

"If this miserable run continues, I'll be done soon." Chad studied his cards again. Then, tossing them on the table, he stood up abruptly. "That's it. I'm done. I fold. Goodnight, one and all."

He gathered up his chips and headed for the staircase. Jake followed. On the higher level Chad led him to the nearby Atrium Bar and Lounge. Oren stood at the bar, close to a young black-haired woman seated on a barstool – the Pequot artist, Jake assumed. Will sat at a nearby table, his head sagging from fatigue or alcohol or both.

Chad approached Oren. "It's time. Ona sent Jake here to gather us up. Big day tomorrow."

"Early start tomorrow," Oren told the woman next to him. "Time for me to be responsible." He sounded clear enough, Jake noted.

Chad walked over to Will, saying, "Come on, barrister."

"A shot of bourbon for the road?" Will slurred.

Although he'd been drinking bourbon, his flushed face had the cast of rosé wine.

"No," Chad said gently. "You wouldn't want Ona pissed off, would you?"

"Oh, all right," Will said, standing up shakily.

He fished in his pocket and threw two twenties on the table.

The bartender, who looked more like a bouncer, had been watching them. "Thank you, sir," he said.

Will attempted a step and stumbled.

Chad took his arm to steady him, saying, "Just like the good old days. Except you gotta be at least fifteen pounds heavier, and me, I'm ten pounds heavier and fifteen weaker."

"Bullshit," Will slurred. "You still whip a lacrosse stick around." He swung a virtual lacrosse stick at Chad's head.

"Walk, frat boy," Chad said, leading him off.

Lies of Omission

JAKE PUT HIS BAG in the back of the Volvo. Chad and Oren, both in peacoats – one black, one green – leaned against the Subaru. Jake saw Oren passing him one of the brand he smoked, Seneca.

Oren had been happy to share his cigarettes with Jake, as he had on the drive to Foxwoods. He'd told him that Grand River Enterprises – a privately, not tribally, owned company, based at the Six Nations of the Grand River Reserve in Ontario – successfully marketed the untaxed, low-priced brand in both Canada and the U.S. Oren's habit was already making it harder for Jake to maintain his shaky resolution to smoke only three cigarettes a day.

Cigarette dangling in his mouth, the young Mohawk started working his phone. Texting? To whom? Jess, the girlfriend back home? The Pequot artist?

Ona walked over to Jake. Her hair hung loose below a multicolored beaded headband similar to Chad's. Under her green parka she wore a black-and-turquoise ribbon shirt. A small suede medicine pouch, similar to the one her grandfather had worn at the sweat, hung from her neck. The Nikon hung from her shoulder.

She touched Jake's arm. "Thanks for helping last night."

"Of course."

"And the photos turned out just fine. Chad's also happy."

"That's a relief."

"Oren says you work hard and he likes your company. That's important since you two will be doing a lot together."

Her words sparked a pang of guilt over the lie he was living. "Nice to hear that, too," he said.

"I want you to get shots of everything today," Ona instructed, her tone now all businesslike. She handed him the camera. "Fire away ... you can't take too many shots of the dancing. There'll be some Mohegan dancers as well as Pequot and probably friends of both. The two nations, business competitors for years, are working together to counter out-of-state competition. We want documentation of our small part in all this."

"Right."

"Be discreet when photographing spectators. Ask permission if you feel it's warranted."

"Certainly."

"I'll be giving the gathering a Haudenosaunee blessing, and Chad, a short talk. Be sure to get shots of that."

"Also of Will?"

She sighed. "It's okay if he's in any but don't worry about it. He'll be dealing with state officials and cops. He's been the advance man, reassuring authorities not to expect any trouble from us. He's also been getting word out to the press. Hopefully they'll show up. Don't forget ... you also function as security. It should all go smoothly. Just keep an eye out. Lots of hate crimes during this hate-spewing time."

"And if there's trouble?"

"Help us get out of the way. Follow Oren's lead. He's sharp. All should be fine. This will be a nonviolent statement of Native self, a way to remind people of Native consciousness beyond gaming. It worked well in Albany. Most of the press was positive since we made sure to keep it low-key yet entertaining. That's why the Pequot and the Mohegan have been willing to take this step in their support of Arrow. They know we're not agitators. Donating money is one thing ... signing on to an event is another. We followed their advice on holding the event at the Old State House, a historic site, rather than at the State Capitol. We're putting a cultural rather than political face on it. It's both of course."

Ona was trusting him, opening up more and more.

"Did they question you about what happened Labor Day Weekend?" he asked.

"Of course. Every event we do proves that what happened was an aberration with absolutely nothing to do with the Arrow Alliance."

Ona's tone made it plain that she was sick of that subject. She looked over Jake's shoulder. "Damn late nights. I wish our partying legal eagle would hurry up."

Will entered the garage as if on cue, garment bag and briefcase in hand. He was pale and bleary-eyed. At least his morning suit looked lawyerly.

He gave Ona a sheepish smile. "Sorry to be dragging."

Chad approached him. "You look like shit," he said. "You can ride with Oren and Jake. Get some more sleep."

Will put his bag in the back of the Volvo, then practically dove onto the back seat. Oren and Jake climbed in the front.

Chad and Ona started off in the Subaru. Oren pulled out behind them.

Will was soon snoring. Oren seemed deep into driving. It was about an hour ride to Hartford. The car heated up, taking the edge off the cold morning.

Thoughts scattering from a suburban road to city streets ... men berating him, kicking him ...

Jake surfaced. He glanced at Oren next to him. Sun streamed in the car window, and Oren had put on sunglasses, making him seem even mentally farther away as he cruised the road.

~

A drum beat staccato. Fancy Dancers, eight of them, stutter-stepped to the rhythm in State House Square. Their brightly colored regalia – bustles and roaches of feather and fur – rippled in the slight wind; the bells and deer-toe clackers on their legs sounded out. The columned building rose up behind them: the lower part brownstone; brick above that; a wooden cornice painted white; and a flat roof with a balustrade and cupola. Occasionally one of the four drummers who sat around the large communal drum of wood and hide would sing-chant. One or two of the dancers would rest while others launched themselves into athletic motion.

Two Native children in street clothes danced nearby, and Jake thought of Little Joe and the other Tiny Tots at the Leesburg Powwow.

Will Thatcher had done his job. The media had come out on this sunny day, as had a decent number of spectators, who still had enough space not to crowd one another. Jake wandered about, snapping photos; reporters and spectators did the same. He made a point of asking permission before close-on spectator shots. Some Native folk, most of whom stood together near the drummers, gave big smiles for the camera. Oren stayed near Chad and Ona as they moved about the crowd, greeting people with namaste bows. Jake marveled how this tradition had passed from culture to culture, especially since the pandemic. Will stood near but not too near the Hartford Police Chief. Other policemen had stationed themselves along Main Street.

After about a half-hour, the drummers and dancers stopped performing and returned to the coterie of fellow Native Americans. Ona climbed halfway up the State House steps. Oren shadowed her. Some folks had exited the State House – staff, it seemed – and watched from the upper steps.

Gripping the medicine pouch hanging from her neck, Ona gave a benediction in Iroquoian. She then added, "We welcome all of you to this gathering of First Nations. The Seneca, Erie, Mingo, Pequot, and Mohegan are all represented here. I am Onatah Makens of the Seneca-Mingo. Chad Catamount next to me represents the Seneca-Erie. The host drum is Pequot. The dancers are Pequot and Mohegan."

Pequot and Mohegan gave yelps of approval and other spectators clapped.

Ona finished: "Now, Chad Catamount will explain why we of the Arrow Alliance are here today."

Chad had taken off his peacoat. He wore the same clothes as the day before at Rainmaker Square, minus the sports coat: headband, ribbon shirt, black jeans, and brown work boots. Jake looked at him as the crowd might, seeing a man of two cultures. The gathering had morphed into a social studies lesson, similar to that in his radio talk. Chad's gently delivered oratory was all about tribal sovereignty and the Native struggle to maintain it what with the hundreds of broken treaties by federal and state governments; about cultural renaissance; and about improving lives for children with revenues from the Native tradition of gaming. He advocated gaming as both a cultural experience and good clean fun. He described past mistakes, including corruption and the polarization and anguish among some First Nations over the gambling issue. Chad's public persona was both confident and relaxed and his dark eyes never wavered.

Jake took a slew of photos. When not watching Chad, he perused the crowd, looking for people's reactions. All seemed genuinely interested, with no signs of hostility. Two men worked their way to the base of the State House steps. Their street clothes – almost-matching wool toggle coats over suits – seemed like uniforms. They studied Chad, listening to every word, unlike

92

much of the crowd who were distracted by their kids or other activity around them. If not plainclothes officers, they were federal agents, Jake suspected. He fought back resentment of them. He assumed they stereotyped Native American activists as threats to order. Recent turmoil over water rights and pollution threats to Native lands no doubt reinforced their suspicions. Then again, he was stereotyping them as bad guys. If there were some kind of trouble, they would become allies helping to quell it.

Chad was wrapping up his speech: "I thank you all for joining with us today in this celebration of Native life and cultural renewal. I hope you've learned a little something about indigenous peoples. I hope you realize that, like you, we Native Americans are pursuing the American dream and that legalized gambling has given us new hope. Hope that we can keep our families intact ... hope that our children can receive the finest educations in all the world ... hope that our children can play safely in our streets ... hope that our children can inherit a clean planet on which to live ... hope that Americans and Native Americans can stand side by side for the good of us all. Thank you, my friends. Enjoy the dancing."

Applause swelled up. Drumming started again and so did the Fancy Dancing. Chad and Ona moved over next to the Police Chief. Two reporters approached them and asked questions. Oren separated from them, descending the stone steps. Jake saw that he was scanning the crowd and did so, too.

An old Native man danced in a relaxed manner off to one side, performing what Jake recognized as the Straight Dance. The man started moving, still in step, toward Oren. His white hair extended below a beaded baseball cap pulled low. His sheepskin bomber jacket, worn collar up, seemed as old as he was. Oren approached him and, looking over his shoulder back toward the State House steps, walked with him away from the crowd.

They talked maybe all of a minute. The old man then moved away from Oren toward the group of Native spectators. But he kept going past them, heading instead for Main Street. On the way he performed one last dance move, a Fancy Dancer move. He jumped slightly, then on landing, he froze in sync with the beat.

Jake looked at Chad and saw that he also watched the old man. The agents – or whatever they were – still had their eyes on

Chad and Ona. One of them followed Chad's eyes, but the old man was gone.

Some in the crowd stayed; others began dispersing. The drumbeat had started up again. Several of the dancers returned to the center of the square to perform. Jake snapped some more photos of their dramatic moves. He decided to get context – the surrounding streets, buildings, vehicles, and pedestrians. Aki might use some of those shots if Ona didn't want them. He aimed the camera beyond the State House Square and clicked away. He rotated slightly and clicked again, then again and again ...

He stopped. He lowered the camera and searched with his naked eye. Had he just seen through the viewfinder the man with the white eyebrows from Leesburg? There was no sign of him now. Could he have disappeared around a corner that quickly? Or moved away in a group of other pedestrians?

Jake, looking at the camera screen, clicked backwards through the recent photos. On the small screen, he couldn't tell for certain what he had seen among all the tiny faces frozen in time.

He needed an enlargement. He had a memory flash, like a camera flash going off in his brain. Michelangelo Antonioni's *Blow-Up* was one of the few foreign films his mother had watched with him. In a blow-up of a photograph from a park – a film print, not digital – a fashion photographer finds evidence of a murder although he never manages to confirm what he suspects. Would Jake?

The drumbeat now was fast and furious. So were the dancers' moves. The wind had picked up as if also driven by the music.

~

Just to the north of Hartford, Oren pulled onto I-91 toward Massachusetts.

"You taking the northern route back?" Jake asked. "Pick up 90 west?"

"Yeah, but only as far as Albany," Oren replied. "From there we go north and west. I wanna stop at Akwesasne on the way home."

"To see your mom?"

"Nah, too much aggravation. She drinks way too much. Just doing a friend a favor. Picking up some cigarettes."

Jake knew that Akwesasne was a center of smuggling for untaxed cigarettes. The waterways and many islands with Native lands on both sides of the St. Lawrence River – along with the confusing jurisdiction among the United States, Canada, New York State, the Province of Ontario, and the Province of Quebec – made for great smuggling opportunities.

"Aren't they cheaper on the U.S. side? Isn't most cigarette smuggling in the other direction?" he asked.

Jake understood that cigarettes were typically shipped to American wholesalers who didn't have to pay taxes levied in Canada by the federal and provincial governments, then sold to smugglers, who distributed them in Canada.

"Nah, depends. We'll get 'em over there to bring back. It still pays off. You got your passport on you, I hope."

"Yeah."

"Good. I woulda had to leave you on the American side while I did my thing."

"Will we stay over?" Jake asked.

"Maybe."

"But not at your mom's?"

"Nah."

"Why don't we stop off at my sister's? We can sleep there. Shaleville is just a short detour. From near there we can pick up 12 North toward Akwesasne. I once drove that route. I forget what I took after that."

"Yeah, I know that way. I had a girlfriend in Boonville. Rough and tumble Rebecca." Oren said, reminiscing. "Yeah ... sure. Meet your sister. Crash there. But we just tell her I'm gonna go see my mother."

"She's cool. No need to hide the real reason."

"I'd rather not get into it."

"Whatever."

"One other thing ..." Oren said.

"Yeah?"

"Same thing with my grandmother and Thomas and everyone else. Don't even mention Akwesasne to them. We'll be spending tomorrow with your sister. Helping her with her house or something. I'll tell my grandmother we'll be back late tomorrow night."

"I got it," Jake said.

Jake hadn't really gotten it. Oren always seemed to be working some angle.

~

Caitlyn was aglow on their arrival, happy to see Jake sooner than expected and, Jake knew, happy to meet the new friend he'd been telling her about. When Oren went off to use the bathroom after a prolonged introduction, Jake fought back the urge to mention the real reason for going to Akwesasne. But Oren had asked him not to. He also wanted to fill her in on other developments, like the possible sighting of White Eyebrows. He would save it all for one of their phone conversations. Anyway, about White Eyebrows, it made sense to first check photo enlargements for confirmation. He'd promised to keep her informed about this case – unlike his behavior during the first one – but no point in worrying her needlessly.

He leaned in close to her and said quietly, "I'm still caught up in my lies of omission about Florida and Georgetown and what led me to Seneca Hills, so don't say anything."

"You don't have to remind me, Mr. Detective," she said.

"Thanks."

"I just hope you know what you're doing," she added.

Did he? "It's all bizarre, but it gives me purpose other than you know what," he reassured her.

"Booze? Hard drugs?"

"I've been good.

"You puff yet with your new friend?" she asked.

"Oren smokes ... I smelled it in our hotel room ... but he didn't offer me any. You've stopped puffing altogether, right? I get to question you on this subject, Ms. Teacher."

"I'm no teacher yet ... just a student again... and students get to party. But I'm practicing life without pot."

"How's that going?"

"I don't miss pot but I do miss puffing with you."

"By the way, Oren sure asked a lot of questions about you on the drive here. And his eyes sure zeroed in on meeting you."

She waved that off. "He's young. I'm not. In fact, I feel middle-aged around all the college kids."

"He's twenty but it's hard for me to think of you as anything post-teen. Not to worry. I'm not matchmaking ... just clueing you in. I don't think an age difference will stop him. I sense a player."

She handed him some dishes, some nice ones that had survived their mother's drinking. "Make yourself useful. Go set the table."

During dinner, Jake filled Caitlyn in on the past weeks – his edited version. Oren gave his version of events, too, leaving out mention of late-night goings-on at the casino. They were eating some lake trout that Caitlyn had thawed on hearing they were coming, along with rice and a salad. And they drank beer Jake had bought on the way.

"I'd love to see one of these cultural celebrations. Any others scheduled soon?" she asked Oren.

"Not yet. Chad and Ona are headed to Philadelphia for a meeting with some Oneida friends about the Museum of the American Revolution. Maybe we'll hold an event there eventually."

Caitlyn kept firing questions and asked Oren about growing up Mohawk and the Arrow Alliance and the work he was doing for it. She also asked him about his teen years and he again mentioned growing up without a father. He added this time that at least his father had taught him how to use a bow and arrow before abandoning him and his mom.

After dinner, they moved next to the fireplace in the living room. Jake built a fire. Oren asked about the Fancy Dancer figurine on the mantel.

Caitlyn glanced momentarily at Jake before answering. "A friend who was visiting Florida gave it to me. You ever dance at powwows?"

"I might someday," he replied.

"Are there traditional steps?"

"Yeah, but Fancy Dancing is about individual expression."

"Can you show us some of them?"

Oren looked uncertain. He finally smiled and stood up.

"There's the toe-heel step," he said, moving in slow motion. "You bring the toes of one foot down, then the heel. There's also the stomp step. You raise the heel and ball of the foot and bring 'em down hard, then hop twice on the toes of both feet. With the drag step, the toes of one foot touch the ground first, then you drag 'em backwards, ending with a downward motion of the heel. The other main step is the canoe step. The whole foot hits the ground, then you tap your toes three times."

Oren's small athletic frame seemed perfectly balanced. He finished his demonstration by jumping in the air, landing gently, then spinning around and raising his arms as if a bird.

Caitlyn clapped.

"There's lots more to it of course," he said. "Different dancers make these moves their own with all kinds of variations. My friend Grant's the best I've ever seen."

Caitlyn's eyes met Jake's. Joe Panther's figurine, along with Caitlyn's shrewdness and warmth, had led Oren to open up to them, even giving a dance demonstration and mentioning Grant. Jake had the thought what a gem Caitlyn was ... how she made people around her feel at ease ... including her detective big brother.

Caitlyn herself was obviously appreciating the socializing. She'd been avoiding men since her breakup, Jake knew, so the attention had to feel good, and Oren was sure attentive, eyes on her a lot of the time. How could he not be? She was one vibrant young woman.

Jake had a vision of her on stage, singing in her band. It had been getting some local traction her senior year in high school. When two of her bandmembers had left town for college, the music efforts had stalled. He'd asked at the time whether the idea of forming a band with other area musicians had been a reason for her staying in Shaleville. She'd answered "kinda," although she never did return to the stage. For a time, he'd thought that she didn't want to admit the real reason for staying was dating Rory, a Shaleville lifer. He'd later concluded the main reason was to be a caretaker of their alcoholic mother. Grace had eventually left town herself, finally freeing Caitlyn of that responsibility. Not of worry though.

The evening continued with brother and sister poking fun at each other over old issues, such as the time Jake had buried their mother's liquor to hide it from her, then how Caitlyn, not understanding, had tattled on him. Jake gazed into the fire he'd built. Cracker – the dog Caitlyn had rescued years before – lay at his feet. Returning each time to what had been his childhood home and getting to know his now-adult sister more and more each time was grounding for him. It gave him confidence he would never drift off again as he had these past years. And he knew Caitlyn was getting to know him better, too, getting a sense of the interesting places his self-assigned cases were taking him and the interesting people he was meeting along the way.

The yawns started. After Caitlyn had led Oren to his room for the night – what had been their mother's room – she returned downstairs to Jake, who was in the kitchen washing dishes. He again had the urge to discuss his new case, especially after their shared evening with Oren, but he didn't want to risk being overheard. He instead asked for an update of her back-to-school experiences.

"Here's one that relates to Jake Maybe-Mohawk," she said. "My theme paper for the semester is on family. My teacher wants us to look at our own, including our ancestors, so we can relate to different cultures and family situations of our future students. It'll be tough writing about mom."

"Therapeutic, I suppose."

She poked Jake playfully in the arm. "And not so easy writing about you."

He feigned concern: "Uh-oh."

"Mr. Shank wants us to make a fictional story out of it to maintain objectivity."

"Creative writing in an education class? Sounds like a creative teacher."

"He's my favorite," she declared.

"He single?"

"No, married ... and gay. Living married for years but just had his wedding. He talks lots about his family and their reaction to his boyfriend and his marriage. He's all about tolerance in life and in the classroom. Some of my fellow students sure need some tolerance. In our case I suppose we have to be tolerant of mom."

"Keep reminding me."

Caitlyn went to the kitchen counter and pulled out what looked like a small glass jelly jar, now empty and clean and without a label. She handed it to him.

"Spit in here," she instructed. "I may do an ancestry test on all of us for my theme paper. Dad agreed to it. I doubt mom will ... if I can even reach her."

Jake did as instructed and returned the jar. "Mom's missing out on a wonderful daughter," he said.

"Not a half-bad son, too."

Jake smiled. "Will you write that?"

She laughed. "We'll see." She then frowned slightly. "I've been going back and forth on whether I should take online courses come summer. I finally made up my mind. I'm taking the summer off, Jake. Got that? You're central to it. What clinched it for me was our talking about a trip together last time you were here. That'll be my reward for studying hard this semester. Please take care of yourself and be there for me. Pinky swear?"

"Pinky swear." They didn't shake pinkies but that expression carried weight between them.

Etch that into your brain, he told himself.

Akwesasne Run

"IF YOU GET QUESTIONED," Oren told Jake, "just say you think you're part Mohawk without tribal affiliation. Just traveling with a Mohawk friend to learn something about the People."

Jake gave a little laugh. "You mean the truth?"

"Sure enough, bro. Shouldn't be a problem. Mohawk have tribal members living on both sides of the border and we can cross without hassle. The fact that I'm with an American not on the tribal roll is the only issue."

Oren pulled up to the booth at the Three Nations Crossing between the American and Canadian lands of the Mohawk Nation of Akwesasne. The rail-thin customs agent, sporting a mustache too big for his narrow face, leaned forward to look through the side windows of the car, front and back.

"Papers, please," he said matter-of-factly.

Jake gave his passport and vaccine certificate to Oren, who passed them to the agent. The agent looked back and forth at the documents and them. He leaned down closer to look past Oren at Jake.

"How long will you be in Canada and what is the purpose of your visit?" he finally said.

"Just seeing my friend's home," Jake replied. "Might stay over one night."

The agent nodded, now as if only half-interested, then waved them through. They drove onto the Seaway International Bridge's South Channel section between the American mainland and Cornwall Island. The wind was up, making the still unfrozen water choppy. Jake could see a number of small boats on the channel between the American mainland and the island. They continued driving across the North Channel onto the Canadian mainland and Route 2.

Oren soon turned onto a side road and drove to Pitt Street and the parking lot of a diner called Spinners. He turned off the car's engine but stayed in his seat. He gazed through the windshield, his thoughts seemingly far away.

He turned toward Jake and emitted something between a grunt and a sigh. Then: "Look, I can't fucking lie. Here's the deal. I have access to a load of black-market ganja on this side of the border and someone to buy it in Salamanca. No worries for you. If something happens, I go down, not you. You won't be crossing with anything. You'll be driving the empty car back across and you'll meet up with me after I cross by boat. You won't even greet the boat. Friends will be waiting."

Jake's exasperation had become vexation. He let some of it out in his own sigh, then asked, "What kind of load you talking about?"

"Four pounds."

"Hell, Oren … what's four pounds of smuggled weed equal in jailtime?"

"Things are looser. Recreational is legal in Canada and in how many states now?"

"Not looser at international borders. People are still getting arrested."

"Not as many."

"Chad know about this?"

"Chad knows I did it before Canada went recreational. Not sure if I'll tell him this time."

"He partake?"

"You mean get high?"

"Yeah."

"From time to time. He never was a stoner ... too much of a jock."

"Ona?"

"No way I tell her. She's tried herb ... says she doesn't like it. Even if she did, she's more paranoid about it than Chad is ... how it could hurt Arrow. I heard him tell her it might help to be honest about it and that booze, pills, and needles are the big problem for Native kids, not herb. I know he's in touch with friends in Colorado who have a license to grow and that he got her some CBD oil for pain she was having. She was open to that. Chad told me you fessed up to past drug issues but still smoke herb and that it helps you avoid harder stuff. That's why I thought you'd be cool about this."

"Yeah, I've done my share of drugs," Jake admitted. "And grass has been a positive unlike the others. But I'm not okay with the legal consequences of a run like this ... for me or for some friend who just sprung something like this on me ... or for the Alliance for that matter."

"It's my deal. Not the Alliance's."

"What about you and other drugs? Be honest."

"You know I'm no alkie. Nor a cokehead. Some pills, but I'm no opioid freak. They fuck with me and they're overrated anyway. I got a script for Adderall ... keeps me focused."

Oren at age twenty sure sounded more self-aware than Jake did about drugs when he was twenty. Yet people rationalize their own drug use.

"It all started with the diagnosis ADHD," Oren added. "They shoulda just branded me badass."

Jake well knew about the ADHD childhood labeling but didn't mention they had that in common.

"What about your grandmother?" he asked. "She know you puff?"

"Of course. But she'd sure flip out about my taking a chance like this so you gotta be cool."

"And Thomas?"

"He's okay with herb but he'd probably also lecture me all to hell about risk."

"With good reason."

"It'll be fine. This is my turf. I'm really just carrying it from one part of the rez to the other, all part of the Mohawk Nation. The other borders were forced on us after treaty violations."

"That's your thinking ... however righteous ... not theirs."

"They're looking most for illegals, bombs, and viruses. I get that they wouldn't mind catching a Mohawk with a load of anything illegal. But I doubt I'd do time."

"What if I didn't bring my passport on this trip?"

"I woulda left you on the other side and lined up someone else to drive the car. I'd rather make it worth your while. Everyone who's part of this is making money. You too. I'll give you four hundred for crossing in a clean car and riding with me and the stash back to Seneca Hills. When we're driving, I assume all the risk and you're just along for the ride. If some fluky bullshit happens, I'd probably just get a misdemeanor anyway what with the laws changing."

"Yeah, but they might keep the car. Busting people for cannabis in the States is now primarily about police departments making money."

"My worry, not yours," Oren stated. "All will work out just fine."

Confidence galore.

"Why didn't you bring this up before, like when you smoked in our bathroom at Foxwoods?"

Oren smirked. "Good nose, eh? I hadn't made up my mind to do the run. I guess I shoulda offered you some. I ..."

"Wait," Jake stopped him. "Did we just cross into Canada with anything?"

Oren gave his half-smile. "Just one joint ... so I can smoke it on the boat. It's good luck."

Jake shook his head. "You're really something, Oren."

"One joint? Big deal. I know the risks and none for you."

"Yeah, but I should be privy to whatever. I'm in the car. When you talked about smuggling cigarettes, you said you were doing a friend a favor. That still true, but a bigger favor ... a lot of cash?"

Oren hesitated.

"I'm here with you," Jake added, "talking about driving the goddamn car. I deserve the truth. You doing this to raise money for Grant?"

"Yeah," Oren finally said.

"He's okay?"

"Yeah."

"Was he the one who drove the car the last time?"

"Nah, some punk. I kept most of the profits from that run. This time's different. Grant needs the money to stay ahead of the Man. That's why Chad might be okay with it ... and maybe even the others since they all think Grant is innocent. But it doesn't matter what anyone thinks. I gotta do this for him."

Oren went on to explain that although Guyasuta had had cash enough to hide out early on, it would take a lot more to cover his ongoing expenses and maybe eventually legal costs as well, if the cops couldn't track down the real killer.

While Oren was occupied with his phone, Jake looked out the car window. Only two other cars were in the Spinners parking lot. At least it was a quiet night for Oren's transaction. The assorted laws surrounding cannabis were Byzantine. What Oren was doing on this side of the border involved an unregulated black-market product. Smuggling cannabis into the U.S. – even into states that had legalized recreational use as well as medical – was still a federal charge.

During his stint on drugs, Jake didn't like the idea he might be underwriting some nasty types, like the drug cartels. But marijuana had helped him cope. He'd started too young admittedly – age fourteen. Caitlyn had held out until sixteen. Their mother had probably been too far gone on drink to care about their secret smoking sessions. Being outlaws together had made brother-sister communication about their mother and other issues flow.

Weed had helped other friendships develop as well. He and his peers had concluded that classifying it as a Schedule 1 drug along with the hard stuff was based on ignorance. They'd become scofflaws together with a healthy dose of cynicism about how society had gotten things wrong.

The occasional anxiety and self-doubt from smoking Jake saw as positives compared to the bravado of booze and the numbing of opioids. Cannabis had been and still was medicine for him, helping him avoid the drugs that had swallowed him up for too long. He'd been known to sound off that people were hypocritical in their anti-pot stance if they drank alcohol recreationally or if they took other medications for pain, nausea, or anxiety.

But he was mindful about cannabis abuse, as with any mind-altering substance. Edibles in particular were tricky. Dosage levels and tolerance were key. Highs could be way too intense, leading to panic attacks.

"This the meeting place?" he asked Oren.

"So, Jake, you gonna drive the car?"

"I'll do it. But no more surprises and forget paying me," he said.

"I can gift you if I want. It's a Native thing. You like Native traditions, don't you, Jake Maybe-Mohawk?"

Jake let that pass, repeating his question: "This the meeting place?"

"Yeah. You'll be inside the diner when it goes down. Let's go eat."

Jake followed Oren into the diner. An elderly couple sat at the counter. They looked Native despite being dressed like a lot of non-Native folks in Shaleville and Seneca Hills – flannel and jeans. Oren headed for a corner booth. A middle-aged woman approached. Her Native features were enhanced by a beaded vest.

"Staying out of trouble, Oren?" she asked.

"You bet," Oren replied. "And you, Ms. Holly?"

She laughed. "Yeah, out of all the good kinds of trouble unfortunately, too. You still living over with the Seneca ... with your grandmother, right? You got a job there, I heard."

"You heard right. My mom tell you?"

"No, my brother. Haven't seen your mother in a while. A long while."

"I'll bring her by my next visit."

"I hope so, Oren."

Oren ordered bacon and eggs; Jake, an omelet. After Holly had walked away, Oren said. "She and my mother had a fight over a man. Stupid shit."

He then went to his phone.

Jake thought about his first time at Akwesasne years ago, rubbernecking everywhere he went. He was less an outsider now but he obviously wasn't going to see much of the reservation this time either.

Jake's mind also returned to Foxwoods and Hartford. Chad and Ona hoped to put a positive spin on Native gaming for the general public, as well as send the message to the casino tribes that the Arrow Alliance was proactive and effective and worthy of financial support. Fancy Dancing was helping build the organization. The powerful movements carried history and meaning in them. The enjoyment on the faces of the crowd at the gathering and the presence of the press attested to all that.

Jake envisioned the old man moving to the drumbeat and then his final dramatic jump before leaving. It was all so youthful. He also recalled how the old man and Oren had been talking ... how deliberate it seemed ... and he remembered Chad's quizzical expression watching the old man.

Jake suddenly connected the last of the dots. Youthful indeed.

He interrupted whatever Oren was doing on his phone. "The old man at Hartford you were talking to ... that was Guyasuta in disguise, right?"

Oren looked up at Jake. "I can't keep anything from you, can I? You're a sneaky, sharp one."

"Funny, that's what Ona said about you although she left the 'sneaky' part out. Well?"

"Okay, that was Grant. He showed up in person to try to talk me outta my run. I shouldn't've told him beforehand."

"Really? Not his idea to do this?"

"He wouldn't ask that of me."

"How'd he get there?" Jake asked. "Quite a risk."

"What's it to you?"

Jake ignored the question. "Chad and Ona catch on that he was there?"

"Not sure yet. Chad might of. If Ona did, she'll be upset. She likes to play things safe."

"And Chad? Would he be pissed?"

"He's a gambler," Oren replied with admiration.

"Like you."

Oren nodded. "Yeah, you can say that."

"And like me apparently."

Oren shrugged. "Yeah, sure, like you. But your bet's a small one. Just some hassle for you if I lose this hand. You don't know about Grant, okay?"

"Okay," he said, thinking he wanted to know everything about Grant.

~

From the diner window, Jake watched Oren. He was leaning on the Volvo, looking at his phone.

A white pickup pulled up, an aluminum crossbed toolbox behind the cab. A man climbed out. He wore a wool cap and brown canvas coveralls. He looked about Oren's age. Oren moved to the front of the Volvo and opened the hood. The man joined him and talked with him a moment. He then walked around to the back of the pickup and pulled out a canvas tool bag from the truck's toolbox. He placed the bag on the ground between the vehicles and, pulling out a wrench, returned to the vehicle's engine. He leaned in and made some adjustments, or pretended to. Oren entered the car and tried the ignition. The car started. Oren stepped back outside and moved to the car's front to close the hood. He briefly talked to the man, then discreetly handed him an envelope. The man put it in his pocket and, wrench in hand, returned to his truck. Oren picked up the canvas bag, opened the Volvo's hatch cover, and placed it next to the other luggage. The pickup pulled away. All very smooth.

Oren glanced at the diner window and gave a summoning wave. Jake left a ten on the table next to Oren's, nodded goodbye to Holly across the room, exited the diner, and headed for the Volvo. Oren now sat in the passenger's seat. Jake took the driver's seat, started the car, and pulled out, Oren pointing the way.

It was a short drive down to the water and the marina parking lot. Jake's nerves made it seem longer.

"This is it," Oren said.

"Whose boat?"

"A rental. I called ahead for the boat and fishing gear. A lot of dudes use speedboats or Jet Skis that can outrun marine patrols. Me, I'm just a young fisherman quietly minding my own business."

"You just leave the boat on the other side?"

"After the exchange with the first guy, I text someone else who gives me a ride to the casino. The first guy returns the boat tomorrow. Part of the deal."

"Does the rental guy know what's going on?"

"He doesn't wanna know," Oren said. He lowered his window. "Wind's died down."

Jake looked at the expanse of river beyond the moored boats. Sunlight glimmered on the frigid water.

"Wicked cold out there," he said.

"Good time for fishing ... around sunset. Other boats will be on the water," Oren assured him. "No prob."

"Sure hope so."

"You want some Adderall?"

Jake thought it over. "I'll pass. It'll remind me of stronger uppers and trigger my craving. I'll stick with coffee."

"Suit yourself."

Oren quickly walked around to the trunk, opened it, and grabbed the canvas bag, a rain slicker, and blankets.

"See you on the other side," he said. "Sticks Sports Bar at the casino. Go east on 37. You'll see signs. Meet you there about ten. I'll text you when close."

He turned and headed for the dock. Jake watched him go, then looked inward. Here he was taking risks in the drug culture again. His was the easy part, he knew. Drive a car across the border, his papers in order. Still, he was tense as he headed for the crossing.

Before reaching customs, Jake pulled over and stepped outside to take photos of the signs and bridge for Aki. She would appreciate them, especially if he told her the whole story ... although she would probably think he was stupid for being involved at all.

He got back in the car and drove toward the customs booth. The American agent – his rotund face just this side of scowling –

looked over his passport, driver's license, vaccine certificate, and the car's registration, finally asking, "Where're you from?"

"Shaleville, New York," Jake dutifully replied.

"What'd you do in Canada?"

"I have some Mohawk blood, my mother tells me, and I'm researching the tribe."

"The car's registered to Onatah Makens."

"She's my Seneca girlfriend. She lent it to me to visit some of the Mohawk reservations."

The man now wore a full scowl but waved Jake through. He'd made it without hassle.

Had Oren?

Jake pulled over again to get photos of the customs buildings and booths. Now to rendezvous at the Akwesasne Mohawk Casino in Hogansburg, near the reservation and the St. Regis River that flowed into the St. Lawrence. The original name for the reservation on the U.S. side of the St. Lawrence was St. Regis. The indigenous name Akwesasne – or *Ahkwesáhsne* – was now more widely used here, too.

Jake easily found the casino. After parking in the resort's garage, he realized how exhausted he was. He had some hours to kill. He set his alarm on his cellphone for 9:15, since Oren had estimated meeting up by 10:00, and pulled his winter coat over him like a blanket.

The day's impressions, like photographs, scroll along his mental screen ... Caitlyn and her kitchen at first light ... the inside of the car, roadside trees, official buildings, custom agents, water, bridge, boats ... and Oren's face showing no concern at all ...

~

The bright lights and noise – the chiming and whirring of slots – were grating after the darkness and quiet of the car. But at least the casino's warmth felt good after the car's cold. Jake passed by the main gaming room and found the Sticks Sports Bar and Grill. He chose a corner table from where he could wait and watch for Oren. He ordered a bagel and coffee from a big-haired, weary-looking waitress. If she were Native, she sure didn't look it. None of the customers did either. The lacrosse sticks mounted on the wall were all that reminded Jake of the Mohawk connection. On the nearest TV was a UFC event. Others showed NBA games.

Jake gave thought to the various Native casinos he'd visited. During Chad's radio talk, in response to the audience comment about casino "cheesiness," he'd mentioned the formula established long ago of glitz mixed with the practical, i.e., making money. Some casinos emphasized the Native connection more than others. The games of chance didn't interest Jake, nor did fine dining, entertainment, or pools and spas. The Native connection and the Arrow Alliance's cause did, however.

He ate slowly, his cellphone on the table in front of him. He ordered and ate another bagel, nursing three cups of coffee. After another hour and a half, he wondered if he would be waiting the whole night. What if Oren never showed up? Check at police stations? Would Jake be on the other end of Oren's one phone call from jail?

Just as he was doubting everything, a text arrived: "I'm hungry! See u soon!"

In under about twenty minutes, Oren walked into Sticks, hands in his pockets. He spotted Jake and joined him, playacting a big greeting. It was now going on 11:00. Oren ordered a burger and fries. Jake didn't ask any questions in the public place, other than about getting a room for the night.

"Nah, I'm good," Oren said. "Adderall sure helps. Trip's about six hours. I can do it, no prob. The weather looks okay ... maybe just some flurries."

"I had a nap in the car," Jake told him. "I can drive if you need a break."

Oren nodded, his head bobbing as if to a pounding rhythm – the fast heartbeat of an emotional high.

~

Once on the road, Oren filled Jake in. He'd made the crossing in stages – first toward Cornwall Island, then eastward along it – stopping from time to time to pretend to fish, then continuing on as if to find a better spot. Other fishing boats had been anchored in or trolling nearby waters, making progress less conspicuous. The critical stretch had been rounding Cornwall Island opposite Îsle

Saint-Régis – the channel serving as the boundary line between Ontario and Quebec – then setting out across the final stretch of open water toward the United States. A patrol boat of any of the jurisdictions might have stopped him for questioning. But no one had checked on him as he made his way to a dock. He'd completed the deal with one accomplice and then texted a second one for a ride to the casino.

Oren went on to open up about his friendship with Grant. The powwow killing and the subsequent manhunt had rocked his new world, as he put it, so he was willing to do anything to help his "brother." He also expressed delight in how Grant was managing to elude his pursuers.

Jake took advantage of the conversational flow to bring up Georgetown: "Chad must be reeling with all the craziness, first at the powwow and now with Grant on the lam. And that suicide in Washington, D.C., when he was about to give a talk. She was a Lumbee Indian, I read."

"Yeah."

"You knew her?"

"I met her at the powwow."

"Didn't she work in Atlantic City for the developer Andrew Sharp?"

"Sharp fired her when he learned she was an Indian," Oren said. "That's what she claimed anyway."

"You believe that?"

"Yeah, I guess. Sharp fucking hates Indians."

The Georgetown students outside E/E had told Jake that a Native American had led her away before Chad's talk – Oren, Jake had assumed. How to bring that up without revealing what he already knew from being on the scene?

"Did she talk to Chad first?" he asked.

"Yeah, I led her backstage," Oren replied.

"She go off on Chad?" Jake wondered how Oren would take that question.

He seemed unfazed. "No, Chad said she was furious and spewing hatred that Sharp didn't show up. When she left, he thought she was heading back to the auditorium. Instead she went upstairs to that window. Maybe she figured she'd get press against Sharp that Arrow could use. Go out as some kind of hero. Probably was proving something to Chad."

"A romance angle?"

"More like a stalking angle. She was sure fixed on him after the powwow. He tried to help her. He knew she was a self-cutter with suicide on the brain."

"How'd he take her death?"

"How do you think? It messed him up. He said he should've known how fragile she was."

"Does he talk about it anymore?"

"Nah, not with me anyway. Maybe with his BFF Ona ... or with my grandmother or Thomas."

Oren eventually burned off the medication fueling him and near Syracuse had Jake drive. He soon fell asleep and now was breathing heavily. Jake turned the radio on and surfed the stations. The nap and all the coffee had served him well and he felt wide awake. He wanted to make good time but, given the cargo, kept the cruise control only five miles-per-hour over the speed limit, letting the big trucks on their nighttime highway runs pass him. South of Rochester some lake-effect flurries further slowed him down.

Oren slept almost two hours. After they'd stopped for coffee, he took over driving again and Jake dozed.

The trip to Seneca Hills lasted seven-and-a-half hours not six, and it was almost dawn by the time Jake crawled into his bed at the Red Jacket Motel. He'd gone through yet another rite of passage on the circular trip to Foxwoods and back – a rite of passage like the sweat. But passage to where?

PART IV: REGIONAL FORAYS

"And yet, there is only one great thing, the only thing – to live to see in shelters and on journeys the great day that dawns and the light that fills the world."
– from an Inuit song

Movie Script

"ALL GOOD?" Jake asked.

"All good."

Just inside Jake's door, Oren reached in his coat pocket and pulled out an envelope, extending it toward Jake, who kept his hands at his side.

"Take it," he said. "Four hundred, like I told you."

"Yeah, but what did I tell you?"

Oren waved him off. "You told me you don't want a payoff. Well, I'm gifting you for going out of the way with me after Foxwoods and helping drive when needed. That's all. It's considered an insult to refuse. Look up the potlatch."

"I know about the potlatch."

"Well then, don't shame me."

Jake thought another moment, then reached for the envelope.

"Okay, I accept it for the reason you said ... for traveling up to Akwesasne with you ... for driving when you wanted me to. Okay? All good?"

Oren nodded.

Jake continued: "Now it's my turn. Take it. Don't shame me. I'm gifting you and through you I'm gifting Grant Guyasuta."

Jake offered the envelope back. Oren settled into his half-smile and, after a few seconds, took it.

"Okay, okay, you win, Maybe-Mohawk. No shame. Your pride and whatever else is intact. On Grant's behalf, thanks for the gift." He headed for the door. "Ona and Chad will be back tonight. My grandmother told me to tell you we all meet at the Turtle tomorrow at nine."

"See you then," Jake said.

He closed the door and walked to his bed, collapsing on it. He'd come up with the idea of regifting the money on the spot. It had all worked out. Oren had helped his friend. The return of the payment would help Grant for what that was worth. It also helped Jake allay his guilt over his grand deception.

Enough ruminating, he resolved. Time to get back into motion. Even without the additional funds, with what he was earning from both Aki and Arrow, he had money enough to buy a laptop. In addition to his investigative research, he could also then create files of his photographs on a screen other than on his cellphone's tiny one.

~

That evening, back in the motel, Jake sat in front of the laptop he'd purchased at an Office Max near Buffalo. He was uploading photos from his phone. At Hartford, while Ona and Chad had chatted with the Pequot and Mohegan dancers after the event, Jake had gone to the car and had done a quick pass to delete the worst of the photos, then transferred files from the Alliance camera to his phone before returning the Nikon to Ona. She knew he regularly did this to have backups of the photos in case of problems with the camera. She also knew he hoped to send some of his shots to Aki. He would first provide Ona with the numbers of those he hoped to send; she would consider Aki's use of them, giving approval or not.

On finishing, Jake studied the crowd shots. On the laptop's screen, in one of the photos, he could make out just enough of one man's hatchet-shaped profile to discern a white eyebrow. No doubt now: White Eyebrows had been at the Connecticut rally.

Craving conversation about all this, Jake phoned Caitlyn. She answered on the second ring.

"Good time to talk?" he asked.

"Sure is. I need a break from textbooks," she said.

"I hate phones but I want to talk to you more about my idea for a movie. I'm working on a screenplay."

"Movie?"

"Remember the idea I ran by you the other day about a young Native character? The Mohawk who has some dance moves?"

She needed a few seconds to catch on. "Indeed I do."

"Remember I brought up his having a mother in Akwesasne?"

"Right."

"There's no scene with her. Instead, I'm thinking he uses visiting her as an excuse to maneuver a character based on yours truly with a deal he's planning."

He could almost hear Caitlyn's thought-wheels turning. "What kind of deal?" she asked.

"Our brother-and-sister medicine. Let's say he wants to raise funds to help a friend in need, the friend on the run who everybody's obsessing about."

"Wait, wait. Tell me ... he and his passenger cross back with it for that friend?"

"No, not like that. He goes by boat with the score. The passenger drives the car back."

She absorbed that and said, "Quite the plot."

Jake related more details about the score and the border crossing and also how the friend in need, still on the lam, as well as a mysterious White Eyebrows character are both at the earlier Connecticut event. He continued to frame everything as part of a movie idea, including the gifted payoff he'd just avoided and his buying a laptop with other funds.

Caitlyn took it all in, letting out an exclamation from time to time, culminating in, "That White Eyebrows character is sure creepy sounding" and "Wow, your lead character, the young Mohawk, sure is a daredevil."

"Reminds me of someone who recently had eyes for you," Jake teased.

"Too young, too intense. Seems to have a good heart though. Takes risks for others. I like the idea that in the screenplay the friend he's doing it all for shows up in disguise and tries to talk him out of it."

"I've been wondering where and when he meets the friend again to give him the money."

"In your movie script, why is the man with the weird eyebrows tracking him? It's not just a bizarre coincidence, is it?"

"That'd be a good thing in real life but doesn't make for a convincing plot."

"Have you made a decision yet about the friend's guilt or innocence?"

"Not yet anyway. I'm working on that."

"Damn, Jake. Mom would sure like this. It would be up there with her all-time favorite movies."

"Maybe someday I'll run the major plot points by her."

"I can lie awake now, thinking about them when I should be thinking about other things, like schoolwork. To change the subject, I'll be drawing up a list of questions for you. I want to get quotes from you about our childhood for my theme paper. I'll be calling you one evening soon."

"Sure, sis."

"In the goddamn meantime, be a writer with an especially watchful eye for detail and plot twists and threats to one and all," she admonished. "I want a happy ending to your movie."

She'd kept the movie theme going, but there was real concern in her voice.

Love Shack

JAKE FOUND HIMSELF in a routine for the first time since he'd left Shaleville for New York City. He and Oren started early in the morning and worked on the grounds until late afternoon. They cut and stacked the wood from felled trees – at the lodge sites and the new parking areas – separating out hardwood from the evergreens and stacking it in manageable lengths near where the garage would be built. On snowy days or days with temperatures in the single digits, they were assigned indoor tasks. such as building shelves in the offices. Most days after work, they smoked up together. Oren had taken his share of the Akwesasne run in product rather than cash.

Jake saw little of Chad, except at the weekly staff meetings, some of which the Alliance leader missed for travel. If not on the go as the Arrow ambassador, drumming up support, he typically stayed in his office. He was warm to Jake when they did cross paths. But he seemed in constant motion, rushing through his days, and they hadn't bonded any further.

Ona was scarce, too, holing up in her office. She slept there most nights now, Jake knew. When in her presence, he tried not to be too attentive. In any case, she acted oblivious. He knew that he should rein in his libido. She and Chad obviously had something deep going on. Jake also knew that any goodwill and respect she'd developed for him would dissolve if she learned what had led him to Seneca Hills and the Arrow Alliance.

Still ... she had that magic. Jake, despite warning signs and obstacles, had succumbed all too often to such magic.

Other than Oren, Jake felt the most comfortable with Thomas and Ehnita. Both tribal elders had a gift for drawing people in through humor. The playful moniker "Maybe-Mohawk" had been the start of it all for Jake. But he recognized the depth of their analytical minds and their dedication to their political and spiritual mission. He'd witnessed Thomas at the sweat and he'd once heard Oren tease his grandmother about how she was an activist about his behavior just like she'd been about everything to do with Akwesasne.

When Jake had commented on Ehnita's spunk, Oren had nodded his agreement. "Yeah, she's a spitfire. She or Thomas tell you the GM story?"

"No."

"She used to work as a secretary at General Motors ... at the plant near the reservation. It came out that animals raised or hunted on the rez and fish caught in nearby waters were polluted with PCBs and other toxins ... way more than the minimum health standard for hazardous waste. The morning that the news came out, my grandma made her choice right on the spot. To hell with her union wage, health benefits, and pension. At what became known as Contaminant Cove she scooped up boxes of soil samples, then dumped them along with some dead fish on her boss's desk. Figured it was a good way to quit."

The next morning, Jake arrived at the Turtle before Oren. Ehnita and Thomas both were in the outer room.

"Hey, Ehnita, I know why you don't drive a Chevy," he said with a smile.

Sitting at her desk, she looked up at him and said drily, "You do? So tell me."

Thomas, at Ona's desk, looked up expectantly.

"The same reason I now want to trade in my GMC van," Jake said.

"I gather Oren's been telling stories ... about Contaminant Cove and all that," Ehnita said.

"Obviously a proud grandson."

"It took me a long time to eat fish after that."

Thomas chuckled.

"Speaking of eating fish," Ehnita continued, "want to join us for dinner at our house this evening, Jake? Okay with you, Thomas?"

"A-okay."

"Jake, you can stand in for Oren. He told us he has to straighten things out with his girlfriend Jess tonight ... for the umpteenth time. What do you say?"

"Love to," Jake told them.

~

Jake was relieved to get a break from the Jack and Jill Diner. Although the food there was decent enough and everyone was friendly enough to him now, making him a de facto goodwill ambassador on behalf of the Arrow Alliance, the sameness of his evenings was getting to him.

Thomas's and Ehnita's "love shack," as Oren called it, stood on the edge of Salamanca, not far from the site of the sweat. It was easy to find being the only partial log cabin on the block. The original central one-story log structure had framed-and-clapboarded additions on both sides.

Jake used the big brass knocker – a ring that swung in and out of a bear's mouth. Thomas answered the door with a big smile, waved Jake inside, and took his coat.

"Dinner's almost ready," he said.

Jake had asked what he could bring and Ehnita had told him vanilla ice cream. He'd stopped at a convenience store on the way and bought a half-gallon.

"Here's dessert," he said.

118

"Great. Ehnita must've told you what I like … as always, taking care of her man. Have a seat by the fire. We've been soaking up all the heat we can. You want a beer? I'm having one."

"Sure."

"Be right back."

The combined living room/dining room had a fireplace along one wall with a woodstove insert burning hot. There were side doors off this central room besides the one leading to the kitchen – to at least three bedrooms, Jake figured, knowing that Ona had grown up here and Oren now stayed here. Off the back wall a sliding glass door led to a snow-covered deck. The small backyard, separated from neighbors' yards with a tall fence, opened to woods in the rear. The view made the setting feel more country than city.

In addition to Native-themed paintings on the walls, a number of Native artifacts adorned the mantelpiece and shelves – sweetgrass baskets, ceramic pots, soapstone animal carvings, a wooden ladle, and a feathered gunstock war club. A plain curved and pointed stick was propped in one corner near a wood chest with a lid. On the chest's sides were painted red and black images, their geometric shapes forming what seemed overlapping creatures.

Thomas soon returned with two Molson's and sat down next to him.

"Quite some chest," Jake said, still studying its designs.

"A Haida friend from British Columbia gave it to me," Thomas told him. "His father, a shaman, used it for ceremonial objects as I do. It's bentwood, everything except the lid made from one piece of cedar."

"By heating the wood?"

"Right, steaming it before bending it into shape, notching it where the corners will be."

"I've had to bend some wood, like on porch jobs. We soaked it." Jake pointed to the curved stick. "What's that for?"

"That's a digging stick," Thomas answered. "Good for seeding or digging up worms or whatever. Simple but effective. I made it based on a Paiute design. I hold it when I'm digging up hard to reach things inside me … forgotten knowledge and memories."

They went on to talk about projected work on the Turtle's shell, scheduled to begin in March. Since the foundation had been finished, framing could start even before the ground thawed, Thomas mentioned.

"Chad lined up a Salamanca contractor. It'll be an all-Native crew," he added.

Ehnita appeared with a tray.

"Time for Ehnita's famous fish stew and homemade bread," Thomas announced.

The stew was delicious and Jake had a second bowl as well as a second beer, ice cream, and coffee. They chatted through and after the meal. Jake asked a lot of questions. Ehnita talked about growing up Mohawk at Akwesasne, then losing her husband in a construction accident when she was in her twenties, then having a hard time keeping her wild daughter, Oren's mom, in line, and ditto for another wild child, her grandson Oren – the last expressed at least part facetiously. Thomas talked about growing up Seneca on the Allegany Reservation and his adult involvement in some regional issues, including the renewal of Salamanca's lease in 1991.

Jake used discussion of local resentment against the Seneca during lease negotiations to redirect the conversation. "The death at the Alliance powwow must make things that much more tense."

Ehnita replied first: "I've heard that the man who was killed ... Baines ... was a bully and not just against Native Americans. Of course some now see him as a hero, standing up against rowdy Natives."

"When Seneca Hills gets another economic bump come spring, people will start appreciating us again," Thomas said.

Ehnita looked doubtful. "Maybe."

"They must realize the case against Grant Guyasuta is circumstantial," Jake offered.

"He's hiding out so they assume he's guilty," Ehnita replied.

"Whites think he's in hiding because he's guilty," Thomas added. "Indians think he's in hiding because he's innocent."

"Based on what I've heard about Grant," Jake put in, "he strikes me as being all about his dancing ... too much so to do something that would interfere with that."

"Thomas says he was always levelheaded about everything except dancing," Ehnita said.

"I know his parents and knew Grant and his sister Anna as kids," Thomas explained. "Always respectful. His dancing got him into traditional Haudenosaunee culture. He was eager to learn. Before the incident, he was pestering me with questions about the path to becoming a shaman. I see him getting there himself someday. He's a nonviolent soul, I know that." He paused, seeming to look inward. "He's a special one. I wish I could do more for him. He's one of those kids, like Oren is ... well, still kids to me ... who you'd lay your life down for."

Ehnita's eyes hung on Thomas after he'd said that, but then she nodded in agreement.

Jake thought about Grant disguised as an old man in Hartford and about Oren making a cannabis run to help him. What would Ehnita and Thomas think about that? They might be okay with it, as Oren had suggested, since they showed such conviction about the Fancy Dancer's innocence. But they certainly would have worried themselves sick thinking about Oren on the choppy St. Lawrence River with four pounds of contraband.

Both certainly seemed worthy of the concept of grandparents being revered in Native culture, as Chad had explained to Jake. He felt honored to be invited into their home and to share a meal with them. Yet doing so made him want to believe in the Fancy Dancer's innocence that much more.

That night back in the motel, Jake lay in bed thinking about the people he knew in this upstate hamlet and at Turtle Island and their intertwined lives. Ehnita's stew seemed a good metaphor for it. Multifarious pieces thrown together that worked together at the right temperature. Yet one had to be mindful while cooking. All could readily boil over.

Digging Stick

WHILE MINING for information online, Jake often thought of Thomas's digging stick – not to plumb himself, the way Thomas had used the metaphor, but rather to seek out buried clues. And he was digging deep.

Grant Guyasuta was the only official person of interest and the prime suspect in the public's eye. Jake imagined him hiding out, sometimes disguised as an old man. He thought about Grant's trying to talk his friend Oren out of taking a risk for him in Hartford. And he thought about all the positives he'd heard from the Alliance folks about him. He traced Grant's dancing career in greater detail than he'd done on his phone, finding more of the Fancy Dancer's winning performances. There was no question Grant was gifted, combining athleticism, elegance, and just enough frenzy.

If Jake presumed Grant's innocence, as his Native friends all seemed to, where else might he look? He had to consider and hopefully eliminate as suspects everyone around him. Ona, Ehnita, and Thomas didn't compute as knife-wielding killers. Oren? As Caitlyn had discerned, he sure had his intensity. But Oren's devotion to Grant and efforts on his friend's behalf showed his heart. None of them were implicated in reports other than the Fancy Dancer.

Chad hadn't been implicated either and Jake didn't want to go there. How could he not if he took the detective mantle seriously? Chad, the seemingly compulsive gambler. He'd revealed his own intensity at the graves of his family; he had contempt for Andrew Sharp; and he was the last person to talk to Salali Jenkins's before her death. His character remained elusive. Did he burn hot enough down deep to stab someone to death? To help get rid of any such notion, Jake had to disprove some past connection between Chad and Richard Baines, like something related to the tragic loss of Chad's family, or a link between Baines and Chad's nemesis, Sharp.

The Alliance website still announced "Under Construction." After creating social media accounts, Jake found summaries of Arrow Alliance's mission and mention of Chad's radio talk. By looking at regional press sites, Jake located more articles on the Salamanca fire. They all reported it as accidental. One mentioned that Chad had been away at college at the time. Another described the funeral for his parents and sister as a traditional Longhouse Ceremony.

Still on Chad, Jake revisited the canceled E/E event and Salali Jenkins's death. The Lumbee Tribe website offered only a short notice: "We have lost one of our daughters. Salali Jenkins passed away on December 17th in Washington, DC. She had been working and living in Atlantic City. We remember her as a dedicated member of the Lumbee Tribe Boys & Girls Club, both as a teen participant and an adult volunteer. She will be missed."

Jake also searched for more on Andrew Sharp, first finding what he already knew – his inherited wealth, his real estate holdings, mostly in New York and Philadelphia, his casinos in Atlantic City and Vegas, his penchant for self-promotion, his frequent use of litigation as a business tool, and his questionable treatment of women. But one thing he read about the mogul further tying him to Chad was that Sharp's son Martin had attended Kenton College.

About Richard Baines, Jake learned he'd worked in the Buffalo Police Department before retiring to Pennsylvania and wouldn't have had any jurisdiction in Salamanca relating to the fire at the Jeffers-Catamount family house. Nor could Jake connect Baines to Sharp. One more article Jake located about Baines's death stated that he'd regularly come to New York during deer season, staying in a friend's hunting cabin in Little Valley, the next town over from Seneca Hills. Had Baines's local friend also been at the powwow? The bearded man with the binoculars on the crest?

Jake would ask Oren about him.

Dead Center

OREN SMOOTHLY NOCKED the arrow in the bow's rest, drew the string, aimed, and released, hitting three rings out from the target's bull's-eye. His second arrow missed by two rings.

That day after work, Oren had told Jake he was going to do some target practice with his bow and arrows. He'd led Jake to his truck to help carry the equipment and handed him a vinyl-covered foam target to carry, then had grabbed a plastic bow case and an aluminum quiver with five arrows.

They'd walked to the edge of the woods near the lodge sites. Oren had told Jake to lean the target against one of the woodpiles. He'd then opened the plastic case and began assembling the bow's components, explaining the process as he did so. He'd inserted the two limbs of laminated and polished wood into pockets on both sides of the grip. He'd called it a "recurve" bow. The unstrung tips curved away from the archer. After having strung the bow with his "favorite" polyethylene brand, he'd mounted the quiver next to the handle. He'd said that he used wood shaft arrows with target points while practicing, saving pricey carbon arrows for hunting.

Oren took pride in all his work, Jake knew. But he oozed it now.

"Didn't you tell me and my sister that your father taught you archery?" Jake asked as Oren strung a third arrow.

"Yeah, before going AWOL on us. I had some homemade bows growing up. I got pretty good with them."

"When you go hunting, you ever get hassled, like by Baines's pals?"

"No, why?"

"I read online that one of them has a hunting cabin in Little Valley. And when Ona gave me a tour of Arrow's lands, we went to the Overlook. Some bearded guy in camouflage was looking at us with binoculars from farther south along the crest. I've seen guys in the diner who could be him."

Oren fired another arrow, this one hitting just inside the edge of the target. "Damn, I suck today," he said, reaching for the next arrow. "Too much goddamn work, not enough of this. Yeah, could be the guy with the hunting cabin. He was at the powwow with Baines. His name is Stahl. Jonas Stahl."

"He's also out of Buffalo?"

"Yeah, one of the suburbs. Works as a security guard."

"Any trouble with him before the powwow? Or at the powwow?"

Oren strung the next arrow. "Not that I heard."

"A lot of locals there?"

"Some. Most of the whites looked like tourists."

"From Salamanca?"

"Probably not. The folks around haven't taken to us Injuns." Oren let the arrow fly. It hit one ring away from the bull's-eye. "

"Closer," he said. "But I'm still a loser."

"Maybe one of them had a problem with Baines. Take him out at the powwow so Indians get blamed."

Oren gave that thought, then spoke: "I wouldn't put that kind of shit past a dude like Stahl. Hell, let's go with that."

Jake let go a little laugh, then said, "I keep thinking about all the good work the Alliance is doing here and what you're up against. The powwow incident happens, escalating ill-will. Can you tell me about that night? What do you think happened? What does Grant say? I read online that Baines was last seen with him before the body was found."

Oren's face clouded over. "Grant says Baines was drunk ... Stahl, too. The two of them made some cracks about Native girls. He told them both to chill. Baines and Stahl said some shit and walked off. That was the only contact between them and Grant."

"Maybe Baines mouthed off again and someone from another tribe took him out."

"Possible, but if so, it was for a good reason. Hate to see someone nabbed for doing us all a favor. Grant would also hate that."

"Would you recognize Stahl up close?"

"I sure would." He looked at Jake a long moment. "You're a goddamn curious one. What're you gonna do if you see the bearded guy in camouflage again? Fire off questions like this?"

"No ... just watch my back."

"A good thing. You look Indian enough to get in trouble around here."

Oren strung another arrow and let it fly. This one hit the bull's-eye dead center.

King of the Block

JAKE SKIRTED Allegany State Park, evergreens zipping by. Roads were clear, plows having cleared the six inches of snow from the night before. It was just over a half-hour trip from Seneca Hills to Bradford, time enough to collect his thoughts.

What was he doing? Here he'd been accepted as part of a team, of an extended family even, and he was playing this undercover game, even looking at Chad as a possible suspect. He wanted to clear the Fancy Dancer. What if he did, only to establish someone he knew and liked as guilty?

125

Other people's business, Jake had glommed onto. What the fuck? He found himself clenching the steering wheel way too hard. He eased off, trying to focus on the positives. Struggling with his own issues had started him down the gumshoe path. He wasn't craving alcohol and pills every day. He was getting context for his possible Native ancestry and moving forward in life. He'd taken this unlikely path leading him to western New York – and, as a state border sign on Route 219 south now revealed, to also western Pennsylvania – and he would just stay on it. Hopefully it would lead him to clear the Fancy Dancer and anyone else he now cared about.

About five miles south of the state border, he pulled into the small city of Bradford. He drove around various neighborhoods at first, getting a sense of the place. It had its Main Street and historic district, including the Old City Hall with a clock tower. It had a college campus, the University of Pittsburgh at Bradford. The city was also the home of the Zippo Manufacturing Company and the Zippo/Case Museum. And it had an oil refinery, oil being central to this region's economic history.

In his ignorance Jake had been guilty of assuming a certain sameness in the communities around here. He was now reminded that each one of them – Salamanca, Seneca Hills, and now Bradford – had unique stories and characteristics. He should have known not to stereotype the municipalities – from small cities to hamlets – having grown up in upstate New York and experiencing differences from one to another firsthand.

Jake had located Baines's address online and now activated his phone's GPS to make his way to Winter Street in the northwest part of town. He was able to park right in front of the white two-story frame house. He turned off his engine, got out, and walked to the edge of the small front yard. A *For Sale* sign greeted him. The neighboring house to the north was blue. A slender elderly man wearing just a sweater, slacks, and gloves – no hat even – was shoveling snow off his front steps. The shovel looked too big for him. No one had shoveled Baines's walkway or steps for a while.

Jake studied the white house, feigning interest. The neighbor watched him. Jake walked along the sidewalk, stopping opposite the man.

"Greetings," he said.

"Morning," the man replied matter-of-factly.

"More snow to deal with."

"Keep waking up to it." The man tossed his head toward Baines's house. "You waiting on the realtor?" He spoke with the flat-A accent typical of upstate New York – and of this part of Pennsylvania apparently.

"No, just driving around, checking out a lot of houses in the area."

"You mean in Bradford?"

"All over. Even across the state line."

"Where you hail from?"

"Near Albany."

The man shifted his weight. Jake could see he had more questions in him.

One came: "You moving to these parts?"

"Got a builder friend who works out of Salamanca. I can work with him. I'll probably just rent for the time being but thought I'd get to know what's available. I like the idea of not living in New York State what with taxes and all."

"They suck everywhere."

The front door opened and a woman stepped out. She wore a big woolen coat over a nightgown.

She looked at the man. "It's twenty-four degrees out and you're dressed like that?"

"I can't shovel properly in a coat." Then to Jake: "Meet the missus."

"Hello, I'm Jake."

"He's interested in next door," the man told his wife. "He's in construction."

"Really now," the women said to Jake. "To flip it?"

"No, just checking out a lot of properties ... for a place to live eventually. I'll probably rent first."

"Where you from?" she asked. "Buffalo?"

"No. Near Albany."

"Good."

"She doesn't like people from Buffalo," the husband said.

"Why would I?" she asked rhetorically.

"The previous owner was from Buffalo," the man added.

"A bad neighbor?" Jake asked.

127

The woman scrunched her face and barked a laugh. "Ha!"

"He's the man who was killed, wasn't he? The retired cop?"

"That's the one."

"What was the problem with him?"

"He's dead," the husband told his wife. "No need to sound off."

She waved him off, still looking at Jake. "He was a bully. Used his once being a cop to get his way with everything."

"Like what?"

"Like letting his yard be a mess and letting his garbage blow onto ours. Like late night loud parties with his obnoxious friends. Thought he was the king of the block. And that girl ..."

The husband shook his head. "We don't have proof of anything."

The wife turned sharply toward him. "Oh, stop it. You and your proof. She was raped. Poor girl."

"Girl?" Jake asked.

"Too young to be with him and that other creep from Buffalo."

"She showed up on our doorstep and asked to use our phone," the husband said. "Called a friend for a ride. She was crying."

"That she was," the wife said, "and I know real tears when I see them. That Baines told us afterwards she came home from a bar with them and it was consensual. Even accused her of being a hooker. Big surprise he would lie and big surprise nothing came of it. Too many goddamn bullies. Groping celebrities, groping politicians, and groping cops, too."

"Not all are bad," the husband said meekly.

"Good riddance to Baines, I say. I hope his friend and everyone like him gets what's coming to them."

"Now you know what kind of neighbor not to be," the husband said with a smile.

Tea and Chips

"GREETINGS, JAKE. What ... no one to hold the ladder?"

Ona had appeared below him, looking upward. Jake was high up on a ladder in the receding light, staple gun in hand, reattaching clear plastic on the back of the Turtle's neck, where the structure would eventually connect to the shell-shaped council room. Winter winds had loosened the temporary covering.

"I'm used to tall ladders," he replied.

"Where's Oren?"

"He's hunting. I told him I could handle the rest of today's punch list. After I finish here, I'll clean and sharpen the chainsaws. He said he told you."

"Oh, right, he's after small game," she said without conviction.

Was she covering for Oren or did she think Jake was?

"I know you might be part Mohawk, making you skilled in high-steel construction," she said with a hint of sarcasm. "But shouldn't you wait till you're both here tomorrow?"

"Almost done with this high-staple construction. No worry."

She gave a flicker of a smile at his play on words. "Hurry up and finish if you must. Stop in my office afterwards. You get a reward for this perilous job ... refreshments. And I have something to show you."

"Sure thing."

Jake used up the gun's remaining staples. He slowly descended, then took down the ladder, leaning it along the base of the structure. He would return tomorrow with Oren and nail on some more battens to make sure the plastic held in high winds.

He walked around to the Turtle's mouth and entered. The big outer office was empty. Oren had told him that Ehnita had left early to go home to Thomas, who was fighting a cold. Chad had flown to Michigan to meet with the Ottawa.

Jake proceeded to the Turtle's neck and back offices. Ona's door, the second on the right, was ajar. He tapped on it and entered. She sat at her desk in front of her computer. With no additional lights on and only twilight streaming through the window, the screen's light reflected from her face. She looked up, turned on a desk lamp, and gave Jake a nod of greeting.

"Obviously you didn't fall off the ladder."

"Still in one piece."

"Some mint tea? Help yourself. I put a cup out. And I opened some corn chips. Let it be known, they're a Native American derived food," she said with a smile, then pointed to an end table near her cot.

"Thanks," Jake said, heading for the refreshments.

"You know about the Three Sisters?"

He turned. "Maize ... corn, that is ... beans, and squash. Traditionally planted together on mounds. The cornstalks support the climbing beans, and the squash act as a natural mulch to keep weeds down."

Ona smiled again. "I see you've harvested information about the People."

He poured tea from a thermos and took a few chips from the bag. He looked around the room. There were some photos on the wall of Ona and friends. In one she stood next to a smiling Chad.

"When you're finished, come around behind my desk," she instructed. "Take a look. I'm finally ready to pull the trigger."

Jake quickly chewed and swallowed chips, sipped some tea, put the cup down, and moved behind her. Her screen revealed a draft of the new Arrow Alliance website. She led Jake through it, pausing on each screen: Home, Mission, History, The Turtle, Tribal Community, Administration, Events, Links, and Contacts. Navigation from page to page was seamless and the designs, engaging. Sample photographs, some of them Jake's, were interwoven with traditional motifs. Sky colors accented earth tones.

"Looks great," Jake said.

"I'll be sending it to everyone on the team ... you, too ... to proof it before the launch. Then I tell the geeks it's a go. Believe me, I use the term 'geeks' with admiration after what we've been through to get this right."

"Who are they?"

"An all-Native team out of Seattle."

Her phone beeped. She picked it up and looked at its screen.

Jake moved back around in front of the desk and took the seat facing her. He sipped more of the tea while she apparently responded to a text. Her brow was slightly furrowed in concentration. She glanced up before he could look away. If she'd caught his riveted gaze, she ignored it.

"Sorry. That was Chad. He just finished meeting with the Little River Band of Ottawa Indians in Michigan. They donated. He's heading now to Wisconsin and the Potawatomi. After that, to Colorado to meet with the Ute."

"On the go."

"Remember, Chad's part Shawnee. I messaged him earlier that he was like the Shawnee leader Tecumseh, who traveled to unite the First Nations against white expansion, while his brother, the shaman Shawnee Prophet, led the people in their village at home ... the village called Prophetstown. I also told him his prophet Thomas Dion'dot has a cold. You know the story of Tecumseh?"

"The big picture of what he accomplished and his death, but not a lot of details."

"I wrote something to read to my grandfather this evening. It's really just for him, but I'll be incorporating it into my talks about Arrow. Have a listen." Ona picked up a piece of paper and read: "There's a Native tradition of medicine men being active in politics. Pontiac had Delaware Prophet to advise him and help unite the First Nations. Tecumseh had his brother Tenskwatawa, also known as Shawnee Prophet ... and Black Hawk had White Cloud, known as Winnebago Prophet. Sitting Bull and Geronimo were shamans as well as war chiefs. The Seneca Thomas Dion'dot of the Arrow Alliance is a modern-day version of this tradition. As was the case with the historic figures, his counseling is a blend of the spiritual and the practical. Even when discussing political strategy, Dion'dot inevitably interjects a philosophical point of view." She looked up at Jake and smiled. "That should rile my grandfather up. I tease him about his modesty. We're all so dependent on him."

"He sure makes me feel better about my existence."

She broke into the biggest smile so far today. "I know what you mean. He has that effect."

She was opening up. Jake wanted to keep the conversation going to get more of her story from her – all of it – not just bits and pieces. He couldn't help but have romantic thoughts about her, despite knowing that she and Chad had a deep emotional involvement, whatever the hell it was. Secret lovers? Former lovers? Lovers to be? Or just spiritual brother and sister forever as partners in a grand project?

"Tell me about growing up in Salamanca," he said. "Tell me how you became an activist."

How would she take his probing? Would she reveal more?

She did. She talked about how her early years, as the first child of a young couple who were building a new life together in a new home, had seemed ideal. Her father had moved east to be with her mother after he'd gotten her pregnant at a shared harvest festival of eastern and western Seneca. She also told Jake that she'd become aware of Native issues as a young child during the controversy surrounding the expiring Salamanca lease. Her parents had been politicized by it and had encouraged her to start reading about history. Chad's parents had been active tribal members as well. Their parents had held meetings in their homes and she and Chad had become friends. Three years older than she, he'd better understood what was going on.

"Chad took the time to explain it to me," she said. "That was our first shared cause. I looked up to him but fought back my little girl crush."

She went on, stating that how, when in high school, she'd lost her parents, Jacob and Willow. A Seneca man, a family friend, returning from a bar – "drunk of course," she said – had run a stop sign and slammed into their car. She'd been raised by her mother's parents – Thomas and his wife Janice – for two years. After her grandmother had lost her battle with cancer, Thomas had continued to raise her.

Ona and Chad had gone to the same schools and, although he'd been friendly whenever they crossed paths, with their age difference they'd moved in different circles. She'd followed his career as a teen lacrosse star, attending many games. She'd also heard stories about his poker prowess. They'd lost touch after he'd gone off to college. His family tragedy had brought him back to Salamanca. But he'd become distant, as if he hadn't wanted to get close to anyone he might lose, as he had his parents and sister. From that time on, she added, he'd thrown himself into Native causes.

Ona had gone off to college when eighteen, majoring in Native American Studies at the University of New Mexico in Albuquerque. She'd spent her summers working and studying in New Mexico on various pueblos and among her ancestral Seneca-Cayuga in Oklahoma. She'd had some contact there with her father's parents, now divorced. For two years after college, she'd lived in Lawton, Oklahoma, with a Comanche she'd met her senior year. He was helping manage his family's restaurant. She'd worked alongside him as a waitress while taking continuing education classes on Native issues at the Comanche Nation College.

"I hated the way my boyfriend treated other staff," she explained. "That brought into focus some other things I didn't like about him and I bolted. I moved back east to live with my grandfather again. Not long after my return, Ehnita entered our lives. I eventually began working at the museum in Salamanca. Chad and I reconnected and we started working on projects together, leading up to the founding of the Erie-Mingo Nation and Arrow Alliance. So here I am."

Yes, here she was, Jake thought. Beautiful, intelligent, driven, calm on the surface but passionate down deep.

She'd finished and Jake spoke: "The Alliance is sure bringing lots of folks together I feel lucky to be one of them."

She paused then said, "You've been a real help, Jake. Not just as handyman and photographer but as a friend to us all. It's been a difficult stretch. Labor Day Weekend was a real setback. Your presence ... an outsider without preconceived notions ... has helped us stay on track."

"Nice of you to say," Jake said, thinking how although his notions weren't preconceived, his secret purpose was. "Being here has really helped me. I'm only about half a year into the new and better me."

"You had to clean up, I understand."

"When I lived in the city, I was way into the hard stuff. My first teen vices, beer and cannabis, have actually helped recently. They serve as medicines to stay otherwise clean."

He wanted to be honest with Ona. He'd never found out if she'd learned about the Akwesasne pot deal that Oren had pulled off with an assist from him and he had the urge to mention it. Yet even under her spell like this, he had enough willpower not to be an unreliable fool and betray Oren's trust.

"Drinking is a curse for many," she said. "The young have to be careful."

"It's all tricky. I sure got tricked myself."

"We all manage to fool ourselves. You've been a good companion for Oren. He'd gotten close to Grant Guyasuta. The whole family, Grant's sister and parents, also made him feel welcome here. But don't assume it always goes smoothly among the different Haudenosaunee First Nations. The Seneca and Mohawk have distinct identities. I think having a friend who fits in both Native and non-Native worlds ... not to mention maybe a Mohawk ... helps Oren. Does he talk to you about any of this?"

"Some. He told me Grant became like a brother to him."

She nodded sadly. "I'm trying to be a real sister to him ... not just an almost-stepsister."

She turned back to the computer screen. Jake wanted to ask more about her thoughts on Grant. He wanted to ask her straight out what she thought really had happened at the powwow. But the silence told him it was time for him to leave. He stood up.

"Time to gather up my tools," he said.

She looked up again and offered one last smile, meeting his eyes.

Jake exited the office. What women did to him, he thought. Ona had welcomed him into her office and world; then through her silence she'd pushed him away; the next moment, with her direct gaze, she'd pulled him back in.

That's where his mind stayed as he loaded his tool bag and bucket.

What's Mixed

WHEN JAKE showed up for work the next morning, Oren was outside, sweeping away the inch of snow that had fallen on the Turtle's walkway. "Chad wants to talk to you," he said.

"You know what about?"

"He and Ona are at it over something. I figured they were in a bad mood because some local came by this morning trying to get us to change electric providers. Ehnita recognized him as one of Jonas Stahl's crowd. He looked around a lot, like he was casing the joint. But I think something else is going on between Chad and Ona."

"Okay, thanks," Jake said, entering the building.

Ehnita, alone in the big outer room, looked up from her computer. "He who was summoned," she said facetiously. "Hurry forth."

"To Chad's office?" Jake asked.

"Yes."

"Should I be worried?"

She gave her version of a poker smile. "Always something to worry about."

Jake walked on through to the back offices and knocked on Chad's door.

Ona's voice: "Come in."

Jake entered. Ona was standing opposite Chad, who sat at his desk, sipping from a coffee mug.

"Have a seat," he told Jake.

Jake took a chair against the wall.

"You know this may backfire," Ona said to Chad, ignoring Jake's presence. "The first time you go back ever and this is the event you choose?"

"We know why he's doing this," Chad countered.

"Exactly. Any confrontation could give him even more for his million dollars."

"Don't worry. I'll be charming as all hell."

"Except when alone with him?"

"Never alone. Jake will be with me."

Ona turned to Jake, her mouth drawn taut. "Chad wants to take you to Kenton College with him. Sharp United is making a donation ... a million."

"To the History Department to be exact," Chad elaborated. "For American studies ... in particular research on the growth of European settlement and development in the region. Starting with Europeans, the announcement says. He's trying to further marginalize Native peoples."

"That's what he does," Ona said. "We know this."

"Why not just a gift to the college like other donors?"

"The potlatch and other gifting ceremonies are similar ploys ... personal aggrandizement, political maneuvering. Our people have played the game that way, too. Let's be smart and not take the bait and make things worse for Arrow."

"How do I fit it?" Jake broke in, looking at Chad. "Will Oren be going?"

"The Kenton trip means I miss the Midwinter Ceremony at Grand River. I want Oren at the opening ceremonies with Ona, Thomas, and Ehnita. I'll be there on the last day for the closing ceremonies if not before."

"You're the compromise, Jake," Ona stated. "I worry about Oren's temper as much as I do Chad's. You, Jake, will be my peacekeeper."

"Sharp may not even show up," Chad put in. "His son and toady Martin, my former classmate, is scheduled to present the check."

"Hated classmate," Ona added. "They once came to blows."

"Just a scuffle between lacrosse teammates," Chad rejoined.

"He's his father's son," Ona said. "He'll turn any controversial attention-getting move you make against you. Your E/E challenge to his father sure misfired."

"Did it? Sharp got exposed as an employer ... someone who would fire a person for being Native."

"The press was divided on that, even with Salali's suicide."

"If anything, we owe it to her to push back at Sharp and my presence does that." His tone had gone from insistent to entreating.

Ona sighed and said more gently. "Wouldn't it just be better to put out an official statement commending the Sharps on the gift to your alma mater and plan a media strategy."

"Sometimes hypocrisy just isn't worth it."

Ona let out a bigger sigh.

"I'm going to Kenton, Ona," Chad added quietly yet firmly. "Some trust, please. I know how far not to go." He turned to Jake. "We'll leave tomorrow afternoon about 2:30. Back late probably."

Jake turned back to Ona.

"Don't look at me," she told him. "You heard him. He's going. And I'm hoping you'll douse any flames."

~

A text from Oren: "Where u at?"

"Just leaving the diner," Jake texted back.

"Come to Chad's office."

"Be there in ten."

Jake had eaten at the diner as usual. For once it had been empty and Jill, responding to his questions, had opened up conversationally while her husband banged about the kitchen. She and Jack had met in kindergarten. She'd been a bad girl and he, a star athlete. Both were from Eden to the south of Buffalo. She'd seduced him while he'd been dating a good girl. At first, Jill had been just a fling for two-timing Jack, but she'd won out in the end. Seeing Jill as a bad girl made Jake appreciate her toughness – tough with a big heart. She made Jake think about Shaleville high-school sweethearts. The stakes had seemed so high at the time, but he'd lost touch with all of them.

Now, in the darkness, Jake drove up the long Turtle driveway, parked, and made his way to the entrance. It was bitter cold, wind chill near zero. He crossed the outer office to the hallway. The office door was ajar and he entered. Chad sat at his desk; Oren, on the cot.

"Hey, Jake," Chad said, then turned to Oren: "Go lock up, okay?"

Oren hustled off. Jake took a chair. Chad waited silently until he'd returned, then reached in his desk and pulled out a tomahawk with a wooden handle and a metal head. When Chad tapped the head on the palm of his hand, Jake realized that it was also a pipe. The opposite end of the head from the blade formed a bowl and the hollowed-out handle served as a stem.

"We're about to head off on a journey, so I thought it would be good to smoke together. You've indicated cannabis has been helpful for you over the years. Oren added it to our blend."

Jake nodded his assent and Chad passed the pipe to Oren, who began filling it from a small ceramic bowl.

Chad looked at Jake again. "I also wanted to thank you for going to Akwesasne with Oren and helping drive. I would've tried to talk him out of his reason for his detour there. Oren explained to you why he did it, he tells me. To help Grant Guyasuta until things settle down. He said he offered you money that you refused ... or rather gifted right back. Whatever your reason for doing so doesn't matter. It helps Grant. We all believe in his innocence. He's far away from those around here who might harm him. When the time is right, he'll come forward. We can hope that those who were responsible will be exposed, so Grant won't have to spend one minute in jail."

The Fancy Dancer far away now? Was that the truth? Was Chad's exposition really what it seemed, or was he just redirecting Jake's thoughts?

Oren passed the now-loaded pipe to Chad. He lit it and took a deep drag, then passed it to Jake, who drew on it. Along with the marijuana he tasted tobacco and other flavors.

"You're smoking *kinnikinnick*," Chad said. "That's Algonquian for 'what's mixed.' This mixture is cannabis, tobacco, sumac leaves, and the inner bark of a willow tree."

Jake exhaled. "Nice taste," he said, passing the pipe to Oren. "And nice pipe."

"European made. French ... traded to the Shawnee for furs. My mother gave it to me. She got it from her Shawnee father."

Jake felt a rush to the brain. *Kinnikinnick*. He would research that further. Cannabis, he knew, wasn't native to the Americas, so this blend couldn't be totally traditional.

"You all packed?" Chad asked. "You have the Nikon?"

"All set."

"Wear that vintage New York Giants baseball cap you have. The one you wore New Year's Eve. Good look for a hip journalist and it might make them think you're from the big city. Any possible psychological edge."

"You think daddy Sharp will show?" Oren asked Chad.

"I bet not. He's molding his son in his own image. It's his money but his son will get more credit this way. He needs it. He was a fuckup while at Kenton. Heavy into the coke. Abusive of girlfriends ... at least that's what one girlfriend originally claimed before being bought off, or so the story went. His lacrosse game sure suffered from his partying ways. The allowances made by teachers, coaches, and administrators have paid off. They're getting a good return on their investment of coddling him."

"What was your fight about?" Jake asked, remembering Ona's words.

"His racism."

"Toward you?"

"Toward a black kid on the team ... Mike Gilley. Sharp wouldn't shut up about how blacks weren't supposed to play lacrosse, like they weren't supposed to play hockey. Big joke, ha-ha. When I'd heard enough of his shit, I told him lacrosse was originally a Native game and Native peoples were fine with whites and blacks playing it, too ... just not rich-prick-daddy's-boy-misogynist a-holes. Or something to that effect. I gave him a little push as punctuation."

Oren chuckled. "And daddy's boy took a swing."

"I was hoping he would. I ducked and clocked him real good. He never picked on Gilley again."

"You think his father knows about all that?" Jake asked.

Chad gave a slow smile. "I've wondered if there's more to Andrew Sharp's stance against Native casinos than just the economics. He's known as a revenge freak in business. In hindsight, it sure looks like I might've been sued. Litigation is Sharp United's weapon of choice. Daddy probably didn't go that route in my case because of possible bad press for his son."

"Is there a plan? Anything I should know?"

"We'll see. Strange the Sharps are donating now rather than at the annual reunion in June. Makes me think old Andrew has something more up his sleeve. Assuming daddy himself isn't there, maybe I'll ask Marty-boy why daddy's too chickenshit to debate me."

Oren laughed again. "And hope he takes another swing at you?"

"After I deck him and make national news, Ona will no doubt be sucker-punching me."

Kenton

THE TRIP INTO Finger Lakes country lasted just over two hours. It was warm for February with welcome sunshine. Chad seemed extra conversational. Nothing like sun for a positive and hopeful outlook on a drive during the long upstate winter, Jake thought. Chad talked about his recent travels on behalf of the Alliance. Nothing more about Kenton though – neither what had been nor what might come – even though they were getting close.

"FYI ... the nearby lake is called Seneca Lake," he said, "but this is Cayuga Indian country. They're brothers and sisters to the Seneca. The lake named after the Cayuga is farther east."

He pulled up to gas pumps at a convenience store just outside the village of Dundee.

"Let's get a snack to carry us over ... maybe eat at the campus center after the talk."

Chad shut off the engine, got out, and started pumping the self-serve gas. On stepping out of the Subaru, Jake stretched, then headed for the store. Near a parked car a couple were squared off in an argument. He couldn't make out what they were saying but he was reminded of the argument in the hallway at the Seneca Allegany Casino during Chad's radio talk. As he strolled the aisles of one of the hundreds of stores like this he'd been in – convenient but limited in selection – his mind then went to Chad's and Ona's recent argument about this trip. She'd placed some responsibility on him to ensure nothing happened counterproductive to Arrow's mission. A lot of responsibility with a wild card like Chad.

Jake settled on nuts and bottled tea. Chad, on entering, grabbed an energy drink at the counter and paid for Jake, too.

On driving again, Chad was silent. College memories stirring? Anything more than that?

They soon reached the small picturesque campus on the opposite side of Dundee. The chapel at its center was easy to spot from the visitors' parking area – a stately stone building with a wooden cupola and a copper roof. Chad and Jake approached along a walkway leading past the back of the building and took an intersecting one around to the front.

The ceremony was scheduled for 5:30 p.m. They waited outside, near the chapel's corner, while students and faculty showed up. The students exhibited motley styles, some borderline extreme. Yet here any piercings, tattoos, or dyed hair seemed more fashion-minded than angry.

"A whole decade and it's like I was never away," Chad muttered.

Even to Jake this all felt familiar. Although he hadn't gone to college, he'd hung out with NYU students in Washington Square Park. And he'd spent a lot of time before that in upstate college town bars, even finding his way into fraternity house parties.

He'd told Aki about the planned excursion to an upstate college, and she'd been happy at the idea of images of a small college campus to work with. To please her, he took shots of both buildings and people.

On an access road paralleling the walkway and closed to the public, a van labeled "WROC, Rochester, New York" pulled near the chapel's opposite corner. Three people climbed out – two women and a man. One of the women, a brunette of medium height in a cobalt blue pantsuit, carried a leather briefcase in one hand and a tablet in the other; the second, a tall blond, wore a fashionable dress and pancake makeup; the man, thickset and bearded, carried a video camera. They hustled along the building's front walkway and up the steps into the chapel.

"A news team in a church?" Jake commented.

"A lot of events are held here besides church services," Chad replied. "Lectures, debates, concerts. The Sharps would only make a presentation where cameras can go."

"You said 'debates'?" Jake asked with a smile. "Like a spontaneous one?"

Chad smiled back. "I like your thinking. Ona sure wouldn't."

"Right, it's on me to make sure you behave church-like."

"No worries ... I want her approval, too."

"So I can relax? Awesome," Jake said, not really sure if he should relax. "What denomination are the services? How does a college handle the religious diversity issue?"

"Unitarian," Chad replied. "The original 18th-century settlement was founded by an Anglican missionary who wanted to convert the savages. Meet Jedediah Kenton." Chad pointed to the quad extending beyond the church's walkway and a bronze statue at its center. "The chapel was built in his honor and the college founded soon after. A number of Haudenosaunee students attended. Algonquians, too ... Mahican, Wappinger, Lenape. They had to convert, but I like to think they did it for the food and not the dogma."

"Any other Native Americans at Kenton while you were here?"

"Two I knew ... both Cayuga from families living nearby ... descendants of the community who stayed in these parts after many tribal members moved away."

"To Oklahoma?"

"Some moved to the Six Nations Reserve in Ontario. Others migrated with Seneca families to Oklahoma, forming the Seneca-Cayuga Nation, my father's people. I connected with the two Cayuga here about that, but otherwise I didn't mingle much with the few other Native students. I'm not proud of that fact. I was first and foremost a jock."

Chad had provided an opening to the subject of his past.

"But you came here as Chad Catamount, not Jeffers," Jake said.

"I was proud of my Indianness as a lacrosse player. I thought the name my father adopted sounded cool."

"I saw online that you were recruited by both Syracuse and Cornell, and it was a big deal that you chose the much smaller Kenton. Why did you?"

"Why else? A girl. A Salamanca High School redhaired-blue-eyed heartthrob. We broke up by the second semester of our freshman year. She was all about getting in the right sorority."

"You never joined a fraternity?"

"I was rushed by a couple of the jock ones, but no. The other reason I chose Kenton was my fantasy of being a lacrosse hero. I was a star here. At the other places I would've been one of many good players. I got to live that life for a while and I dated a lot of girls after that first one. I wasn't meant to be in a fraternity, or at a place like this at all really. The loss of my family woke me up to that."

Chad scanned the campus quad and the limestone buildings flanking it. Jake didn't interrupt his thoughts.

Chad spoke again: "Here's a good one ... Martin Sharp left Kenton my sophomore year soon after I did. He finished the semester, I didn't. But he never got his degree either. He also lost a family member ... an aunt. His story goes that he grew up mostly in his uncle's and aunt's home. After daddy Sharp divorced his mother, she returned to Sweden with a boatload of money and had nothing more to do with the family. Andrew, who started dating model after model, placed little Martin with his brother Theo Sharp. I was hoping that losing his aunt might've changed Martin, like losing my family changed me, but he's jumped right in with dad and uncle, taking over the role of hatchet man at Sharp United."

Students were approaching the chapel from all directions.

"We better get seats," Chad said. "Looks like a full house. I guess millennials like to watch money being tossed about."

"Isn't this Generation Z?" Jake corrected him. "Don't you and I qualify as Generation Y, that is, among the infamous millennials."

"Ha, that's right! This is Gen Z, the end of the alphabet."

"Yeah, then what's after that?"

"I've heard Gen C among other labels used since the pandemic ... that sure works ... covers the virus family and the disease. These labels become all-too-easy insults between age groups."

"I used to refer myself as one of the Gen F for fuckups ... proudly, while acting fucked-up, I should add."

"So as not to continue in that vein, better take your hat off. A no-hat tradition in the chapel."

Jake pocketed his cap, then followed Chad up the chapel's stone steps toward the large white doors. Inside the vestibule Chad angled to a winding staircase on the right. It led to a balcony that wrapped around three sides of the big room. It was filling up fast. They headed to the left side where there were still empty seats.

The chapel had beautiful interior carpentry, including mahogany pews. At the room's far end, the raised portion of the floor had a podium at its center – not a pulpit. Five folding chairs now flanked it.

Two dolled-up female students sat down on the opposite side of Jake from Chad. Even at the safe distance, he could smell perfume. Cheap or expensive, it didn't work on him. The crowd settled in and quieted down.

College dignitaries – three men and a woman – took the stage and the chairs, and Jake had the thought that today, even though it was a Sunday afternoon, the podium served as an altar to academia, if not to a particular god.

Martin Sharp was directed to the middle seat. Jake recognized him from press photos. The fact that the younger Sharp was balding for his years – and would probably end up with garish implants like his father – helped offset his shiny baby face. He wore a tapered black suit. He looked fit, as fit as Chad. A fight between them now might end in a draw, Jake figured.

Chad pointed below. "See that big guy with the slick-backed hair in the dark blue nylon jacket at the end of the first pew ... the one who looks like he could be a linebacker on the Kenton football team?"

"Yeah, a linebacker on steroids," Jake said.

"I'll give you odds he's Sharp's bodyguard."

"I know better than to bet with you. You want photos of the ceremony?"

"Just a few. The local press will be covering it."

"I don't see Andrew Sharp."

Chad only nodded. Disappointment?

One of the dignitaries stood up and approached the podium. From his shock of white hair and faded complexion, Jake guessed he was in his seventies. But he was spry and animated, his energy seeming to rumple his tweed herringbone suit from the inside.

"Greetings, one and all, students and faculty and any other visitors to our campus. As many of you know, I'm Reginald Hunter, chair of the Kenton history department. I have the honor of speaking first at this Sunday afternoon event ... this special event ... in which one of our extended family, Martin Sharp, has returned to bestow a generous gift upon our beloved Kenton."

Hunter looked at Sharp. Students applauded, not by clapping hands but rather by snapping fingers.

"Damn ... the finger-snapping," Chad muttered.

"A Kenton thing?" Jake asked.

"Yeah, a tradition here. It always bugged me."

Hunter went on: "I see that the press is in attendance. The *Ithaca Journal* is here as is the Rochester television channel WROC, both so essential to this region. And let's not forget our student journalists from *The Kenton Bugler*. Welcome, all!"

More finger-snapping.

"The generous gift from Sharp United has been earmarked for the History Department. That's why I'm the first to welcome you. As those of you who've attended my classes well know, I'm passionate about the story of humankind. I'll get things rolling with some of my favorite quotes ... first, Cicero, who said that 'History is the witness that testifies to the passing of time ... it illumines reality, vitalizes memory, provides guidance in daily life and brings us tidings of antiquity.' And Theodore Roosevelt ... 'The more you know about the past, the better prepared you are for the future.' And President Abraham Lincoln ... 'We cannot escape history.'" Hunter paused, then stated, "Here at Kenton we don't let you escape history!"

Finger-snapping.

"I'll leave you with those thoughts. Dr. Henry Franklin, our Provost, will now speak."

Franklin stood up and stepped to the podium. He looked considerably younger than Hunter – he was probably no more than fifty – and, unlike the history professor, not the least bit rumpled. With his groomed gray hair and expensive gray suit – perhaps as expensive as Sharp's – he could have been the CEO of a Fortune 500 company. Before speaking, he looked around the room dramatically.

"This moment is about the History Department, but it's also about Kenton's history." His voice was as smooth as his appearance. "These are the historic moments that have helped Kenton fulfill its mission of academic excellence." He turned to look at the donor. "I thank you Martin Sharp, and I thank your father Andrew Sharp."

Finger-snapping.

"Please welcome to the podium Janet Clarkson, our Dean of Students," Franklin concluded.

Again, the finger-snapping. The woman stood up and moved to the podium.

A student yelled out, "Our Janet!"

Janet Clarkson beamed, her smile big and bright. Jake estimated mid-forties for her age. She, like Franklin, was well groomed. Her clothes showed some color, however – Kenton's colors in fact, maroon and white.

"I'm delighted that so many of you have come out today to celebrate as a community. Although we staff and faculty set the stage for activities at Kenton, you students play the leading roles. One such student has returned from his life elsewhere to share that stage again. He was here before my time at Kenton so I can't share any stories about him. I do know he chose business as his major, taking a history course one semester as we recommend to all business majors. I also know he excelled at lacrosse on a winning team. Let's give Martin Sharp a round of two-handed applause."

The crowd obliged, offering traditional clapping.

Chad turned to Jake with an expression communicating disbelief. "I'd like to pass on some Martin Sharp stories to this

Janet Clarkson," he said. "And with the latest primped provost Franklin. And with Professor History himself, Dr. Hunter."

"Were you in the same history class as Sharp?"

"Yeah. He never said a word. But I did hear him outside the classroom bitch about the stupid requirement for a business major."

"Was that Hunter's class?"

"I took history both my years here, planning to major in it, but Hunter only taught advanced courses."

The clapping subsided.

"Now," Clarkson continued, "please welcome our president, William Minton."

The crowd reverted to finger-snapping.

Minton stepped forward. "Don't applaud me," he said. "All the applauses should be for the gift-giver, Martin Sharp."

More scattered two-fingered applause.

Minton was probably in his sixties. He was an unlikely-looking number one what with his small frame, pointed ferret face, drab suit, and wire-rim glasses. He looked more like a high school social studies teacher than a college president. Yet he sure had a resonant and commanding voice.

"Those of us who speak to you today all make the same point. Two-hundred-year-old Kenton is part of history and has focused on history. We strive to maintain its centuries-long high academic standards and to grow in ways that keep us relevant to modern times. We're a family that recognizes important moments such as this one. Another family has reached out to us with a most generous gift. We are moved when an alumnus returns with a contribution to our mission. Let us all express our gratitude to Martin Sharp, who has come back to us with the purpose of helping Kenton grow." He turned to Sharp. "Martin, please come forward and share some of your thoughts."

Hoots and clapping filled the chapel, bouncing around its walls.

Sharp stood up and angled toward Minton. Minton stepped forward, gesturing him toward the podium.

More applause, clapping morphing into finger-snapping.

The student next to Jake spoke: "He's kinda cute."

"And single," her friend said.

"I hear he likes to beat on girls," Jake interjected, a little surprised at himself.

Both co-eds showed confused expressions. Chad gave him a congratulatory grin.

Martin Sharp waited till the crowd quieted down. Then: "Yes, this is a way we at Sharp United ... my father, uncle, and I ... can offer thanks to Kenton College for all it gave to me." He spoke in clipped words, but flatly with no apparent emotion. "I didn't graduate ... I was here for my freshman and sophomore years ... but those two years were critical to my growth. My time here prepared me for my work at Sharp United. The history course I took gave me the global perspective I need." He reached into his jacket pocket and pulled out a bank check. "Let me present this to you," he said, extending it to Minton, still standing nearby.

Minton extended his hand in return. The two held the check and looked forward. Cameras flashed. The WROC cameraman moved in closer along the center aisle.

Hands clapped, fingers snapped. What a love fest.

Not for Chad. "A small price to pay for a corporate facelift," he said. "Just a paltry million," he said. "Okay, let's get out of here before I earn Ona's wrath and invalidate your presence."

Chad and Jake descended the balcony stairs, walked through the vestibule, and stepped outside. The sun had set and dusk enveloped the campus. Chad led the way down the stone steps over to the chapel's corner where they'd stood before. He looked down at his feet, biting his lip.

Jake finally asked, "That's it? We go?"

"No, it's time to confront him."

"Uh-oh."

"Not me. I'm staying out of sight. You. You're going to talk to him." He leaned in. "Here's what I want you to ask ... on camera if possible ... put your hat back on."

~

Chad bet Jake five dollars it would be thirty-five minutes before the press interviews and chit-chat with hangers-on had ended and Martin Sharp would be led out of the chapel by Kenton

147

dignitaries. Jake guessed thirty minutes. Sharp and the Kenton administrators appeared after thirty-seven minutes.

Jake handed Chad the five dollars. "Like I said, I should know better than to bet with you," Jake said.

"You ready for your role as big-city ace journalist? Got the talking points sorted out?"

"Sure ... I'm ready ... what the hell." Jake touched the brim of his baseball cap.

"Break a leg."

"You mean *his* leg?"

"We'll wait on that."

Jake, pen and pad in hand, moved up the steps toward Martin Sharp. The dignitaries – President Minton, Provost Franklin, Dean of Students Clarkson, and Professor Hunter – and the press representatives hung close. The latter included the two WROC women – the brunette with the briefcase and tablet and the Barbie Doll blond – plus their cameraman. A dissolute-looking man, with camera around his neck and a canvas bag dangling from his shoulder, also had a press tag. From *The Ithaca Journal* mentioned by Hunter, Jake assumed. Mr. Steroids in the blue nylon jacket held up the rear. Jake smiled inwardly. It was a good thing he hadn't also made the bodyguard bet with Chad.

The group paused on the chapel steps to look out over the quad while the last of the students passed them. Only two lingered, watching the group from the quad – a college-age, athletic-looking young man, wearing a Kenton maroon-and-white nylon team jacket, and a second man, somewhat older, in a gray winter parka.

Jake seized the moment and approached Sharp. Mr. Steroids turned toward him, hawk-like eyes zeroing in.

"A question, Mr. Sharp?"

Sharp turned toward Jake. "Yes?" It was supposed to sound neutral but had an impatient edge.

Jake glanced at the cameraman, who in turn glanced at the brunette. She gave a quick nod, and the cameraman hoisted his camera and pointed it at Jake and Sharp.

Jake, trying to call up a reporter's tone and syntax from TV News, spoke: "Given the ongoing dispute Sharp United has with Native American casinos ... as illustrated by the tragic death of the

Lumbee Indian Salali Jenkins, who claimed she was fired from the Pelican Wing Casino because of her Native ancestry ... would you say that the million dollar donation is in some way an affirmation of Kenton College's questionable early history with regard to Native peoples? Why exactly is all the money earmarked for research on European settlement? Aren't American studies about all peoples?"

Jake's line of questioning, hovering like a drone, got everyone's attention. It seemed Sharp would return missile fire, his eyes locked and loaded.

"We at Sharp United have a great interest in the specified historical subject matter and hopefully can apply any new findings to future projects."

Hunter jumped in. "Ah, history is in the air today ... this is a good thing."

"I thank each and every one of you for coming out today," Franklin, the Provost, said with finality. "We at Kenton College are honored by the interest our regional press has in activities here on campus. We now are taking our generous donor to dinner. Have a nice evening." He stepped next to Sharp, took his arm, and led him away, followed by Kenton's bigwigs and the bodyguard, who looked hard at Jake on leaving.

The members of the press watched them hustle off.

The WROC brunette turned to Jake. "Whom do you represent?"

"I'm freelance."

"I'm Rhonda Fields, producer of this segment. Do you mind if we air the question and response?" Her eyes twinkled and her tone was conspiratorial, as if she appreciated the controversy contributed by Jake.

"Not at all," Jake said, his eyes smiling back at hers.

"Even though this is obviously a press-covered public event, we'd prefer if you signed a release," she added.

"No problem."

She pulled a piece of paper from her briefcase and handed it to Jake on a clipboard. He scanned the standard release form, then signed it, using Caitlyn's address, and passed it back. She glanced at it.

"So, Jake Jakes ... do you have any articles published?" Rhonda Fields asked, sounding genuinely curious.

The way her brunette hair dangled over her intelligent hazel eyes he was certainly curious about her, too. Yet with all the others present and the solo reporter raising his hand as if to speak – Jake now could read his *Ithaca Journal* tag – he felt he should move along rather than become the story himself.

"I'm just a concerned citizen. I'll send more info," he said, bowing his head in goodbye as he moved away.

Chad no longer stood at the corner of the chapel. Jake headed that way, then followed the walkway around the building. Chad waited near the far corner, smoking a cigarette and contemplating the campus. Jake joined him.

"Success?" Chad asked.

"I made all the points you wanted. Sharp played it as neutral as he could. He claimed great interest in the narrow field of study and said it might help with future projects. But he sure looked uncomfortable."

"Future projects?"

"That's what he said."

"What ... appropriating reservation lands? Or maybe polluting them?"

"The Q&A was videotaped and might be part of the coverage of the entire event. The WROC producer had me sign a release."

"Good, good. I'll have Ona track it," Chad said. "How'd the Kenton powers-that-be respond?"

"Hunter tried to deflect it by celebrating the history slant. After that, Franklin took charge, getting Sharp out of there fast."

"Well done, Jake. Thanks for being the messenger and allowing me to keep my cool."

"You think Sharp United will scope out the messenger?" Jake asked, adding, "I said I was freelance."

"No doubt. What address did you use?"

"My childhood one, now my sister's."

"Since you don't reveal anything personal in your social media accounts, they'll probably reach the conclusion that you're just a nobody making trouble. Sharp United gets lots of flak online."

Chad headed around the chapel's rear toward the parking lot. Jake followed.

A voice sounded out from behind them: "It *is* you ... Chad Catamount!"

Chad and Jake stopped and turned. The fellow in the gray parka had rounded the chapel corner. The younger man in the Kenton team jacket also came into sight.

Chad eyed them as they approached. "Keith Dryden?"

"The one and only. This is Nick, my little brother. He goes to this prep school for the privileged that calls itself a college. Good to see you, my man."

Chad now had a big smile on his face. "This is my friend Jake," he said. Then, to Jake: "Keith played lacrosse with me."

"How cool is this," Jake said.

Fist bumps followed.

"Did you come back for the same reason I did?" Keith asked Chad. "To see what our former teammate is up to?"

"Sure enough. You talk to him?"

"Yeah, I gave him a hello inside the chapel. He barely acknowledged me, but then again there was a crowd of fawning students to meet and greet. It's been a long time since we all played together. He still comes off as a cold bastard. I guess I should be happy he's helping the college my little bro goes to."

"Bet you it was his dad's idea," Chad said.

"Yeah, to make up for his son's asshole behavior here. I didn't see you talking to him?"

"No. I was afraid of what I might say and do."

Keith turned toward Jake. "I saw you talking to Marty boy. What was that about?"

"Just some questions from the Native American point of view."

"How'd he take it?"

"I don't think he likes me."

Keith smiled and looked at Chad. "I've been following what you're up to. Mighty impressive. I see that sometimes Will Thatcher works with you. How's that madman?"

"The same. Now, he's a madman with a law degree. What about you? You still live in these parts?"

"Yeah, the Finger Lakes won't let go of their grip on me. I'm a social worker. It took me a while to get there. I decided it's a better life path than making sandwiches in a deli." He looked at his brother. "Got that, Nick?"

151

"Same old propaganda," Nick said with nod and a smile.

"I'm just a half-brother," Keith joked, "so he only takes me half-seriously."

"What year are you?" Chad asked Nick.

"Junior."

"Your major?"

"He means besides golf," Keith joked again.

"Communications, *minoring* in golf," Nick replied, then turned to Keith with another smile. "How's that for half-serious?"

"Don't forget poker," Keith added.

"Really?" Chad said that without licking his lips, but he might as well have.

"Chad wasn't just the lacrosse teammate you've heard me talk about," Keith informed his brother. "He was a poker buddy, too." He smiled at Chad. "Where're you guys heading?"

"I saw that Hondo's is still up and running ... I miss that greasy spoon."

"How about this?" Keith said. "We eat there together, then rustle up a campus poker game?" Then, to Nick: "What do you say, little bro?"

He feigned tough decision-making, then announced, "Writing that paper can wait."

"See what a good influence I am? And I know just the place to set up a game. For old time's sake. The dungeon. Can you make that happen, little bro?"

"Not a problem," Nick confirmed.

~

Over beers, burgers, and onion rings, Chad and Keith reminisced. Jake sensed that, thanks to Keith, what had started as a painful return to Kenton College for Chad had evolved into a cathartic reunion. The two celebrated escapades as mythical.

Keith claimed the "keg affair" as a favorite of his. He, Chad, and Will Thatcher – at Chad's urging – had broken into the football players' favorite fraternity during house-party weekend, cutting the glass to a basement window to open it and climb on through. They'd located the reserve keg sitting in an ice bucket and, while a band had played loud music above them, they'd drilled two holes through the stainless steel, letting the beer drain out. They'd done the deed as sophomores because some of the varsity football players in the fraternity had picked on a freshman lacrosse player.

After buying more beer in a convenience store, they returned to the campus and made their way to the "dungeon," a basement room in South Dorm. Humming fluorescent light revealed a mishmash of stored boxes and cleaning supplies under exposed pipes. Out of some of the boxes, students had made a table and chairs in the center of the small room. Nick had lined up three fellow students to play with him, Keith, and Chad. One of them brought a girlfriend. With her perfect makeup and color-coordinated sweater and skirt, she looked like she might be held in a movie dungeon for ransom. None of the students hobnobbed with the visitors, other than during perfunctory introductions – not even when Nick described his brother and Chad as among the first to use the secret poker room. This was serious business, even though the game was for low stakes, dollar bills only.

Although invited to join in on the game of Texas Hold'em, Jake declined. He'd learned the standard hand values of poker, from high card to Royal Flush. He also had a good sense of the rules of this popular variation of the game from friends in Shaleville. But he'd never gotten proficient. He would rather just watch ... and observe Chad.

Nick and Keith hadn't let on to his poker buddies about Chad's reputation other than as a pioneer to the dungeon. That gave Chad some advantage besides his skill level.

He acted reserved, letting Nick announce the house rules without any comment. Jake of course knew Chad was thoroughly engaged. He wasn't the only one studying Chad. He noticed that the young woman – she was introduced as Sharon – couldn't take her eyes off him. He had magnetism all right.

After a couple of hours, Keith, Nick, and two of the other students had busted out, and the game came down to Chad and a slight and intense student named Lyle. Earlier, on a bluff, he'd reduced Chad's stack of dollar bills by about two-thirds. But then Chad won with a straight in the final round against Lyle's three of a kind.

Chad's take: twenty-seven dollars. Big-time ... symbolically anyway, reaffirming his legendary status to Keith, who teased his brother about it afterwards.

~

Chad stopped at another convenience store. He asked Jake to drive, then entered the store and bought more beer. On the way to Seneca Hills, Chad drank three more bottles. Emotions spilled over. He talked about Martin Sharp's victimizing behavior. About Andrew Sharp attending an away game and yelling louder than anyone else. About the team's perfect record up to the NCAA tournament. About missing the tournament because of his family tragedy. About the team losing in the first round without him. About how much his little sister had loved to watch him play lacrosse.

Reunions telescope time. Old memories become fresh. Old wounds bleed. Chad was showing some of that blood.

PART V: LOCAL FORAYS

"Mine is a proud village, such as it is. We are at our best when dancing!"
– from a Makah song

Spring Equinox

THE FIRST DAY of spring came. The sun was out and the temperature had climbed into the forties, making for decent enough weather for Arrow to hold its equinox ceremony without a rented tent. It was held on the grounds where the Turtle's shell would be erected. Some guests attended – all indigenous, mostly Seneca.

Thomas, the host, welcomed them in both Iroquoian and English, then chanted and danced while one of the Seneca men drummed. He did his version of the Straight Dance, wearing his traditional single-feathered headdress and holding a short wooden dance staff also topped with a feather. His understated moves seemed effortless. Others, including Ehnita, Ona, Chad, and Oren, joined in and danced in parallel lines behind him, then formed a circle. Ona beckoned Jake and he entered the circle, becoming part of the flow, trying to match her footwork. The smiles were infectious and Jake found himself smiling as well.

A traditional Native ceremony around a natural phenomenon such as the equinox indeed carried significance, a point Chad had made to Jake on New Year's Eve. The change from winter to spring wasn't just an arbitrary human-derived number on the Gregorian calendar. Despite the continuing cold temperatures and chance of lake-effect snow, the sun was higher in the sky and the seasonal change, well underway. Day and night seemed in balance, a concept that helped Jake – for the moment anyway – find inner equilibrium. Life here was comfortable for him, he sensed more than ever, while watching Thomas draw people into motion.

Too comfortable?

That night, Jake woke up from a dream. He couldn't remember much of it ... only that the hostility of others seemed to swell up out of the Earth itself and envelop him ... and, along with the hostility, Caitlyn's disappointment in him for not following her heartfelt words of advice: *"Be careful ... careful ... careful ... care ..."*

The sound of her voice, like a bird call, echoed in his thoughts as he slipped back into sleep ...

Construction

WITH MOSTLY warmer days, construction could proceed. Oren and Jake began further prepping of the lodge sites, pulling out tree stumps with the tractor and using its plow attachment to level ground. If not early-spring snow or ice, the mud sometimes defeated them, and they would return to their chainsaws and the felling of trees.

The first week of April was scheduled for full-on construction. Arrow had hired the architect Niles Maskeet, a Cree Indian from Quebec, who had studied architecture at McGill. A rotating all-Native crew worked for a Seneca contractor out of Salamanca, Mark Tama. A second crew under Don Tarbell, an Onondaga from the Six Nations of the Grand River Reserve in Ontario, consisted of a Seneca also from Grand River, two Mohawk from Kahnawake in Quebec, and a Tuscarora from the Tuscarora Reservation in Lewiston, New York. The Tuscarora nicknamed Roof was Don's righthand man. All the workers were non-union. But all had been vaccinated, Ehnita assured Jake.

When the construction finally began, so did the noise from trucks, generators, and power tools. Tama's crew worked on the Turtle and the garage; Tarbell's crew, including Oren and Jake, began the lodges. Working from Nile Maskeet's plans, they laid out the circular foundations for the structures, each with a diameter of twenty feet. They then set limestone blocks below the frost line along the outer edges, and poured cement flooring inside the circles. They would do all the foundations first, then begin work on the walls and ceilings, using geodesic dome architecture, with wooden two-by-four struts and plywood sheathing to create the triangular panels, a replacement for the bent saplings of traditional wigwams. Cedar shakes would be used instead of bark to repel the elements.

Jake's building experience – the skills he'd developed in his teens and twenties – served him well. He became a liaison between Chad, Maskeet, and Tarbell. His time as a builder in Shaleville had been a whirlpool of drug use, pulling him down ever deeper. After his transformation into a sculptor in New York City, the whirlpool had fed a bigger maelstrom. Now, even though he sometimes felt the pull of eddies, his commitment to work helped him tread their currents.

His salary had been increased to four hundred a week – not a lot for this kind of work. But he still received lodging at the Red Jacket, now with some friendly company since Tarbell's crew stayed there as well. The motel was completely booked for weeks. Sam, the owner, had to be happy about that, although he never looked happy. Perhaps late-night noise kept him up. Or more likely, he just couldn't get past resenting Indians for being Indians.

Don Tarbell, although no more than five-and-a-half feet tall, had a powerful leadership presence. His squat, muscular frame seemed immovable. The default smile on his moon-shaped face along with his teasing humor helped keep everyone motivated. He liked to joke that, as an Onondaga, he was the best suited to making sure everyone on the job got along, since the centrally located Onondaga Nation near Syracuse hosted the Iroquois League's Grand Council and its tribal members were the keepers of the confederacy's continuously burning Council Fire.

After dinners at the Jack and Jill – Jill at least expressed some appreciation for the extra business – the crew regularly played poker in Tarbell's room at the Red Jacket. Chad often joined them, typically leaving with some of the workers' salary in hand. Jake's game improved and he once won a thirty-dollar pot, even with Chad present.

Most evenings, Jake streamed movies to keep his mind occupied. He tried some new ones – that is, from the last couple of decades – and looked for Native-themed ones in particular. He also, true to form, sought out mysteries. Yes, he was his mother's son. And his Mohawk father's?

While lying in bed trying to fall asleep, after he'd mentally reviewed that day's building details, Jake's mind inevitably returned to the Fancy Dancer mystery. He engaged co-workers on the subject a couple times but learned nothing new and gave up trying to lead others to that topic. He did know from a conversation he'd overheard between Ehnita and Ona that Ona had Grant's name flagged on the Alliance computer. Jake flagged it on his, too. If there were any mention of Guyasuta's name in news sources, a notification would come in. His arrest would start a flood of notifications. But nothing new appeared.

Jake and Caitlyn still talked regularly, usually on Sundays. He kept her informed of events, such as what had happened at Kenton College and progress with construction. He'd stopped hypothesizing to her about the Fancy Dancer puzzle. She had her own undertaking – studying to become a teacher – and it was consuming her more and more. She needed to vent about the craziness of all that. Jake kept the stress of leading a double life inside.

Webcast

ONE EVENING, Chad brought his laptop to Don's room for a viewing of a segment about Kenton. The day after Chad's and Jake's trip there, the channel WROC out of Rochester had aired a brief spot on the ceremony and Sharp United's donation. Yet it had omitted Jake's questioning of Martin Sharp. All these weeks later, Jake was surprised his questions and Sharp's answer had finally made it on air, part of a series of podcasts focusing on western New York universities and colleges.

Chad, Don, Jake, and the rest of the crew watched the give-and-take. Toward the end of the segment, the blond commentator quoted the comment by Dr. Hunter, the chair of the history department: "History is in the air today ... this is a good thing." The webcast's host, a middle-aged man with an academic look himself, went on to say, "The remark originally served to deflect any controversy, but there are many views of history and there will be more debates, as there well should be at centers of higher learning."

Did Rhonda Fields, the producer, have to convince her superiors to air the controversial segment? Perhaps including it as part of a broader subject had been a compromise at the channel. The talking head's last sentence had probably been written by Fields, Jake guessed. The piece raised the question of Native causes, without revealing intent to do so.

Jake hadn't sent his promised contact information to Fields. He was simply introduced in the segment as a concerned citizen. Maybe he should have kept the connection current for the sake of the Alliance. But then again, if she asked about what had led him to the Arrow Alliance – for a personal or professional reason – he would have to lie to her, too.

Oren, who had had stayed on in Seneca Hills after work to watch the webcast, said to Jake, "You nailed that toady."

Don called Jake "a crack investigative reporter."

Roof told him, "You look like a film star."

Chad added, "Jake Maybe-Mohawk did us proud."

Lubricated by two beers, Jake basked in the goodwill. The feeling was fleeting, however. Despite all the good times – capped by this one – he still felt like an outsider. Duplicity does that, he reminded himself.

Fuck it, he told himself, the alcohol helping expunge guilt. Just stay on all tasks, deceptive or otherwise.

Outreach

THE METHODIST CHURCH on the southwestern end of Eagleton had a baker's dozen people spaced out in its pews. One of them was the minister Reverend Davis's wife; Chad, Ehnita, Ona, Oren, and Jake made up another five; the other seven were non-Natives – regular congregation members, it seemed.

Ona had arranged the outreach event on a Wednesday normally slotted for Bible studies. Davis – a progressive–minded man of the cloth, the way Ona had described him – had liked the idea. Yet he obviously hadn't managed to get many of his flock out.

The church, like the Kenton Chapel, had historic stonework and woodwork. This building's windows, however, had stained glass adorned with biblical scenes.

Reverend Davis, a pink-faced and tired-looking man in his sixties, appeared from a side door and went to his pulpit. He briefly introduced Thomas, who approached from the same door. Davis then sat down next to his wife in the first row. The Alliance shaman was decked out traditionally like at other events, wearing a beaded leather shirt and a headdress over his braided hair. He looked around at the faces dotting the pews. His deep-lined face smiled.

"Thank you for coming out on this spring evening. I'm honored to be here and I thank Reverend Davis for inviting me to talk. I'm currently serving as shaman of the Arrow Alliance, now a part of the fabric of Seneca Hills. We've been working on what we call the Turtle, where we have our offices and will have a council room. All of you should feel free to stop in and see our progress firsthand."

He paused and gave another smile. His offer came across as heartfelt.

He continued: "I'm calling this talk Native American Religion and the Holy Spirit. My intention is to give you some understanding of Native traditions with regard to spirituality. Let me begin by saying that discussing Native spirituality as one great world religion is a modern interpretation. Native Americans have a wondrous variety of beliefs and rituals. Yet the myriad Native belief systems have much in common. First and foremost, they typically involve intimacy with an all-pervasive spirit, often referred to as the Great Spirit. This is a monotheistic concept. The Seneca and other Iroquoian-speaking peoples use the name Orenda. Algonquians speak of Manitou ... Siouans, of Wakenda. Other English translations you might come upon include the Great Mystery, Mystery of Life, Master of Life, Master of Breath, All-Power, or simply Medicine."

Thomas paused again. Jake already knew him as an effective teacher, like his granddaughter and like Chad. From the third row next to Oren, he glanced at both of them sitting in the front pew next to Ehnita. Both their profiles, even when in repose, revealed intensity.

Thomas continued: "The Great Spirit is understood as formless, a kind of divine essence, magic, and medicine existing in everything ... in all matter and natural phenomena and in every life form. This is a holistic as well as a monotheistic way of thinking. Regarding holism, in traditional Native belief systems the natural is inseparable from the supernatural. Reality is interpreted through myth. Native languages in fact typically have no word for religion as a distinct part of existence. Spirituality is a function of all activity ... social and political organization, healing, the food quest, shelter, transportation, arts and crafts, and warfare. Prayer for instance is used in conjunction with hunting and fishing techniques. Incantations accompany herbal remedies in healing."

Jake wondered if others listening heard Thomas as reassuring and therapeutic like he did, making them more open to the subject matter. He glanced around. The guests seemed attentive enough. If church regulars, they were no doubt entrenched in their Protestantism, but politely so. This talk would more likely light some fires at a university, pro and con, Jake reflected, remembering the vocal audience at Chad's radio talk.

"Manifestations of the Great Spirit can be referred to as Spirit Beings," Thomas continued. "The Faces of the Forest, part of the False Face tradition of the Seneca and other Haudenosaunee nations, are an example of Spirit Beings. So are the kachina of Pueblo Indians. The fact that Spirit Beings are all thought to emanate from the Great Spirit reinforces the notion of Native religion as monotheistic as opposed to polytheistic, the latter often associated with European pagan traditions."

Jake heard the door to the church opening and looked over his shoulder, hoping that several people might be entering, making the event a less bleak endeavor. It was just one stooped-over elderly man. The man took a seat in the last pew. Thomas nodded a greeting to the late arrival, then continued:

"This sense of an all-pervasive spirit ... a holy spirit ... is a Christian concept as well. That's one reason why, over the centuries, some Native peoples have opened their minds to Christian teachings. Some continued to practice their own religions in secret and often at great risk, even if integrating Christian teachings into their traditional beliefs."

"Many Native revitalization movements of the latter half of the 19th and early 20th centuries incorporated Christian practices. One example, the Handsome Lake Religion, also known as the Longhouse Religion, originated in these parts. It helped people adapt to a new way of life on reservation lands under the pressures of non-Native settlement."

Oren stood up, sidestepped along the pew to the passageway along the wall, then headed for the back of the church. Jake heard the church's front door opening and shutting again. He looked to the rear again. Oren had apparently exited.

Thomas elaborated on Handsome Lake's founding of Gaiwiio, the Good Word, and then described other historical examples of Native revitalization movements that drew on Christian practices – the Dreamer and Indian Shaker Religions of the Pacific Northwest.

Jake had a spark of realization and looked over his shoulder once again. Sure enough, the old man was heading for the door. Jake recognized that gait. Of course. Another meeting between Oren and Grant.

Thomas was now talking about the Ghost Dance Religion, a revitalization movement that had spread among Plains tribes. Yet Jake's thoughts were outside the church.

The shaman wrapped up his talk: "The Native example is about a reverent state of mind, being in the spiritual moment, with an appreciation of shared experience and a respect for all life and the natural phenomena and resources that sustain it. Native spirituality is about opening one's senses to the moment and carrying inside the continuing wonder of nature and existence."

He smiled with his final words: "Thank you, one and all."

He received warm applause, enhanced by his friends. Reverend Davis stood up to thank Thomas and announce that refreshments would be served in the rectory.

All attendees – minus Oren and the old man who Jake was certain was Grant – made their way there. The room's paneling was stained the same dark brown as that in the church. Portraits of past reverends lined the walls, with dates of their service.

Davis's wife, a tall, slender, gray-haired woman, stood behind a table with a punch bowl and cookies. Like her husband, she also looked tired but repeatedly thanked people for coming. Jake overheard Davis's comment to Chad and Ona that the poor turnout was probably because of the forecast of freezing rain.

Jake's phone vibrated with a text – from Oren, asking where they were. He responded and Oren soon entered the rectory from the church. He walked over to his grandmother and spoke to her. She looked concerned. He found a wall to lean against.

Jake approached him and said, "That old man who left the church just after you did ... I recognized him."

Oren smirked. "Maybe you did, maybe you didn't." Then: "By the way, there's a protest going on."

"Say what?"

"Outside. Some locals have gathered to complain about us Injuns in their backyard?"

"The New Year's Eve crowd?"

"No, mostly women. Mothers against Injuns or something. That's what reaching out gets us."

Jake watched Ehnita say a few words to Thomas, Chad, and Ona. Thomas then spoke to Reverend Davis, no doubt passing on news of the demonstrators.

"What about the old man?" Jake asked.

"He came and went. Satisfied?"

"I'm involved now, remember?"

"Yeah, yeah."

"Anyone else recognize him?"

Oren's tone softened. "I don't know. Chad and Thomas probably caught on if you did. Thomas looked right at him."

Chad joined them and said almost cheerfully, "The reverend has informed me we can leave by the side rectory door to avoid any unpleasantries with the protesters, as he put it. I'm assuming the guests will take him up on the offer. Thomas and Ehnita will stay here for the time being. You two come with me. Let's go make nice."

"What about Ona?" Oren asked.

Chad smiled. "She's coming. I told her she has to keep an eye on me. She suggested you two do the same."

"Good. That means she's not keeping an eye on me."

"I wouldn't bet on it."

Chad left the room, Oren right behind him. Jake waited as Ona separated from the others and caught up to him. She didn't have to say anything as she and Jake crossed back into the church and followed Chad and Oren to the front door; her expression of world-weariness said it all.

They joined Chad and Oren on the stone steps. No freezing rain outside yet. On the sidewalk in front of the church, five women and one man were lined up. One held a sign: *No violence in Seneca Hills!*

On seeing Chad and the others, the six protesters started chanting the slogan.

"At least they don't outnumber the folks who attended the talk," Chad said lightly. "Come on, Ona, time to meet and greet. Oren and Jake, you keep an eye out. The crowd might grow."

Chad started down the steps. As Ona followed, Jake saw her expression transform from weary to purposeful, and, on nearing the protesters, even to welcoming. She'd shapeshifted into a peacemaker. She followed Chad right up to the woman with the sign. The sign carrier and fellow protesters stopped chanting and moved closer to the sign bearer to listen to them.

Jake looked over at Oren. His eyes were in the distance and Jake followed his gaze. A van pulled up a short distance away on Eagleton. A group of five men exited from it and approached on foot – Jake had seen at least two of them at the Woodbine. A cop car approached from the other direction and parked. That was a good thing, Jake thought, since only one of the five approaching men looked sober. The designated driver? They were about to join the public conversation, but one of the cops reached the protestors first, and the men held back. The cop said something to Chad, who spoke in return. The second cop meanwhile had moved up onto the church steps near Oren and Jake.

Chad separated himself and Ona from the protesters and walked with her toward the church parking lot. He looked over his shoulder and gave a little wave summoning Oren and Jake. They descended the steps and followed. The five men from the van eyeballed them.

On passing them, Oren began chanting a Native song, just loud enough for the men to hear. A war song, Jake assumed.

"Cut the mumbo-jumbo," one of the drunks said. "This is America."

Ona looked back over her shoulder. "This is America ... so cut the racism," she parried.

So much for public relations.

Oren's fists were clenched. Jake felt his own hands forming fists, too.

Chad slowed down to wait for Oren and Jake. Ona followed suit. Oren had turned and now stood facing the five agitators.

"Lucky there're cops here," one of them said.

"Yeah, you *are* lucky," Oren shot back.

Chad took Oren's arm and directed him toward the parking lot. The young Mohawk begrudgingly turned to go but chanted even louder.

Shedding

THE SPRING THAW had finally come to stay, the string of freezing or near freezing early spring days having ended. Liquid was in play – seeping, dripping, flowing – and the stubborn patches of snow that blanketed the woods were receding, revealing browns.

Jake had fond memories of this change from his upstate childhood, the grand shedding of wintertime to spring, giving the promise of summer vacation. He would walk to the end of the paved stretch of Elm Street beyond his home, then continue on gravel that hadn't been plowed all winter, extending a mile and a half out of the hamlet and ending at another paved road. From the seasonal unpaved stretch Jake would either climb the hill to a perch or descend to a swampy area. In the woods he could think about things far away. His favorite teen spot had been a stand of tamaracks halfway up West Hill. One bit of Native American culture had stayed with him from his schooling – middle school, it had to be since, in his high school experience, Native studies were presented just as a footnote to U.S. history: *Tamarack* was an Algonquian term for this species of larch, meaning "wood used for snowshoes."

In his present unexpected life, Jake could also escape to nearby woods in order to clear his head and seek answers. So many undercurrents stirred in Seneca Hills and beyond in Little Valley. At the Turtle, the day after the Methodist Church outreach, he and Oren had been present when Chad had informed Ehnita and Thomas that, before the rowdy latecomers and cops had arrived, he and Ona had made the case to the protestors that the Arrow

Alliance was committed to keeping violence out of the region, that what had happened at the powwow back in September was an aberration, and that they were doing everything they could to help authorities solve the case.

Ehnita had commented that it had to have helped to some degree.

"You kidding?" Oren had responded. "It's hopeless. It's been the same shit for five hundred years. That's why Grant can't return."

Chad had turned away as if in resignation.

Thomas had looked pointedly at Oren and said, "We have to endure. Let's all stay calm and focused."

At Turtle Overlook Jake could better cope with his own slow burn and maintain the long philosophical view of these issues. Aiding in that effort, he drew on Thomas's teachings. He imagined the Spirit Beings the Alliance shaman had referenced in his talk: Wind Spirits, touching the face; Tree Spirits, their bough arms bending and their leaf-fingers quivering; and Rock Spirits, ever still.

Jake sometimes wandered into the deeper woods. Oren hunted these woods. Every time his friend headed out with bow and arrows, Jake wondered what would happen if he encountered the man with the binoculars, presumably Stahl. He'd asked him, remembering that Oren had once asked him what he himself would do on meeting up with Stahl.

With his half-smile Oren had replied, "We'd talk about the weather and hunting conditions. When finished, we'd walk our separate ways and I'd put an arrow in his ass."

That comment had stuck with Jake. Did Oren have that much violence in him? Certainly as much as he'd experienced inside himself over the years. There were times Oren and everyone seemed a suspect. Ona even? Ehnita? Why the hell not any of them? Were they all playacting Grant's innocence because each and every one was guilty? As the mystery played out in Agatha Christie's *Murder on the Orient Express*, was this a group thing? Did the entire Turtle bunch participate in killing Baines?

It was a good thing that he had these solo excursions to clear his dark thoughts and his nervous system top to bottom ... that is, clear them without a drink, pill, or line.

166

Encounters with wildlife were curative as they'd been his whole life. Jake usually chose a spot to sit and observe, with camera ready on Aki's behalf. More than once, he'd photographed deer as they meandered by. They would inevitably freeze in place and look in his direction. A noise he made? His smell? The deer would then dart off, stirring up the woods. At one spot Jake had encountered a porcupine. Seemingly ancient – fat, faded, and missing quills. On sensing Jake's presence, it had waddled away, then climbed a tree to a safe spot above the intruder.

Jake also had photographed a variety of birds. From some locations he had a good view of the sky and could watch flocks of birds returning from the south – especially ducks and geese. Other birds seemed to appear magically – robins, cardinals, wrens, chickadees, blackbirds. Solitary travelers? From where? Some had never left these hills, enduring winter. Their various songs became a soundtrack for Jake's time apart. He once startled a gang of turkeys, mother and offspring. They scurried away from him, but not before he'd clicked some photos. Another time, he startled two quails and they in turn startled him. They flapped away too fast to capture with a camera.

After his latest walk, Jake considered calling his sister for further distraction but didn't want to interrupt her schoolwork. Instead he called Aki. They hadn't talked in over a month.

"Jake! Good to hear from you. At least I know you're alive from the photos you send."

"You okay with them?"

"You're doing just fine. You'll know when you're not."

"Yeah, I figured that you were satisfied, based on PayPal payments. I've got a new batch to organize and send. Forest scenes ... deer, a porcupine, birds."

"Sounds like my next collage," Aki replied. "How's everything else? What's going on with your Fancy Dancer?"

"Crazy stuff with the locals. Some folks, mostly women, picketed a talk Thomas gave on Native spirituality. Some men who showed up looked like they wanted to cause trouble, but cops came just in time. The locals sure seem to believe the Fancy Dancer's guilty. Everything I learn about him makes me think different. I'm doing construction most days. That's helping me stay on the straight and narrow."

"Whatever it takes not to end up sleeping in doorways." Aki typically sounded like she was joking, but her messages came across loud and clear.

She then filled him in on her growing success ... and the problematic people that came with success, both those in the art business and the wannabes who networked the scene. Jake took it as a good sign she didn't mention germs they might be carrying.

The human condition, Jake had the thought, not sure after the conversation if he wanted any part of it. So much for distraction.

He headed for bed.

~

Jake awoke from a convoluted dream – not surprisingly involving animals and shapeshifting – to intermittent thunder and lightning signaling an approaching storm. A flash filled the room with eerie light, followed by a distant thunderclap. Then, once again, the quivering blackness and loud silence. He pulled himself upward, walked to the front door, and opened it.

Wind Spirits hit his face. He waited until the Rain Spirits joined them, then returned to bed in a better psychological place.

Boys' Night Out

WILL THATCHER spent a week in Seneca Hills, helping get Arrow's finances and permits in order. That was daytime. Nights, it was all about drinking and playing poker.

On Oren's twenty-first birthday, the party began at the Turtle just after work, Ehnita offering cake and coffee to everyone present, including both crews. The two different crew foremen each gave Oren power tools – a Sawzall and a planer. Chad's gift to Oren in addition to a beaded leather pouch – and Jake's and Will's, too – would be a night on the town, now that the young Mohawk had reached legal drinking age.

Ona couldn't help but show disapproval before they left, telling Oren in earshot of the others, "Be safe this evening. You're twenty-one now. Be the adult in this group if you have to." She frowned at Chad and Will, then glanced over at Jake, her expression imploring.

The Woodbine was closed for some repairs, so they drove to the next nearest bar, the Duckbill Tavern in Little Valley. Someone would have to be the designated driver on the return trip. Jake – the relatively abstaining Jake of the past year – volunteered.

~

The Duckbill was a good-old-local-boy hangout and the good old boys were out in numbers. They eyed the outsiders as they entered. Yet they showed no reaction beyond the long looks, returning to their drinks. Country music was playing. A television mounted on the wall behind the bar broadcast a swamp-country reality show without any audio. The back room was empty, and the pool table, free. Chad led the way to it.

"Birthday boy and me against Will and Jake," he said. "Eight Ball? Beer and shots for everyone? First round's on me."

"Just a beer for me," Jake said.

Chad went to the bar. Oren and Will removed their coats and settled in.

On returning, Chad produced a handful of quarters to feed the table. The bartender soon followed him with a tray. They gathered up their drinks.

"Two bucks from each team per game," Chad said. "Let's play ten games if no one else wants the table."

They each placed their bets next to the quarters. Jake wondered if Chad hustled pool the way he did poker.

Chad handed Will the triangle. "You rack. Birthday boy gets to break."

No one else entered the back room and the table remained all theirs. Oren was the best at this game and ran the table a couple of times. It turned out Chad was no shark. Will, who had been hitting a flask on the ride there, held his own until the additional drinks took hold. Jake, a streak shooter, to his surprise had more good streaks than bad.

Oren, after the second round of drinks and the sixth game, announced his new singlehood.

"What ... no more Jess?" Chad asked.

"Not for me. Too much drama. I'm letting it fade. Into friendship, my grandmother insists. Not sure I want that though. It'll just mean more drama."

Will held up his glass. "To drama-less relationships."

This experience was rare for Jake, watching others get drunk around him while he stayed sober. He'd already had his two allotted beers. He'd better start drinking something else to be ready for the drive back to Seneca Hills.

He headed to the bar and ordered a ginger ale. The bartender, old but fit and spry, seemed agreeable. The others at the bar ignored him, although there was a pause in their conversation as he asked for the soda. No mocking tittering anyway. He looked around the room and froze internally.

At a corner table sat White Eyebrows, alone. The man with the hatchet face and distinct eyebrows, whom Jake had seen in both Florida and Connecticut, had a cocktail and glass of water in front of him. He wasn't touching either when Jake glanced at him. Jake looked away quickly but felt the man's eyes on his back.

He had the absurd thought that he was in the George Stevens western *Shane*. The movie's title character, played by Alan Ladd, goes into town to go shopping at the general store and enters the adjoining bar to order a soda for the son of his new farmer friends. He gets laughed at by the cattlehands for ordering a "sody pop." One of them throws whiskey on him. Shane later gets his revenge in a bar fight, prompting the rancher ring leader to send for a gunfighter. Fast forward to a scene at the same bar, when Shane encounters the hired gun Jack Wilson, played by Jack Palance. He sits at a table and silently watches Shane, his own hatchet face in a perpetual sneer. The story of course ends in a showdown between the two of them.

Jake, with his own sody pop, returned to the back room. Chad and Will were arguing – half-seriously – about an Eight Ball rule. Jake seized the opportunity to ask Oren to check out the man at the corner table.

Oren headed to the men's room. On returning, he told Jake, "Never seen him. What's the deal?" He sounded drunk.

"He was at Hartford."

"You sure?"

"Not a doubt," Jake replied – without mentioning he had a photo to prove it.

Oren's blurry eyes narrowed.

They played several more games and had one more round of drinks. Chad called for one final game, the tenth. While Will was trying to focus on the cue ball and Chad watched his former college friend from the opposite side of the table, Oren nudged Jake and tossed his head in the direction of the front door. A man had entered and was taking off his coat, revealing a camouflage vest over a bulky frame. He had a brush cut.

"Is that your guy minus all the hair and the beard? The guy you saw on the ridge?" Oren slurred some of his words.

"Could be. Same build. Same vest."

"That's Baines's friend ... Jonas Stahl ... the security guard from Buffalo. Seems he's cleaned up."

Jake looked hard at Stahl then glanced at Chad, who also was looking at the newcomer. Chad's demeanor changed. He even scratched on the eight ball, giving Jake and Will only their second win.

They gathered up their coats. Stahl seemed to ignore them all as they passed the bar on their way out. Jake looked at White Eyebrows one more time. He still sat alone, silently watching the room.

Chad's mood lifted once they'd pulled away in the Outback. Jake drove, Chad riding shotgun.

Chad spoke: "How you doing back there, birthday boy?"

"Aces," Oren replied, except it sounded more like "ayshez."

"Yeah, now you're rich with winnings," Chad joked.

"And me, I'm poor!" Will blurted out thickly.

"And let's give a round of thanks to our DD ... designated dude."

"Here ... here," Will managed.

"Ayshez," Oren repeated.

"It's a good thing I'm designated," Jake said. "Look what's behind us."

The others turned. A flashing red light closed in on them.

"The cops hang near the bars, waiting for out-of-towners," Chad said. "Good thing our lawyer is with us."

"Drunken lawyer," Jake commented.

"I'll observe and offer my expert counsel," Will managed.

"And I'll fume," Chad added.

"I'll tell them it's my birthday," Oren announced.

"All of you just let the designated dude do the talking, okay?" Jake stated.

He pulled the Subaru along a shoulder. The vehicle following them also did so, parking about thirty feet behind. Its headlights went dark; the roof light kept flashing. A second vehicle pulled up behind it and also turned off its lights.

Two figures stepped out of the first vehicle and approached, each with a flashlight. One was rail-thin; the beefier one hung back.

"This is bullshit," Chad said.

"See, Jake? I told you it was hopeless." Oren wasn't slurring his words now.

The skinny man reached the driver's side window. Jake lowered the window. The man shined the light into the Outback.

"License and registration," he ordered.

Jake started to reach in his pants pocket for his wallet.

"Don't give it to him," Chad said with icy clarity.

"Huh?"

Chad leaned across Jake and spoke through the window: "Where's your uniform?"

The second beefier man had also stepped up to the window, his face obscured by darkness. The flashlights pointed into the car were blinding.

"Don't get smart. We're plainclothes," the second man said.

"Is that right ... cops in a pickup truck?"

The second man turned and gave a summoning wave toward the vehicles. In the side mirror Jake caught a glimpse of five other figures exiting the second vehicle and fast approaching. He turned and looked through the back window. Was one of them White Eyebrows? He couldn't tell.

"Step out of the car," the second beefy man said.

"Not a fucking chance," Chad said. Then, to Jake: "Let's go."

Oren lowered his back window and spoke to the beefy man: "Hey, Stahl, are all security guards wannabe pigs?"

Jake hit the door lock just as Stahl was reaching for the exterior handle. He peeled out. As they sped away, something hit the back window.

Chad, seething, said, "Stahl and some of the local yokels followed us from the bar. It's good racist fun harassing Indians."

"They threw something," Will said.

"A beer bottle probably," Oren said.

"That's assault." Will sounded like an attorney again.

"They'd deny it," Chad said. "Didn't even get their plate numbers."

Will had more counsel to give: "At least you'd make them sweat. Especially Stahl. And you'd get press out of it."

"And more hostility. And if we could get Stahl to admit it, he'd just say how he was acting out because of his friend's death at the powwow and he was oh so sorry. He'd get a slap on the wrist, nothing more. No, we forget this. We don't even tell Ona and Ehnita. It'll upset them, especially so soon after Thomas's talk."

"And get us a lecture for going to a bar on my birthday," Oren put in.

Jake kept glancing in the rearview mirror. Had a third car joined the others? It had seemed so. But the lights were receding now. He eased off the pedal.

He was reminded of some incidents back in Shaleville. Back then he and his pals would have gotten out of the car for a good fight.

"Just more of the same local shit," Chad said. "Nothing to obsess over." After a moment, he added, "Good driving, Jake. And nice one-liner, Oren. If you want to avoid a jail cell, probably not a good idea to reference pigs to cops, but, gee, why not go there with a wannabe cop?"

He was minimizing events to them, Jake thought. A good leader, keeping their spirits up. But Jake could sense the rage beneath Chad's calm delivery, rage like his own on so many past occasions.

Now silent, Chad was undoubtedly processing all that had happened and strategizing what to do about it.

PART VI: KEEPING WATCH

*"The world is rolling around for all the young people, so let's not love
our life too much, hold ourselves back from dying."*
– from a Tlingit song

Worthy of a Lodge

JAKE REACHED OVER and shut off the alarm, then sat up,
stretched, and scanned the interior of the lodge. The rounded walls
and domed ceiling had been plastered and painted a beige color,
making them look adobe. The small bedroom on the structure's
south side had a built-in bed and above it a small curtainless
window, letting in the morning sun. Through the bedroom's open
door, Jake could see the larger living room/office with desk and
chairs and the kitchenette separated from the rest of the lodge by a
counter. There were two other windows, on the lodge's north and
west sides, with the doorway facing east.

This was Jake's first morning waking up on Arrow's grounds.
No more Red Jacket Motel for him; as promised, he'd been
provided with a lodge. Chad and Ona each lived in one; Thomas
and Ehnita shared another as a second dwelling; Oren had moved
into the fourth one the week before. Now, with Jake in the fifth
lodge, there were only two remaining ones to be completed. Like
his, they would house long- and/or short-term guests.

Today was the weekly Alliance meeting, held during this
construction phase on a Sunday, the only quiet morning of the
week. Jake stood up and crossed to the tiny bathroom that shared a
partition wall with the bedroom. Afterwards, he moved to his desk
in the central area. All the lodges had WiFi. He checked his email,
finding one message from Aki telling him to check Instagram for
her latest works. He did so. One was called "Refuge," based on
photos he'd taken of the Kenton Chapel. Her collage made it look
more like a different place of worship – a dance club with disco
lights. The second work she'd posted was also based on Jake's

photos, an array of animal and people shots. Birds were on the ground; other animals were airborne above them, including some amorphous human faces, as if they represented the grounded birds' dreams. She'd named this one "Fauna Fantasy."

He also checked the Arrow Alliance's Instagram page and the other social media sites Ona used for its postings, as well as the Arrow website. She'd obviously been up early to post the news of the completion of one more lodge. No mention was made of Jake as the lodger. In a meeting some weeks ago, there had been discussion of how much attention to give individuals in their postings – either staff or advisers from member tribes – in order to personalize the Alliance for other possible members. It had been decided, given the ongoing tension in and around Seneca Hills since Labor Day Weekend, not to use names.

Jake had about an hour to get ready. He made himself coffee, then went to shower and dress. The appliances and other furnishings felt luxurious compared to his room at the Red Jacket. After his shower, with twenty minutes to spare, he sat down in the high-back reclining office chair and read the news on his computer. It depressed him, a lot of articles affirming the cultural divide of national politics, making the divide in Seneca Hills seem that much more daunting.

At 8:50 a.m., Jake stepped through the door. It was the first week of May and happily it felt like it, the sun having already burned through the morning chill. He saw Ona leaving her lodge, situated three down from his. She carried her tablet. She spotted him and paused to wait on the red flagstone walkway as he hurried to catch up. She wore jeans, an embroidered blouse, and a suede vest. The sun, peeking over the Turtle, caught her face. Her determined expression gave Jake some hope regarding humankind's well-being.

"Sleep well? Enjoy your lodge?" she asked.

"Sure did."

"You've earned it," she said with feeling.

"I appreciate that."

They veered from the new walkway flanking the lodges onto one leading to the imposing Turtle. Its exterior had been completed just over a week ago. The cedar shakes on its domed roof gave it the feel of a traditional longhouse. Skylights provided a modern touch.

Tama Construction was now focusing on the interior: The shell would serve as a large council room; the legs would be guestrooms; and the tail would be for storage. Since the Tama crew used the recently completed garage for its equipment and supplies, Oren and Jake and the rest of the freelance crew working on the lodges kept tools and materials in the tail for the time being.

Jake worried that he looked hungover despite the shower. He, Chad, Oren, and some of the crew had partied to celebrate his moving in the day before, going late at his new digs.

It seemed as if Ona had read his mind. "You guys went late," she said.

"Did we keep you awake?"

"I was up working. But this sure has become a period of heavy drinking. I worry it'll continue even beyond construction."

"It hasn't been too bad weekdays."

"Oren likes it too much. Ehnita even said so. Chad assures me you all have it under control. I'm not convinced."

"I think I do. I'm not how I used to be."

"And Chad?" she asked.

How to handle this? Jake looked down, then back up at Ona's tense face. "To me he seems more about the card games," he finally said.

"Gambling too much to keep from drinking too much?"

Jake took that as a rhetorical question. They reached the walkway along the Turtle and headed toward the entrance.

Ona was still on topic. "What about Oren?"

"He's still enjoying his legal drinking age. We all talk about the risks, short and long term. And we all have Will as a model for too much drinking."

"Right, Will. But he's still astute as a lawyer. Not everyone can stay competent and drink like that. He might be a bad example."

"I think Oren understands that."

"He should by now."

They reached the Turtle's mouth and started through the door.

"Thanks for sharing," she said. "The nationwide statistics about alcohol use and related tragedies among Native peoples are scary. I won't let any of you forget how scary."

176

"Right," he replied, even though he felt ambivalent about their talk. On the one hand, he felt closer to mysterious Ona. On the other hand, he felt like she'd just recruited him as her spy.

They entered the outer office. Ehnita sat at her desk. Chairs had been set up around it. Chad and Don sat to one side of her; Thomas, the other. Ona and Jake took two of the three remaining empty ones.

Ehnita looked up. "Any sign of Oren?"

"No," Ona replied.

"I'll call him again. He probably fell back to sleep."

Ona's glance Jake's way communicated that this was what she'd just been talking about.

Ehnita talked into her phone: "We're all here. Hurry up, grandson."

Those present chatted together. Jake enjoyed times like this. The informality of idle conversation brought them all closer. They talked about the changing season and what it meant for wildlife.

Oren arrived after about ten minutes and moved to the last empty chair. Jake was relieved to see he looked fresh and eager. It had to be an act for Ona's sake, given what he'd consumed the night before.

Chad spoke: "Since Mark isn't here, Don will speak for both his crew and for Tama Construction. First, let's hear from Jake about his first night in the newly completed lodge."

Jake nodded and smiled. "I love it. It's a great design. Comfortable but with meaning. I'm honored to be there."

"We all know you've been a big help working on the lodges," Chad said.

He'd been thanked for his help before. This was the first expression of gratitude at one of these meetings.

"Hear, hear!" Thomas called out.

"Ditto," Ehnita said.

Ona smiled at him.

Chad turned to the foreman. "Don?"

Don Tarbell related how Mark Tama's crew had just finished the Turtle's outer shell and had started on the interior. He went on to say that he and his own crew would soon finish the final two lodges and do some touching up on the others. He sprinkled his report with his typical humor, using animal analogies for the different workers. Roof, the Tuscarora, he described as half-giraffe and half-gorilla because he was the tallest and strongest; Oren, he compared to a ferret for being able to fit anywhere; and Jake, he compared to a beaver for his engineering skills. He also suggested that, since there were more than enough of his workers to finish the final lodges, perhaps Oren and Jake should work on the grounds – clear rocks, rake, seed the lawns, and so on.

"And move the logs from the parking area to the stacking area behind the garage," Jake suggested. "We now have several piles worth."

"We also have to decide what lumber to use for the woodshed and take that to the sawmill," Oren added.

"We still haven't decided on the woodshed's exact location," Chad reminded them. "Let's take a walk after the meeting to discuss it some more. Don, Oren, Jake?"

"Sounds good," Don said.

Oren and Jake nodded approval.

Don finished his report by saying that he and Mark agreed that both teams would finish their contracted work by mid-June.

Chad took the floor again: "Great. My feeling is that we should commit to the week of the summer solstice for the next Alliance powwow and start firming up plans. This one we can ease up on social distancing to some degree compared to last year's Labor Day event. Consult with SNI first to make sure there are no scheduling conflicts. We can discuss the idea at the tribal council meeting on Thursday."

He was referring to the Erie-Mingo council meeting, open to anyone part of that tribal entity, as well as to members of all six Haudenosaunee nations because of their shared ancestral connection to the Erie and Mingo – which meant everyone here except Jake. Jake knew that five men and six women from the Seneca Nation of Indians along with two men and a woman from the Grand River Reserve had joined the Erie-Mingo so far and attended monthly meetings.

"I'll also check for scheduling problems with the Mohawk and other nations," Ehnita offered, "and with non-Native events in the area ... that is, if we're opening our gathering to the general public."

"I've asked Ona to make a recommendation on that," Chad said.

Ona let out a sigh. "I've agonized over this. Our failed attempt at the Methodist Church to reach out to the community at large proves we have to be circumspect, given the public's perception about what happened here last year. I've come to the conclusion that we should hold a grand council of all tribes on a Saturday, then have an open powwow on Sunday. Thoughts?"

Chad didn't hesitate. "I agree."

"I do as well," Ehnita said.

"Thomas?" Chad asked.

"Yes, with music and dance on Sunday for all our guests ... a celebration of the Arrow Alliance. We shouldn't be cowed from that."

"And the host drum?"

"Why not the Grand River Six Nations?" Thomas suggested. "All the Haudenosaunee nations would then be represented."

"Will you talk to them?" Chad asked.

"Affirmative."

"As for dancers, we should probably do it by invitation to keep the numbers manageable," Ona said. "Let's not overreach and risk any kind of trouble."

Jake thought of Grant Guyasuta, as he assumed the others now were as well.

"We can ask member First Nations to recommend people," Ehnita said.

Chad looked around. "Do we have consensus? Any other concerns?" When no one spoke up, he continued: "We've been doing our best to get the most out of membership and donated funds this first year. Since the tragic incident, we've had only a few new nations join the Alliance and we've only had minimal donations. Growing as an organization continues to be our primary thrust. A lot depends on the Solstice Gathering ... we'll call the event that ... for our continued growth. So please everyone, stay focused on our shared mission." He looked around the room again before continuing: "One last matter ... we'll be putting in an order for our flags to fly over the Turtle ... both Arrow and Erie-Mingo flags." He looked at Ona. "Give us your talk on Native flags. I've heard it at the museum. Everyone should get to hear it."

"Okay," Ona agreed. "I'll go all teacher on you but give you the short version." She took in her audience, like Thomas had done at the church.

When her eyes passed quickly over him, Jake couldn't help but feel like a stupid schoolboy with a crush on teacher.

"Flags are a custom Native Americans borrowed from other cultures," she began. "Native peoples traditionally used pictographs ... carvings on rocks and paintings on hide tepees and shields and carved totem poles and other objects." She spoke slowly, letting her words sink in. "And they kept totemic sacred objects, such as those representing First Nations in medicine bundles. They had their imagery and symbolism. But the use of flags is pretty recent among First Nations, from the late 19th century on. Most now have them. The SNI flag shows the outlines of their three reservations plus eight animals symbolizing the clans. The Seneca-Cayuga of Oklahoma have thirteen animals symbolizing the eight Seneca clans plus five Cayuga clans. As for the Erie-Mingo and the Alliance, the same designs as on our signs will be the basis for our imagery." She paused and flashed a smile. "Questions, class?"

"Exciting," Ehnita stated.

"Sure is," Don agreed.

"Even with any unexpected problems, we should have our flags in plenty of time for the powwow," Chad said. "Any other comments?"

No one had any.

"Okay then, meeting adjourned."

Everyone started getting up, except Thomas, who seemed either tired or in deep thought.

Chad spoke again: "Before we go about the rest of the day, there's something I want you all to see." His expression showed he wasn't happy. He looked at Ehnita. "May I use your computer?"

"*Our* computer," she said, getting up from her desk.

Chad sat in her chair and began searching. "Okay, everyone, have a look."

They formed a semicircle around the computer screen to look at the WGRZ news channel. Chad clicked on a story entitled, "Hunt continues for suspect in powwow killing." The text stated:

"Authorities have no new leads in the death of Richard Baines, a retired policeman from Buffalo, who had since moved to Bradford, Pennsylvania. He was found stabbed to death on Saturday evening of last Labor Day Weekend, during a powwow on the grounds of the intertribal organization known as the Arrow Alliance in Seneca Hills, New York. The prime suspect is still at large."

Chad clicked on an accompanying video. Jonas Stahl, described as a Buffalo resident, a bank security guard, and a friend of the deceased, was being interviewed:

"I miss my pal. Rich was a great guy. We hunted deer together. He was my friend and someone killed him. Gotta believe someone targeted him because he used to work as a policeman before he retired. Someone could've had a run-in with him. The prime suspect grew up in Salamanca and has a lot of friends around here. Maybe in Canada, too. Could be the authorities already passed it off to the Canadian police. Someone's hiding him out. I don't care how much time passes. I know the police have a lot to do and can put in so many man-hours in each case. But there's no dropping this."

Chad clicked off, stood up, and spoke: "Notice he never specifically mentioned Indians. If he had, they probably wouldn't have aired it. He might as well have though. A lot of people won't stop blaming Grant or all Seneca and other tribes in the area or the Arrow Alliance. That's what we face. I just want to remind you all what we're up against. Okay, back to work."

As Jake also stood up, he saw Ona pull Chad aside. The two walked over to the shelf that held periodicals. She talked forcefully. Chad listened, head tilted downward, then spoke briefly. Ona returned to her desk. He headed for the back offices. What was bothering her? The partying the night before? Ending a positive meeting with the Stahl footage?

Each of them so powerful, Jake thought. So star-crossed but so apart. At least it seemed that way publicly. And so much unresolved for them. Deep in their psyches, the killing. How deep?

The Arrow Alliance was like an arrow in rapid forward motion. But its feathers were uneven and it wobbled.

History Fun World

TWO DAYS LATER, Jake and Oren again looked at the computer screen on Ehnita's desk, this time just with her. Martin Sharp's puerile face looked out at them from an online newscast. He stood against the backdrop of a huge open field.

A few steps behind him stood his father. Jake recognized Andrew Sharp from news photos. No mistaking him: the puffy woven faux yellow hair; the bloated all-too-shiny cheeks; the smug expression even without a smile. Proud father but obviously the power behind the enterprise.

The younger Sharp spoke in his clipped fashion:

"We at Sharp United are excited to announce our latest project. No, my friends, I'm not here to talk about a new casino or a high-rise. I'm here to talk about an amusement park ... an educational amusement park. We're calling it History Fun World."

Martin Sharp went on to describe its attractions. The different parks within HFW, as he referred to it the second time, would be Explorers Park, Colonial Park, Birth of a Nation Park, Destiny Park, Wartime Park, and Future Park. Each would have themed rides, interactive displays, shows, characters, shops, and restaurants, much like Disney parks.

He further announced:

"South-central Pennsylvania will be the home of History Fun World, a rural area between Harrisburg, the state capital, and Philadelphia, the historic city where the Founding Fathers of this great country met to sign the Declaration of Independence and the Constitution. Ground will be broken next month. The targeted date of completion is July of next year."

The younger Sharp signed off with a forced professional smile, stating he would be overseeing this "wonderful project" for

Sharp United. His father had remained frozen in place the entire time. Jake mused that it might have been a cardboard cutout.

So that was one of the "future projects" Sharp had referenced at Kenton. The PR angle regarding this project had to be part of why Sharp United had donated a million to the History Department.

Ehnita spoke: "No mention of Native Americans. Chad says this is a slap in the face to the casino tribes in general and to him in particular."

"You'd think they'd go PC on this," Jake commented.

"PC?" Ehnita asked rhetorically. "The new PC, thanks to potty-mouthed politicians, is 'pettiness' and 'cruelty'."

Oren was fuming. "Chad in his office?"

"He and Ona took a walk to the Overlook. She's trying to calm him down so he doesn't do anything rash."

"I know what I'd like to do," Oren said.

"Easy, Oren," Ehnita told him. "Ona suggested Chad write a statement. I'll keep you posted."

"Where's Thomas?" Oren asked.

"He drove back to Salamanca. He didn't feel well this morning and needs more sleep. It's too intense around here anyway. I'll call him later."

~

That evening, Jake saw Chad's response on Arrow's website:

"We at the Arrow Alliance are always happy to see new projects relating to accurate history, whether books, plays, movies, or museums. Sharp United has announced the opening next year of a theme park in southern Pennsylvania devoted to U.S. history. History Fun World, they are calling it. We congratulate them on their entrepreneurial spirit. Yet we are disappointed to see that in the description of History Fun World there is no mention of Native Americans. In fact, one of the categories mentioned by Martin Sharp, the son of Andrew Sharp, is that of 'destiny.' We're assuming that Destiny Park is a reference to the concept of Manifest Destiny – in effect the dispossession of Native American lands and culture – as ordained by a higher power. Many academics now avoid this phrase other than in discussing the prejudices of the past, recognizing it as an insult to indigenous peoples. We would hope that Sharp United would admit to its insensitivity and henceforth have the representation of First Nations in the shaping of this theme park. If not, we at the Arrow Alliance would recommend boycotting History Fun World."

Chad, probably with Ona's approval, had fired off another volley. Jake fell to sleep wondering how the Sharps – father and son – would react to the posting. If the Sharps were true to their basic natures, the Arrow Alliance could expect incoming.

Payday

TUESDAYS WERE PAYDAY. Jake and Oren typically stopped by the Turtle during their lunch breaks to pick up their paychecks for the prior week. Ehnita inevitably made a game of it, pretending she'd lost them or telling them they'd been docked pay for slacking off.

Today, she handed the paychecks over, saying, "We may have to fire you by the end of the week. We've lined up two high school kids who'll work for half of what you get."

Oren looked at Jake. "This means we go to the Buffalo Raceway today, okay?"

"Gee, yeah, love to," Jake replied.

"Great idea," Ehnita said. "You could make a fortune, Oren. Buy your grandmother that house in Costa Rica."

Thomas entered from the Turtle's neck, a newspaper in hand. His movements were somewhat labored as they'd been all week. Showing his years? He joined them at Ehnita's desk and held up the paper.

"*The Salamanca Press* has an article on the Weather Hermit," he said.

"What about?" Ehnita asked.

"It's in the local lifestyle section ... about how, despite all the weather coverage on television and online, people stop by to discuss the weather with him. When they interviewed him, he predicted a cooling spell, explaining how around the full moon the moon's gravity pulls the jet stream south and lets cold Canadian air reach us."

"It's been quite a while since a visit," Ehnita reminded Thomas.

"Over a year," he said. "But we talked after Labor Day." He turned to Oren and Jake. "Myron's been one of the region's best diplomats between Native and non-Native folks."

"Let's invite him to dinner?" Ehnita asked.

"He's quoted as saying he rarely leaves his house now ... gets his food delivered."

"Okay then, go see him soon," Ehnita said. "He's ancient and we're right behind him."

Confession

THE FOLLOWING FRIDAY MORNING, Jake received a call from Ehnita, telling him he would be driving Thomas to the Weather Hermit's house in Olean, about twenty miles east of Salamanca. She explained that Thomas didn't feel like driving himself, especially with rain predicted. Jake could take her car and leave in about an hour.

On walking to the Turtle, Jake saw two Native-looking men sitting in a van with Canadian plates in the staff parking lot. He entered the outer office. Ona and Ehnita were at their desks. A young Native-looking woman wearing a blue sweater and a long floral-patterned dress sat opposite Ona. Jake joined Ehnita.

She stood up, saying, "Let me introduce you to someone."

Jake followed her to Ona's desk.

"Ona, may we interrupt?" Ehnita asked.

"Certainly."

"Jake, this is Anna Guyasuta. Anna, this is Jake Jakes, also known around here as Maybe-Mohawk."

Anna – Grant's sister, Jake assumed – managed a hint of a smile at Ehnita's playful name for him. She looked wan and weary. She carried more weight than Ona, with a rounder face. Yet she was just as lovely in her own way ... and just as guarded. Any stress and suspicion she revealed was understandable, Jake thought.

"Happy to meet you," he said.

Anna nodded back at him.

"Jake's been a great help to us," Ehnita said. "Anna grew up here and is a great help, too. We're delighted to see her again."

"We love her dearly," Ona spoke.

Anna looked down with a hint of a smile again. Ehnita led Jake back to her desk, turning to him before sitting back down.

"You remember how to get to my house?" she asked.

"I think so ... and I have GPS."

She handed Jake her car keys. Chad and Oren entered from the back offices. Chad nodded to Jake. Oren looked toward Ona and Anna.

"All set?" Chad said to Anna. "They expect you. Oren will go with us."

"Good," Anna said.

Oren looked serious, his eyes now fixed on Anna. Even when serious, he rarely looked this serious. Anna stood up.

Ona also did so and hugged her. "Don't worry. This is just routine. You carry the truth. Just be your honest self."

Anna followed Chad and Oren toward the front door.

"*Konoronkhwa,*" Ehnita called after them as they exited.

"Grant's sister, right?" Jake said. "Is she back for good?"

Ona heard his question from her desk and answered before Ehnita could: "Anna left the area because she was being harassed after the powwow killing. She returned from New Mexico to see her parents who've been staying in Grand River since Grant's disappearance. We all felt it might help calm things down if she reported to the police that no one in the family has seen her brother. Chad arranged a meeting. Two family friends from Ontario drove her here." Her tone was perfunctory.

"I see," Jake said, standing up.

"You'll like Myron, the Weather Hermit," Ehnita told him. "He's a kindred spirit."

"Get a picture of them together," Ona said as Jake headed for the door.

He turned back to give her a nod but saw that she was again looking at her computer screen.

"Will do," he said.

~

Jake drove Ehnita's Ford east from Salamanca along Route 17, Thomas next to him. The wipers fought back steady rain. Thomas was explaining how Myron's mother had dated a Seneca after the death of his father and, as a teen, he'd learned something of Seneca belief systems, leading to his fascination with natural phenomena, in particular the weather. He and Myron had met in their twenties at a benefit for the Salamanca Fire Department, at which time they'd discovered that their respective girlfriends were sisters."

"Seneca sisters?" Jake asked.

"No, non-Native," Thomas replied. "Neither relationship lasted long. But Myron and I became good friends and we started taking house-painting jobs together. About a year later, I married a Seneca woman, Janice, and we had a daughter together, Willow. Out of her marriage with a Seneca named Jacob sprung Ona. Janice passed away from cancer not long after Ona's parents Willow and Jacob were killed."

Jake wanted to say something, but Thomas continued quickly.

"Myron never married ... lived as a hermit. As for me, I had my willful granddaughter to deal with and I never dated anyone seriously until Ehnita."

They drove some miles in silence.

Thomas finally spoke again: "I've been meaning to talk to you about your heritage. I want you to know that the subject has become an issue with me and mine."

"An issue?"

"You've probably caught on that Ehnita's a strong-willed woman," he said, his tone trending to facetious.

Jake responded in kind: "Uh ... yes."

"She told me she wants me to encourage you to get a DNA test sooner than later, so you can find out if your father was indigenous. I've told her it shouldn't matter. You've proven you belong to what we're doing at Arrow whatever your ancestry. This is a private matter you should get to in your own good time ... if you so choose."

"When it first came up, Ona said I should know whether I have Native ancestry even without a test. I think about that."

"That sounds like Ona."

"My sister talked about getting the test for both of us for a college paper. Maybe I'll know soon."

"The point I made to Ehnita ... and to my granddaughter ... is that, like Myron, you have an ancient and wise soul whatever your ancestry. If you seek to join a tribal nation, then the test makes sense. If you are part Haudenosaunee, then you can join the Erie-Mingo Nation. We sure need members and it would be great to have you in on tribal as well as staff meetings. And other members who don't know you might be more open to your opinion if you have any Native blood at all. Maybe you'll eventually want to be a Mohawk tribal member and walk their path. My advice, despite what my better half says, is do it at your own pace if at all. Maintaining a sense of identity means being supportive of others and knowing when to suppress individual wishes for the greater good. It also means accepting one's dependency on other life forms and maintaining a sense of humility in the face of Nature. I see all that in you regardless. As a proven staff member, you're one of us now. Know that Ehnita, who prompted this conversation, was the one behind hiring you in the beginning. It didn't take long for all of us to agree you'd make a great addition to the team."

"Thanks, Thomas. I'm honored by all of it. An 'ancient and wise soul.' I'll carry that with me."

"You're certainly welcome."

"And coming from the Arrow Alliance shaman."

"Ha! That title is moot. Ehnita recommended I use it for Arrow. I would have settled for advisor or, better yet, simply team member. But strong Haudenosaunee women ... the bearers and bringers of life, like Mother Earth itself – are the bearers of practicality, too."

"Also the cause of angst in men?"

Thomas laughed. "I forgot to mention that your sense of humor fits with the Native psyche. That's also important, Maybe-Mohawk."

"Your talk at the church was really helpful. I can see why Ehnita lobbied for the title."

"I'm glad I reached someone in the audience, whether I deserve the title or not. Although I've been making a study of many First Nations' spirituality my whole life, I'm not a member of any of the societies. Since Arrow is about many First Nations, it makes sense to have a wide-ranging approach to represent them all. My age ... the stereotype of the wise old man ... also helps me fit the bill. Regarding Native humor, I try not to take myself too seriously. You know about the clown societies?"

"A bit," Jake replied.

"I've been reading up on them myself. They're an approach to existence common to many Native peoples. Members of the Contrary Society of the Cheyenne ... also called the Bowstring Society ... perform the Crazy Dance, all their actions backwards. The Lakota Sioux have the Heyoka, who perform the Clownmaker Ceremony. Similar societies exist among the Pueblo Indians. Maybe at the Solstice Gathering, you'll see a Clown Dance. I'm hoping Grant will be able to dance publicly by then. He was working something up when all this happened. That's between you and me for now. Keep it a surprise for the others if it should happen. Surprise laughter is a good thing."

Jake seized the opening. "A lot of heavy stuff has sure been going down ... Grant and all. I also read about Salali Jenkins. Did you know her very well?"

"Ah, Salali, a tragic figure. I spent some time with her the weekend of the powwow. She asked a lot of questions ... looking for answers that I guess never came. I wish we could have helped her."

"Oren said she was a self-cutter with suicide on her mind."

Thomas's brow crinkled in reflection. "Some folks talk about doing it, some don't. I guess it adds up. She told me she was raised by whites who didn't acknowledge her Indianness even though she knew her mother was Cherokee. She was raised as Sally, later changing it to the Cherokee name Salali. She ran away from her home in South Carolina as a teen, living on the street for a time before finding support among the Lumbee in North Carolina, who accepted her as a tribal member."

"The Lumbee? A small nation?"

"They're a people of combined ancestry of southern First Nations. They themselves struggled to establish their tribal identity using different names before they started calling themselves Lumbee after the Lumber River. That wasn't until the 1950s, I think. Salali told me she settled in Pembroke because that's where the Lumbee have their headquarters. She later found work in Atlantic City at the Sharps' casino. Salali seems to have gotten caught up ... I mean emotionally ... in Chad's history with the Sharps. After what happened to Salali, Chad's contempt for both father and son grew even more. I know he felt guilty for pressing her to go public about Andrew Sharp."

"About being fired?"

"Right. She reported that but not about being groped by Sharp the day before ... and not about how he supposedly whispered to her when she was being led out of the Pelican Wing by security."

"What'd he say?"

"Chad told me she reported Sharp's words as 'You could've kept your job ... and with a raise ... if you'd been a friendly little squaw.'"

Oren hadn't said anything about that part of the story to Jake in their discussion about Salali. Jake wondered if he knew.

"Do you know why she held that back?" he asked Thomas. "You'd think with MeToo and Times Up, she wouldn't do so, knowing she'd get support."

"Feeling shame for letting herself be bullied, thinking no one would believe her, fear of getting sued, a Sharp United specialty? Who knows? Such a violation goes deep." Thomas paused, seemingly too weary to continue, then said, "This whole Sharp thing can easily get out of hand. First Salali's death at Empathy / Empowerment and now History Fun World."

Jake glanced from the wet road back over at Thomas. The Alliance shaman looked ashen with concern.

~

Myron lived in a ranch house on the edge of town – a double-wide modular home. Thomas told Jake it was only two years old. He'd last visited Myron just after the new home had been wheeled in, the original ramshackle building on the lot demolished and hauled away in pieces.

The side garden had a narrow slate walkway winding through a tapestry of plants. The rain had stopped and the sun peeked through the last of the clouds. The plants, wet and glistening, looked healthy and eager, ready to burst into flower.

Myron opened the door and greeted them. He was tall and lanky – a little too lanky with an unhealthy-looking paunch. And his skin was too weathered even for his advanced age, probably from time in the sun. He gestured them inside.

The house was a mess, the floor unswept, surfaces covered with possessions. Piles of books and magazines – especially copies of *National Geographic* – competed for space with kitchenware and an array of pads, pens, tools, and hardware. A big orange tabby cat, its presence contributing to the house's odors, slept on a beat-up couch.

"Your place looks great," Thomas told Myron. "I feel much more comfortable this visit now that it's cluttered like your old home."

His tone was ironic and Jake was reminded of their conversation about Native humor.

"I get that a lot," Myron replied, taking an armchair. "I'm glad my staying true-to-form makes all my friends comfortable."

"The garden looks great as usual."

"I use up all my orderliness out there."

Thomas sat on the couch, next to the cat.

"Hello, Powwow," he said, petting him.

The cat didn't stir from its deep sleep.

Myron offered Jake an armchair opposite, then set about making them coffee to drink with pastries Ehnita had sent. On returning with three full mugs on a tray, Myron sat on the couch to the other side of his cat.

The two friends were a good conversational match, whether they talked about the weather, the state of the planet, current affairs, the Erie-Mingo Nation, or the Arrow Alliance.

Myron asked for an update on Grant Guyasuta. Before Thomas responded, Myron told Jake that he and Thomas had painted the Guyasuta home when Grant was ten and Anna, seven. Thomas reported that, as far as they all new, Grant was laying low, hopefully far away among supportive friends, waiting for a break in the case.

"How's Anna doing?" Myron asked.

"She's been in New Mexico. She returned to talk to the police. She's informing them that no one in the family knows where her brother is. Poor girl is trying to help her parents cope. They've been at Grand River, afraid to return to Salamanca because of all the hostility."

That led them to reminisce about past discord and Native activism in the area. Myron had joined Thomas on the Seneca side of the barricades in various demonstrations relating to the tribe's sovereignty. Thomas also brought up Jake's ancestry to his friend. Myron's advice, like Thomas's, was not to worry too much about it one way or the other.

He added, "I like to think I have some Indian in me ... that one of my ancestors found a love interest among the Seneca. But as long as my Seneca friends tolerate me, I feel like a family member."

"You're my big brother," Thomas teased.

"Right, by three whole years. I deserve respect!" Myron teased back.

"You up to date on your vaccines?"

"Of course, or I know you'd sic Ehnita on me."

To oblige Ona, Jake asked permission to take a photo. Myron took the tabby in his lap and the two men moved in closer to each other, offering big smiles without any prodding from photographer Jake. Thomas looked even more pallid. He joked that he wished he had Myron's magic youth potion. The cat jumped off Myron's lap and, after rubbing on Jake's leg, sidled over to the front door.

Myron stood up, walked to the door and opened it. "No magic potion," he said. "I learn from Powwow and I stay active. See? He wants to go on the prowl again. He was out all night and here he goes again. Hey, Thomas, want a kitten? I know someone with too many kittens."

"Don't we all." Thomas seemed to struggle to get the words out.

They said their goodbyes. The visit had been inspiring for Jake. He just wished Thomas looked better.

~

They'd barely left Myron's house, nearing the interstate back to Salamanca, when Thomas spoke again: "We're not going home. Take me to Olean General Hospital. It's on Main Street near Route 16."

His voice trembled. Jake looked over from the wheel. Thomas was clutching his left arm with his right hand.

"Okay," Jake said, trying to sound calm although doubting he did.

He pulled over, picked up his phone from the door tray, and activated GPS. He got to the screen he wanted despite the adrenaline coursing through him.

"Okay, I have directions," he said and launched back into the midafternoon traffic.

Moments had the gauziness of a dream. The car felt as if it were on automatic pilot, taking its ailing passenger where he needed to go. The hospital's emergency drop-off area presented itself. Jake rushed from the car. Just inside the hospital door he met up with an orderly wearing a mask and gloves."

"My friend's outside," he said with urgency. "Apparent heart attack."

"Okay, go be with him," the orderly said.

Jake returned to the car and stood next to Thomas's window. The shaman was still upright in the seat but with his chin on his chest.

Before Jake knew it, Thomas was being wheeled into the hospital. He followed and, while reporting the situation to a check-in desk, watched as Thomas was rushed to hidden rooms.

Jake collapsed onto a waiting room chair. He pulled out his phone, located his contact screen, and clicked on the Turtle's number. Ona answered.

"Thomas is sick, really sick," he said. "He's conscious but I think he had a heart attack. We're at the Olean General Hospital. They took him inside. I'm in the emergency waiting room."

After a pause, Ona said feebly, "Okay ... coming."

Jake settled even deeper into the seat. He realized now how drained he felt. He closed his eyes. The recent events raced through his brain. He opened his eyes as other people came through the door. A woman led a young boy past him, his left hand wrapped in a bloody white shirt.

Hospitals, dreaded and depressing ... but life-saving.

At least some of the time.

~

They all arrived together, each tense and forlorn – Thomas's partner Ehnita, his granddaughter Ona, his step-grandson Oren, and his friend and leader Chad.

Ona nodded slightly to Jake on spotting him and, holding Ehnita's arm, led her to the emergency room desk.

Chad and Oren approached. Jake stood up. Without their asking, he recounted what had happened.

"Any earlier signs before he clutched his arm?" Chad asked.

"He seemed okay on the way. He was conversational, even laughing. I did notice his color was off just before we got to Myron's and during our visit."

Chad looked around the room again as if searching for hope. "The Chest Pain Center here is first-rate," he came up with.

Oren hadn't said anything yet. He watched his grandmother and Ona disappear into the back rooms. He finally let out, "Oh, man."

An hour crept by. Chad sat motionless, his eyes downward. Oren's eyes were closed.

Ona reappeared without Ehnita and joined them.

"Yes, heart attack," she said. "They didn't use the word 'massive' but they might as well have." She spoke evenly but struggled to do so. "They'll be taking him to the ICU soon."

"Did he talk to you?" Chad asked her.

"With his eyes."

"How's Ehnita?"

"Keeping it together. Barely. I don't think we'll get to see him again for a while after they move him. I'll text when I know where they're taking him. Maybe in the meantime you all want to go get some coffee or something."

She turned and left.

Going for coffee in the cafeteria gave them something to do. Chad, Oren, and Jake sat together and sipped without talking. Life seemed normal at some of the tables, staff or visitors eating. Other tables resembled theirs – zombielike.

When finished, they returned to the emergency waiting room. Chad collapsed into one of the chairs and closed his eyes. Oren also sat down and went to his phone. Jake sat next to him. He wondered what Oren could be doing on it now. Texting? When

Oren shifted in his seat, Jake got a glimpse of the screen and saw a hand of solitaire.

Ona returned after another hour or so. "He's conscious and insists on seeing us all, which scares me. It might be because he thinks he's saying goodbye, and maybe the doctor thinks that, too. He's on the second floor. Oren, you'll be going in with your grandmother. Chad, he wants to see you and Jake together."

They went to a small visitors' lounge on the floor above. Ehnita was already there.

"Come with me," she told Oren.

Grandmother and grandson exited. Jake was relieved to have changed locations – new walls to look at. He studied a painting's nature scene and its bright colors, thinking how the artwork didn't make him feel any better. Ona had stayed with them and gazed far off into the distance.

Chad's and Jake's turn came. They crossed through swinging doors and walked down a corridor. They donned masks and gloves handed to them by a nurse. They entered the ICU room. Thomas, under sheets except where wired up, seemed tiny in the midst of all the equipment. He was ghostly pale. He remained motionless other than his eyes following them as they neared. He struggled to raise his right hand. Chad took it.

Thomas spoke in a near whisper: "Move closer, Jake."

Jake stepped up next to Chad.

"Both of you, listen. Can you hear me okay?"

They both said they could.

"I may not make it through the night. I have something to tell you. Chad, you're the face of Arrow and you have to do what's right. Jake, you're new among us and can be an objective witness. This will count as a deathbed confession."

"Confession?" Chad said. "I don't see a deathbed but we're listening."

Thomas took as big a breath as he could muster, then spoke: "I killed Richard Baines. I did it because he was threatening Anna. I did it with Baines's own knife that I threw in the Allegheny River. That's all. Now go."

Jake looked toward Chad. His eyes were still fixed on Thomas.

"You sure about this?" he said.

"Yes, yes, yes …" Thomas's whisper tailed off.

False Face

JAKE WOKE UP only a few hours after he'd managed to fall asleep. The lodge that had been a comfort to him these past nights now suffocated him. It was still dark. He needed more sleep, although not as much as he needed fresh air. He made coffee and ate a granola bar with it, then dressed and readied the camera.

Outside, he walked southward along the row of now-empty lodges. Chad had dropped Jake off and soon headed back to Olean, and Jake was alone on Alliance property for the first time. Being alone in darkness made flora and fauna seem that much more present.

Jake couldn't get his mind around Thomas's confession. The communication on the ride to Myron's had felt like such a breakthrough toward deep friendship. The confession after the heart attack seemed to come from some other person, not the Thomas Jake knew.

Two things he had to worry about now: Thomas's health *and* his guilt? The shaman was at the philosophical center of the Arrow Alliance. But the final arbiter of life and death for another, granted even a bully like Baines? He'd said Baines had been "threatening Anna." What did that mean? A possible rape? Jake could see Thomas as a judge, but only a lenient one who understood differing points of view, even bigotry passed down over the generations – not a hanging judge and certainly not an executioner who would stick a knife into someone.

On the ride back from the hospital, he'd asked Chad if he believed the confession.

"No, he's protecting Grant," Chad had asserted. "It has to be that. Grant's been condemned by all but his people. This is a way to end the insanity and let him return home."

"If both Grant and Thomas are innocent, then Thomas ends up protecting the real killer."

Chad had responded without pause: "Whether that occurred to Thomas or not, he knows how much the ongoing hunt for Grant is hurting all the Seneca people as well as the Alliance."

"What'll you do?"

Chad had had a ready answer for that as well: "Talk to Thomas again. That means until I do, we say nothing about what he told us ... not to anyone. I'm not sure yet who I'll share this with. Maybe Oren, but not Ehnita or Ona. They don't need added stress. Okay?"

"Of course."

Jake's thoughts kept swirling. Thomas, back when Jake had had dinner with him and Ehnita, had said he would lay down his life for Grant. Was he doing that now because of his condition? That made the most sense, like Chad had suggested. If Thomas were to pass, would Chad try to use that deathbed confession to clear Grant? Would the authorities believe him? Jake himself was supposed to serve as a witness to the confession.

Oren's lodge came into view. He'd only recently moved into it, just a week and a half before Jake had moved into his. He'd expressed relief to have his own place. Would he move back in with his grandmother if Thomas were to pass? Would Ehnita herself stay at the "love shack," or just make her Arrow lodge her permanent home? Or would she return to her daughter in Akwesasne? Would Ona want to keep the house she'd grown up in spite of her new life on these grounds?

Endless speculation. Stay in the present, Jake told himself. Thomas was still alive. Chad had promised to notify Jake right away if the worst happened, and his cellphone was mercifully silent. He continued along the deserted walkway, reaching Thomas's and Ehnita's lodge.

He froze in place. Pine needles on a tree beyond the lodge suddenly seemed to vibrate with light. The effect, he realized, was caused by flickering light coming from the lodge's southern window. Someone was inside. It wouldn't be Ehnita. Chad returning to retrieve something? He would have informed Jake of that.

Jake moved quickly past the closed door around to the lodge's far side. He heard a sound – a rattling. The small window on the lodge's south side was at eye level and he could peer inside. Two candles cast lambent light within the bedroom. He could discern that they'd been placed at each of the built-in bed's outer two corners.

A human shape moved away from the bedroom's door into the shadows of the lodge's main room. Jake caught a glimpse of long white hair. Someone was dancing while shaking a rattle – a turtle shell rattle, similar to ones Jake had seen at the museum in Salamanca. He could now hear chanting – a man's voice.

The rattling and chanting became louder as the figure turned back toward the cubicle and the candles. A shaman performing a healing ritual?

Should Jake make his presence known? It didn't feel right to interrupt. He stayed at the window, hoping to catch a glimpse of the man's face before deciding.

The man reached the bedroom's doorway. The candlelight illuminated his features.

Jake innards jumped and his body jerked slightly backwards. The face wasn't that of a man – rather a creature with ridged black skin, bulbous cheeks, and thick red lips twisted in a sneer. The eyes were round and deep-socketed; the white hair, long and stringy.

Jake, after the initial jolt, looked again and saw the face for what it was – a painted wooden mask with attached hair. He'd seen masks like this before – Haudenosaunee False Faces.

Jake's sudden movement had alerted the man behind the mask, who was now frozen in place and staring out the window. His eyes – the real eyes gazing out through the mask's eyeholes – had found the voyeur.

The masked man lurched back into motion, extinguishing the flames with his left hand, while the right hand still held the rattle. He then disappeared.

Jake moved quickly back around the lodge to the walkway and front door just in time to see the masked man exiting the lodge. The man froze again, as a deer would on encountering a human in the forest. Or was Jake the startled animal? Too startled even to reach for the camera?

They stood facing each other in the pre-dawn light.

"Hey, I didn't mean to ..." Jake said.

The man raised a hand to silence him. His piercing gaze hung on Jake for another few seconds. He nodded at Jake as if in understanding. The mask's twisted mouth suddenly seemed to be smiling. The man then turned and glided away, darting along the lodges – again like a deer, Jake thought. Beyond the final lodge the man hesitated to look back over his shoulder. With a powerful jump he cut left into the woods up the path leading to Turtle Overlook.

Jake, walking quickly, headed back in the same direction along the lodges toward his own. He was still keyed up, emotions raw. He felt bad about interrupting the ceremony no doubt meant to help Thomas. But the man had managed to communicate with his upheld hand and nod that Jake shouldn't fret over that.

Jake had another emotion coursing through him, pushing aside others – excitement. The apparent athleticism of the dancer and his jump up the hill reminded him of the old man at State House Square in Hartford, Connecticut, who had given a jump before departing. The pretend old man. Had Jake just stood a few feet away from Grant Guyasuta?

Back in his lodge, Jake phoned Chad. He didn't respond at first but called right back before Jake left a message.

"You phoned?" he asked.

"First, how's Thomas?"

"Nothing new. Still stable as far as we know."

"Good, good. I'm calling because someone was in his lodge. I couldn't sleep and took a walk. I saw a light inside and looked through the window. Someone had lit candles and was dancing with a rattle and chanting. Whoever it was wore a black-and-red mask with white hair ... I figure a False Face mask. He stopped dancing and after coming outside and encountering me, he ran off and disappeared into the woods behind the lodges, up the path to the Overlook."

Chad hesitated before saying, "I requested this. This is something Thomas would want since he hopes to join the False Face Society. Did he tell you that a while back he dreamed that he should be a member? A dream is one path to acceptance by the Society. Those cured by a False Face also can join. I'm hoping the dancer will be able to soon spend time with Thomas."

"He's Seneca?" Jake asked.

"Yes."

"Why come and go through the woods?"

"The masks represent the Faces of the Forest, the forest spirits who control disease. The dancer felt it would increase his power. I gave him directions. I'm not sure where he parked."

"I feel bad I interrupted his ceremony."

"My fault, not yours," Chad reassured him. "I should've warned you. I didn't know he'd dance last night. Did he say anything to you?"

"No. He held his hand up for me not to speak, then nodded before running off, heading back up the hill. It came across as reassuring."

"Okay, all good. If he plans to return to the lodge, I'll let you know. No more surprises. Thanks, Jake. I'll check in with you later."

Jake had been on the verge of bringing up Grant but didn't after Chad's quick explanation. Chad would likely cover up his presence as Oren once had. Would Grant perform such a ritual? Had he, like Thomas, dreamed of being a Society member, or had he already been cured in a False Face ceremony?

Jake went to his desk and laptop and began searching for information on False Faces. He read how they're believed to frighten away the malevolent spirits that cause illness. They're carved on living trees, then cut out ceremonially, with prayers and tobacco offerings. Both men and women can join the society, either because they've been so instructed in a dream or because they've been healed by the society's ceremonies, confirming what Chad had said. Women, however, do not wear the masks. A False Face Dance or series of dances are performed for sick individuals – more confirmation – or as general healing rites at festivals such as the Midwinter Ceremony.

While wondering about Chad's explanation and reading about the False Faces, Jake felt like an interloper treading on sacred ground. He reminded himself that in a way he himself had been healed that night, at least psychologically. Something edifying had seemed to pass from the False Face Dancer to him.

Yet he still had his suspicions that the False Face Dancer had been Grant. And, if so, he couldn't help but resent Chad's not trusting him, even after his helping Oren on the Akwesasne run.

Jake needed more sleep, he well knew – at least a couple more hours to be ready for whatever the immediate future held. But his thoughts leapt about like False Face Dancers and his emotions couldn't keep up. He was still adrenalized. Would he ever sleep again? He moved from his back to his left side and tried to keep his mind on empty darkness ...

Circles Within Circles

DREAMING HE'S NOT dreaming although he's not sure how or when he arrived at this place. He's outdoors and the stars are the ceiling. The stars begin swirling as do dancers adorned with feathers, performing for men in overalls gathered in a circle to watch. Some of the dancers leap upwards and transform into birds. Has Jake misidentified them as people or is this actual shapeshifting? The birds hover above. Only one of them, a young woman, remains on the ground in human form. The circle of men closes in on her, eyes glowing like embers. Before they reach her, the birds aloft dive back down, striking at the men with beaks and claws, extinguishing their burning eyes. The woman also becomes a bird and flies away, cawing in mocking celebration. A chime answers the cawing and the dream starts to dissolve ...

Jake opened his eyes to his phone's chiming. He'd reprogrammed his phone's ringtones so he knew ahead of time if a call were from Chad, Oren, Ona, or Arrow's office number. This was from Chad.

"Hey," he said, trying to clear his head. He knew he dreaded what he might hear next.

"Hi. Jake. You go back to sleep?"

Heavy equipment sounded outside. The workday had started. Jake looked at the time on the phone's screen. 9:43. He'd slept another three hours since the encounter.

"Some more tossing and turning."

"I could use even that," Chad said through his exhaustion.

Jake asked the big question: "Is Thomas okay?"

"Stable. That's all we know. We're waiting for a detailed update. It'll probably come by early afternoon after some more tests. I'll stay here all day. Ona is heading over to pick up some things."

"I can make the trip to Olean if that's easier."

"No, it'll probably do her good to get out of here for a bit."

"What should I tell Don and the others?"

"Don't say anything for now. I'll give Don a call at some point. You don't have to work with the crew today. Just make the rounds, keeping an eye on things. Take pictures of construction progress. Until you hear otherwise, that's your assignment for the day, okay?"

"Understood," Jake said. He wanted to add something hopeful. "When you talk to Thomas, tell him I had my first False Face encounter."

"I will."

Jake pulled himself out of bed. He'd slept in his clothes. He walked to the front door, opened it, and stepped into a beautiful May day. To the northeast some of Tama's crew were unloading materials from a truck into the Turtle's tail. From the southeast beyond the Turtle's head came machinery noise.

Jake was glad to have something to do. He went back inside. He reheated coffee, downed a cup, then set out, camera strapped to his neck.

In the field where the amphitheater would be located, two of Don's crew manned bulldozer and backhoe, removing the last of the tree stumps and leveling the ground, while four others followed up with shovels and rakes. All seemed happy to pitch in on this sunny day, smiling on seeing Jake and even mugging for the camera. They were caught up in the present and looking to the future. Jake, however, carried the recent troublesome past with him.

Inside the Turtle's shell Tama's men also seemed energized, as if charged by the sunlight streaming through skylights and the classic rock blasting from a radio. Jake stood in the center of the domed space and documented progress in photos. The cement floor with radiant heat tubing had been poured, wiring installed in the walls and ceiling, foam insulation blown in, and mesh stretched between the beams. The workers now applied a plaster mix to the mesh.

The council room would soon be finished. After the adobe-colored plasterwork had been applied, he and Oren would help stain the beams. After that, Tama's crew would lay tile over the subflooring.

Jake sent thoughts Thomas's way: Make it, Ancient Soul; live to see the Turtle completed. And Thomas's mind-boggling confession? How would that change things if he recovered? Jake did his best to tuck that question away.

Back outside, he started toward his lodge for something to eat. He heard a vehicle and turned to see Ona's black Volvo enter the parking area and pull up. She climbed out of her car and approached Jake. She appeared drained of all emotion but, on reaching him, let more out, bursting into tears. He stepped closer and, sliding the camera to one side, put his arms around her and hugged. She didn't resist, letting her hold him for ... what ... a total of three seconds? It felt much longer. When she pulled back slightly, he let go and stepped back himself.

"Sorry," she said. "I'm barely keeping it together."

"Chad told me you should know more this afternoon."

"Right. We haven't even gotten to see Thomas this morning. I'm heading right back."

"And the others? How're they holding up?"

"I'm afraid Ehnita will also end up in the hospital. Chad's being the rock. Oren is just acting remote, giving nothing away." She looked around. "I'm glad we have you here watching over the place ... for us ... for my grandfather." Her eyes welled up again. "I have to gather up some things from the office, then go get cleaned up."

"You know my thoughts are with you all."

"I know," she said and headed into the Turtle's mouth.

Jake walked back toward Don and his crew clearing the field. In his mind he was still holding Thomas's granddaughter.

~

Chad phoned in the late afternoon. He reported that the doctor's report was encouraging, based on the fact that Thomas's heart was consistently beating without irregularity. The next day, depending on his vital signs, the medical staff would decide if he were strong enough for an angioplasty. Ehnita and Ona had seen Thomas but he hadn't spoken. The three of them would spend another night at the hospital. Oren would sleep at Thomas's.

Jake had walked around the grounds two more times after Ona's departure, taking more pictures. He now sat at his kitchen counter in front of his computer screen, searching information about heart attacks and angioplasties.

Enough of that. He needed to keep moving. He turned off the computer, drank a glass of water, picked up the Nikon, and exited.

The sky had clouded over. He walked northward, following the escape route the False Face Dancer had taken the night before.

He reached the opening in the woods and took the now-familiar pathway up the hill.

At the Overlook he got the full effect of the Turtle's reptilian-inspired architecture – head, carapace, legs, and tail. Directly below, the lodges' shake roofs peaked through the evergreens. The grounds were quiet, the workers having departed at 4:30. The quiet gave clarity to the view, even with the threatening clouds and the Turtle's now grayish cast. Jake clicked some photos.

He moved away from the Overlook and walked through the woods, paralleling the crest southward. The False Face Dancer had to have a good sense of geography to have found his way in the dark through the forest to Thomas's lodge. Had he navigated just by moonlight or starlight? A flashlight seemed incongruous for an embodiment of the Faces of the Forest.

Jake soon reached the second overlook where the man with the binoculars had stood in wintertime. From this different angle, Jake took more photos of the vista below. On the far edge of this small clearing, the tree-line opened up to what seemed like a path angling southwestward. He followed it. The trees and undergrowth played tricks on him. He sometimes veered off the path and had to backtrack to locate it again.

He stopped from time to time to listen, sensing he was being followed. He heard no human sounds – only bird calls. Native hunters and warriors were adept at mimicking birds.

Grant might know these woods well. Perhaps he'd hunted them with Oren. One more reason to think Grant had been the False Face Dancer. Jake wanted to talk to Oren about that possibility. Grant might even have a hideout nearby.

Scanning the woods around him, Jake saw a patch of color different from the bark of the other nearby trees. At first, he thought it must be a solitary white birch standing among other hardwoods. But then he saw that it had grayish brown bark with only one small off-white area. From all the firewood he'd cut over the years, he knew trees well enough to identify this one as basswood with its domed crown and ovate leaves. Leaving the path, he approached it.

He touched the tree's moist, gaping wound. This was not just weathering from natural elements. Someone had recently carved out a piece – a piece the size of a False Face mask. The masks were carved from a living tree, Jake had read, so that they also would be alive.

Wouldn't an established False Face Dancer already have a mask? Grant, a novice, might have to make one. More evidence pointing to him.

Jake was in a forest that was already special to him, standing before a tree with special meaning. He took a photo of the mask's birth spot. Was he violating the Tree Spirit with a photo? He remembered the reassuring nod of the False Face Dancer. He bowed his head and thanked the basswood for its offering, asking for reassurance and protection for all those he cared about.

Even as he did so, he couldn't help but self-reflect. Roleplaying being Native, like roleplaying detective? He pushed aside doubting thoughts.

Drizzling rain began to fall as he returned to the path. He continued southwestward, soon finding himself on a slope, leading him downward to his left. He had to step carefully, resisting the pull of gravity. He activated the compass app on his phone and determined that he was now walking eastward.

Jake eventually reached the bottom of the hill. The hemlock stands had been logged, as indicated by the stumps and remnants of treetops and brown needles blanketing the ground. The path had disappeared but he saw the ruts of a logging road a bit farther to the east.

The rain had increased and some water had pooled up in the ruts. Jake, stepping more carefully, followed them. They ended after about an eighth of a mile, and he found himself on the shoulder of an empty stretch of paved road. It was Eagleton, he realized.

His clothes now soaking, he followed it northwestward. At the entrance to Arrow's grounds, he started up the long, inclined driveway. He finally reached the Turtle and beyond it, his lodge.

Jake had completed a big circle and was entering a circular structure. His thoughts had kept circling from question to question, from person to person. Circles within circles. He knew that Native Americans traditionally regard the circle as a symbol for existence, as in birth to death and in the recurring seasons. It holds mystery even as it elucidates the mystery. Each of the circles around and inside Jake had a center.

Align those centers, he told himself, to arrive at the answers he sought.

B&E

JAKE AWOKE CONTORTED in body and mind. If he'd just been dreaming, he'd already lost recollection of it.

It was almost 3:00 a.m. On returning to the lodge after his walk, he'd removed his wet clothes, showered, dressed again, and poked around his kitchen for food, settling on cheese and crackers. He'd then sat down in his reclining office chair in front of his computer to upload photos from that day. He'd fallen asleep there. Another day had started for him in the middle of the night. He stood up and stretched.

Where was the False Face Dancer? Had he returned to finish his curative dance? Not likely. Nevertheless, Jake, the de facto Arrow watchman, would take another walk, even if just to wander among unseen animals and Spirit Beings.

He stepped outside, camera in hand. The rain had stopped and the clouds had dispersed, exposing the moon. The air was damp and chilly. He went back inside to don a sweatshirt.

Outdoors again, Jake ambled along the row of lodges. All were dark. He turned onto the walkway that led toward the Turtle. On reaching the walkway around it, he headed south toward the entrance.

Light flickered from a window along the Turtle's neck – Thomas's office. Was the False Face Dancer now purifying that space? Had Chad given him the front door key? He'd promised no more surprises. Had Jake missed a text while sleeping? He took out his phone. No messages. He put his phone on mute.

He waited, watching. The light had vanished. Jake continued toward the Turtle's head. No vehicle occupied the staff parking lot, other than his own. He moved around to the Turtle's eastern side and saw another light in the closest window – Ona's window. He crossed the lawn and peered inside. Through the curtains he could see the beam of a flashlight. He couldn't make out who held it.

Clutching the Nikon like a football, he broke into in a quiet run northward along the Turtle's shell. He half-expected a beam of light on him or a shout. No reaction came, friendly or otherwise. Jake reached the end of the tail and saw that no vehicle was parked in the guest lot. He quickly moved to the door at the tail's tip. He found the key he wanted on his key-ring and slid it into the lock. He pushed the door open and stepped inside.

Using the soft light of his phone's home screen, he navigated through the tail filled with building materials. He opened the door to what would be the council room inside the Turtle's shell. Moonlight filtered through skylights, and Jake no longer needed the artificial light. He entered the big room, avoiding any obstacles from the ongoing construction. He reached the door to the Turtle's neck at the room's opposite end and cracked it open. He saw light bouncing along the neck's inner walls and a shadowy figure.

A man's voice spoke: "There's a computer in here. Looks like it's the bitch's office."

Another voice: "The hot one?"

The first voice again: "Hey, I found a photo you'll like."

"Don't touch anything!" a third voice called out. "Remember, it's just about the message."

"How much time you need?" the first voice asked.

"The computers are networked so I can download files off any one of 'em. But it'll take a while. Like a long fucking hour. You can check every door but leave everything as you found it. Close any doors behind you that were closed. Wait for me in the front. One of you keep an eye out. The other write the message."

"First I'll take photos of all the rooms," the first voice said. "Might come in handy someday."

"Yeah, do it. Good to know the layout."

A camera light flashed. Jake gently closed the door and receded back into the council room. Boxes of ceramic tiles were stacked to one side. He hustled over to them, slipped behind them, and waited.

After several minutes, the door opened and light danced about the big room.

"Just a jobsite," one of the men said.

"Maybe we should burn it down and save 'em the trouble of finishing it."

Jake, peering around the edge of box, could make out the shapes of the two men standing a few feet inside the doorway.

A camera flashed a couple of times, and Jake instinctively pulled back. Relative darkness came and the sound of the closing door.

He'd seen and heard enough to be convinced that the two men were Stahl and his friend, the skinny guy who posed as a cop outside of Little Valley. Was White Eyebrows the third man telling them what to do?

Jake moved back toward the tail and through it out into the night. He darted for the garage across the driveway and around it. Leaning against its back wall, he looked for Chad's name in his phone's contacts. He found it and clicked on the number.

Chad answered sleepily on the first ring: "Hold on, Jake." Then, a few seconds later: "What's up?"

"Three men are inside the Turtle. I'm pretty sure one is Stahl and the other guy, the wannabe cop who hassled us. A third one gives orders. He's downloading files while they take photos. He also said something about leaving a message but that they shouldn't do anything else we'd notice."

Chad let out a quiet "fuck," then said, "Probably so we won't know they hacked us."

"What should I do ... scare them off? Call the police? He said the download might take an hour."

"Let me think."

Jake waited. Chad's grinding thoughts seemed to intermingle with his own breathing.

He finally spoke again: "You know how they got there? You see a car?"

"No. Maybe they came through the woods like the False Face Dancer."

"More likely they parked on Eagleton or somewhere along the driveway. They could've heard about Thomas being in the hospital ... maybe they've been casing our comings and goings." Chad went silent before adding, "I can't leave the hospital right now. Oren shouldn't either."

"Is Thomas okay?"

"The nurse called in a doctor. Something's up. We're waiting."

"Hell."

"Okay, listen. Here's what we do. No cops. The publicity will hurt us. This bunch will just claim they're trying to solve their best friend's killing. A lot of the locals will support them.

Instead, I'll rouse up Don and the crew. Maybe he and his boys can intercept them. I'll have them wait at it if they can locate it. You follow these fuckers and see which way they leave. You have Don's number, right?"

"Yeah."

"Report to him. There's nothing in the files that they can use on us ... we release all our financial info anyway ... and nothing about Grant ... but we can't let them get away with this. I'd like to shake them up a bit to discourage them from any more harassment. Stay out of sight in the meantime. But try to get photos, including license plate numbers."

"Okay."

"I'll head over as soon as I can."

"Right."

"Keep me posted. Text," Chad finished.

Jake headed back along the Turtle's shell and beyond its head to his van in the staff parking lot. He crouched behind it at a good angle to watch the front door.

After about ten minutes, one of the three exited the Turtle's mouth and lit a cigarette. Jake could see him clearly in the moonlight. He'd been right. It was the skinny pseudo-cop. He wore a black wool skullcap, pulled down around his ears, and a black baggy sweatshirt on his bony frame. Jake considered taking a photo but doubted he would get anything without a flash even in the gibbous moonlight. He didn't want to alert the intruders before Don had a chance to organize his men.

The man had smoked two more cigarettes by the time a second man appeared in the doorway.

No question, it was Stahl. He also wore all black – a similar skullcap and a commando-style sweater, with suede shoulder and elbow patches.

The minutes crawled along. Jake, motionless, felt the penetrating damp chill. He thought about all the hours spent waiting and watching while on his first case. Those times he'd been staking people out while uncertain anyone would show. This time he knew a third person was coming.

He finally did. It wasn't White Eyebrows. He was taller and looked more in shape. He had slick-backed hair and wore a dark blue nylon jacket. Jake thought he recognized him. From the Duckbill Tavern?

"All set?" Stahl asked.

"All set ... mission accomplished," the tall, muscular man replied.

Where had Jake seen him? A bubble of realization rose up and burst in his brain. He'd seen him at Kenton. The third man was Martin Sharp's bodyguard.

Other thought bubbles rose up. They'd have to wait. The intruders hustled along the edge of the parking lot. Jake held back until they reached the driveway, then followed, keeping pace.

About halfway down the driveway, beyond the three men, Jake could just make out a parked SUV, facing in the opposite direction toward Eagleton. As they neared the vehicle, Jake stopped long enough to ready the Nikon, then ran at them, shouting, "Hey, assholes!"

They turned to look. He pulled up and clicked photos with the flash on.

One of them blurted out, "Fucking hell!"

Jake dashed off the road into the woods. He found a large tree to crouch behind and wait. He hadn't gone far and could hear them over his own panting.

"Whatta we do, go after him? Break his ass and his camera?" That sounded like Stahl.

"You want to run around the woods at night? Photos aren't proof of anything. They could be taken anywhere." That had to be Sharp's man.

Maybe not conclusive proof, Jake thought, but a good start.

"All right, let's go." Stahl again.

Jake heard the SUV's doors slamming shut. He pulled his phone from his pocket and called Don.

"Jake, where you at?"

"They reached their vehicle. They're heading down the driveway. I'm following on foot."

"Okay, good, we've got them. Hurry up," Don told him. "Join the fun."

Jake returned to the driveway and broke into a run. After about a hundred yards, on rounding a bend, he saw the back of the SUV with its brake lights on. Four pickups, were lined up side-by-side, facing it, blocking its exit. Jake continued close enough to get some photos of the SUV and its license plate.

The pickups' headlights came on nearly simultaneously, making the scene look like a nighttime movie shoot. Three of Don's crew – carrying an axe, a sledgehammer, and a wrecking bar – appeared out of the woods and surrounded the SUV. They ordered the intruders out of the vehicle. Don and three more of his crew climbed out of the pickups and approached. Don and one of his men cradled hunting rifles; the two others held hand tools. Don waved them forward away from the SUV, then held up his hand for them to halt. The three men who had approached from the woods backed away, forming a semicircle.

Jake ran past them and moved up next to Don.

Don spoke: "You're on private property. We have evidence of breaking and entering." He looked to Jake for confirmation.

Jake caught his breath. "I got lots of photos. Hey, Stahl, I see you and your buddy aren't pretend cops tonight ... just real-life felons."

"Fuck you," Stahl said. He had what looked like white chalk on his sweater, pants, and boots. His mouth twitched.

"Oh, so you know this loser?" Don said to Jake. Then, to the captives: "We don't want a big fuss. We understand you think we're harboring a fugitive here or know his whereabouts. Well, you're wrong. We understand that emotions get heated when it comes to losing a friend, so we don't want to kick the shit out of you. And we don't want to take a sledge to your vehicle. We just want to see your licenses. And we want you to give us any stolen items you might have in your pockets. Please don't make us strip off your clothes and send you on your way. That sight might haunt us the rest of our lives."

Stahl looked at Sharp's bodyguard who nodded.

"Fuck you all," Stahl said and emptied his pockets onto the ground.

The others did the same. Sharp's man gave up four flash drives.

"Roof, search 'em to be sure there's nothing else," Don said. "Afterwards, search their vehicle."

Roof, the Tuscarora – whom Don once had described as half-giraffe and half-gorilla – stepped forward. He was as big and buff as Sharp's man. He patted them each down twice.

"Nothing more," he reported, heading for the SUV.

Don turned to Jake: "There's a pen in my truck and something in the glove compartment to write on. Get all their info, then report to Chad. Ask him if he wants us to hang the trespassers upside down from a tree."

Sharp's man looked hard at Don, then at Jake. Did he recognize him as the reporter from Kenton? No matter, Jake thought. He decided not to reveal for now that he recognized him as someone with a direct connection to the Sharps until he asked Chad about it.

Jake grabbed up the three wallets and two phones – Stahl's skinny friend didn't have one – along with the flash drives, leaving other miscellaneous pocket possessions behind on the road.

Don spoke again: "I see we have two phones. Give us the passcodes or we keep them."

"Go on, keep mine," Sharp's man said. "You won't be able to access it."

"No passcode on mine," Stahl said.

"Confirm that," Don told Jake.

Jake hurried to Don's truck. Inside the cab he snapped pictures of the licenses and to be certain copied their names, addresses, and ID numbers. Stahl's friend was Stanley Adams; Sharp's man was Travis Tillman. Stahl had a Cheektowaga address, and Adams a Buffalo one; Tillman, a Bronx one. As expected, Jake couldn't activate Tillman's phone. He was able to open Stahl's and looked for photos of the Turtle. There were at least two dozen. There were also a lot of a young provocative girl. Jake deleted all recent ones. On Stahl's contact list he found Tillman's number and took a photo of that. Lastly, he wrote down the SUV's license plate number.

Still in the truck's cab, Jake phoned Chad and reported what had happened.

On Jake's mention of Sharp's bodyguard, Chad said, "Sharp and son sent their man who must have recruited local lowlifes. I'm glad you didn't let on to Tillman that you recognized him." His voice was flat but the flatness gave it extra intensity.

"No. Even if he recognized me, he doesn't know I recognized him."

"Good. We'll keep that between you and me for now. Tell Don to be sure he gets all the flash drives, then let them go. You stay at the Turtle until I arrive. Also tell him to post Roof and a couple others at end of the driveway in case they return with reinforcements. I'd be surprised if they do."

"Right. Anything new about Thomas?"

"We'll be here a while," was all Chad said.

Jake exited the truck and returned to Don's side and quietly passed on Chad's instructions.

"Roof, give 'em back their stuff as promised," Don said. He waved the flash drives. "Except these."

"And this," Jake added, holding up Tillman's phone.

Tillman looked hard at him.

Roof collected the possessions to be returned and did so. Jake took more photos of the three captives – they didn't look happy – and a video of them as they piled into their vehicle and drove off.

Stahl shouted his favorite retort out the window: "Fuck you all." But this time he elaborated: "This ain't over, fucking Injuns!"

Don, watching them disappear into the night, said, "I've met worse though not much worse." He turned toward his crew. "Roof and Tucker, park near the end of the driveway in case they show up with reinforcements. I'll join you soon. The rest of you can go back to the motel but keep your phones nearby."

The crew dispersed. Don drove Jake back up the driveway. The Turtle's front door had evidently been pried open with a bar or a flatiron, the casing damaged. They passed through and entered the Turtle's outer office. Jake turned on the lights.

"What the hell?" Don said.

Wheres the murderer had been written in chalk in various places on the walls, the apostrophe missing in each. Pieces of white chalk lay discarded on the floor. Chairs were out of place, obviously used to write high up.

"Nice of 'em not to use paint," Don commented.

"Maybe so we'd think it was just minor vandalism," Jake said.

"I wonder what they wanted with the data."

"To try to hurt Arrow in some way. Chad says they wouldn't have found anything anyway."

"Sure is some crazy shit. You want help with cleanup?"

"Chad will want to see it as they left it."

"Good thinking."

Don turned to go.

"Thanks for the muscle," Jake said.

"We just flexed it. Didn't have to use it."

"Well, you flexed it just right."

Storm Clouds

THE CLOUDS HAD RETURNED the next morning. A storm was brewing, thunder and lightning predicted. Chad stood in the middle of the Turtle's outer office, looking at the chalk writing on the walls. Don had gone for water to start the cleanup.

To everybody's surprise – the doctors' apparently, too – Thomas had rallied in the morning and was even conversational. After talking to Ehnita, he wanted time alone with Oren. Chad had returned to the Turtle by himself.

Taking in the defaced walls, he asked, "You get photos of all this?"

Jake, blinking away sleepiness, replied, "I'll send them to you. They sure went to a lot of trouble for just one message."

"Probably an attempt at misdirection. Deface the office with the question on everyone's mind to distract us from the more serious violation ... the data heist."

"How do you think the Sharps managed to hook up with a security guard from Buffalo?"

Chad again had a ready explanation: "The Sharps follow everything on us. They see Stahl on TV talking about Baines ... and they probably already knew about Stahl being at the powwow with him. After our statement about their theme park, they decide to play hardball to discredit us. They contact Stahl to see how they might use him. Baines's toady would love the idea of a break-in at the Turtle. Stahl could've gotten word from someone at the hospital about Thomas and decided it was a good time to make a move. They probably thought they could get something about our being in contact with Grant and also get some financial dirt on us.

214

It could've been like that. Whatever their stupid plan was, it failed thanks to your watchfulness."

"I'm glad I took a walk when I did."

"Get one more round of photos as backup before you clean up. Leave one of the messages for Ona to see," Chad instructed, then headed to the back rooms.

As Jake took more photos, he thought about the spray paint used by graffiti artists as in his last case.

Don returned with a bucket, sponges, sponge mop, and a roll of paper towels, setting them down in the middle of the room. He grabbed the mop, dipped it in the bucket, and started on the high writing. Jake used a sponge to wipe off the chalk within his reach.

Chad returned soon after they'd finished. "A photo's gone from Ona's wall," he said. "One of her and me. It wasn't on them when you searched them?"

"If it hasn't turned up, I guess we missed it," Jake replied. "I heard them mention a photo when they were inside."

Chad, Don, and Jake stood in silence, looking at the one remaining *Wheres the murderer?* Their thoughts seemed to be taking on energy, like the static electricity building in the air outside. Jake knew discharges would come, matching whatever the elements had to offer.

Road to Recovery

TWO DAYS AFTER the break-in, while atop scaffolding working on a lodge roof with the two Mohawk from Kahnawake – Tanner and Tucker – Jake saw Chad's Outback pull into the staff parking area. He and Oren climbed out of the vehicle and, rather than enter the Turtle, they approached the lodges. Chad headed toward the workers; Oren gave a quick wave to the crew and angled toward his own lodge. Jake hadn't seen him or even talked to him about any of the recent goings-on. He probably needed to unwind.

Chad reached the worksite, nodded a greeting to those on the scaffolding and stuck his head into the lodge's doorway. "Hey, all … come outside."

Don and Roof and a Seneca named Tobias exited.

215

"Some good news," Chad announced. "The doctors told us today they're happy with Thomas's progress. He'll probably be discharged later this week. He'll need some time to recuperate at his home in Salamanca but should be returning to the Turtle soon enough."

Don gave a big smile. "Yeah, that sure is good news."

Others echoed the sentiment.

"I'm happy to report he's the Thomas you all remember ... sees and tells things like they are ... no more hospital hallucinations." Chad glanced Jake's way.

Had Thomas retracted his confession?

"We need him to keep us clearheaded," Chad added.

"That we do," Don agreed. "We're in the final stretch. We hope to finish this lodge and caulk all the others one more time each before end of the week."

"If Thomas is back home as scheduled and the lodges are done, we celebrate on Saturday," Chad announced.

Don looked at his men. "Hear that, you all? Keep your asses moving."

Roof gave his oversized smile, saying, "They'll be moving, you can be sure of that."

The crew returned to their tasks. Chad headed for the Turtle.

Jake gave an inward sigh of relief as he pulled his measuring tape back out from his toolbelt.

~

Early that evening, Jake knocked on Oren's door. When he finally opened it, he looked as if he'd been sleeping in his flannel shirt and denim jeans.

"I wake you?" Jake asked.

"Sleep's been scarce."

"Sorry. I just wanted to celebrate with you a bit over the good news about Thomas."

"Yeah, we should. I'd smoke up with you now but I think I'm fighting something. Too many all-nighters. I kept Thomas's house going for my grandmother but I couldn't sleep much wherever I was. I heard you had some action over this way."

"Yeah."

"You put it to some of my favorite locals, along with Sharp's bodyguard. Sure weird he's part of this shit."

"And you heard about the False Face Dancer at Thomas's lodge the night before that?" Jake asked him.

"Yeah."

"I thought maybe it was Grant."

"I don't know anything about that," Oren said too quickly. "Okay, I'm gonna hit the sack again. I'll probably take tomorrow off. Not sure."

"We've just about wrapped up work on the lodges," Jake reassured him.

"Yeah, that's good. See ya'," Oren said and stepped all the way back inside, closing the door.

Jake, disappointed, returned to his lodge. He would call Caitlyn with the good news. That was a kind of celebration. Assuming the doctors had it right, all of Thomas's friends could breathe easy.

How easy? Grant was still on the lam. Stahl and his buddies were no doubt planning revenge. The Sharps probably, too. Oren was still in a distant, seemingly troubled, place. And Chad seemed primed to take action against all enemies.

So much still to go wrong.

PART VII: FULL CIRCLE

"In the very earliest time, when both people and animals lived on Earth, a human could become an animal and an animal could become a human. Sometimes they were humans and sometimes they were animals and there was no difference. All spoke the same language."
– from an Inuit narrative chant

In Deeper

"I'VE TRIED THREE TIMES. Oren doesn't answer," Chad told Jake. "Go get him, will you? See if he's well enough to join us."

Thomas had been discharged from the Olean General Hospital on Friday. Ona and Ehnita had stayed in Salamanca with him. The crew had met at the Turtle the next day to celebrate Thomas's recovery and the completion of the lodges. People had gotten too drunk, including Chad, but all had made it back safely to where they had to go. Oren had kept to himself and had left early after just one beer.

Work on the amphitheater was set to begin on Monday morning. Instead of a staff meeting, Chad had asked Mark Tama – along with Don, Oren, and Jake – to meet with the architect Niles Maskeet at the jobsite an hour before the rest of the crew to review the blueprints. Oren, despite the meeting's importance, was a no-show.

Jake left the others in the cleared portion of the south field and headed for Oren's lodge. It was a cloudless day, an encouraging start to a hoped-for productive week.

He knocked on the lodge's door. No response. He tried again, knocking harder. Still nothing. He tried the doorlatch. Open. He stepped partly through the door.

"Oren?"

No reply. Jake entered the rest of the way. He could see that the bed was empty. He took out his phone and called Chad.

"He's not in his lodge."

"You sure? His pickup's still here. Maybe he doesn't hear you."

"The door was unlocked. I'm inside."

Jake waited for Chad to speak again.

When he finally did, Jake heard suppressed concern in his voice: "Take a look around, will you? Look for his bow. Text me."

Jake did as instructed. The lodge was messier since the last time he'd been there, with dirty dishes, empty beer bottles, and clothing strewn about. He found no bow or quiver – only some arrows without feathers. He texted Chad to let him know, then waited.

Chad's response: "Hunting on a workday? Come back here for the meeting and if he still doesn't show or answer, we look for him."

~

Chad had them conduct their search in approximately quarter-acre segments, moving parallel to each other north to south. He'd told Jake to make noise and call out to Oren. From time to time, Jake heard him doing the same in the distance.

Not far from the False Face tree he'd come upon the afternoon before the break-in, Jake spotted something – two arrows protruding from a hemlock trunk.

"Hey, Chad, over here!" he yelled.

Chad soon arrived at Jake's side and they approached the tree. Chad touched the arrows' fletches. Jake could see that sap had trickled down the trunk from the embedded arrowheads.

"Yeah, Oren's brand," Chad said. "Look at the sap. This was recent."

"Target practice?"

"Probably to fine tune his bow."

Chad's jaw was tight. To Jake he suddenly looked older than his years. He pulled his phone from his pocket.

"Come on, Oren, answer, will you?" He gave up quickly and put the phone away. "If he's anywhere around here, he's heard us by now. We'll work our way down to the logging road just to be certain." He didn't sound hopeful.

The descent proved fruitless. From the logging road, rather than follow it to Eagleton, they headed back up the slope and along the ridge to the well-trodden path they'd taken from the grounds below. They descended and walked along the lodges. They could hear the crew working again after their lunch break. Oren's lodge was still empty. Jake waited outside while Chad entered.

He returned after about ten minutes, holding up a set of keys. "Truck and lodge keys, and I think the one to Thomas's house," he said, pocketing them. "You stay nearby. Keep an eye on his lodge. He might slip back in. I'll inform Ona, then take a drive on some of the back roads, hoping he shows up on one of them. Make sure your phone is charged."

Jake returned to his lodge to grab something to eat and the Alliance camera, then began a series of walks between the Turtle and the lodges. He tried to keep his mind far away as he whiled away the hours. He took photos for Aki in every direction to help pass the time.

He was leaning on the side of Oren's lodge in the descending darkness when his phone beeped.

"Oren came and went without a word," Chad reported. "Seems he has an extra set of keys. No one saw or heard him. We should've staked out his truck rather than his lodge. Meet me at the Turtle."

Jake hurried to the outer office. Ona, at her desk, put the phone down as he entered. Chad stood nearby.

Ona spoke: "No, still not at the house." She sounded forlorn. "Ehnita doesn't need this stress. Thomas is sleeping fortunately." She rubbed her eyes with the heels of her hands. "Oren, Oren, why make things even harder?"

"Maybe he's driving to other state lands," Chad said. "Dobbins or Cattaraugus. He probably saw or heard us looking for him. Wants to be alone."

"What do you think set him off?"

"He's finding solace in the wilderness. That's what he does. Things built up here at his new home and around his new family. It got to him. He's following his own path."

Family, Jake thought, ever determining and challenging. Oren had also grown up without a father. In Thomas he'd gained a grandfather figure; in Ona, a sister. And Grant had been like a brother to him, he'd said. Chad and Jake, also like brothers to him. Had Oren's new family become so important to him that now he was acting out because of them? Acting out how? Abandoning them all for the wilderness?

"Do we notify the police?" Ona asked. "Someone might have ..."

Chad cut her off: "Let's keep the police out of it for now. We ..."

His phone beeped. He looked at its screen, then pocketed it. "Just Don," he announced, "with nothing to report from Seneca Hills."

"Where're you going?" Ona asked.

"We'll check out Little Valley," the Arrow leader said. "Unlikely Oren would go to the Duckbill alone, but who knows? Maybe he stopped for a quick drink."

Ona looked hard at him. "Goddamn bars," she said.

"If no luck there, we might head to Salamanca and ask around. It's getting too late to search other state lands. You just stay put. He might wander in here soon, an animal carcass slung over his shoulder."

"In the meantime, don't you go missing," she said bleakly.

Chad and Jake left the Turtle and headed for the parking area.

Before reaching the Outback, Chad turned to Jake and said, "Oren brought you into his smuggling deal at Akwesasne. I'll bring you in even deeper. Don't mind getting in deeper, do you?"

"Of course not."

"I wouldn't ask for help if I didn't trust you." He tossed his head toward the vehicle.

Jake followed him and also climbed in and fastened his seatbelt. Chad pulled out of the parking area and headed down the driveway.

"We're not checking the bars," he finally explained. "That wasn't Don who texted. That text was from a friend. He says Oren plans to stake out Stahl's house. I didn't tell Ona. I just couldn't put her, Ehnita, and Thomas through the worry until I know what exactly he's up to."

Jake absorbed that. He remembered Stahl's hometown from his license.

"So we go to Cheektowaga?"

"I'm hoping we don't have to. My friend is trying to convince Oren to meet us in Salamanca."

"Is your friend with him?"

"He reached Oren by phone. I hope he agrees. I think Thomas's heart attack and confession ... Thomas's trying to take on the blame ... hearing about the break-in ... the inaction ... became too much for him. He's been in some distant place since the hospital."

The "friend" talking to Oren had to be Grant, Jake figured but let that deduction go for now.

Instead he asked, "Thomas also confessed to Oren?"

"Yeah. He helped me convince Thomas to drop that act."

"Thomas admitted he was trying to help Grant?"

"That he did," Chad said, reaching over and turning on the car radio. He set it on a Buffalo station. "Wish I had a goddamn scanner," he said.

Jake processed the fact of Thomas's retraction. A commercial blared. Chad turned down the volume. Local news came on but nothing relevant to their concerns.

They drove along Eagleton, then turned onto 353 toward Salamanca. The news droned on. Jake's mind left the radio noise behind, trying to make sense of Chad's, Thomas's, and Oren's behavior. Of all of them, Oren had revealed the least emotion just after Thomas's heart attack. It must have festered inside him along with everything else. And Stahl was a good target for anger.

They neared Salamanca.

Chad spoke: "We're close."

Jake recognized the turn-off leading to the ruins of Chad's childhood home. Chad soon turned onto and drove up the gravel driveway, parking along the remnants of the stone wall, as he'd done the night of the sweat. They exited the vehicle. Jake looked in the direction where the sweatlodge had stood. He knew it had been stored at the Turtle because of concerns about vandalism. It was to be reassembled on Arrow's grounds at a place of Thomas's choosing when he was healthy.

"I'm going to pay my respects," Chad said. "You stay here."

He stepped over the stone wall and walked toward his family's headstones. Jake leaned against the Outback. A gentle wind had come up, rustling leaves on nearby trees. He could see Chad's outline at the burial place, his body still, his head bowed. Native peoples had their sacred grounds. Some were natural features; some, structures; some, burial sites; some had ruins on them. This was indeed a sacred place for Chad.

Jake could see the Arrow leader lighting a cigarette and remembered how on the night of the sweat he'd spoken of tobacco in Native rituals. On hearing the distant hum of an engine, he turned and saw a white car approaching. Oren? No, this was a sedan, not a pickup.

Chad rejoined Jake just as the driver stepped out of his vehicle. It was an old man, wearing a beaded baseball hat, a western shirt, and blue jeans. Jake had seen this "old" man twice before. In Hartford, Connecticut, and at the Methodist Church in Seneca Hills. Grant Guyasuta in disguise.

Shapeshifting Grant nodded to Jake as he went to hug Chad. Jake recognized the piercing eyes. Those of the False Face Dancer.

"I understand you two sort of met," Chad said. "Let's make it official. Grant Guyasuta, this is Jake Jakes. And, Jake, this is Grant Guyasuta."

Grant gave a namaste bow, and Jake bowed back. Jake could see that he'd applied yellowish base color to his face, using dark brown makeup to create the effect of shadows under his eyes. He'd also used the brown to highlight wrinkles and to draw vertical lines on his lips. The brim of his hat created real shadows, helping hide his actual age.

Grant spoke: "I've heard lots of good things about you, Jake Maybe-Mohawk."

Jake had heard this voice chanting in the lodge. Some of the melodic chanting still seemed to resonate.

"Same here about you. Sorry I interrupted your dance for Thomas."

"A simple misunderstanding." He turned to Chad. "I just heard from Oren again. He's not coming here. He's already at Stahl's. He won't change his mind. He's going through with it whatever it is. I think I convinced him to wait for me. I told him I'd help him. I didn't tell him I was meeting up with you first."

"Okay, let's go. Grant, you follow us. We'll take 219 to 90 East, then exit at 52A."

"Right."

"And stay the old man, right? Just in case."

"Yeah, why not? All this has made me old for real."

Native irony, Jake thought as he climbed back into the Outback – humor tinged with sadness.

He had questions galore. Time to get some answers. He'd been taken in deeper and he was owed a full explanation. Sorting out his questions, he let Chad drive back to the paved road and get up speed before speaking. Where to start?

"Did you know beforehand about Grant's False Face Dance?"

Chad took one hand off the wheel and rubbed his brow, like he was trying to give his brain a deep massage.

"No, but I assumed he was the dancer when you contacted me about it. I knew he was nearby. He decided to return from Michigan when Oren told him about Thomas's heart attack and confession, even though Oren says he encouraged him not to. He called me soon after your encounter at the lodge. Sorry I wasn't forthright."

"Has Grant been in contact with you and Oren all along since hiding out?"

"Once in a while. Thomas, too. Mostly Oren."

"Taking chances."

"He's been using friends' phones, speaking with hidden meanings."

"He didn't dance at the hospital like you said the Fancy Dancer might?"

"No way I'd let him risk that. Sorry again."

Jake kept firing questions. "Why Michigan?"

"Hiding out with the Anishinabe. One of them lent him the truck."

"Anishinabe?"

"Another name for the Chippewa ... Ojibwe's another. Grant's been moving around a lot. Different reservations. I told him it's better if we don't know where he goes. We hoped he'd made it to an Anishinabe Reserve in Canada until all this got resolved but he never tried."

"Did you know he was at Hartford and at Thomas's talk?"

Chad nodded wearily. "Yes. He keeps risking his freedom. Thomas also took a risk by trying to take responsibility. Oren is doing so by going after Stahl. Around and around we go."

"Do Ona and Ehnita know Grant's back?"

"We've spared them worry regarding his comings and goings."

"What do you think Oren plans on doing?"

Chad ran his hand through his hair and sighed before speaking. "He's acting out. Stahl came after us, accompanying Sharp's errand boy Tillman at the break-in. Maybe Oren wants to reciprocate, hoping to find some kind of evidence. Let's hope he waits for Grant."

It occurred to Jake he'd been brought along as added muscle in case of violence. He doubted he was getting the full story, Chad confiding in him as needed.

"What's our plan? Just try to talk him out of doing anything stupid?" he asked.

"We're all his friends. Maybe he'll listen."

"And if he doesn't?"

"We're all his friends. We protect him."

~

Darkness had fallen. Chad hadn't said much the last leg of the drive, except to ask Jake to use his phone's GPS to locate the address so he didn't have to bother with his. He did mention that Cheektowaga was a Seneca name for the region after the big red berries of the once-abundant Hawthorn trees.

"Wonder if it torments Stahl to live in a town with a Native name," he added, "and that he lives on Cayuga Creek Road taken from a tribal name."

"And a Mohawk is now after him," Jake said.

"Let's hope the Mohawk keeps his head."

Not far off Route 90, on nearing Stahl's house, Chad pulled over in front of a chainlink fence and a commercial building behind it. He turned off his headlights. Grant pulled in behind them, his lights illuminating the Subaru's interior for a moment before he also turned them off.

"Be right back," Chad said. "Text Ona, will you? Tell her I'll be filling her in on developments soon. Nothing more."

Jake imagined her impatient, frustrated expression.

"Will do."

Leaving the Outback running, Chad got out and hurried to the sedan. Jake texted Ona as instructed. He saw that a message from Caitlyn had come in, telling him she had a nasty spring cold – a fever even – and had already missed two days of classes as the semester wound down. Even knowing she'd gotten the vaccine, his mind flashed on Covid-19. He would call after things settled down here or if things got even worse – perhaps his one call from jail.

Ona texted back, "Tell Chad to call soon!"

Chad returned, climbing in the driver's seat again. "Grant just spoke to Oren. Stahl's not there. At first, he was upset you and I came along but then said he has something he wants to show all of us."

They drove three more blocks along a row of residences and the forest opposite. Lights dotted some. Stahl's house was dark. They passed it and parked along the woods opposite another dark one. Grant pulled past them and also parked his vehicle.

Chad and Jake met Grant along the shoulder.

"Okay, time to rescue Oren from himself," Chad said.

They walked along the tree line back in the direction they'd come, stopping on the shoulder opposite Stahl's address.

"Over here," came Oren's hushed voice.

In the moonlight Jake could see his head sticking out from behind a tree. He waved them into a stand of maples and used the light of his cellphone's home screen to direct them to the largest tree and to shelter behind it. He wore all black – a black hoodie, jeans, sneakers, and a wool cap – Ninja-like. He'd also smudged his face black. Propped against the tree was his bow and quiver with four arrows. A fifth was leaning against the tree next to the bow.

"Listen for a returning car," Oren instructed.

"How long you been here?" Chad asked.

"Going on three hours." Oren's voice, gravelly with exhaustion, was still intense.

"Just here?"

"I've been inside."

"Oh, brother, how long ago and how long were you in there?

"I went in after I last spoke to Grant. Maybe for about ten minutes."

"You wear gloves?"

"Of course I did. Found his photo collection. He converted a heater cabinet into a file cabinet," Oren kneeled down behind the tree. "Have a look," he said levelly, suppressing rage.

Chad crouched to one side of Oren; Grant, to the other. Jake leaned over Chad's shoulder. Oren turned on his flashlight app and handed the phone to Grant.

"You're gonna be sick," Oren said.

He reached into a black leather knapsack and pulled out a pile of papers. He thumbed through them, holding them at different angles for each onlooker to see. Grant tracked them with the light.

They were images of children, predominantly girls. Most were computer-paper copies of photos. Some were clippings from magazines. In some girls were half-naked in sensual poses. Others were candid photos of women and kids from public settings.

"That one was taken at our powwow," Chad said icily.

One of the young women standing in front of the Turtle's head, Jake realized, was Anna. Another photo showed Richard Baines walking next to Anna, looking over his shoulder, leading her toward the woods beyond the driveway. The flash of the camera had revealed the glint of something in his hand, next to his side. A knife. On Baines's face, a sickly smile.

"Oh, man ... oh, man," Grant uttered under his breath.

"Look at this one," Oren said.

He held up the photo of Ona from her office wall, with Chad's image torn away. Jake remembered Roof searching Stahl and the others the night of the break-in and had the sickening thought Stahl had stuffed it down his pants.

"Quite a collection," Chad said, like a volcano about to blow.

Oren reached in the black bag and pulled out a knife.

"Thought this might come in handy," he said.

The same knife as in the photo?

"Is that Baines's?" Grant asked. "I'd like to stick it in Stahl ... for real this time," he said quietly and evenly.

"You told us you'd ditched it," Chad said to Oren.

Oren shoved the photos back in the bag but put the knife in his sweatshirt's front double pocket.

"I kept it for a night like tonight. Stahl also deserves to die. I do it for all of us, then turn myself in. It's time to finish this." He looked at Grant. "Bring you back in with your name cleared." Then, to Chad: "Keep Thomas from spouting his bullshit about being the guilty one." He looked at Jake. "I'm gift-wrapping myself for the cops with a final act."

Chad spoke: "You know there's a better way, Oren. Don't make it worse. These photos will prove what Baines was and what Stahl is. There're more like this in the house?"

"Lots more."

"The cops will find them. We don't even have to sneak back in to replace these."

"Oh, he'll skate. You know how it is with the good old boys."

"Not all the good old boys are pedophiles and rapists," Grant said.

"I'm doing it for Anna."

"I say don't do it for Anna," Grant countered, now with emotion showing. "It'll just add to her suffering."

"She'd be better off having her brother back and Baines's sicko friend off planet Earth."

Chad and Grant looked at Oren, searching for more words. Jake wondered if he should try another angle to reach Oren. Was it his place? He'd been proclaimed one of the family. Go for it, he told himself.

"By getting this evidence, you've already lived up to the Warrior tradition, like your father," he said. "It's time to return to your loved ones and celebrate."

Oren's eyes locked on his but he didn't say anything. He turned to Grant, saying, "Thanks so much for bringing him along to mention my father."

"What if we ..." Chad didn't finish. A car approached, its light bouncing along the road and nearby trees.

Jake looked and recognized the vehicle from the night of the break-in. "It's the sicko's SUV," he said.

Oren had grabbed up his bow and quiver and dashed away from them toward another smaller tree closer to the road.

Chad hurried out of the woods onto the shoulder, yelling back at Oren, "We'll have some words with Stahl ... give him a scare! But that's all!"

Grant ran to follow, his nimbleness contrasting the old-man disguise. Oren stayed half-sheltered by the smaller tree.

Stahl rolled his vehicle into his driveway. He shut off the engine and climbed out. Chad had reached the center of the street.

"Hey, pervert!" he called out. "Yeah, you, Stahl! You got some company!"

Grant also yelled: "Time to talk, sicko!"

Stahl turned to look, his moonlit expression going from surprise to alarm.

Jake glanced over at Oren, still standing next to the second tree. The Mohawk held the bow up, slowly drew back the arrow, and aimed. His wiry frame was taut, like a bow itself ready for release.

Jake was already running. He launched himself and slammed into Oren just as he let the arrow fly. The two of them tumbled to the ground. Jake, disentangling himself, sat up far enough to look across the street. Lights in the two flanking houses had come on. Stahl was looking toward his door. The arrow was embedded in it.

Grant ran back to them. He grabbed the bow off the ground. Oren sat up and looked toward the house.

"Fuck, I missed," he said without anger ... just despair.

Grant helped Jake up, then turned to Oren. "Anna will be happy you did."

From the street came Chad's voice: "You can keep the arrow, Stahl. A trade-off for a sampling of your photo collection."

In the distance a siren sounded out, becoming louder and louder. Stahl had disappeared into his house. Chad, still in the middle of the road, waited for the approaching cars. There were two sets of headlights, Jake saw.

Grant, now helping Oren up, told Jake, "Get the bag and quiver." He then spoke to Oren: "Come on. Here's what you can tell the cops ..."

"Fuck that," Oren interrupted. "I'm telling the truth ... all of it."

Grant lowered his head, then looked him in the eyes. "You sure?"

"Dead sure."

Grant quietly said, "Okay, Oren."

Jake, trying to make sense of it all, followed as Grant led Oren toward the road.

The siren stopped. Two cars, the second unmarked, pulled up. Chad, still in the middle of the road, had spread his arms.

Two state police, hands on their guns, climbed out of the first car. One turned his attention to Chad; the other, to Grant, Oren, and Jake.

"Drop the bow," he told Grant. "You, drop the rest," he told Jake. "All of you, hands up."

They did as instructed. The passenger side door of the second car opened. A tall figure emerged. It was White Eyebrows. He looked at all four of them, then at the house, and then back at them.

One of the Staties spoke first, "Up against the car ... all of you."

"That's Jonas Stahl's house. He's inside," Chad said, pointing. White Eyebrows nodded. "We know where he lives."

Morning After

"THANK YOU for your statement, Jake Jakes. We're now turning off the recorder. The time is 6:30 a.m."

White Eyebrows – John Borsa was his real name – sure looked the part of a tough cop. All that was missing cinematically was a cigarette dangling from his mouth. But his voice was gentle. A stone-faced woman, sitting nearby in the borrowed office of the Erie County Correctional Facility in Alden, turned off the recorder.

"You must be tired," Borsa said, stretching himself. "Your statement helps us. It confirms pretty much my understanding. Like I told the others, Oren Feather has confessed to the killing. Your friends ... Grant Guyasuta and his sister Anna Guyasuta and Chad Catamount ... share in the coverup blame. Not sure what we'll do about that. But know that they've taken responsibility in a convincing manner and cleared you. And your story fits their accounts."

Jake was indeed exhausted but his thoughts still churned. "Oren told us when you showed up that he was finally going to tell the truth," he said. "Probably feels good for him to get it out."

"No doubt," Borsa said and stood up. "Grant probably feels good about that, too."

~

Jake rode with Chad again. Ona had driven Anna to the Correctional Facility and both had given statements, as had Grant of course. Chad's Subaru and the sedan lent to Grant by a Chippewa friend had been towed from Cheektowaga but had been returned to them upon their release. They were all heading to the Turtle in their respective cars. Anna rode with her brother. They would spend the night in one of the empty guest lodges.

During his ride with Chad, Jake kept asking questions until he'd finally gotten his mind around the powwow killing and its aftermath.

Oren Feather, Mohawk from Akwesasne, friend and co-worker of Jake ... guilty. Not Grant Guyasuta, the Fancy Dancer and, until now, a fugitive. And not Thomas Dion'dot, the Alliance shaman, who had given that false confession from his hospital bed.

The man at the Brighton Casino had declared that Fancy Dancers don't commit murders. Grant, the Fancy Dancer in question, hadn't done so. Oren, with his own aspirations to be a Fancy Dancer, had killed once and might have done so a second time if his arrow had flown straight.

Jake of course had known all along that the blanket statement he'd overheard in Florida was just one man's opinion. But he couldn't keep from having imaginary dialogue with that man whose words had shaped his recent life. If given the chance, Jake would tell him that maybe as a group Fancy Dancers, dedicated to their art, were unlikely murderers. So were ballerinas for that matter. Yet people of all callings were full of surprises.

As Borsa had told Jake, Grant, Chad, and Anna had all admitted covering up Oren's guilt. Grant had fled, allowing suspicion about the killing to fall on him because he knew Oren loved his sister and had prevented her rape. Grant had encountered Baines at the powwow as originally reported. He'd even told him to stop harassing girls. He'd then gone to change out of his dance clothes. Soon afterwards, Oren had spotted Baines leading Anna into the woods at knifepoint. He'd also seen Stahl taking the picture found at Stahl's house and that served as proof of what they'd all claimed. And Oren had seen Stahl heading to the parking area, evidently to get Baines's car so they could readily leave after the attack. He claimed that Baines had thrown Anna down, then had pinned her with his legs. The retired cop had started unbuckling his belt with one hand, the knife in the other. Oren, silent hunter that he was, had snuck up behind Baines and snatched the weapon out of his hand, thrusting it twice in his kidneys.

Thomas, like Grant and Chad, had known the truth since the night of the killing. Ona and Ehnita had not known, however. Thomas on his presumed deathbed had claimed guilt for the actual killing so that Grant and his family could get their former lives back. When the shaman's recovery was certain, Chad and Oren had convinced him to drop his attempt to assume guilt, and it had never reached the authorities. Nor had Thomas's part in the coverup.

Jake had been duped by the others. Understandably. And they'd been and still were being duped by him.

Dancing Fancy

BITS OF DIALOGUE, revelations, and repercussions were bouncing around Jake's brain – along with apprehension about seeing Thomas and Ehnita – as he drove to their house for lunch. Ona had expressed how Ehnita, like Ona herself, was distraught about Oren's incarceration. Thomas was reportedly doing well. Jake wondered if the shaman would still have a calming effect on those around him, given his frail condition.

The fact that Oren was so open and resolute in his confession, providing details confirmed by others, had resulted in an indictment on two counts – homicide regarding Baines and attempted homicide regarding Stahl.

Public opinion, even among a surprising number of non-Natives in the region, seemed to be on Oren's side. He'd stopped a rape – the rape of someone he loved. He'd exposed the rapist's friend, a pedophile.

Oren's lawyer – a Buffalonian who had handled other Native cases – had advised that he plead guilty to manslaughter in killing Baines, with the hope that the additional charge of the attempted murder of Stahl be dropped.

Oren was ready for the consequences. He'd claimed to Chad and Ona that he was fine with doing time after witnessing what Grant's sacrifice had led to.

"I manned up," he'd told the judge when arraigned.

He'd further informed everyone that he didn't even want bail posted. Chad had had to convince Ona and Ehnita that it was a good idea for Oren not to be out of jail before the trial – and the center of too much attention – and they'd relented.

The DA still might push for a homicide trial. Baines, an ex-cop, had apologists, even if he'd tried to rape a young woman and even if his friend Stahl had been indicted for child pornography as well as for aiding, abetting, and covering up an attempted rape.

There were no charges against Oren's friends about their shared coverup of the killing. Chad had considered charging Stahl with the breaking and entering into the Turtle, but had decided not to do so. Oren's attorney had pointed out that, although the B&E could help explain his client's motivation against Stahl, it would probably be dismissed as irrelevant to his case and might just confuse things. He preferred focusing on the young love angle along with that of protecting women and children from sex offenders.

Chad and Ona had invited Jake to accompany them on their second jailhouse visit. Oren had acted civil yet distant to him, as if still processing events. Jake wondered if the comment he'd made about Oren's Warrior father still rankled him, along with Jake's slamming into him and ruining his aim. But he knew not to make too much of his own concerns. Others were living through greater emotional turmoil.

After the visit, during the drive back to Seneca Hills, Chad had offered the following perspective: "Maybe Oren could've found a way to stop Baines without killing him. We'll never know, will we? His way sure proved effective in the heat of the moment. Effective yet impractical because of all the consequences. Anger, especially anger fueled by love, sure makes for the impractical. I think his finally taking responsibility is the practical path. Grant says he grew up while hiding out, getting a better perspective on things. Oren's time in jail might mean the same for him."

Ona's response: "I just hope he doesn't get sent somewhere where it's fight or die."

Chad had taken the conversation elsewhere: "He was sure happy to hear that Anna worked with you today."

"Anna gives him purpose. I hope they make it," Ona had said, her matter-of-fact tone terminating the conversation.

Jake eventually pieced together more about the case through other conversations with Chad and Ona. The killing hadn't taken place on a reservation. But given the Erie-Mingo connection to the Seneca and that tribe's federal status, and also to the federally recognized Seminole through Grant's ancestry, and because a federal agent could better check on leads to Grant's whereabouts in other states, John Borsa had been assigned to the case.

Borsa and the New York State Police had made it to Cheektowaga and Stahl's house so quickly the night of Oren's arrest because someone in one of the neighboring houses had spotted him exit the house and head for the woods.

Borsa had admitted to Chad that he'd come to the area – after looking for leads about Grant among the Seminole in Florida and after trying to get a sense of Alliance activism at the Connecticut event – not just in the hope of locating Grant, but also to get a sense of Baine's activities leading up to his death. He was also concerned about more violence at the upcoming powwow that was now being publicized. He'd been staying at a motel in Little Valley, claiming to be a traveling salesman and frequenting the Duckbill Tavern as well as the Woodbine. He'd known that Stahl and his cohorts had followed and stopped the car the night of Oren's birthday. He'd told Chad that he decided to follow them on seeing them leave the bar just after Chad and the others departed and that he was about to pull up next to the roadside goings-on just before their car had peeled out. When Stahl's bunch turned around to head back to Little Valley, Borsa had returned to his hotel.

Chad had also asked Borsa if he'd known about Stahl's proclivities as proven by his photo collection and he'd replied that Baines and Stahl were considered to be of questionable character by many ... by coworkers and neighbors alike.

On hearing that, Jake had thought of Baines's neighbors in Bradford – the snow-shoveling husband and the outspoken wife – but hadn't let on to anyone about his own excursion there.

Borsa of course had also checked out everyone at the Arrow Alliance, including Jake. He knew Jake had been at Hartford. But he didn't know he'd been at the Leesburg Powwow in Florida. Jake had maintained the partial truth that his ending up in Seneca Hills was about his own ancestry.

Chad had told Jake that Borsa had expressed understanding Jake's quest, since he himself was part Crow and was proud of the fact that some of his ancestors had worked as scouts for the U.S. Army during the Plains Indian wars. So Joe Panther's doubts about Borsa really being part Crow had been proven wrong.

Chad had also asked Borsa if he'd suspected Oren. As he'd relayed it to Jake, Borsa's response was "No more, no less than anyone else. I'm glad no one else got hurt and I'm glad he fessed up and is taking responsibility. I like the kid and I like that Anna girl he did it for. And I like Grant Guyasuta, who gave up his Fancy Dancing for running and hiding in order to protect a friend, as foolhardy as that was."

At those words Jake had had the thought that the middle-aged hatchet-faced man with the white eyebrows, who reminded him of a ruthless killer from a movie, not only had a blood connection to Native America but had also developed a soft spot for the three young Native Americans at the heart of the case.

Proof positive yet again, Jake had mused, that people were full of surprises.

~

Ehnita must have heard the car. She was there to open the door without his using the knocker with the bear's face.

"Jake," she gently said.

Jake gave her a big hug. "Ehnita, I've missed you."

She hugged back. "Damn, boy, we've missed you. Welcome to our home again." She led him inside. "You hungry?"

"Need you ask when you're doing the cooking?"

"Go join Thomas. We'll eat in his bedroom. He wanted the couch but I'm being stubborn."

"I'll back you up."

"Atta boy."

"Should I go in now?"

She pointed. "That door."

He started for it.

"Jake, one thing first."

He turned to look at her again.

"I want you to know that I'm doing okay. It's still hard to grasp it all. I'm working at it. Oren's a hero to many now. He may be some kind of hero but I see him as a stupid one. Not for his original act in rescuing Anna but everything since then, dancing fancy around the truth and almost killing again. I just hope he gets easy time." Tears welled up. She took a breath and rallied. "It could have been so much worse. I want to thank you for what you did."

"I was the closest to him. I just reacted."

"That's the point. You reacted right."

"Thanks, Ehnita."

"I have my grandson still," she added. "I have my man still. And Ona and all the rest of you." She forced a smile and headed for the kitchen.

Thomas was in bed but not the way he'd been in the hospital bed. He now sat upright. He'd also regained his color along with his wry smile and the twinkle in his eyes.

"Jake, the man of the hour," he said.

"Somewhat of an overstatement, I'd say."

"Chad described how you protected the Turtle and its computer system. And I know how you caused an arrow to miss its mark."

Jake shrugged away the compliments, then said with a smile, "And you must've heard I interrupted a False Face Dance being performed on your behalf."

"Not till the dancing went on long enough to cure me. I'm living proof."

"I think Ehnita thinks you're acting too cured for your own good."

Thomas managed a laugh. "She's using you to bolster her case for more convalescence."

"I agree with her ... as long as you keep allowing visitors."

"Deal. As long as I can direct the conversations with the visitors."

Jake smiled again. "For example?"

"I want to hear it all, starting with the break-in ... your side of it ... since I went down for such a long count."

"As long as I get to ask questions, too. You have to help me understand."

"People's behavior? Like Oren's and Grant's and yours truly's."

"Exactly."

Thomas nodded, his sadness showing through. "It's all been such an ordeal. So, please, fill me in."

Jake recounted his version of recent events, of course omitting any thoughts or suspicions related to his hidden agenda. Thomas listened intently, often nodding in a smile.

"Such excitement," he said when Jake had finished. "You certainly did yourself and the Alliance proud."

Ehnita entered with a tray of food. Fish tacos. She ate with them. During the meal, she, like Thomas, asked questions about the night of the break-in and the night of Oren's arrest.

A phone rang next to Thomas's bed. He answered. "Greetings, Oren." He listened a moment, then replied, "I'm feeling better and better, no lie. I have a visitor for tacos. Jake's here. I'll put your grandmother on."

Ehnita left the room. Thomas waited until she'd picked up another receiver, then hung up.

"He sounds okay," Thomas told Jake. "My turn."

He delved into Oren's choices – as well as Chad's, Grant's, and his own– for keeping the truth from Ehnita and Ona. He confided in Jake that Ehnita still didn't know how he'd tried to take responsibility for the powwow killing. Thomas said he hadn't confessed to her because she wouldn't have believed it for a second and she might've started suspecting that he was doing it not just for Grant's sake, but for the actual killer's – her grandson.

"I told my granddaughter the other day about my lying confession. After scolding me yet again for not sharing the truth with her about Oren and Grant all this time, Ona agreed it best for now not to burden Ehnita with yet another layer to all this, given her worry and heartache over Oren."

"It came from a good place."

"Maybe. I'm glad the truth finally did come out. Too many lies. I think it will all be okay now. I think Oren will be okay. We can all now be our real selves."

And Jake's own real self? As a way to cope with guilt over his ongoing deception, he asked Thomas about his dreams, some involving shapeshifting, and possible meaning.

Thomas said he didn't believe in interpreting the details of other people's dreams, but, teacher that he was, he did give Jake context: "According to many different Native belief systems, images seen with the eyes closed ... either in wakefulness, half-sleep, or dreams ... are glimpses of and messages from the Spirit World relevant to the individual or even to an entire tribe. From visions people receive guidance in choosing a totem, such as an animal, and a path of life and in healing. Even though visions don't necessarily provide the answers to specific questions ... I sure can attest to that ... they can help us understand ourselves and, in that way, offer guidance. I need that guidance. We all do, especially after all this stress."

Thomas had just wrapped up the conversation, Jake realized. He looked spent. It was time to go.

On the ride back to Seneca Hills, Jake thought about all the lies from the past months that had been exposed and the effect of it all on Thomas and Ehnita. And his own lies? All still buried. The big lie and all the other related small lies he'd been carrying – the reason for his trip all the way from Florida to Seneca Hills, his digging for information, his suspicions about Salali Jenkins's death. What effect would they have on everyone if they were exposed? And on him?

He sure was tired of dancing fancy himself.

Lots to Tell

"DID YOU START with Tiny Tot dancing?" Jake asked Grant.

"Sure did. Both my mom and dad danced. My dad thought I was too bookwormish and got me going with it."

Jake thought of Joe and Jolene Panther in Florida and how proud of their son Little Joe they were. "Does your sister dance?"

"They encouraged her to do so. She's damn good when she does. She's promised to practice with me now that things have settled down."

Grant and Jake sat at the counter in what had previously been Oren's lodge. Although Grant had agreed to work for the Alliance, he'd said he didn't feel right taking over Oren's lodge while looking to his friend's future release. Jake had been present in the Turtle when Ona had convinced him otherwise.

"Don't be silly," she'd said. "The lodges are for rotating staff and guests and no one's a permanent resident. Everyone would feel better if you take Oren's former home for now rather than having someone else in there ... and your sister gets to use it whenever she wants. When he comes to work for Arrow again, he'll have a lodge again. He knows that."

Grant had invited Jake over to the lodge, the day after he'd moved in, for what he'd called a kind of housewarming. He'd told Jake not to bring anything for dinner, saying he wanted to pay him back for his part in the Akwesasne deal, adding that it was reckless of Oren but a big help. He'd also told him that, during one of his visits to the jail, Oren had managed to communicate where he kept his stash. They now were smoking some of it from a glass pipe.

Grant's face was roundish like his sister's, with the same sloping eyes and mouth. He wore his hair longer than Chad or Oren did. In online photos and videos Jake had seen his hair in braids, dangling below a multicolored headdress. It was hanging loose now. He possessed such a powerful physical presence on the dance floor, like a warrior. These past weeks, however, Jake had come to know more of Grant Guyasuta beyond the dancer and the shapeshifting fugitive. He had a warm presence. He had a curious mind. Like Thomas, Ona, and Chad, he was a thoughtful student of Native history. He did indeed come off as bookwormish.

"Tell me about your sister," Grant said. "Oren says he met her."

"Caitlyn, adorable and smart. She went back to college to become a teacher. She's in the middle of exams right now."

"No other siblings?"

"Just Caitlyn."

"Same for me. Just Anna."

"You should meet Caitlyn."

Grant smiled. "That wouldn't be matchmaking, would it?"

"Ha! No, this big brother isn't allowed to do that."

"Me neither."

"I didn't realize how Oren was pining for Anna," Jake said. "He had that girlfriend Jess and eyes for others, it seemed."

"Like your sister? Just a distraction for him. He said dating Jess was a way he could get a sense of what people around here were saying about the case. I thought maybe it was a good thing so he didn't obsess over Anna. She was freaked out by what happened ... I mean not just to herself but to him and me, too. Heavy stuff to deal with. Even though Oren saved her that horrible night, I think she blamed him for my hiding out to protect him." Grant nodded to himself. "Now, her brother is back ... and she's back as well, living with our parents in our childhood home. Before all this happened, she wanted to move out. She's now happy to be there. And to see Oren regularly."

"How often did you talk to Oren while hiding out?"

"Lots."

"Kind of risky."

"We never used our names. I was Coyote and he was Magpie."

"Both Trickster figures."

Grant smiled. "You've picked up some stuff about the People. That was us all right ... Tricksters. If anyone listened in, they'd hear two Indians talking about who was living the greater adventure. Everything became codified. Sometimes we stumped each other with our references but we worked through that."

"You surprised him at the Hartford event, he told me."

"I'd left the Mohawk community of Kanatsiohareke ..."

"I know it. It's not far from Shaleville on the Mohawk River," Jake said.

Grant smiled. "That's right, your turf. The heart of the original Mohawk homeland. Oren told me over the phone about his plans for the Akwesasne deal while you two were at Foxwoods. He told me he hoped you'd be the driver to bring the car back across. I went to Hartford to try to talk him out of it, afraid he'd get caught and the truth would come out about the killing and he'd be charged. But he'd made up his mind. I assume you've caught on about how things go when he makes up his mind. He also told me you figured out who I was despite my disguise."

"You came and went fast but I caught on."

Grant offered the pipe again. "I appreciate how you gifted back what he gifted you for your help. He said you outfoxed him."

"I was worried about him risking the crossing. I'm just glad he pulled it off without consequences."

"I think taking chances on my behalf helped him cope with his guilt in letting me be the fall guy for the killing. We both hoped I'd eventually be dropped as a suspect. But that sure didn't happen."

"Maybe down deep he wanted to be caught," Jake offered.

"Yeah, I had that thought."

Grant lit and passed the pipe again.

"How many different Native communities you visit through all this?" Jake asked.

Grant stared in the distance, counting in his mind. "Seven total, I think. "I just stayed at some a few days. In addition to Kanatsiohareke, I spent time with the Onondaga and Oneida in New York, the Narragansett in Rhode Island, the Nipmuc in Massachusetts, and a Mohawk family in Brooklyn. I'd only been to the big city once before, so I was into sightseeing."

"You get to see a lot of it?"

"Also your turf, right? Yeah, I wandered all over. My last stay, the longest, was with the Anishinabe in Michigan. I was returning there from Brooklyn when I stopped at the church. Oren said you recognized me there as well."

"Right. It was Oren's leaving Thomas 's talk to go outside that convinced me. How much did you confide in the folks you stayed with?"

"Just that my sister was almost raped and the perpetrator had been killed. That was all that mattered to them, not who wielded the knife. You know we different nations bicker a lot, but folks on all the reservations sure united behind me. I was planning to travel to Oklahoma ... I have Seminole relatives both there and in Florida. I heard about Thomas's heart attack and returned. I stayed with a Seneca family in Buffalo. I came to Seneca Hills to dance for Thomas. You know about that dance."

"Once again, sorry for interrupting."

"No matter. Thomas got well. I like to think my dancing helped. That night, I almost told you who I was. I knew I could trust you based on what Oren had told me about you. But then there'd be one more person having to lie to protect me."

"You came to Salamanca when Oren got it in his head to take out Stahl?"

"Right. He told me he was going after him, then would turn himself in. I stalled him by telling him I wanted to be part of it ... be the lookout for him ... and that we'd meet there. I should've known he'd go straight to Stahl's. Luckily we got there in time."

"Some journey you've been on," Jake said. "Quite a story."

"That's for damn sure."

"How'd you pass the time when holed up?"

"I exercised. I worked on my dance moves. I read up on the tribes who put me up. I reflected on my life and what I want to do with it."

"Besides dancing?"

"I want my dancing to be more meaningful. A dream about False Faces led me to that path. I want to join a society and dance as a healer."

"Will you continue Fancy Dancing, too?"

"I've been talking to Chad and Ona about that. They want to sponsor me as a goodwill ambassador for the Alliance. Do dance workshops. Tomorrow, I head to Quebec City to meet with a Huron-Wendat shaman to talk about all this. He used to do the intertribals. Thomas set it up." Grant smiled. "You know, Jake, yours is also quite a story."

"Sure is ... lots to tell."

And, once again, as it was with Thomas – as it was with all his Native friends – Jake wanted to confess all his lies of omission that amounted to one big lie. But he didn't.

Have Faith

ONCE AGAIN, Jake woke up to a knocking. Once again, like at Foxwoods, he opened the door to Ona. And, once again, as she had at the casino, she asked him to go after Chad. This time though the stakes were much higher.

"We went through this with Oren." Her voice cracked. "Now Chad. It's been building in him. I thought I'd talked him out of any kind of confrontation."

Jake collected himself. "Chad? What?"

The early morning sun was rising behind Ona and her face was in the shadows. But there was no question she was fighting back tears. A cool breeze stirred her loose-hanging hair. She wore jeans and a black and red t-shirt with a stencil of all of North America described as *Native Territory*. Jake stood in the door in a blue t-shirt and boxer shorts.

Her words cascaded: "Chad left a note, telling me to 'have faith.' I don't. The other day, I walked in on him making copies of photos of the break-in and of news clippings. When I asked him why make extra copies now, he said he was reorganizing his file on the Sharps to be ready. That means ready now, I'm sure of it. I bet he's planning to confront them. I've been calling him. He must've turned off his phone, just like Oren did when he took off. It's even occurred to me to call Martin Sharp and warn him and his father to prevent something horrible happening. I just looked in Chad's lodge. He bought a new tomahawk recently. It's gone."

"Not more weapons," Jake had the thought, then realized he was saying it out loud.

"I'm going after him. I want you to go with me. Will you?"

"Of course. Come in and make coffee while I get dressed."

Motion seemed to help Ona get a grip. She walked past Jake toward the kitchenette. He went to his bedroom cubicle to dress.

"You know what time he left?" he called out through the partly open door.

"I'm not sure. When I woke up a couple of hours ago, a light was on in his lodge. I shouldn't have gone back to sleep."

"That means he has no more than a couple of hours on us. Was that all the note said ... to have faith?"

"That and 'All will work out,' which makes me think it won't."

"The Sharp United building is in Manhattan, right?"

"I wrote the address down. What do you think ... should I call them to warn them?"

Should she? Jake thought about Chad the college student, the lacrosse player, the poker player, the organizer, the activist, and the leader. He thought about the power broker Andrew Sharp and his sleazy son Martin and the operative Travis Tillman. He thought of his friendship with Chad and Ona. With Ehnita and Thomas. With Grant, Anna, and Oren.

He would be spending hours sitting in a car, agonizing over what Chad might intend to do and what he himself could do to stop it, wondering if he would ever be able to look Ona in the eyes again if something bad happened to Chad because she hadn't given the Sharps warning. Or because she had.

If only Thomas were far enough beyond the point of convalescence to burden him with the dilemma. If only Grant, whose presence reassured everyone, hadn't left for Quebec and could go along and help them decide to make the phone call or not.

All these considerations passed through Jake's mind in a flash – just a few seconds total. And a couple more for the sense of stupefaction that Ona was asking him this question at all.

"No," he said. "Don't call."

~

Jake was at the wheel of the Volvo, very much aware of the distraught, vibrant Ona sitting next to him. They hadn't spoken since leaving the Turtle. He wasn't about to try cutting through the layers of emotion filling the car. He glanced over at her from time to time. Her eyes were fixed on the road ahead, her thoughts beyond the horizon.

After about an hour heading eastward on Route 17, she spoke: "Oh, hell, Jake, should I be this freaked out? Chad drives me crazy with his ways ... dealing with stuff on his own like this, despite all we've been through together."

"Maybe he wants to spare you ... out of love."

The word could mean a lot of things. Jake had no idea how she would take it.

"He's afraid of love because of loved ones lost," she said. "I sure understand that. Some people want to get closer after such a loss. I do. Others opt for avoidance."

That said so much.

"Even so, you two are hopelessly entangled," Jake found himself saying.

Would Ona catch on to the fact that there was an unintentional question in that statement? She went silent, not denying it, and he took that to mean she and Chad had more going on than they let on.

After probably a minute, she finally did admit more: "Entanglement, you sure got that right. But what if you start thinking that someone you love isn't the person you think you love."

"You have to explain that one."

"Okay, here I go. Some of the time before the truth about Oren came out, I actually suspected Chad was the one who'd killed Baines, and that Grant was hiding out to protect Chad because he's so essential to the Alliance. That made the most sense to me.

What does that say about my love? And what does it say about Chad ... that he's so damn distant that I'd expect him to lie to me even about something like that? I even wondered about Salali's death ... that he'd been having an affair with her and she killed herself because he broke it off. Half the time I had these thoughts and half the time I dismissed them as paranoia and jealousy on my part. But how about the way he lied to me about Oren, hiding the truth from me for nine months! That was real!"

"He was trying to protect all of you. In his way. Probably best that you and Ehnita didn't have to worry all that time and fret over what Oren and Grant should do."

"Maybe not his grandmother who helped raise Oren, but I would've been a good schemer myself. Chad should've known that. And maybe someone who would've helped them find a less risky path. Oren almost killed a second person."

Jake didn't want to delve any deeper into all the convoluted happenings. He just said, "Chad's intent was good."

"Even so, my suspicions about him, along with my worries over Grant, were as painful as my worries over Oren would've been. I even fainted at the sweat. You remember?"

Did he ever. "Yes ... can't forget that."

"That night, when I heard Thomas say he saw Chad taking action, doing what is necessary, I visualized his taking action against Baines. I had a vision of him wielding the knife."

"Didn't you ask him outright if he was the one?"

"Of course."

"And ..."

"He scoffed at the idea."

"A mistake, I agree, not to confide in you about Oren. But understandable, right?"

It suddenly felt like he was talking to a sister, playing big brother as he did with Caitlyn ... in other words, not talking to the object of some unrealistic romantic notion.

"What stupid human behavior isn't understandable on some level? And I'll forgive him even if he's again taking stupid action and leaving me out of it."

An end was needed for this conversation. Jake improvised: "Because of all you two share, I suppose you have to do what he told you and have faith."

"Easier said than done."

Indeed, it was. Knowing Chad, Jake didn't have faith himself.

~

If Jake had been in a noir movie from the 1940s, he might be driving a stylish Packard or Studebaker and he would simply pull it up to a curb, allowing him and his femme fatale passenger to jump out and rush into the Sharp United building. But real life in congested Manhattan meant real-life parking issues, as he'd experienced before and after Florida, living out of his home-on-wheels. So here he was strategizing parking as he pulled off the Henry Hudson Parkway into the heart of the city. He didn't want to spend too much time looking for a metered street or parking garage. And he didn't want to risk having the car towed away if he parked illegally. But he wanted the car close for a ready escape.

Before their departure, while in his lodge, Ona had looked up a street view of the Sharp United building on her tablet. He should have had her also search online for a garage. The "have faith" concept ... did it apply to convenient parking? He had the absurd thought in his moment of doubt behind the wheel that web-sleuthing didn't fit with either Sam Spade or Philip Marlowe. He kept his desultory thoughts to himself. Ona didn't need a discussion of parking issues right now or how they related to noir fiction.

The parking part of things worked out at least. Before even reaching the Sharp United building, Jake spotted a garage, located conveniently on the north side of West 57th Street between 10th and 9th Avenues. He pulled up to the garage entrance and, stepping out of the car, he handed the keys to the attendant.

"We shouldn't be long," Jake told him.

"What's that mean?" the attendant asked.

The man then looked over at Ona getting out of the car and brazenly took all of her in.

Ah, the big edgy city, Jake reflected ... here he was, back again.

"That means an hour or less," Jake said without emotion. "If we take longer than that, we'll cough up an extra twenty if we can get the car back promptly."

The man's expression changed to agreeable. Jake suddenly felt big-city-film-noir competent, then felt foolish for the thought.

Ona joined him.

"That way?" she asked, pointing east.

Jake nodded. Clutching her tote, which held her tablet and the Nikon, Ona broke into a semi-jog past other pedestrians. He hurried to follow.

At the corner of 9th Avenue, they had to wait at an endless red light. Ona leaned forward in anticipation. The light finally changed and she launched, stopping suddenly on reaching the corner.

"There it is," she said, pointing to the opposite side of the street.

The Sharp United building rose up mid-block to the east, a giant rectangle of black steel and glass, both materials in the early afternoon sunlight. Ornate gold lettering spelled out the company name over the entranceway.

"Gold can sure look ugly," Jake commented.

"Ugh," Ona muttered.

While they waited to cross 57th Street at another red light, she pulled out her phone and tried Chad yet again.

"Damn him," she said. "Still goes right to voicemail. If he checked his messages, he knows we're on our way to Sharp United. I wonder if that would change anything. Maybe he'd just hurry up with whatever the hell he's doing. If he's not here, we may end up in a meeting without him."

"And say what?"

"I don't know ... that I think both Sharps are vile and I hope they finally get what they deserve? The meeting would probably be convened within seconds."

The light turned green and she again launched into motion.

They hustled along the long crosstown block, reaching the front of the monstrous building. A uniformed man, dressed in a pseudo-military doorman's outfit, didn't offer to open the door like a doorman would but eyed them like a security guard might. Ona looked too intense. Jake took her arm to calm her, roleplaying the male part of a couple. She caught on and looked at him with a strained smile. He directed her to the revolving door situated

247

to one side of the oversized swinging one. They took turns pushing through.

The lobby maintained the stark modernism of the building's exterior, but here by means of unmitigated whiteness – white walls, white columns, a white tile floor, and a long white metal desk blocking easy access. No artwork adorned the big not-so-welcoming room; just security cameras placed high up.

A man in a gray business suit sat behind the desk. A man in a security uniform – blue shirt plus black hat, tie, pants, shoes, holster, and pistol – stood nearby. At least they weren't wearing all white, Jake thought. The lobby was otherwise empty.

Jake and Ona approached the seated man. He looked them up and down as the doorman outside had. Before leaving, after starting the coffee for him, Ona had returned to her lodge to change. She was wearing the same black pantsuit – or one like it – that she'd worn at Foxwoods, a silver and turquoise pendant hanging from her neck. She looked both stunning and businesslike. Although the clothes Jake wore were clean, he hardly looked the Manhattan businessman in brown Dickies pants, beige t-shirt, and a black denim jacket.

"May I help you?"

Ona spoke: "My name is Onatah Makens. This is Jake Jakes. We're here to see Martin Sharp."

The man studied his logbook. Then, looking back and forth at them, said, "He doesn't expect you."

"We work with Chad Catamount who, we understand, is here or on his way here. He may have arrived before us. Or he may be delayed in traffic."

"Please step to the side," the man said and pointed them over next to the security guard.

They obeyed his instructions. He picked up a phone and spoke discreetly into it. Jake contemplated what they should do if Chad hadn't come here, or if they weren't granted access to join him. Give warning to this functionary of a possible risk to Daddy and Son Sharp? Ask to speak to Martin personally via the house system?

The man looked at them with a certain disdain but said, "You can go on up. Forty-first floor."

The security guard broke his stern silence. "Please empty your pockets and open your bags."

They obliged. Jake had nothing but his wallet and cellphone. The guard poked through Ona's tote, pulling out and examining her phone and tablet, then putting them back inside. He reached behind the desk and pulled out first a thermometer gun to check their temperatures, then a hand-held metal detector to scan their clothing. Satisfied, he waved them toward a small side room and the bank of elevators.

Only one went to the top floors, listed as "41-44." Jake pushed the wall-mounted "up" button, then turned to Ona and gave her a comforting smile. She herself didn't look as if she had any smiles left in her.

"Thanks for being here," she managed.

They waited as the elevator descended to them. The doors slid open, revealing a sumptuous chrome interior. They stepped inside. Jake pressed the desired floor. The doors closed.

The seconds passed, red floor numbers ticking by on the digital display. Jake glanced at Ona's profile. The set of her jaw and angle of her cheekbone spoke to him of Native struggles over the centuries.

The elevator eased to a stop. The doors slid open.

This small lobby, done up in shades of gray rather than white, was as stark as the white-themed main one downstairs. A youngish woman, blond hair in a tight bun, sat at a silver-gray desk, empty except for a computer and phone. On the slate gray wall behind her, raised gold lettering announced *Sharp United*. As if there were any doubt. Again, no artwork. The receptionist looked up.

Before she could speak, a familiar voice said, "So much for faith."

Ona turned to look. "Chad," she said. It came out as a sign of relief and reprimand both.

Chad sat in an adjoined waiting area to the right, his colorful Native shirt and headband in bright contrast to a taupe leather couch. She headed for him.

"You're here for the Chad Catamount meeting," the receptionist stated to Jake with no hint of emotion.

"That we are."

"Please have a seat," she told him, again sounding preprogrammed.

Jake headed for the waiting area. Ona was hugging Chad ... or more like clinging onto him.

Chad looked over Ona's shoulder at Jake, raising his eyebrows in resignation. "How can I be mad with a greeting like this?"

They separated. Chad sat back down and Ona joined him on the couch.

"Who should be the mad one?" she asked rhetorically. Then: "You haven't met with anyone yet?" she asked in a near-whisper, her eyes calling attention to a camera mounted in the corner of the room.

Jake took a leather chair opposite.

Chad leaned in and replied quietly, "He's kept me waiting an hour and a half. As could be predicted." He frowned, adding, "You didn't have to come. Really."

"Yes, I did, mystery man ... he who hides the truth."

Jake thought he saw Chad flinch ever so slightly at that.

But he rallied: "You didn't have to bring reinforcements." He glanced at Jake.

"How would I know that?" Ona fired back.

"What does 'have faith' mean to you?"

She replied with another question: "Why didn't you just ask me to come along?"

Chad met her eyes. "We would've ended up analyzing all the consequences ad nauseum ... goddamn flow charts even. You would've had me doubting any course of action. And I had to act."

She glanced at Jake as if to seek confirmation, then back at Chad.

"My first analytical query ... or do I mean psychoanalytical? ... would've been why take a weapon? A Native weapon at that."

That gave him pause. "Nothing gets past you," he said resignedly.

Chad opened his large messenger-style briefcase. It held a notebook and two packages wrapped in brown paper.

"I don't have a weapon on me now, do I?"

"What's in the packages?"

"You'll find out. They got past security, didn't they?"

"The tomahawk must be at the front desk," she said with an edge.

"Just be patient, Ona. I was asked by the receptionist if you were here for the same meeting as I was. I said yes. I could've told them to have you wait downstairs. So please, just bite your tongue and take it all in. I called this meeting and I think you'll be okay with my risk assessment."

"You *are* the Arrow Alliance chairperson ... lead the way," she said in exaggerated compliance.

They fell into a loaded silence. Jake, exhausted after the drive and anticipation, closed his eyes ...

He steps out of the car to see what he struck. A dog ... no, a coydog. A truck is barreling down. He cries out in warning to the passenger still in the car ... Ona ... no, Caitlyn ... "Get out!"

"You asleep, Jake?" Chad's voice interrupted the nightmare. "Ona has run you ragged. Come on. I'm about to make my pitch."

Jake shook off the dream and stood up, falling in behind Chad. He saw that a familiar figure – a muscular man with slick-backed hair, wearing a blue sweater instead of a blue nylon jacket – was walking Ona toward a metal door at the far end of the waiting area. Travis Tillman. Bodyguard. Would-be data thief.

Tillman ushered Ona through the door, then held it for Chad and Jake.

As he passed him, Jake said, "Yo, Travis, I keep running into you."

Tillman showed no reaction at all, except in his flashing eyes. Chad gave a quiet but pointed laugh.

The four of them passed through a short hallway. A security guard, dressed in the same blue and black as the guard in the lobby, sat on a stool next to a second metal door. Tillman opened it and they all stepped through into a big room. Tillman shadowed them.

Martin Sharp was standing at a wall of windows, looking out over the city. Jake had seen this same scene in too many movies: the mogul taking in the cityscape from high above. He wore a mauve sweat suit. His office was neither white nor gray, but black: black tiled walls and flooring; black metal lamps hanging from a black tile ceiling; black security cameras in two corners; a shiny black desk that looked like obsidian; a black leather inclining desk chair with wheels, and, opposite the desk, three black steel chairs with black leather cushions. The desk held a laptop – black of course – and neat stacks of brochures, magazines, and newspapers. The only other item on it was a pipe-tomahawk, similar in design to the one with which Jake, Oren, and Chad had smoked *kinnikinnick* at the Turtle.

"Hello, Martin," Chad said.

Sharp turned from the window. His face was shiny with sweat. "Chad Catamount and motley others," he said, sounding bored.

"This is Ona and Jake. They decided at the last minute to sit in on our meeting."

Sharp scowled. "I know who they are. And you know who my man Tillman is, so let's get on with it. What the hell do you want? To split open my head?" He looked at the pipe-tomahawk.

"Not my style. Nor is punching anyone anymore. You?"

"I'd like to land a good one." Sharp said.

Chad smiled ever so slightly. "Point taken."

Sharp moved from the window toward his desk. He walked slowly, making them wait that much longer. With his sweats and baby face, he still looked a college student to Jake. And Chad, standing opposite Sharp, now did so as well.

"Everybody, sit down," Sharp instructed. "I need to get off my feet. I just walked miles on my treadmill."

He sat down in his desk chair. Jake waited till Chad and Ona had each chosen a seat, then took the remaining one. Tillman remained standing behind them.

Sharp made a show of gathering his thoughts, then asked, "So whattya want, Catamount?"

"I requested your father's presence, too."

Sharp's eyes narrowed as they had outside the chapel at Kenton when Jake had fired questions at him.

"He has other business to tend to. What is it, Catamount? Spit it out."

Chad didn't spit it out. His delivery was relaxed, his tone neutral: "Martin, you and I have had personal issues, no question. I'm putting them aside to negotiate, as I hope you will. I speak as a Native person who cares about issues beyond you and me. Before coming to you, I asked myself what really matters here. Not any lingering personal feud ... not one-upmanship. Rather, this is about a centuries-old struggle for fairness. That being said, I'll use whatever legal means we have to achieve that fairness."

He paused. Sharp gave an ambiguous grunt.

Chad continued: "I'm here to discuss Sharp United's History Fun World. It could be a worthwhile project but not as originally presented. I won't get into possible reasons you've shaped it with such a glaring omission ... that of the critical role of Native Americans in U.S. history. I just want to point out that that this omission negates your stated purpose of fully enlightening people. Even if the project were to be a financial success, I think it's to your advantage to give a broader view to spare Sharp United criticism. But I won't try to reason you out of your choices. Instead, I'll barter for them."

Sharp looked at him long and hard. "And how's that, Catamount?"

"We want a Native American historian on your History Fun World team. We want him to help you create a park that includes the Native American story and those of other minority groups, as a replacement for one of the six parks you've listed ... Destiny Park. It can be called something like Diversity Park. I have suggestions for your hire, but you can headhunt your own employee as long as he or she has proper credentials and is a person of color. That's what I want ... that's what we want. Here's what you might very well want ... our silence." Chad opened his briefcase and pulled out the two folders, placing them on Sharp's desk. He continued: "In these you'll find photos and photocopies. Those in one folder serve as proof that your man, Travis Tillman, broke into the Arrow Alliance headquarters and tried to steal computer information. It might've been a good idea for us to let Tillman keep the downloaded files so you could have marveled at our transparency. And maybe even learned from it. But then again, it's rewarding in itself to thwart felony breaking and entering. Those in the second folder show what your employee's fellow felon, Jonas Stahl, was all about. He's already a public figure, charged with all kinds of vile things. I doubt you want Sharp United associated with him in any way."

Jake glanced over at Tillman, who remained frozen in place. Sharp, however, shifted around in his seat, biting his lip. He didn't pick up the folders.

"Blackmail, eh Catamount?" he said.

"I prefer thinking about it as a poker move," Chad replied softly. "At the end of the game, the hands we played are forgotten.

Once again, I'm doing you a favor. It's a win-win for you. We don't press charges for a break-in, and your theme park gets a much better response from the academics and from its visitors as well, given the public's growing fascination with Native America."

Sharp's eyes couldn't be any narrower and still be considered open. He again looked at Tillman – with the same disdain, it seemed, as he had for the others in the room.

He picked up the pipe-tomahawk and asked. "What the hell is this about?"

"It's a gift," Chad said. "It's symbolic. We bury the hatchet."

Sharp gave a sarcastic laugh. "Good one."

"It's also a pipe. I was hoping for the additional symbolism of smoking a peace pipe." Chad smiled. "Nothing exotic. Just some tobacco."

Sharp threw his hands up. "Okay, enough. Enough of this bullshit. You've laid down your cards. You can go now. You'll hear from Sharp United."

"When?"

"When we make a decision. Now go. I want to finish my workout."

Sharp put down the pipe-tomahawk, hit a button under his desk, and stood up. Part of the wall to Jake's left slid open. Through the now-exposed doorway, Jake could see exercise equipment in the adjoining room. Sharp, without looking at any of them, walked around the desk and passed on through.

The wall in the adjoining room was mirrored floor to ceiling. Jake caught a glimpse of a second figure, also in mauve sweats. A reflection. But it seemed like a refection in a funhouse mirror. At first, he saw it as a bloated version of Martin Sharp, except it wore a yellowish hat. Or rather a wig.

Andrew Sharp.

The younger Sharp extended his right hand, apparently pressing another button. The door closed behind him.

"You heard him," Tillman said. "Out."

Jake was the last to leave. As he stepped through the door, Tillman turned to him and said, "I hope we get the chance to meet again. Just you and me."

"Aww, touching," Jake replied, now feeling like a college student himself.

~

On the long elevator ride down from the 41st floor, Jake offered to drive alone on the return trip so that Chad and Ona could ride together. He figured they had lots to sort out. Chad accepted his offer, asking him to share a meal before leaving. Ona seconded that idea. But Jake declined, saying he would eat something on the road.

Ona said, "We'll walk you to my car."

Jake decided not to mention Andrew Sharp's presence in the exercise room – at least not yet – the elder Sharp no doubt monitoring the meeting via the cameras or a hidden microphone. Jake didn't want to provoke an extreme reaction from Chad, who seemed to have missed the mirrored image. Better to have some distance from all this.

Outside, pavement again under his feet, Jake thought about past moments on city streets. They felt far in the past, even though it seemed as if he'd never left Manhattan. The city had that effect, every other place seeming so distant when one is here.

He noticed a pigeon, flying toward a building's windowsill, where another pigeon was perched. What would they shapeshift into? Rats, maybe, another predominant wild animal species here. Pigeons after all were something called "fly rats." Or maybe other predominant birds, the invasive starlings and sparrows. Or maybe those who were more likely to soar high and frequent parks, birds of prey like hawks. Or maybe parakeets to get regular meals inside people's homes.

At the parking garage's booth, when Jake started to settle up with the cashier, Chad reached in and paid. The same attendant as before, on seeing them, set off to retrieve the car from inside the building. He soon pulled through the exit to one side of the driveway, got out, turned over the keys to Jake, who tipped him a twenty even though it hadn't been quite an hour. The attendant gave him what sounded like a relatively sincere "Thanks." Jake smiled inwardly at the price he'd paid for big city politeness.

Chad placed his briefcase on the car's hood, opened it, and removed one of the two packages.

He turned to Ona. "Guess what arrived yesterday."

"Our flags," she said.

"I was going to open the packages with you today. When I made up my mind to come here, I brought them along with the idea of opening them in front of the Sharps to communicate our longterm commitment to what we're all about, but decided not to bother after Sharp Junior so readily dismissed the concept of a peace pipe."

Chad tore the first package open and pulled out a piece of folded fabric. He unfurled it and held it up. It was a flag about two by three feet. It had the same design as the Erie-Mingo sign at the Turtle: a deep red background, the tribal name written in black, and two crossed arrows inside a double-lined hoop.

He handed the flag to Ona, reached in the briefcase and removed and opened the second package, revealing a second flag that he unfurled. This larger one, three by five feet, had the same design as the Turtle's Arrow Alliance sign, with lettering and four connected circles in black over dark green. He looked at Ona expectantly.

"They're beautiful," she said.

Chad went to her and hugged her. She'd lost her recent pallor, her cheeks now flushed.

He turned to Jake, saying, "Ona lined up the Tlingit weaver in British Columbia, renowned for her Chilkat blankets. These are the first flags she's ever made."

"Beautiful," Ona repeated.

Chad folded them and handed them to her. "You're the flag-keeper."

In this moment, things felt right to Jake, as if all would work out for Chad and Ona and his other Native American friends. The Arrow Alliance and the Erie-Mingo Nation would thrive, he had confidence, despite the Sharp United father-son team and their anti-Native ploys.

Things would work out for himself, too, he thought. His first case had started in New York City and this one had ended here. In the course of that full circle, he'd been further healed from past missteps.

With the emotional letting go, Jake longed to see his sister and share with her all he'd experienced ... in person, not just in fragmented bits of phone conversations. It was high time to be there for her and do some work on her house as he'd promised.

And they could take that hoped-for trip out West. He would always have a second home in Seneca Hills and a second family. It was now time to return to his primary home and the closest person on the planet to him ... Caitlyn.

Construction at the Arrow Alliance was near completion. Jake wouldn't be needed as before. He would give notice, then head back to Shaleville. He could return to Seneca Hills with Caitlyn for the Solstice Gathering and introduce all his new friends to her.

He took a deep breath. Right now, even New York City air seemed clean and life-sustaining.

Summer Solstice

"SEE WHAT I MEAN?" Jake said.

From the Overlook he and Caitlyn gazed at the scene below. Along the walkway around the Turtle, wooden poles held the flags of all Arrow Alliance member nations, including that of the Erie-Mingo that Chad had first shown Ona and Jake in Manhattan. The Alliance flag Jake Chad had also shown them that day was mounted above all the others, next to the Turtle's head. The stirring of the flags in the wind made the building appear alive, like it might lurch forward in a reptilian gait. And the surrounding grounds pulsed with activity. Visitors – Native and non-Native alike – wandered about on this intensely bright June day with just enough of a breeze to counter the heat.

In the cleared field to its southeast, on the far side of the Turtle's head, stood the open-sided amphitheater, log posts supporting a hexagon roof. Talks and workshops – the current one about flint-knapping for kids – had been held all morning. Behind the amphitheater a sizeable tent served as a backstage area. Beyond the backstage tent, poles supported a giant canopy under which artisans and vendors had set up tables. Parked farther to the southeast, along the south branch of the driveway, were the food concession vehicles. Directly to the east, partly blocked from their view by the Turtle, the area between the two driveway branches had been paved over for public parking. Seneca youth volunteers directed cars to open spots. Beyond the Turtle's tail, at the edge of the field flanking the driveway's north branch, were rows of portable toilets, and beyond them, camping sites.

On this Sunday, the second day of the Solstice Gathering, as decided back in May, Arrow had sponsored a powwow open to the public. The day before, representatives from member nations had taken meetings. Jake and Caitlyn had arrived in Seneca Hills on Thursday and they'd both helped with setting up. They were camping in the north field next to the van, outfitted for a cross-continental trip. They'd just completed the first leg of their journey – Shaleville to Seneca Hills – and, after the gathering, they would push on westward to visit Caitlyn's father in Alaska. He expected them. They would then make their way southward back into the United States and head eastward by way of Oklahoma City, where they hoped to see their mother. Grace had fallen out of touch with them yet again, despite expressing enthusiasm about their visit a few weeks earlier.

The day before, at Chad's invitation, Jake and Caitlyn had attended the Grand Council inside the completed Turtle's shell and had experienced an invocation by Thomas and a Navajo shaman by the name of Hastin Daagi. They'd heard talks by Chad and Ona, summarizing the first year of the Arrow Alliance and its plans for the future. And they'd heard the give and take of ideas among the tribal representatives of member nations.

"Yeah, I sure do see what you mean," Caitlyn responded. "It's grand all right, like a panorama of history." She extended her arms as if to hug the entire vista, then added, "My brother's recent history, too."

"Lots of memories ... and now new ones with you."

Caitlyn squeezed his arm. "Shared memories. Keep them coming."

They stood in silence, absorbing the moment.

Jake broke the spell: "Already a decent turnout."

"I know you were worried," Caitlyn said. "I've been counting cars myself. I'm just a tourist but I sure feel connected. Weird. All because of a lab test."

To provide data for her term paper, Caitlyn had sent off the DNA samples of herself, Jake, her father, and their mother. On Caitlyn's instructions and a promised gift of a check, Grace had finally submitted a saliva sample. That gave them some hope that she would be in a good enough psychological place to spend time with her kids.

From the tests Jake had learned that he wasn't half-Native American, rather just an eighth. Caitlyn's results, despite her having a different father, also showed an eighth, indicating that the indigenous lineage was through a great-grandparent of their mother. A specific tribe couldn't be identified through DNA, but the test's geographical indicators were consistent with the fact that Grace had been born and raised until age fifteen in Millville, New Jersey, not far from Bridgeton, the location of the state-recognized Nanticoke Lenni-Lenape Tribal Nation headquarters, making a Lenape a likely candidate as an ancestor. In addition to their shared Native ancestry, Jake and Caitlyn both had what was most likely British and French DNA through their mother. Jake's unknown father didn't seem to be Sicilian – the other candidate cited as his possible father by his mother – but seemingly part Germanic and part Slavic. Jake and Caitlyn had racked their brains, trying to remember some other "sperm donor" in that period of their mother's life. In any case, they both were indeed mutts, reflecting centuries of people on the move, interacting in Europe and North America.

Ehnita had dropped the Maybe-Mohawk moniker and now was calling him Jake Lenape or Jake Delaware. The alternate English name Delaware had been given by European settlers to the river at the heart of Lenni Lenape ancestral lands, draining parts of New York, New Jersey, Pennsylvania, Maryland, and Delaware, and had been passed on to the tribe. Chad called him Jake Algonquian after the language family of the Lenape, teasing him because, through much of their history, Iroquoian- and Algonquian-speaking peoples had been traditional enemies. Thomas, on hearing the news, had come up with Jake Real People as a moniker since in Algonquian Lenape meant "people" and Lenni meant "real" or "true."

Jake had known how welcome his Arrow friends would make Caitlyn feel. But he didn't know how Oren would receive her. Before leaving Seneca Hills for Shaleville, Jake had visited him a second time and their interaction had again been awkward, even with Grant and Anna present. But Oren had seemed much more at peace on Jake's and Caitlyn's visit on Friday. The DA had agreed to his plea bargain of manslaughter, the final sentencing to come soon. Caitlyn had been her warm self, asking question after question as she'd done when Jake and Oren had visited Shaleville on their way to Akwesasne. Oren, again apparently charmed by her, had opened up about his daily life in jail. He'd also talked about his plans for the future: working for Arrow, entering both archery and dance competitions, and starting a family with Anna. He'd been exercising and looked fit.

Chad seemed in a positive place as well. Sharp United had released a statement that, because of watershed and other environmental issues, it was cancelling History Fun World in Pennsylvania and investigating other potential sites before recommitting to the project. As a gesture toward ongoing historical education, as the press release stated, Sharp United had decided to make another donation to Kenton College's History Department. Andrew Sharp and chip-off-the-old-block Martin had made a brief appearance at the college's June reunion weekend to bestow the second check of one million. Had this press event been orchestrated by Martin or his father to save face in his feud with Chad, buried hatchet or not? Did this mean no History Fun World at all? That seemed to be the case as of now. The younger Sharp was presently in Florida, overseeing the building of a new resort called Sharp Beach Town. Chad had joked that this new enterprise was just a "town" and not a "world." It had also been rumored that Sharp senior was going into politics.

"A laughable but all-too-scary concept," Chad had said about that.

He'd also informed Jake that Rhonda Fields of WROC, Rochester, had called to inquire about the Solstice Gathering and would be covering it for their "Life" segments, which included stories on multicultural events in western New York. On her call to inquire about the powwow, she'd asked about Jake. Chad had reported to her that he'd learned he was part Lenape and was taking a leave of absence from Arrow to travel with his sister through Native America.

Chad had advised Jake to be careful not to reveal anything about a vendetta with the Sharps and the fact that he'd put Jake up to his Kenton encounter with Martin. He'd also told him not to mention that Grant Guyasuta was currently on staff, hopefully to avoid a reference to the last powwow and anything about Oren. WGRZ out of Buffalo would also be covering the event. Theirs supposedly would also be a lifestyle piece. Print media would be out and about, Chad had warned, undoubtedly inquiring about the larger story of Arrow's goals and past problems. Be wary, he'd advised Jake, as had Ona.

After one last panoramic scan on both their parts, Jake led Caitlyn away from the Overlook through the woods to see Grant's carved False Face tree and Oren's target tree, the two arrows still embedded. As always, she asked a lot of questions and Jake recounted how these woods had been a refuge for himself as well as for both Grant, the False Face Dancer, and Oren, the hunter. Caitlyn had listened spellbound.

They returned to the hillside pathway and followed it downward to the Alliance grounds. Caitlyn asked to walk by the lodges again before heading for the Turtle and they detoured along the walkway past the seven domed structures. The Navajo shaman Hastin Daagi was staying in Jake's former lodge. On Friday, it still had been empty and Chad had taken them inside so that Caitlyn could see where her brother had lived. He'd been apologetic about offering up the three unoccupied lodges to special guests for the weekend and not keeping one for Jake and his sister. Both had assured him that camping under the stars on these lands was perfect, a great way to start their trip.

Jake checked the time on his cellphone – an hour plus until the dancing. They reached the Turtle and entered the mouth. Ehnita was at her desk in the outer office that now served as the official welcome area for visitors.

"*Kwekwe*," she said with a smile. "I have to learn the Lenape greeting, too."

"*Hè*," Caitlyn said proudly. "I found that online."

"That's an easy one." Ehnita said, turning to Jake. "Your sister's doing her homework. Are you?"

"She's the academic in the family."

"Well, don't be a slacker. Hit the books."

"I've been schooling him," Caitlyn said.

"That she has," Jake said. "I've already learned the Manhattoe might have been a Lenape subtribe."

"My brother claims that's why he ended up on the streets of Manhattan," Caitlyn added.

"Maybe we should call him Jake Manhattoe," Ehnita said.

"And we've also been checking out the different Lenape groups in different states and in Canada," Caitlyn added.

"History has dispersed the Lenape as it has the Haudenosaunee. Anyone tell you about the Munsee Lenape community at Grand River?"

"I had no idea," Jake replied.

"I saw you talking to some folks from the Delaware Nation of Oklahoma yesterday. Your mother's in Oklahoma, right?"

They were hoping that was still the case, Jake thought.

Caitlyn spoke: "Yes, we talked to them and plan to stop at their table."

Ehnita gave a thoughtful smile. "Wonderful. Remember, you both also belong where you are right now. You're part of the Arrow family."

Some more visitors arrived and headed toward her desk. Jake and Caitlyn started to move on.

"Don't forget about the brunch at our house tomorrow," Ehnita advised.

"I can't wait," Caitlyn said.

"Don't eat any corn soup today. Wait for my recipe."

"We sure will," Jake said.

He and Caitlyn headed for the door to the Turtle's neck. They crossed into the hallway and continued past the office doors, all of them closed and locked. Chad had shown Caitlyn the offices the day before, and she now recited which door was which as she passed them, reminding herself.

They entered the council room. The large domed space was alive with people. Members of various tribes sat at tables offering information; visitors milled about. Colorful Native artwork, representative and abstract both, adorned the walls. Arrow had requested pieces from all the member tribes.

Ona sat at the first table to the right of the door. On the table in front of her were brochures about both the Arrow Alliance and the Erie-Mingo Nation. She was talking to a family of seemingly non-Native parents and two teenagers. Looking radiant, she wore a white buckskin dress with multicolored beadwork trim. Silver combs held back her black hair. She glanced up and smiled at Jake and Caitlyn, then went back to explaining the history of the Erie and Mingo. Jake flashed on that day she'd taken him on his first walk to Turtle Overlook and had informed him of the same. Behind her, mounted on the wall, was a glass case with photos of the various stages of construction of the Turtle and outbuildings, most of them taken by Jake.

Jake and Caitlyn circled the big room along the different tables. Caitlyn stopped at many of them, collecting brochures. They spent the longest time talking to a representative of the Delaware Nation of Oklahoma and what they might visit in and around Anadarko.

Outside again, they walked past the amphitheater that was now emptying of children and parents after the flint-knapping workshop. They could see through an opening between rows of seats that Roof and others from Don Tarbell's crew were sweeping the clay floor for the dancing to come. Jake and Caitlyn continued on to the food concessions and ordered some frybread.

They ate standing up, then proceeded along the driveway's south branch to an area of open field. Four men and two women – including Chad, Grant, Will Thatcher, and one of the Seneca from Mark Tama's crew, along with Anna and a young Native woman Jake didn't know – had formed a loose circle and tossed a lacrosse ball among them. After a catch and a toss to Grant, Chad greeted them with a wave. Jake had never seen him play. The legendary lacrosse player, who had given up his college and a possible professional career in the sport, flipped and sliced the netted stick through the air as if waving a two-handed conductor's baton. Grant moved athletically but his stick motion wasn't as smooth as Chad's. The ball he tossed went to Anna, who caught it with ease. She made a mercifully slow throw to Will, who missed it, stabbing awkwardly with his stick. After running to retrieve it, he made a wild throw to the other young woman, who couldn't help but laugh at him. Grant, after one more catch and toss, left the circle. Anna joined him. They approached Jake and Caitlyn.

"The dancing starts soon," Grant said, keyed up. "Thomas and Hastin will do the benediction, then there's a welcoming dance. I've worked up a new one, so don't miss it. Then there'll be some social dancing followed by the competitions ... Fancy

Dancing last." He looked at Caitlyn. "You'll join in on the social dancing, won't you?"

"Of course," Caitlyn said.

Anna looked back and forth at Caitlyn and Jake. "Sit in the front. I'll find you."

"And you promised dinner afterwards," Grant said to Caitlyn. "You bet."

Grant smiled and he and Anna headed toward his lodge.

Another familiar face approached Jake and Caitlyn. Rhonda Fields. She wore slacks and a cotton tunic, tablet in hand. She gave a warm, knowing smile, her hazel eyes smiling as well.

"Hello, Jake Jakes," she said.

"Great to see you again. Meet my sister Caitlyn. Caitlyn, meet Rhonda Fields, producer for WROC out of Rochester. She produced the Kenton segment."

Both started to extend their hands but pulled them back and laughed off the pre-pandemic ingrained custom. Instead, they nodded at each other.

Caitlyn said, "You made my brother look good."

Jake let out a laugh. "I took some ribbing by the folks around here but all for the better. Thanks for caring about Native issues. And thanks for covering this event."

With another knowing smile, Rhonda said, "I'm a concerned citizen, too. Chad Catamount told me you found out that you're part Lenape." She looked from one to the other. "I'd like to interview both of you."

"Have you scheduled interviews with any of the Alliance folks yet?" Jake asked.

"I've lined up Catamount, Onatah Makens, Thomas Dion'dot, and Ehnita Feather. You, Jake, an employee here, and both of you with an upstate New York background, might have an interesting view of things. Everyone I talk to will get just a sound bite in this piece. Without a reporter on this assignment, I'll be off-camera asking the questions. We'll add a narrative in the studio, setting up each bit. So what do you think? Are you willing and able?"

Caitlyn replied first: "I'd be happy to say something."

"That'd be great," Rhonda told her. "I'll find you after the dancing, okay? Darren's on B-roll now."

She pointed toward the driveway. The bearded cameraman Jake remembered from Kenton was videotaping people walking from the parking lot toward the amphitheater, concessions, and the Turtle.

Rhonda turned back to Jake. "What about you?"

He had a lot of good points to make about the Alliance but he didn't want to lie about what had led him Seneca Hills. "Caitlyn can speak for both of us on camera. Why don't you and I talk over dinner? Maybe I can give you some context. Have you been to the Jack and Jill Diner?"

"No. I spotted it though. Darren loves the local taverns and has his eye on the Woodbine. I prefer diners."

"Meet at seven-thirty? At the Turtle welcome area? Then we can head over."

Rhonda gave her bright smile, although this time it came across a little less professional. "See you there. The welcome area. Seven-thirty."

She moved off. Jake's eyes followed her. Another talented, attractive woman with a calling. He didn't want to declare Ona-like, but like Ona she seemed a match for any and all. Spoken for? She wore no rings.

Caitlyn must have read his mind. "Both of us with dinner dates ... uh-oh, could be trouble."

"I'd say," Jake played along. "Probably a good thing we're leaving town tomorrow."

They entered the canopied area and wandered about the artisans' tables. Caitlyn bought a beaded barrette for herself along with two carved soapstone turtles made by an Oneida sculptor – gifts for her father and their mother.

On the far side of the tent, Jake saw familiar faces from the diner, those of Big Ben and his wife Little Nell, the traveling recreational bowler. It was good to see some of the local folks participating. Jake wondered if any at all would have come out – even good-natured Ben and Nell – if the Baines killing hadn't been resolved.

Jake and Caitlyn moved out from under the canopy. Near the food concessions, Thomas and a Native woman Jake didn't recognize had stood up from a picnic table. He assumed it must be Lily Feather, who, he'd been told, had been staying with Thomas and Ehnita while recovering from an illness. Thomas waved them over. He wore a fringed tan suede shirt. The woman wore jeans and a fringed blouse.

"Jake, Caitlyn," he said, "this is Lily Feather, Ehnita's daughter and Oren's mother."

The Mohawk woman gave a slight nod. Like her mother and son, she was small-framed. She looked haggard, aged beyond her years, with deep lines and bags under her eyes. Ehnita, for all her years, projected more vitality. But Lily's fine features were evident, and Jake could see both Ehnita and Oren in them.

"Jake's a close friend of Oren's," Thomas told her.

His color was good and he seemed as vigorous as he'd been before the heart attack. He was on medications, Jake knew, but the weakened and bedridden version of the shaman seemed a distant memory.

"We saw Oren on Friday," Jake said.

Lily nodded again.

Thomas picked up on that. "He's holding up well and so are his mother and grandmother." He put his arm around Lily and gave her an encouraging squeeze. "Lily, like her mother, is a beautiful *wathonwisas*. That's Iroquoian for a woman who sways like a tree in the wind."

Jake noticed that Lily's earrings of liquid silver swayed as she moved her head, adding to the effect of Thomas's words.

Thomas turned to Caitlyn. "You're also a *wathonwisas*. Jake's a lucky brother."

"And I'm a lucky sister," Caitlyn said, smiling at all of them.

Thomas had a healing effect on all around him, as did Ehnita, with her comparable calm, wise presence, and hopefully they were helping heal the morose Lily. Oren had described her to Jake as a heavy drinker and she sure looked it. Jake wondered if he and Caitlyn could similarly help heal their mother after all this time. Maybe bring her to the Turtle?

"Lily, why don't you sit with my friends ... Oren's friends. I have to join Hastin and take our assigned seats. Ehnita, too."

Lily nodded again, this time managing a slight smile.

The amphitheater was filling up. Jake led Caitlyn and Lily along a passageway leading through the circular rows of seats. They found some empty ones in the second row and climbed up to them. Caitlyn sat in the middle between Jake and Lily. Jake heard his sister asking Lily about Akwesasne and Oren. She offered just the right amount of concern, he thought. A good trait for a teacher.

Jake had worked on the open-sided structure with the hexagon roof. The clay, circular floor had a diameter of forty-eight feet. The seats, eight rows deep, were redwood. A second passageway interrupted the rows, this one for performers. It led to the backstage tent. The bottom row had two other open areas – one now being used for the Host Drum; the other, opposite, for the judges' table.

The participants had started entering. Six men sat down in folding chairs around the large communal wood-and-hide drum. They represented the Six Nations of the Grand River in Ontario. Don Tarbell was the lead singer. Four judges sat at the table opposite – three men and one woman. Thomas had suggested that the judges represent the Four Directions. Ona and Chad had invited a Seneca to represent the East; a Creek, the South; a Ute, the West; and a Chippewa, the North.

The judges entered and took their seats. Ona, Ehnita, Thomas, and the craggy-faced Navajo elder Hastin Daagi sat in the front row near them. Also sitting in the front row were members of the press, including Rhonda and Darren.

The drummers began pounding the communal drum with drumsticks also made from wood and hide. Don broke into song. A second man soon joined in, followed by all the other drummers, creating a vocal collage. The Grand Entry had started. Chad led the way into the amphitheater. Some thirty dancers followed him – children and adults – lined up by height, shortest to tallest.

Chad paraded by. He now wore a plain tan buckskin shirt – the same color as Thomas's – and black jeans. He carried an Eagle Staff – a rod wrapped in leather with dangling eagle feathers – a symbol of nationhood used by many tribes.

The dancers, circling the clay floor, looked striking in their multicolored costumes of leather, cloth, fur, feather, shells, and beads. Jake recognized just Anna and Grant – Anna walked in the middle of the procession, and Grant to the rear. Anna wore orange, yellow, and white. Grant stood out because of a red-and-black shawl blanket over his shoulders, torn blue jeans, and mismatching moccasins.

Chad led the procession out of the amphitheater toward the backstage tent. He reappeared without staff and walked to the center of the floor, holding a cordless microphone.

"Welcome, friends of all nations," came his words, amplified from speakers mounted beneath the roof. "Welcome to the Arrow Alliance's home. We give thanks to our Mother, the Earth, which sustains us. Today, we will have a traditional prayer-song from one of the Navajo Ways, performed by our Diné friend from Arizona, Hastin Daagi. Thomas Dion'dot, the Arrow Alliance's shaman, a Seneca from Salamanca, will give the translation."

The tall, lean Hastin Daagi – dressed in a plain brown cotton headband, a collarless black velvet shirt, and black cotton trousers – stood up and moved to the center of the clay floor. Chad handed him the microphone. Thomas, who had donned his single-feathered Seneca headdress, also stood up. He swung by the judges' table for a microphone, then joined Chad and Hastin.

Hastin spoke in Athapascan. As his voice intoned in his Native tongue, Thomas translated each sentence: "Let evil be given the wink. Let all the forces of evil be driven away in hordes. Let evil sail off like a feather. Let evil be worn down. Let all the weapons of evil move away from me."

Hastin passed the microphone back to Chad, then returned to his seat. Thomas followed, returning his microphone to the judges' table.

"Thank you, Hastin and Thomas, for the blessing," Chad said. "The Arrow Alliance is growing for the good of all Native peoples and their friends. We've drawn on the wisdom of our ancestors in the hope of achieving unity of all peoples. But as individuals, let's not take ourselves too seriously. Let's start the dancing with laughter!"

On "laughter," Don let out a cry and pounded the drum. The others encircling it joined in. Their drumming was more disjointed this time and their singing, cacophonous. Chad quickly hurried to his seat.

Grant, the blanket still around him, suddenly appeared, running backwards. He feigned dizziness, then tumbled to the ground.

"His Clown Dance!" Jake said to Caitlyn.

Grant rolled into a backwards somersault and, leaving the blanket on the clay floor, stood up, revealing a patchwork shirt, made from clashing pieces of cloth. It hung loosely to his tattered jeans. He staggered about, jerking and twitching his arms, legs, and head to the erratic drumbeats. He unexpectedly did a nimble back flip but, on landing, staggered again. The crowd applauded.

The drumbeat got syncopated, finding a groove. Grant now mimicked popular dances, such as Breaking, the Moonwalk, and the Texas Two-Step. He kept getting tangled in his own feet and falling down, only to leap up and try again. The crowd loved it. He danced spasmodically backwards all the way out of the amphitheater. Jake looked at Thomas, Ehnita, and Ona; they all wore big smiles.

The social dancing followed. As she'd said she would, Anna located Jake and Caitlyn and summoned them along with Lily into the big circle that moved around the amphitheater. She crossed her hands and had Jake cross his, then clasped them. Grant joined them and did the same with Caitlyn. Hastin paired up with Ehnita, Thomas with Lily. Other hosts invited audience members to join them. The big circle moved around the floor twice. The goodwill seemed contagious, even among those guests who stayed in their seats. The social dancing ended in a flurry of drumming, and hosts and guests found their seats.

The competitive dancing now began. Jake knew that Chad and Ona had agonized on what dances to include and had settled on the following lineup: Tiny Tot Dance for small children; Ladies' Jingle Dress Dance, one for adolescents and one for adults; Ladies' Shawl Dance for all ages; Men's Traditional (or Northern Traditional) Dance, one for adolescents and one for adults; Straight (or Southern Traditional) Dance for all ages; and Fancy Dance, one for adolescents and one for adults. In this intertribal event, given its relatively small size and its purpose of fostering tribal unity, the only prizes offered were items donated by artisans – and of course bragging rights.

The dancing and award ceremonies lasted a good part of the afternoon. Spectators came and went, some taking breaks between the different competitions to buy food or use the Porta-Johns. Jake and Caitlyn stayed for all of it, as did Chad, Thomas, Ehnita, Ona, Hastin, Rhonda, and Darren.

What an entrancing array of shapes, colors, and movement the afternoon presented. On seeing feathers and garments swirling and bodies contorting like animals, Jake more than once flashed on his shapeshifter dreams. But then he would hone in again on dance techniques. The dancers' moves, from head to feet, were keyed not just to rhythm but also to the singers' pitch, tones, melodies, and words.

Jake and Caitlyn made a game out of guessing the winners. They both picked the little boy who excelled in the Tiny Tot Dance, a Seminole who seemed a mini-Grant, and he won. They also agreed that a Potawatomi teenager had been the best in the Ladies' Jingle Dress Dance for adolescents; so did the judges, although neither Jake or Caitlyn guessed the adult winner, a Creek. They both picked Anna to win the Shawl Dance; she was the runner-up, a Cherokee woman taking the prize. Neither of them chose the winners of the two Men's Traditional Dances, an Oneida teenager and a Sioux adult. Caitlyn thought a middle-aged Apache had been the best in the Straight Dance; Jake bet on a Seneca. The Apache won. Neither picked the winner of the Fancy Dance for adolescents, even though it was a Munsee Lenape from the Grand River reserve who won.

Both Jake and Caitlyn were of one mind about the dancer in green and white as the winner of the Fancy Dance. With his great athleticism yet remarkable subtlety, Grant stood out as the best. Many of the spectators apparently thought so, too. Jake took his eyes off Grant long enough to see how fixated they were by his dramatic moves. The intensity of the applause after his performance further confirmed their appreciation.

The day before, Thomas had told Jake and Caitlyn that Grant was dedicating this dance to Oren. Its meaning: winning out over life's unrelenting challenges.

When Grant was receiving the top prize – a figurine similar to the one Jake had purchased in Florida for Caitlyn – Jake overheard a middle-aged man to his right tell the woman accompanying him, "That's Grant Guyasuta. He's a famous Fancy Dancer. He's the one everyone was looking for before they figured out who really killed that Buffalo cop."

"Ex-cop," the woman corrected him.

Jake closed his ears to any other snatches of conversation. Enough sleuthing for a while. This was Caitlyn time.

EPILOGUE

"Thanks, my father, my mother. This day, following your road, yonder with prayers, I will make my road stretch forth."
– from a Zuni chant

"YOU SURE ABOUT THIS?" Caitlyn asked Jake.

"It'll be okay."

She wasn't convinced. "Maybe you've done this kind of thing, Mr. Detective, but I haven't."

"And I pulled it off."

"Still ..."

"No one can see us," Jake told her.

"Toothless might check on things."

She was referring to the manager of the trailer park, a man probably in his forties who looked an unhealthy sixty with his blotchy skin, sunken cheeks, and no teeth. From meth, Jake guessed. Given his own past with that nasty drug, he was relieved Toothless wasn't his doppelganger.

"Probably too busy shooting up," he said.

Under the big Oklahoma sky, just inside Oklahoma City's eastern limits, Jake and Caitlyn were crouched behind an abandoned vehicle, looking at a rundown trailer separated from the rest of the trailer park by junked cars. Less than ten minutes ago, they'd pulled the van off the paved road onto a dusty dirt one, parked it next to a stand of trees, crossed a dried-up streambed, and scaled a chainlink fence at a spot where razor wire had previously been cut away and not repaired. They'd moved from one junked car to another to reach one with a view of the white trailer with blue trim.

"We could leave a note for mom with Toothless and get a motel," Caitlyn said.

"And probably be right here the same time tomorrow, agonizing again."

"Or just leave a note on the trailer, so less risk?"

She was manifesting a childhood nervous tic, blinking her eyes hard.

"We've come this far," he said gently. "We have to check inside. Remember mom's last message insisted that we stop by her home."

"Oh, hell ... just tell me what to do."

Jake kept a tool bag in the van for emergencies, although not this kind of emergency. But the flat pry bar was just what he needed.

The manager had told them that another tenant had seen Grace Jakes leave by taxi about a week and a half ago with some luggage, and no one had seen her since. Jake had explained their reason for coming to Oklahoma and had asked permission to enter their mother's trailer. The manager had insisted that Dust-Bowl Trailer Park rules prohibited that when the occupant wasn't home. Jake had tried to bribe cooperation with a twenty, but the manager had declined. Jake had offered him another ten, asking him to call the owner and explain their worries about their mother's health. The manager had taken both bills and had ambled back to the shed just inside the trailer park. Jake and Caitlyn had returned to the van, parked at the front gate, to wait. Toothless had finally returned after almost a half-hour to tell them sternly that the boss said the rules were the rules.

"How about I call him and speak to him directly?" Jake had asked. "She could be sick in there and no one knows. Another twenty?"

Toothless had hesitated then said, "No can do. No way. It's my job to know these things. No one's there. She left and hasn't come back."

He'd walked away again

"As if he even called," Caitlyn had said.

Afterwards, Jake and Caitlyn had gone off to a late breakfast at a diner about a mile down the road to discuss options. Seeing their mother had been their final goal on their trip, and Jake, after finding nothing online about the company that owned the trailer park, had managed to convince his sister of his plan to get inside her home.

But he knew she still had her doubts. How could she not in this apocalyptic junkyard setting?

"You good, sis?" he asked her.

"I miss Cracker," she said.

That response gave Jake pause. She'd expressed that only once before on the trip, on telling him she was ready to end the visit at her father's. Maggie of Maggie's Bowling Alley and Bar was taking care of their childhood dog. An odd way to deflect the tension, but certainly Caitlyn-like.

She waved off her comment, saying, "I'm okay, I guess, because you act like you know what you're doing."

Jake gave her a reassuring smile, then said, "I miss him, too."

~

The drive across North America by the northern route into Canada was a maiden voyage out West for the two of them, and their first time seeing the Mississippi River, the Great Plains, the Rocky Mountains, and the Pacific Ocean. It had been a bonding experience. They'd developed an efficient routine at campgrounds, setting up their tents and cooking over a portable propane stove. In some of the big cities, they'd stayed in motels. Taking photos for Aki had given Jake additional purpose and continuing income.

Their first stop had been at the Six Nations of the Grand River Reserve in Ontario near Brantford, Ontario, the largest First Nations reserve in Canada and the only one with members of all the Haudenosaunee tribes. Don Tarbell, along with other Iroquois that Jake had met, lived there. Grant's parents had stayed there while Grant was in hiding. The Solstice Gathering host drum had come from there.

On his first visit all those years ago, prompted by his possible Mohawk ancestry, Jake had visited a gift shop at Oshweken, the village where the reserve's administrative offices are located. That time, Jake had had a long conversation with the owner about the Mohawk actor Jay Silverheels and had bought a photograph of him for his mother. This time, when talking to the owner's daughter about Silverheels, she'd informed them that another well-known actor – Graham Greene, an Oneida – had also grown up at Grand River. Jake and Caitlyn had first become aware of Greene in two films they found in a box of used videotapes their mother had bought at a yard sail – *Dances with Wolves* and *Thunderheart* –

when households were abandoning the VHS format for DVDs. Grace must not have known about the Grand River connection or she certainly would have gone on about it. In any case, here was another perfect gift for her – a photograph of Greene.

He'd also bought her and Cailtyn beaded bracelets—made by a Lenni Lenape woman, the owner's daughter, a Cayuga, had told them. What Jake hadn't realized about Grand River was that there was also small Munsee community living on this most populous reserve in Canada. Yet another coincidental connection to their ancestry, he and Caitlyn had marveled on setting out again.

While driving through Midwestern states, after the Grand River Lenape experience, brother and sister had made a point of detouring to Bowler, Wisconsin, to eat at the North Star Mohican Resort and Casino, owned by the Stockbridge-Munsee Community, consisting of Mahican and Lenape whose ancestors had relocated to the area from eastern states in the 19th century. After playing the slots and eating lunch, they'd driven around the area. Visiting a gift shop there as well, they'd talked to two tribal members, who, on learning of Jake's and Caitlyn's part-Lenape ancestry, had opened up about their own experiences. They of course had bought more gifts, this time books on Lenape history and culture.

After angling through Minnesota, they'd reached Portal, North Dakota, from where they'd crossed into the Canadian province of Saskatchewan. The van had proven ever-reliable. In Alberta, although its alternator had failed, they'd been able to reach a garage outside of Edmonton on battery power. With a new alternator, they'd crossed British Columbia into Alaska, finally making it to Caitlyn's father's home in Anchorage.

The reunion with Hugh Edmonds after so many years had gone well enough. He wasn't drinking and had mellowed with time. He'd seemed a lot smaller than Jake remembered him. He hadn't been in their life very long, moving out when Caitlyn was six and renting a place closer to Schenectady and his job at the General Electric factory. He'd visited Caitlyn from time to time over the years and, after moving to Alaska, he'd sent her money to buy the house outright from their mother and Jake.

During the father-daughter reunion, Jake had remained scarce. Hugh – or Hughie – had never given much attention to his daughter's older half-brother, "some other man's bastard kid," as he'd once expressed during a fight with Grace in earshot of Jake. This visit was Caitlyn's emotional journey, not his, and, during it, Jake had had just one detailed conversation with his erstwhile stepfather. He'd asked Hughie about his life first as a fisherman out of Anchorage, then as a worker in a cannery. Hughie was better at talking about himself than asking questions and listening, and Jake had been fine with that on this occasion. Hughie had mentioned a girlfriend but hadn't suggested they meet her. After two days as guests in her father's tiny house, Caitlyn had told Jake she was ready to move on.

Still camping along the way, they'd returned to the lower states through British Columbia, crossing into Washington near Seattle. From there they'd driven southward through Oregon into California. On a stopover in Los Angeles, they'd stayed with one of Caitlyn's high-school friends, who had followed a boyfriend there, then broken up with him. Like Caitlyn, she'd enrolled in classes to become a teacher. She and Caitlyn had been corresponding just this past year, having reconnected via social media. After one overnight there, brother and sister had headed back eastward. In Arizona they'd detoured from Route 40 to the Grand Canyon and camped there. They'd continued on 40 through New Mexico and the Texas Panhandle.

Jake had been sensing Caitlyn's growing anxiety as they neared Oklahoma. Their mother had responded by letter after Caitlyn had written about the results of the DNA test, and once after that, when Caitlyn had proposed the idea of a visit just before departing Shaleville. Grace had encouraged them to come and had even given them directions to the trailer park and her white-and-blue trailer, adding that it had a second bedroom for Caitlyn and a couch in the living room for Jake. But Caitlyn hadn't heard from her again despite attempted phone calls from the road before getting a message that the number was no longer in service. She'd sent a letter from Wisconsin, asking Grace to contact them one way or the other, with a check to cover the cost of a new phone and had arranged for a friend to collect her mail in Shaleville. The friend had reported that no letter from their mother had arrived. Grace's latest disappearing act wasn't about resentment over their visiting Hughie, they knew, since Caitlyn had decided to tell her about it in person. Jake had reminded Caitlyn daily that going incommunicado for long stretches was typical of their mother and that she was probably just nervous about a reunion. Caitlyn of course knew he too was worried.

They'd reached Oklahoma by midnight the night before and had camped out one last time before continuing to Oklahoma City. They hadn't gone to a campground but had sought out an isolated spot off the highway and had slept in the van.

Early that morning, Grace finally had contacted them – a text message from an unrecognizable number: "Be sure to stop by my new home while out West. I don't have a shadow of a doubt - a good phrase for a title - that you'll make the attempt. Don't bother trying to reach me at this number. Pinky swear!"

Any relief to have heard from their mother at all had quickly passed. The strange text had raised new questions. During their childhood years, Grace had established a pinky swear as a meaningful family custom and, under these circumstances, it struck Jake as a codified way to communicate insistence. As a result, they'd followed instructions and hadn't messaged back.

~

Now, while looking over at the supposedly empty trailer, then back at his sister's strained face, it was hard to call up even an iota of hope. Jake tried. Their mother may have simply left home to avoid them. That would be bad enough. But maybe the manager hadn't really checked the trailer and she was there right now, maybe sick, maybe ...

Enough with speculation, Jake thought. Time to act.

He pointed. "See that junker over there, sis ... the fourth one ... the yellow one without a windshield?"

"Uh-huh."

"You should have a view of the gate and shed from there. Get behind the far side of it and keep a lookout. Text me if all clear or if anyone's heading our way."

Caitlyn wiped the sweat and dust off her face. "Okay."

"If necessary, you can call. I'll keep my phone on vibrate. Same with yours. Once I get inside, I'll text you and let you know whether to join me. We won't stay long. Just a quick look."

277

"Okay," she sighed. "Here I go."

He watched her slender, athletic body dart from one abandoned vehicle to the next and take up position behind the car he'd pointed out.

A text came in: "Clear view of gate and shed. No one in sight."

"Here I go," Jake texted back.

Still crouching, he moved out from the junked cars and walked quickly toward the white trailer with light blue trim. Some broken glass and other trash littered the front yard. Beneath the dirt were traces of a slate walkway.

Jake reached the trailer's aluminum front door, its window covered by a frayed piece of plywood. He knocked gently and waited, then knocked somewhat harder. No reply.

Although the dented door looked as if it might open with a kick, he used the pry bar, wedging it between the lock and the door frame. The door resisted. He jammed the bar in deeper for more leverage and tried again. The door sprung open. Jake stepped inside, pulling the door shut behind him.

Remembering his mother's housekeeping, or lack of it, and given the condition of the trailer park and its trailers, Jake had expected a mess on entering. To his surprise, her living space was orderly and clean.

He hurried through the trailer's small rooms – combined living room/kitchen, two bedrooms, and bathroom. The trash had been emptied. The beds were made and the bedclothes looked clean. Possessions were carefully placed or stored away. He came across no empty liquor bottles, an all-too-familiar sight during his upbringing.

Jake recognized two items, gifts from both her children: the signed Jay Silverheels photo hung from her bedroom wall; a mug from Caitlyn offering an inscribed pearl of wisdom – "Grace, an ability to give as well as to receive" – sat on the kitchen counter.

A metal stand – supporting a small analog television, with a VHS video player on its middle shelf and videotapes stacked neatly on the bottom one – struck Jake as a shrine to the past. Some months before, Grace had told Caitlyn she'd bought the TV and VCR at a thrift store and asked her to ship one of her stored boxes of tapes to this address. She'd requested one of the boxes she'd labeled as containing tapes passed to her by her father.

Caitlyn had done so and made Jake find room in the van for a second box of the same.

Time to summon Caitlyn. He worded the text to let her know the trailer housed no tragedy: "No one here as expected. Come if all still clear."

"Coming," she immediately replied.

Jake didn't expect to find a loaded tape in the VCR, given that his mother had taken atypical care of her VHS collection, often scolding her kids for failing to rewind, eject, and re-sleeve tapes, but he turned on the player anyway and hit the eject button. A tape popped out – Alfred Hitchcock's *Shadow of a Doubt*.

Jake's thoughts and emotions convulsed, remembering that Grace had referenced that title in her text. He quickly scanned the stack of tapes for the film's sleeve. There it was, in between *The Stranger* and *Laura*. Jake pulled out the empty sleeve with his free hand so abruptly that he dropped it. He reached down. As he picked it up, a piece of folded notepaper fell to the floor. He grabbed it.

The door opened. Jake looked over and watched Caitlyn's face as she took in the surroundings.

"Whoa, it's nice in here," she said. "Didn't expect this."

"Yeah, quite a shock," he replied.

Caitlyn headed for the bedrooms. Jake unfolded the notepaper. It was a letter in his mother's handwriting, although neater than he remembered it. He began reading:

"Dear Daughter:

I've changed my life. Just before I learned of your trip, I became involved in something that motivated me to stay clean. I've had one relapse but that provided new motivation to stay on course. Your planned visit deepens my resolve even further. Keeping my poor excuse for a home respectable helps me do so. It sounds like Jake has turned his life around for real. I'm determined to make the same real for me. Some redemption is called for.

Thanks for the money to buy a new cellphone. I may get one soon. I have work now and I have some money. I also have a phone through my work but I can't use it for personal calls. Absolutely not. It's through this job that I've decided to do some good in my life. Well, indirectly, that is. I just want you to know that it's my failure as a mother that has prompted me to do what I feel I have to do.

I can't explain anything more than that for now. If you arrive at the trailer park when I'm not there, you'll have to go to the manager who stays in a trailer near the gate. Politely ask him if you can use the trailer to clean up. But tell Jake, given his new calling that you say I helped inspire, he should take a special interest in local characters. Both of you stay curious and alert!

Maybe we should just meet at some other place. That's probably a better idea. Possibly a friend's workplace. It's meaningful to me that your recent discovery about our ancestry and your advice led me to this new friend. I want you to meet her one way or the other. She's really just an acquaintance, but we connected in a special way. Track her down, promise?

I'm not sure where to send this letter since you're on the road. I don't want it to be returned and fall into the wrong hands. I feel better for having written it though and maybe you'll eventually get to read it. I'll try to figure out an alternate way if necessary.

Right now, I'm going to watch two other favorite movies from two other favorite directors, Orson Welles's *The Stranger* and Otto Preminger's *Laura*, both about a stranger hiding in plain sight, like in *Shadow of a Doubt*. How apropos, these masterful character studies!

Love,

Your Mother Grace (trying to live up to that name)"

Caitlyn returned to the living room.

"What's that?" she asked.

"A letter. She led me to it though her text."

He held up the film's sleeve. Caitlyn eyes widened. Jake handed her the letter and watched her read it. Any stress she'd shed on seeing that their mother had made a nice home for herself returned.

Caitlyn looked up and asked, "What the hell? What's she talking about? Where is she? Why didn't she just find a way to call?"

Jake of course had no answers.

"What'll we do now?" Caitlyn implored.

Jake, his jaw clenched, looked around the trailer.

"What now?" his sister asked again.

Jake met her eyes. "Solve this mystery, that's what. We're going to find mom."